The Imagination of
the Heart

Also by Judith Glover:

Sister and Brothers
The Stallion Man

JUDITH GLOVER

The Imagination of the Heart

St. Martin's Press
New York

Library of Congress Cataloging-in-Publication Data

Glover, Judith.
      The imagination of the heart / Judith Glover.
         p.   cm.
    ISBN 0-312-03847-X
    I. Title.
  PR6057.L64I43   1990
  823'.914—dc20   89-27046
                                          CIP

First published in Great Britain by Hodder and Stoughton.

First U.S. Edition

10 9 8 7 6 5 4 3 2 1

He hath shewed strength with his arm; he hath scattered the proud in the imagination of their hearts.

Luke 2:51

I am certain of nothing but the holiness of the heart's affections and the truth of the imagination – what the imagination seizes as beauty must be truth.

Keats

1

Catherine March.

That was the name she had been given twenty years ago. Catherine, because it happened to be next on the overseer's list; and March, after the month in which she'd been found abandoned on the steps of Tonbridge Orphanage.

She hated the name. It was an institute name, a label to identify an unwanted child; and in defiance she'd always called herself Kitty, which wasn't half as grand but at least was something of her own choosing. Kitty was the real her, a very private yet spirited young woman kept hidden carefully from the world, whereas Catherine March was a different person entirely – the outward skin which she wore as protective disguise. And it was Catherine March who this morning was to be married to a man she did not love, a man she scarcely knew, a man of whom Kitty for all her brave mettle was secretly a little afraid.

Oliver van der Kleve.

That Mr van der Kleve was a gentleman of some wealth, holding a good position in society, ameliorated the situation only somewhat. He was twice Kitty's age, a widower with a daughter; though he was not unattractive, the coldness of his manner and the superior detachment he adopted towards her had caused his wife-to-be a good deal of puzzlement as to his reasons for wishing to make her the second Mrs van der Kleve.

She was not a vain young woman, but she had only to look in a glass to know that she was beautiful, and only to see the admiration reflected in the eyes of men to know that she was desirable. Therefore it seemed strange that her suitor had never once spoken either of beauty or desire, but only of compliance, and docility, and dutifulness, words she had heard all her young life from the overseers of one institution or another, but which went ill with what she supposed was the tender intimacy of marriage. On the day he had asked that

7

she become his wife, Mr van der Kleve had made his proposal a command, not an invitation; and she who had been trained to obey authority from infancy had complied, acknowledging the extraordinary honour being paid to her – a no one, a foundling, a charity child – with "if such is your wish, sir" longing, but not daring to enquire of him the reason why.

Kitty yawned and arched her back, easing away the slight stiffness from her shoulders; and rising from the edge of the bed, crossed the dim room to the casement window. Dawn was breaking at last to end the dragging hours of the night, hours in which she'd lain staring into the darkness while the slow tick of the long case clock outside the door marked off the seconds taking her towards this changing point of her life. The past lay charted out behind her like a road running through familiar country, signposted along the way with memories. Ahead, the future covered an entirely new landscape through which she must now journey; a foreign country beckoning her with its promise of a world of which before she could no more than dream. She was terribly afraid – yet at the same time exhilarated by the dazzling adventure she was about to embark upon.

She pushed aside the piece of net at the window and looked out into the street. In the east, above the rooftops of Tunbridge Wells, the pale grey light of an April morning was beginning to creep across the skyline. Beyond the open slopes of the Common where sheep and cattle grazed, the gas lamps were being extinguished slowly one by one along the length of Mount Ephraim. When a new dawn broke, the world would still be the same; but she would be in a different room, bearing a different name.

Catherine van der Kleve.

The young woman repeated it out loud, her warm breath clouding the glass. However many times she said it, it sounded awkward and unfamiliar still, that of a stranger. Catherine van der Kleve. Oh, but what a fine ring it had, to be sure – a name to impress tradesfolk. Once it was hers, would it change her at all, she wondered with a sudden nervous thrill of excitement. As Catherine March, of unknown parentage, she'd had only her striking beauty to speak for her, that, and her quick intelligence; but as Mrs van der Kleve, wife of a well-to-do merchant banker, she would acquire all the advantages of

8

class which such a position in society was bound to attract.

Could she still remain the same? Still, beneath all the traps and trimmings of wealth, the same Kitty who had learned from the unloving years of the orphanage and the spite and mockery of being a charity scholar at Miss Meyrick's Academy, how to protect herself from hurt and loneliness behind the façade of being Catherine March? Who could say? Only one thing was certain, that the whole tenor of her life was about to be altered in the most radical fashion.

She rubbed away the condensation from the panes, and leaned to look out to the left along the dawn-lit street towards the blackly silhouetted spire of St Bride's Church. There in five hours' time, she would be required to repeat a formula of words, receive a ring upon her finger, and thereby bind herself to a man whom she regarded as the personification of authority, to be obeyed in all things and in every way.

The thought of it sent another little shiver running through her, though whether that was the anticipation of the wedding ceremony itself, or the realisation of what an extraordinary future was being offered her, she could not tell.

"Oh, beg pardon, miss —"

The sudden unexpected sound of a child's voice made Kitty turn quickly.

"Only I didn't knock in case you was asleep still."

The small face peering in a halo of lamplight round the opened door was almost hidden beneath the frills of a large and not very clean muslin cap which Kitty recognised as the uniform of the workhouse children employed here at the Academy as domestic labour.

"Madam said to light you a fire first thing," the child continued, advancing herself a little further through the doorway, "on account o' you wanted to bathe yourself, miss."

There was a smile. "Yes. Yes, that's right."

The cap promptly withdrew and reappeared again moments later together with the rest of its owner's small thin body, accompanied by a scuttle of coal which was brought into the room by the simple expedient of dragging it backwards across the carpet to the black-leaded grate.

Kitty observed this exercise in pitying silence. During her first year as a pupil here at Miss Meyrick's Academy for Young Ladies, she too had been required to rise at dawn and see to the lighting of fires in the private quarters of the large, draughty house, and she well recalled the weight of a coal scuttle carried up four flights of stairs from the back yard.

While the child fetched in the lamp from the corridor, the young woman took up her wrapper from a chair and drew it over her high-necked flannel nightgown before seating herself. Last night at supper in the dining hall below she had been treated to a most sickening display of deference from Miss Meyrick, as though this forthcoming marriage to one of the board school's principal benefactors had expunged the past entirely and wiped clear all memory of the unhappy humiliations she'd been made to suffer at its proprietress's hands. She who had formerly been the despised charity scholar had found herself invited to a place at the top table; and it had proved a most curious experience indeed to be up there on the dais looking across the bowed and silent heads of pupils to the bench at the back of the hall where once upon a time she'd been required to take her own meals apart.

She could never call this place home; yet from the age of eight she had lived here, her board and education paid for by the orphanage scholarship she'd won, and after the past two years spent abroad it was the only roof she had to return to from which to be married.

Interrupting her thoughts, the little skivvy clattered the coal tongs into the hearth and twisting round awkwardly on her knees, said cheerfully, "I'll make you up a good bright fire, shall I, miss? You won't want to be a-catching a chill for the church, I'm sure."

Kitty responded with another friendly smile. Then, for the sake of sharing a kind word, asked, "What is your name, may I know?"

"It's Em'ly. Em'ly, miss."

"Well, Emily, and have you been working here long?"

"Only since Christmas, miss." The small hands, already scullery-roughened and red, began laying sticks of kindling across the screws of oily newspaper in the grate.

"Do you like it?"

There was a hesitation, and then a too-hurried nod of the muslin cap.

Seeing that was all the answer she would get to her question,

Kitty went on conversationally, "And how old are you, Emily?"

"Twelve, miss."

"Twelve? What a big girl you are, indeed. I came here first when I was eight."

"Lor' –! You was no more'n a little 'un, was you, miss." A shower of sparks from the Vesta match lit the child's face for a moment.

"And I remained for ten years before leaving."

Emily directed a look over her shoulder as if she could not quite believe that anyone could stay so long in this place and not bear some outward scar of the experience. "Meself, I'd be dead afore then," she commented philosophically, turning back to tend the small flame kindled among the paper.

There was a short silence; then, on a note of some caution – "Beg pardon for asking, miss, but is it true? Is it true what Cook says, that you've been away in foreign parts?"

"Oh, is that what Cook says?"

"Yes, miss. France, she says."

"I wonder how she knows of that."

"Oh, she knows everything, does Cook, Miss. To hear her talk, you'd suppose there wasn't a thing could happen in Tunbridge Wells wi'out her being first to learn of it."

"And what is it she has to say of me?"

"Well –" The child seemed embarrassed suddenly.

Kitty at once regretted letting her curiosity prompt her to ask that question, and was about to change the subject when the answer came a trifle awkwardly.

"She says the gentleman you're to wed paid money to have you turned out a lady, miss."

Turned out a lady . . . Put like that, it sounded so cold, nothing more than the business investment which, in truth, it no doubt was for Mr van der Kleve.

"You're not offended, I hope?" The pinched face under its incongruous cap looked towards her with something approaching real fear. "It's lies I'm sure, miss. Anybody can see you're quality born. Janet says."

"Janet?"

"The scullery maid, miss. It's her as is fetching your hot water up directly."

Having suddenly reminded herself of this fact, Emily at once began heaping lumps of coal upon the crackling wood, at the same time continuing hurriedly, "You went to France to be finished, that's what Janet says. To learn how folk there dress theirselves, and mind their manners, and talk, an' all. She says belikes you dined off frogs' hind legs and snails – you didn't truly, did you, miss?"

This last was added almost disbelievingly with another snatched glance across the shoulder.

Kitty shook her head. Such questionable gastronomic delicacies had not been part of the fare offered to those young women attending the English finishing school in Paris to which Oliver van der Kleve had paid for her to be sent two years earlier, in 1863. It was true, though, that she had learned to be 'a lady' – to conduct herself at all times with dignity and decorum; to understand the art of entertaining and the management of a good table; to control servants and inferiors with fair yet firm discipline; to hold pleasing conversation on divers topics; to appreciate the etiquette of dress; to know the significance of social customs such as 'at homes' and visiting cards and be able to observe them correctly – all these and a hundred other things which marked the invisible boundary of class and cultural division in Victorian society.

"There –" Emily announced, jerking her head as sounds from without indicated the arrival of the water jugs. "That'll be Janet now."

Rising from her knees she made for the door, the lamplight throwing the shadow of her cap grotesquely against the ceiling, and a whisper of conversation ensued outside in the corridor before both came in together and set about preparing the hearth, fetching an enamelled hip-bath from the dressing room, filling it, and erecting a screen around to give the bather both privacy and some protection from draughts.

When the pair had gone, two peas from the same pod almost, dipping curtsies from the door, Kitty discarded herself of wrapper and nightgown and got into the tub while the water was still pleasantly warm. The fire had burned up now, taking the edge off the chill in the room, and she sat for some minutes with her knees up beneath her chin enjoying the sensation of gentle heat on her nakedness. While she'd been a boarder here at the Academy, pupils were required to bathe dressed from chin to ankle in a coarse grey sackcloth garment so that no part of the body was exposed: only the worst type of female showed her limbs, said Miss Meyrick, and it was an offence verging upon grossness to look at oneself or one's neighbour whilst in a state of undress.

Kitty's friend Harriet – her only friend – said that gentlemen actually paid to see ladies thus. And worse, that husbands slept quite naked with their wives (though for what purpose she was unclear). The thought of sharing a bed with an unclothed man, husband or no, had quite horrified Kitty at the time; and it horrified her still, though with a tinge of curiosity. Would she be expected to oblige Mr van der Kleve in such a fashion? Would he demand that she removed her drawers and chemise and allow him to see her with no other cover to her shame than a bedsheet?

The blood coloured the young woman's cheeks. Slowly she lowered her knees to glance down at herself, pushing back the heavy waves of honey-pale hair from her shoulders. The firelight gilded the tips of her full, firm breasts and glistened on the drops of moisture pearling her skin. "A vessel of corruption, fair without and foul within" – that was how Mr Pugh the minister had often described the female form in his hour-long Sunday homilies to Miss Meyrick's pupils. "The Devil's own bait to lure menfolk into sin." Perhaps that was why he had married a wife with a face like a dead cod, Harriet said – to keep himself from being tempted.

Kitty took up the cake of hard yellow soap and began to lather her legs. The dancing master at her finishing school had complimented her frequently upon the grace of her carriage and had one day embarrassed her greatly by referring to the length of her *jolies jambes* as though long legs were a most admirable asset to a woman. She herself had never given much thought to them, apart from being thankful that they were straight and not bowed apart by rickets, or else lamed like poor Harriet's so that one was shorter than the other. The same dancing master had complimented her, too, upon the trimness of her waist; and in her final week at the school had even gone so far as to kiss both her hands at the end of a polka waltz, a gesture which had thrown her into considerable confusion.

Kitty looked down at herself once more in critical examination; then, ashamed at such indelicacy, applied the soap with increased vigour until her skin was covered with a lather of

13

iridescent suds. If indeed husbands and wives slept together in the same bed unclothed, as Harriet said, might that perhaps have something to do with the begetting of children? She had no idea how a woman came by babies, except that they were formed within her body through some association with the monthly courses. Would her future husband wish her to bear him a child? She supposed so. He already had a daughter by his first wife, but no son to inherit his place in the family bank of van der Kleve Lindemanns.

True, he'd never spoken of wanting an heir; but then, their conversations together had scarcely invited such confidence, being the stiltedly overpolite exchanges of almost-strangers. The only occasions upon which he ever passed personal comment were when he expressed satisfaction with the gowns and the jewellery which he himself had chosen and bought for her.

"He has a heart somewhere, to be sure," Harriet Seymour had put when writing to Kitty upon her betrothal in the summer of the previous year. "I pray that you find it, dearest, and when you do, that you discover it is not made entirely of marbled stone."

Rinsing the lather from her creamy skin, the young bride-to-be fervently hoped that such might indeed be the case, and that once they were wed her husband would reveal a warmer and kindlier side to his nature. He had invested a good deal of both time and money in having her fashioned into the type of wife he seemed to desire, therefore he must at least like her. That was something upon which she must endeavour to build, for where there was a liking, affection was bound to follow in due time. Such things, Kitty reflected in a spirit of brave optimism as she reached for the towel, were surely a natural outcome of the married state.

Her life so far had been a cold, unloved existence, a joyless discipline of regulation and rule. This union with Mr van der Kleve offered security and comfort and status, the opportunity to reach towards undreamed-of horizons, to be mistress of the kind of household where she might very well have found herself employed as servant had Fate gone otherwise.

It would have been unthinkable to reject his proposal.

"Wilt thou have this man to thy wedded husband, to live together after God's ordinance in the holy estate of Matrimony?

Wilt thou obey him, and serve him, love, honour, and keep him in sickness and in health –"

In the echoing stillness of St Bride's the minister's voice had a sepulchral quality to it.

"– and, forsaking all other, keep thee only unto him, so long as ye both shall live?"

Kitty's lips parted but no sound issued from them. Beside her she was aware of Oliver van der Kleve, and behind him the small congregation, all waiting for her to make her response. Mutely she stared at *The Book of Common Prayer* held open in the minister's hands, and sensed rather than saw her bridegroom's head turn towards her and his mouth tighten impatiently.

There was a clearing of the throat and the Reverend Mr Edward Terris repeated himself.

"And, forsaking all other, keep thee only unto him, so long as ye both shall live?"

The young woman met his eyes. They held a professional smiling sympathy. She was not the first bride who had been struck dumb at the altar rail, nor would she be the last.

He leaned forward with a prompting murmur. "Say 'I will', my dear."

The trembling cascade of orange blossom held beneath her breast betrayed the rapid pounding of her heart. She felt herself shaking in every limb with a nervousness that was part apprehension and part a strangely heady excitement.

She drew in a breath; then, huskily, with a quick little nod – "I will."

But it was Catherine March, not Kitty, who spoke that promise; and Catherine van der Kleve, not Kitty, who a short while later lifted back her wedding veil and offered her mouth to her husband for his kiss.

2

From the first, Beatrice van der Kleve had not approved of her brother's proposed marriage. While he'd remained a widower she was in effect mistress of his house; but another wife meant she must yield her place and be forced to hand over the management of the household into the care of the newcomer.

Being a woman who enjoyed her superior position, she could not stomach being thus deprived of all authority. For the past six years, since the death of her sister-in-law Maria, she had devoted herself to the running of Sion Place with a meticulous discipline which was reflected in every aspect of the domestic scene. Each minute of each day had its routine and rule and regulation, and woe betide the servant who forgot. She was respected by the tradesmen of the town, but not liked; she was liked by her few friends, but not loved. In fact, the only one person ever to love Beatrice van der Kleve was her motherless niece Angelina, and that was with the fawning, self-interested affection of a spoilt child.

She was now in her forty-fifth year, a tall woman with strong, square features framed by heavy plaits of dark hair, and watchful, unsmiling eyes which seemed to hold criticism of all they looked upon.

Those eyes at this moment were observing the second Mrs van der Kleve, seated beside her new husband at the wedding breakfast in the terrace room of Sion Place.

What on earth had possessed Oliver to cumber himself with the wretched girl, Beatrice could not think. His decision was his own, and she must of course respect it; but the wisdom of such a choice left itself greatly open to question.

"She is a work of art which it is my intention to acquire," he had answered one day when his sister pressed him for some explanation of his behaviour. "Should I say, an unfinished thing of beauty which I believe may be moulded into the ideal."

He had first set eyes on this 'unfinished thing of beauty' some four years ago, when little Angelina had gone as a day pupil to Miss Meyrick's Academy for Young Ladies on the London Road. Catherine March was then sixteen, a quiet and seemingly tractable girl being educated on a charity scholarship awarded annually by the Church Orphanage Trust, to enable a suitable female to be trained for the post of governess.

For some months Oliver had covertly followed Miss March's progress, and on her seventeenth birthday had arranged that she remain at the Academy as assistant teacher to the reception class. The first intimation Beatrice had of his personal interest in the girl was a tearful complaint from Angelina that Miss March was wearing her Mama's best India shawl; and upon making enquiry of her brother, she was informed that indeed, he had given the shawl as a gift, feeling pity for the girl that her own was so patched and darned.

That he should pay such a singular favour – that shawl had been his late wife's favourite – had set Beatrice against Catherine March from the beginning: had she been a person of any moral sensibility she would have refused to accept it, not flaunted it about her shoulders for the admiration and envy of her fellow boarders. Then, two years ago, the sly creature had accepted Oliver's offer to send her abroad to a finishing school to put a gloss upon her manners; and naturally, when he later proposed marriage, the answer was a foregone conclusion.

Beatrice van der Kleve eyed her new sister-in-law with narrowed dislike. To look at her, sitting there so quiet and demure in her Westbourne Grove wedding gown, one would think butter wouldn't melt in her pretty pink mouth.

Aloud she said smoothly, "You gave us all quite a fright, Catherine dear, when you faltered in your responses at the altar. We thought perhaps you may have had a change of mind."

"That was nerves, Beatrice! Nerves, nothing more." The Reverend Mr Edward Terris spoke up in Kitty's defence before she could answer for herself. "I've scarce ever known a young woman not stumble upon her words. A good sign, that. Shows how solemnly she has set her thoughts upon the gravity of her marriage pledge."

He inclined himself with a smile towards the bride, the smug assurance of his expression emphasising the slight pomposity of an otherwise handsome countenance; and at the sight of that smile Beatrice's pale, narrow lips tightened a little more.

Edward Terris was her brother's friend, and a frequent guest at Sion Place. He was of that breed which attracts itself strongly to the emotional hunger of a certain type of woman, being both a bachelor and a clergyman; though in the case of Mr Terris, his lack of a wife was not due to any fear of the female sex, but simply to the fact of having been wounded in love early in life. He had yet to meet another woman with sufficiently pleasing attributes to win his whole-hearted affection. Beatrice had long hoped that she might be that one. She had inherited an independent income under the terms of her father's will, and had given generously to St Bride's Church over the years; but while Mr Terris repaid her with the unction of friendship and conversation, he was careful to avoid any turn of talk which might lead towards a deeper and more personal involvement.

To see him now, being so attentively agreeable to Oliver's new wife, added further fuel to the older woman's resentment, and she came back just a little sharply with – "Nerves, you say, Edward? Indeed? I thought myself how remarkably composed the bride appeared. As cool as a lily. Did you not think that too, Oliver?"

Her brother broke off his discussion with the guest upon his right and glanced towards her. The soft April light filling the room through the tall double windows lent a flush of warmth to the pale, elegant features, a warmth echoed faintly in the smile which curved the corners of his mouth while failing to reach his eyes.

"Perhaps Catherine herself should be the one to answer that."

Conversation from the half-dozen or so other guests at the table quietened at something in his tone subtly at variance with the lightness of his words.

"Well, my dear?" He turned to his bride. "Let us not wait in further suspense. Which is correct, Edward or Beatrice? Was it sudden want of courage which caused you to fall silent, or a considered review of your desire to become my wife?"

His grey eyes, beneath dark straight brows, made a critical study of Kitty's expression as she raised her face to him.

"Well –?"

"It was a moment's confusion, sir," she answered obediently, not meeting the appraisal of his glance but looking beyond him to Harriet Seymour, further down the table.

Harriet winked.

"And I apologise to Mr Terris for causing him to have to repeat himself."

"My dear Mrs van der Kleve – upon my soul, if every bride were to apologise for so slight a matter, I should very soon weary of hearing it!" Mr Terris exclaimed at once, helping himself to some more of the excellent mayonnaise of cold salmon.

Then, shifting the conversation with an adroitness born of practice – "I must congratulate you, Oliver, upon the magnificence of the wedding breakfast. My goodness me, you have a treasure indeed in your kitchen if your Cook prepared but half of this." A gesture of the head indicated the starched white linen cloth decorated with silver *epergnes* of artificial silk mock-orange flowers, and laden with assorted cold dishes to accompany the Bouchie Fils et Cie champagne.

"Cook prepared it all," he was pertly informed by young Angelina van der Kleve, "and I heard her declare that she hoped it would poison the lot of us."

"Now, Angelina – " her father sought to silence her sharply, "that is enough of your silliness, if you please."

"But, Papa, she did!"

"I said, that is enough."

This time there was a note of warning in the admonishment, and Angelina's face coloured up, reddening the cluster of pimples around her sulky mouth.

At fourteen years old, she was a plump, plain child, her features betraying the stolid Dutch blood of her paternal forebears, without any of the delicate fine-boned grace which had been her mother's before that lady's untimely death in childbirth in 1858. Neglected by a father who could not bring himself to love her, and over-indulged by an aunt whose toleration only served to encourage her sulks and tantrums, Angelina had grown into an unlikeable young person who expressed herself in acts of petty spite if thwarted of getting her own way. The servants disliked her, and with good cause: her tale-bearing to her aunt had brought about the dismissal of more than one member of the kitchen staff for supposed laxity or insolence, and dismissal without reference for a maid was a disgrace almost as serious as pregnancy.

Her attitude towards her father was an ambiguous one. Resentful that he should show himself so indifferent to her existence, she tried to win his attention by behaving in a noisy, pettish manner, creating scenes over imagined grievances, or suffering phantom illness to arouse his pity, or boasting falsely of the praise which her teachers paid her schoolwork at the Academy.

Her pique when she had discovered her father's interest in Catherine March soured quickly to a child's angry jealousy – jealousy fostered and fed by her Aunt Beatrice. It was rooted in several separate resentments: Miss March was a nobody, a nothing, a common workhouse foundling, trying to pretend she was as good as her betters; Miss March was stealing Papa's attention and occupying the notice he ought rightly be paying to her, his own daughter; Miss March would replace her dear, dead Mama if she could, and feather her own nest in the process, as Aunt Beatrice said; and worst (and most unforgivable of all) Miss March was beautiful and people admired her, even liked her.

Seeing her father's eye still coldly upon her, Angelina ducked her head and began picking sullenly at the fringes of lace trimming on her sleeve. I hate her, she thought with a sudden furious intensity; I *hate* her. I'll make her wish she'd never come to live here. And Cook did say that, she did, she did. I heard her tell Rose Maguire she hoped we'd all be sick as cats.

The attention of the wedding party was now with a Mr Lockyer, chairman of the governors of Tonbridge Orphanage, who had been invited to give Kitty away in marriage. Finding herself ignored, Angelina slid from her chair and left the table. They were all making such a fuss of *her*, the detested new stepmama, it made her choke just to see it. She wanted to rush over and hit her, pull the creature's horrible gold hair to make her scream, scratch her china-doll cheeks and spoil her silly, pretty face so that Papa wouldn't want to look at her any more.

Grinding her teeth with temper, she flounced out through the door. Several rooms away, in the deserted entrance hall of Sion Place, a table had been set to display the wedding gifts. Among the pieces was a fruit bowl of cut crystal, a beautiful thing presented by Mr Terris which the new Mrs van der Kleve had particularly admired. Angelina picked up the bowl in both hands and stared at it, hating it; and in an outburst of uncontrollable rage suddenly hurled it from her with all her force down upon the black and white squared marble of the floor.

When the child returned again to the wedding breakfast, Mr Lockyer was still in full flow, regaling the company with an account of the number of pauper children successfully placed in employment by his orphanage in recent years.

It was observed that Mrs van der Kleve, unused to drinking anything as strong as champagne, was beginning to look a trifle pale; and as soon as she politely could, she asked to be allowed to excuse herself from the table.

As she went out, her friend Harriet Seymour rose and accompanied her into the adjoining ante-room.

"What you want is a good sniff of sal volatile," Harriet said practically, hunting about in her reticule for the smelling salts she always carried.

"No . . . I need some air, that's all," Kitty told her. "I'll feel better in a while . . . just let me walk up and down."

"As you wish, dear. But lean on me, do." The other held out an arm fashionably encased in a wide pagoda sleeve and fell into step at her side, walking with an awkward, limping gait slowly back and forth across the crimson plush carpet.

"I must say, I don't envy you your new relations," she went on tartly. "That sister of Mr van der Kleve's has a face that would curdle milk if she smiled. And the daughter –" Harriet's own mobile features pulled a long expression – "well, if she were *my* daughter, my hand would be itching to apply itself often and sharply to her nether anatomy."

Kitty responded with a sigh of resignation. "It grieves me that she should resent me as she does," she said after a moment. "I've tried to make myself agreeable whenever we've met . . . but since the engagement, Angelina will have none of it. Nor

Beatrice. However hard I try, all my overtures have been spurned."

"Jealousy, that's what it is," Harriet asserted roundly. "Plain old-fashioned jealousy. Neither of the pair has a feature between them to redeem their drab looks. You should've seen Bea's expression when Mr Terris paid you his oily compliments! Clearly she admires him rather more than might be supposed."

"You think so?"

"Of course. I've seen the way she watches him. You don't make a habit of observing folk as I do, Kitty dear. It's a pastime which affords infinite grist for the mill of my curiosity."

Harriet Seymour paused for a moment to rest her leg. She herself was a plain enough young woman, with a sharp little nose and chin giving her a mouselike appearance. Her features, however, were constantly enlivened by the humour of their expression, a humour reflected both in her conversation and in her attitude towards the world; and though her lameness – the result of a midwife's clumsy birthing – was a physical hindrance which made her often appear ungainly, she had acquired a stoical acceptance of the handicap entirely lacking self-pity.

She and Kitty March had made one another's acquaintance at Miss Meyrick's Academy years before. Mocked by her fellow boarders with the cruel tag of 'Peg Leg', Harriet had felt a sympathetic affinity with the charity scholar who was used as an unpaid servant and treated as an inferior by all and sundry. Her own family were gentry, landowners farming several thousand acres around the village of Frant, on the Sussex border beyond Tunbridge Wells; and as the two of them grew older, she had occasionally been allowed to invite Kitty to stay with her and her younger brother William during holidays. This childhood intimacy had flourished in time into a firm and enduring friendship which was knitted together by the bonds of mutual trust, support and affection.

"I wish it were I who had married first," Harriet declared, resuming her clumsy walk at Kitty's side. "Not for want of a husband, you understand, my dear, but so that I might have the experience of a wife to impart to you, that you might be better forewarned."

The new bride made no response to this generous thought,

and after a further few moments the other went on, "'It is a mystery to exercise the minds of maids' – now who said that, I wonder? Ah well, no matter. Whichever way one views it, wedlock is a chance leap in the dark –"

"Oh, Harriet, if only I had you with me," Kitty interrupted her in a sudden, fearful manner. "How I am dreading this wedding tour . . . *dreading* it."

"That I can understand. Fourteen days at Weymouth with Mr van der Kleve is hardly likely to provide much in the way of diversion."

"It's not the days which occupy my fears so much. They will be tolerable enough, I dare say . . . we shall visit Lyme Regis and the Isle of Portland, and Dorchester. But the evenings . . . the nights . . . dear God, I know nothing of men. What will happen to me?"

"What happens to all wives, I suppose."

"Poor consolation!"

"It's all I have to give. But those who are married seem well enough satisfied with whatever it is a wife must endure from her husband's attentions."

Kitty paused in her pacing to and fro, and looked fretfully towards the door into the terrace room. "They will miss me . . . I suppose I must return." Then, clutching again at her friend – "Oh, Harriet, Harriet, give me some comfort, do. Those tales you used to tell me at Miss Meyrick's – they weren't the truth, were they?"

"Which tales?"

"Those about . . . babies."

"Ah, *those*." The other gave an enigmatic look. "Well, infants are not found beneath gooseberry bushes, rest assured of that. Neither are they delivered to the door in carpet bags."

"You swore it was gospel truth that they crawled from between the bedsheets."

"And so they do, in a fashion."

"But how –?" Kitty gave a soft cry of exasperation. The nagging fear which was haunting her showed itself in the darkening violet of her lovely eyes. She looked so vulnerable, thought Harriet sorrowfully – a child-woman in her bridal gown of Nottingham lace, and her soft shining hair threaded with a garland of mock-orange blossom. Like Ophelia, or Tennyson's Mariana.

Aloud she said with a note of reassurance, "I'm sure you have no need to feel afraid, dearest. Mr van der Kleve would not have wished to marry you did he not care for you – and if he cares for you, he will treat you with kindness and consideration."

"But *does* he care for me, Harriet?" The other pressed a hand to her lips and averted her head. Almost in a whisper she went on after a pause, "He has never said so . . . never spoken one single word of love, or need, or tenderness."

"Perhaps that is not his way. It may be that now you're married he will behave with more affection. Have courage and believe that!"

"If only I could –"

Kitty would have added something more, but a sudden commotion at that moment made her turn her head quickly towards the arched doorway leading in the direction of the entrance hall. From the noise, it sounded as though someone had been hurt and was now crying bitterly.

She exchanged a glance with her friend; then, casting a hasty look back into the terrace room and seeing them all engaged there still in conversation, she moved towards the arch.

At one side of the hall, crouched against the wall by the wedding display table, the two young women came upon one of the housemaids, her cries quietening to sobs now as she struggled to control herself. Close by her lay the shattered pieces of Mr Terris's crystal fruit bowl, its thick glass reflecting a prism of colours across the marbled floor.

"Mrs van der Kleve –"

Kitty looked round to see who it was had spoken her new name with such cold correctness. At the other side of the hall, where a recessed door opened beneath the wide sweep of the staircase, a woman was standing whom she recognised as Jane Perrins, personal lady's maid to her sister-in-law Beatrice.

"I am sorry, Mrs van der Kleve, but as you can see, there has been a most regrettable accident."

Miss Perrins moved towards them, black bombasine skirts rustling, and made a cursory indication of the damage done to the bowl.

"I'm afraid Miss Beatrice will need to be informed."

"Beatrice?"

"Yes, madam. The accident was entirely due to this girl's clumsiness —"

"It wasn't, ma'am! It wasn't, I swear!" The maid struggled to her feet against the wall, and the vivid red mark standing out across one cheek showed the reason for the cry of pain which Kitty and Harriet had heard. "It wasn't me broke it, ma'am. It was like that when I come up from the scullery and found it —"

"Clumsiness compounded by lies and evasion," Jane Perrins continued, prim lipped, "and Miss Beatrice will not tolerate such behaviour among the domestic staff."

"I don't see what business it is of sister Bea's," Harriet remarked out of the corner of her mouth, turning her head so that only Kitty heard. "You're mistress of the house now, remember, dear. This is your responsibility."

Kitty looked again at the young maid, a well-formed girl of about seventeen years with dark curling hair tidied neatly beneath her starched lace cap.

"How did you mark your face like that?" she asked her quietly.

Hesitating to answer, the other cast a quick, fearful look towards Jane Perrins.

"Did *she* strike you?"

There was a dumb nod.

Kitty felt the sudden warm flush of anger begin replacing her previous nervousness. Too many times she herself had been spitefully used, and often for no other reason than being looked upon as an inferior by those who liked to hurt her. Hating cruelty, harshness and bullying spite — all of which she had experienced to some degree during her childhood — it was her nature to take the side of the underdog against those whose regard for their own superior worth made them callously indifferent.

"What is your name?" she asked the girl, disregarding Miss Perrins's rapidly chilling expression.

"Rosie, ma'am. Rosie Maguire."

"And was it you who broke the bowl, Rosie?"

"Oh no, ma'am, no. Truly it wasn't. I found it done already —"

"I must insist, Mrs van der Kleve, that Miss Beatrice be informed," Jane Perrins tried again to interrupt.

"Why?"

"Why? Why, madam, because she would wish it!"

"Miss Perrins, I believe that the management of the servants in this household is now *my* concern," Kitty told her steadily, marvelling at her own cool authority. "And if Rosie says this damage was none of her doing, then I am inclined to give her the benefit of the doubt. Physical violence will not alter the truth. However, the accident must be investigated of course, and I shall see that my husband is told as soon as I return to him. In the meanwhile, may I suggest that you confine yourself to your own duties?"

The haughty expression on Jane Perrins's face shifted to one of indignant outrage.

"Very well, Rosie," Kitty continued, ignoring her to turn again to the other, "you may return below. And ask Cook if you might bathe your cheek in cold water."

"Yes, ma'am. And – thank you, ma'am, thank you ever so!"

Rosie Maguire dipped a curtsy, and accompanied it with a smile trembling with gratitude.

As she went back to take her place again at the wedding breakfast, Kitty knew that she had made one friend at least in this house; but by the same token she had also added to the list of her enemies.

3

No one came forward to admit responsibility for the damage done to Mr Terris's crystal fruit bowl and the incident cast something of a shadow over the conclusion of the wedding breakfast. Had the gift been of less value and from someone outside Oliver van der Kleve's immediate circle, the episode might merely have provoked moderate regret; but Edward Terris was a close acquaintance, and that bowl had cost him a pretty penny at Jackman's in the High Street.

The expression upon the bridegroom's chilly features spoke clearly of his annoyance that the morning should have ended on such an awkward note – his friend pained at the careless usage of his gift, the servants unsettled, his sister resentful that his wife had interfered in the matter, and his daughter treating the whole thing with giggling stupidity.

This dark mood remained with him into the afternoon, lasting the length of the railway journey which took him and his bride up to London to spend the first night of their wedding tour. It was only as the train rattled between the crowded tenements of Southwark and its smoke cleared to give them a fine view of the Thames and riverfront buildings that he unbent sufficiently to address a few stiff remarks.

Whatever small pleasure Kitty may have had in her wedding day shrivelled again into a nervy, silent tension.

There had been an incident earlier, before the start of this journey, when she might even have warmed a little to her husband, except that his stern humour robbed the moment of potential promise. After their guests had departed from Sion Place, he had conducted her upstairs to the large, handsome suite of rooms they were to occupy as man and wife, and taking a key from his waistcoat pocket had unlocked the double doors of a mahogany wardrobe. Inside, still shrouded in the dressmaker's calico wrappers, were hanging some half-dozen or more gowns, ordered for Kitty as his wedding present.

Nor was that all. In a drawer of her dressing room, undergarments of silk lay between scented tissue, and further drawers contained pairs of French kid gloves, embroidered Swiss lawn handkerchiefs, and finest cambric nightgowns. There was a cupboard of hat boxes, another of hand-lasted boots and shoes, a leather travelling portmanteau embossed with her new initials – C.K. On a small table in the window a jewellery case held a triple choke collar of matched pearls together with a pair of drop earrings.

"These were my grandmother's," Oliver had said, indicating the pearls. "I presented them to my first wife but they will suit you better . . . you have the skin to complement them. Maria was always too sallow."

He picked up the collar and held it against Kitty's cheek, and at the touch of his fingers she had flinched a little.

"Yes, wear them tonight at dinner at the hotel," he said tersely, "with the *moiré antique* gown."

Kitty wished that she could like her husband more, that she might show him the full extent of her gratitude. He was providing her with so much – position, security, the trappings of affluence. It took her breath away to see these beautiful things which he'd bought, and she longed to go running from one to another, trying the gowns against her, touching, feeling, holding, like a child let loose in a toyshop to enjoy itself. To have all this, she who had always had so little in the past, seemed a fairy-tale come true.

Finding his eyes upon her still, with that disconcerting intensity which always made her feel nervously ill at ease, she had said, "You're very generous, sir. And indeed, I do thank you."

Polite words, spoken by one stranger to another.

Now, as they arrived at their destination, alighting from the hansom cab outside the entrance to Brown's Hotel in Dover Street, she was wondering whether they would continue to treat one another with the same cold and distant courtesy once they'd spent this first night together as man and wife, or whether the enforced intimacy of a shared bed would bring about any beneficial change in their relationship.

Having as yet no lady's maid of her own, Oliver had arranged through a domestic agency in the City for a suitable woman to be engaged in his wife's service. She attended upon them punctually at four o'clock in their hotel suite, a quiet, efficient person of middle years named Miss Dobby who, having unpacked Kitty's portmanteau and put everything neatly away, retired to the servants' accommodation until required again before dinner.

"If she suits you, Catherine, you may perhaps like to engage her for the entire tour," Oliver suggested, seeming impressed with Miss Dobby's competence. "It would save your having to use a hotel maid at Weymouth – the standard of service in these places can be wretchedly unpredictable."

This was the first time, in the several years of their acquaintance, that Kitty could ever recall her own wishes being considered, and taking it as a hopeful sign for the future, she began preparing herself for the evening with a slightly less heavy heart.

Miss Dobby dressed her hair beautifully, piling up the heavy gold-blonde waves into a chignon and leaving just a few loose tresses to be crimped into ringlets to soften the nape of her slender neck. It was a style which displayed the van der Kleve pearls to perfection, and worn with the gown of ivory *moiré antique*, added a flattering note to the warm, smooth texture of the young bride's shoulders.

At eight o'clock precisely, when she presented herself to be taken down to dinner, there was a moment's fleeting expression upon her husband's face of unguarded admiration and pleasure as he beheld her; and for the briefest instant the usually closed, cold features were transformed, like an iron mask being lifted. Then the visor was clamped down again and he said briskly, rising to his feet, "Excellent! A most charming effect. Thank you, Miss Dobby." And holding out an arm for Kitty – "We shall not require you again this evening. My wife can attend to herself before retiring."

The dining room of Brown's was not yet as full as it would be later when the theatres closed, and the two of them were able to have a pleasant table by one of the windows. At their entrance, a number of the diners turned to look at Kitty, examining her with critical interest as she went by; one gentleman in particular seemed especially taken, even shifting his chair so that he might have a better view round the brass-potted palm between their tables.

Several times during the course of the hors-d'oeuvre Kitty

glanced up to find his eyes still fixed upon her, and in trying to avoid him found herself inadvertently looking in his direction whenever her gaze wandered.

"I trust you are not attempting to encourage that fellow," Oliver said with sudden sharpness as the main course was being served them. "You appear to be paying him a good deal of attention."

Kitty's face coloured. "He happens to be seated where I can see him, sir."

"Then change your place. Perhaps that will discourage the flirtation." He rose to his feet and casting aside his napkin, went round to the back of his wife's chair and took hold of it. Conversation at nearby tables halted as fellow diners turned to see what was happening, and a waiter came smartly over to give his service.

"My wife wishes to be seated towards the wall," Oliver announced, making it sound as though this were some personal aberration. "Be so good as to lay her another place."

"Certainly, sir. If Madam would permit –?"

Without a word, Kitty got up and allowed herself to be given a chair at the opposite side of the table; and it was only the rigid self-discipline learned at Miss Meyrick's Academy which prevented her from betraying any other sign of emotion than the slight flush still staining her cheek.

"Come, eat your food before it spoils," her husband told her, seeing her slow to take up knife and fork again. "Now that the meal has your full attention you may enjoy it better."

Obediently she bent her head, but it was as much as she could do to finish even half of what was there, and she had to force herself to make a pretence of emptying her plate.

When, finally, the dessert course had been ordered, and silently picked at and cleared away, Oliver requested brandy to be served him upstairs and rose to escort his wife from the table. Again, eyes were turned to look at the lovely young woman with the face of a Sistine madonna. This time there were glances cast too at her husband, as though in curiosity that a man with such a beauty for partner should appear so icily impervious to the pleasure of her company.

Once back in the privacy of their first-floor suite, he waited in silence until the brandy came, standing at the tall window to look out on the bustle below in Dover Street; then, when the waiter had gone again, added a splash of soda to his glass from the siphon and went to seat himself in an armchair. During this brief interlude Kitty had stood irresolutely near the door, not knowing whether she should go into the dressing room to prepare herself for bed, or whether it might not be wiser to wait until her husband gave some indication of his wishes.

Perhaps sensing her indecision, he drained his glass at a single sudden gulp and got up again to refill it from the almost full bottle on the tray.

Over his shoulder he said peremptorily, "Stand here – here beneath the light. I want to look at you."

And when she had done so, moving to the centre of the room where the overhead gasolier shed its pale yellow incandescence upon her – "Now turn yourself around, slowly . . . Good. And again. Yes . . . very good."

Glass in hand he came across in front of her and reaching out, caught her small chin in his fingers and tilted it.

"But raise your head, Catherine. You spoil the effect by hanging it so. What has become of your spirit?"

The light upon his face chiselled the elegant features into sharp, angular lines, lending to their expression a touch of cruelty. Kitty looked back at him and immediately dropped her glance, finding it impossible to meet the concentration in those grey eyes.

He gave her chin a little shake and released it.

"You are very beautiful, my dear. Has any man ever told you? No? Then I shall be the first. You are beautiful . . . and it was for that beauty that I made you my wife, to own it, to have it as mine before some other man should come along and claim it. I am a connoisseur of lovely things. I admire perfection. You are both lovely, and very close to perfect. It would have been a tragic waste to allow something so unique to pass into the possession of a common boor who in a few years would destroy it."

Kitty supposed that this was her husband's way of making love to her but was at a loss to know how to respond to such coldly formal speech. Should she thank him, she wondered? And would he be angry if he knew he was not the first to call her beautiful? There had been a boy, a half-grown youth, who one day had caught her by the hand in the Rue St Honoré in

Paris, and before she could stop him had pressed his lips to her cheek and declared, "*Ah, que vous êtes belle, mam'selle!*" before disappearing again into the crowd. The warmth of that kiss had burnt itself into her flesh, just as the words had branded themselves upon her memory.

"There is something occupying your thoughts." Oliver's voice had a sudden strained edge to it. "I want to know what it is. Tell me."

"I – I was thinking of the kindness of your compliment, sir."

"Nothing more?"

"No."

He looked at her a little oddly, then, tilting his glass to his lips, moved away again towards the window. In the ensuing stillness Kitty could hear the thud of her heart in her ears, above the background sound of horse traffic from the street below. She stared at her husband's strong back, waiting; the only outward sign of her tension being a slight trembling of the pearl eardrops and the whitened knuckles of the hands clasped in front of her.

He finished his brandy.

"You won't mind if I undress you?" he asked, without turning.

The breathy hastiness of her answer betrayed her. "Oh, there is no need . . . I can see to my own undressing."

"But it is my prerogative as your husband. You are not fearful, are you, my dear?"

"Yes. A – a little, sir."

He examined his glass with studied deliberation and put it aside, then came over to her again, closer than before, so close that she could smell the brandy on his breath. Taking her by the hand he led her across the room through the bedroom door, and closed and locked it behind him before releasing her.

"There is no need to fear me," he said calmly. "I shall try not to hurt you. What I am going to do is perfectly natural." He removed his double-breasted frock coat, laying it over the back of a chair, and went on, "First, my dear, I wish to kiss you . . . kiss those inviting lips . . . a pleasure I have denied myself until this moment."

He took Kitty's face between his hands and drew her against

him, bending his head so that their mouths almost met. She shut her eyes tightly; and in another moment felt his lips upon hers, hard and possessive, crushing the soft flesh against her teeth.

"Open your mouth to me," he whispered.

She tried to do so, anything rather than endure that bruising hurt, but the sensation of his tongue being forced into her was so disgustingly repellent that she thrust herself away, squirming to escape his grasp.

"You don't enjoy my kisses?" he said savagely, holding her fast by the wrist. "Do you not know how a man gratifies himself?"

"No! I know nothing of such things. For pity's sake – you said you wouldn't hurt me!"

"Then let me do as I wish, Catherine. Don't deny me what I want of you tonight."

•She shook her head, and looking away from him said in a low voice, "I cannot deny you, sir. But, please – if you must kiss me, then not like that."

"We shall see. Now . . . allow me to undress you."

He twisted her round and began unhooking the back fastenings of her gown, drawing down the sleeves to expose her bared shoulders. Without bothering with her skirts, he unlaced her corset, and when that was undone, tossed it aside leaving her standing naked from the waist up with no other covering than the pearl collar at her throat. Kitty tried to fold her arms across herself, but he pushed them away and putting his own arms round her from behind, cupped her firm breasts in his hands.

Hot with shame and embarrassment she stood rigid as a statue, staring ahead, not wanting to look at him touching her; but the glass of the wash-stand against the further wall threw the image back at her – Oliver van der Kleve's dark head bent over the pale gleam of her shoulders, his hands holding her nakedness, exposing the pink thrust of nipples between his fingers.

He pressed his mouth hungrily to the nape of her neck, running his tongue beneath the pearls, then turned her to face him and bent to kiss her breasts.

"Sweet . . ." he murmured, his lips moving against her softness, "so sweet . . . Are you as lovely below the waist, my

33

pct, as you are above. Let me see . . . let me explore you and see."

Unhurriedly he started undoing the hooks of her skirts, letting the garments fall one by one around her ankles, beginning with the *moiré antique* silk, then the cotton petticoats, and then the whalebone cage of crinoline hoops, until she was left standing in nothing but her drawers and stockings.

"Don't tremble so," he said, almost harshly, and in the soft-hued light of the gas jets Kitty could see the perspiration beading his forehead as he knelt in front of her.

Tears of humiliation filled her eyes. She felt soiled, defiled, dirtied, by what her husband was doing, and it was as much as she could manage to control the shuddering of her limbs as he began stroking his fingers up and down her legs, each time lingering on the silk-smooth skin of her thighs above the lace-trimmed garters.

Just when she thought she would scream at the vileness of it all, Oliver suddenly rose from his knees and began to undress himself, pulling at his clothes with a kind of controlled excitement which frightened her. Like most women of her time she had seen men naked before, either in paintings and sculpture or from a distance swimming off river banks, but this was the first occasion she had been near enough to have the details of sexual arousal forced upon her reluctant gaze, and what she saw now when Oliver had stripped himself made her feel almost sick with shock.

"What are you going to do – ?" she cried out at him as he reached to take hold of her.

For answer he pulled the combs from her hair, and then the corrugated pins holding it in place, and when the heavy waves had fallen loose about her shoulders, caught her up in his arms and carried her to the bed. There he threw himself down at her side, his cruel, hard kisses bruising her mouth afresh as he forced her face round to his, his hands everywhere on her body so that she was left in no doubt at all now of his intention.

When he took her, it was suddenly and violently, tearing her apart.

How long the nightmare continued, Kitty had little recollection afterwards. The pain of what her husband was doing to her was disgusting. Crushed and winded by his plunging, panting body, she felt she was suffocating in some unimagin-

34

able hell, her nostrils filled with the sour acrid smell of his sweat and her ears throbbing with a dreadful groaning wail which she realised later had been coming from her own throat. When, finally, this crucifixion of rape was finished, he rolled away and lay sprawled across the bed, his head turned from her, one arm flung over his face as though to shut himself behind its barrier.

After a time he said thickly, "I'm sorry . . . I did not mean to use you with such force."

She made no answer. There was none to give him.

"I hope I have not hurt you too much. The first time can be . . . painful for a woman, I know."

Still, she lay silent, tears of shame and hopelessness trickling slowly from the corners of her closed eyes. The private places of her body throbbed and burned from the violation she had suffered, and there was the taste of blood in her mouth.

"I have had to wait so long for you, Catherine . . . so long. It was that which made me greedy . . . the desire to possess you made me forget myself. I will try to be more gentle with you next time."

Oh God, did there have to be a next time – and a next, and a next? Kitty could not bear even to think about it. To be made to endure this gross and terrible obscenity over and over again, night after night. She would rather be dead.

Something broke inside her and she began to weep, great sobs tearing from her throat and shaking her slender body. She felt Oliver move, and his arms go round her. In her fear and her horror of him she screamed out, lashing with clenched fists to rid herself of the touch of his nakedness.

He released her abruptly and sat up.

"Am I so repellent to you now?" There was something in his voice which she had never heard there before. "Catherine? Catherine – answer me. Do I repel you?"

She turned away on her side, curling herself into a small defensive ball.

"Answer me!"

"I am your wife, sir," she managed to choke through her tears. "It is my duty to submit to you."

"I do not want submission. I want . . ." There was a long hesitation. Kitty sensed that her husband was struggling to say something, but whatever it was, he did not complete the sentence. Instead, he got up from the bed and she heard him dress himself, then go through into the other room.

He did not return. By morning, the bottle of brandy was empty upon its tray.

4

The Royal Gloucester Hotel, Weymouth,
Monday, the 24th of April, 1865

My dear Harriet,

Well, here am I in Dorsetshire, and a whole week gone already. The weather has been mixed, tho' more good than bad – I am able to go out each morning before breakfast and walk a short way up and down the Esplanade to take the air.

Weymouth is a fine old town – indeed, it has been much patronised by the Royal Family, and I am told that our Hotel was formerly used as a private residence by our Queen's grandfather, George the Third. Imagine it, His late Majesty dined in the very rooms which are now used by the public, and his private sitting room is still to be seen, tho' much changed.

I am attended here by a maid hired through an agency in London, a most obliging woman and very neat and efficient. I wish that she might remain with me upon my return to Tunbridge Wells at the end of the week, but alas, she prefers temporary service only because of an aged mother whose health is inconstant. I trust that I may have my own maid at Sion Place, since I should not care for it were Jane Perrins to attend me – nor do I think she would serve me well, being Beatrice's creature.

Oh Harriet, the thought of Sion Place fills me with dread, I do not know why. No – ! that is untrue. I know very well what it is that makes me so ill at ease. But this shall be a cheerful letter, and therefore I will not permit myself to write of such things.

I have been on a number of pleasant excursions. Last week, I (– I suppose I should write rather, *we* –) sailed in a steamboat along the coast to Lyme Regis, which is a quaint and crooked little town almost tumbling down upon itself into the sea. There are some most interesting fossil remains to be found there – I saw several displayed in a window of a shop which looked for all the world like giant snail shells.

On Thursday morning we went by trap into Dorchester, which is not far distant from here and most agreeable to visit. It being a market day, the streets were thronged and there were also a number of soldiers from the garrison who made a fine display among the crowd. I must confess, I could not readily understand the speech of the country folk, which is very broad and slow and drawling and not at all like our own in Kent. On the way back toward Weymouth we passed a great hill at the roadside which is called Maiden Castle and is an ancient Earthwork.

The weather remaining pleasant, in the evening we made an excursion by steamboat from Weymouth to Lulworth Cove, during which harps and violins provided music for the company to dance upon the deck. In the moonlight, and with coloured lanterns hung above, it made a very pretty scene. I did not dance. I had no heart for it, and you will understand why, knowing the gentleman I would have had for partner.

The newspapers are full of the dreadful news concerning the murder on Good Friday of Mr Abraham Lincoln, in Washington. What a fearful thing this war is which is being fought between the American States, and how I do hope that your brother William is safe. I cannot remember to which part it is he has gone. How I do envy him! Not for the danger of his situation – but because he has plucked up courage to seek for himself the adventure of life in a New World. I wish that I, also, had such courage to escape.

I had a dream last night – shall I tell you of it? – that you and I together shared a pleasant house in Dorchester, where we kept a school for Young Ladies (tho' nothing at all like Miss Meyrick's!)

Ah, Harriet, would that dreams came true.

Kitty

Kitty was unaware of Oliver van der Kleve's regret that his behaviour as husband had caused her the revulsion it had. On

38

the night of their wedding he had known that his wife was an innocent young woman, utterly inexperienced in the ways of life and knowing nothing – or very little – of the nature of physical intercourse. It was this very naïvety and guilelessness which was a part of her attraction for him; that, and her extraordinary beauty. But the desire to possess her had been uncontrollable.

He had lived with his desire from the moment he first saw her, an undernourished girl of sixteen dressed in the cast-off clothing of the Academy's more fortunate pupils, yet even then displaying the most remarkable natural dignity. There was something in her attitude, something indefinable – like an aura almost – which had made her seem remote, apart, in a time of her own, unaffected by the sullying influences of life around her. He had known within a few weeks of that first meeting that he wanted her for his wife.

During the intervening years of their acquaintance she had never given a single sign, not a word or gesture, of her feelings towards him, but had always behaved on every occasion with a passive, compliant docility which attracted him still further. She was like one of the china-faced dolls in his daughter's nursery: a silent, flawless creature looking into some hidden world of her own with those lovely violet eyes, untouched and almost untouchable.

Oliver knew exactly what he wanted in a woman, and he had found it in Catherine March. He wanted unquestioning obedience, and respect and constancy; he wanted social grace, good taste and elegant manners; someone to fulfil his physical appetites and be a robust mother for his sons; a beauty he could parade upon his arm for the admiration of his fellows, and clothe and bejewel as an advertisement of his wealth; a woman who would be seen but not especially heard, who did not complain, nor cause mischief, and above all, one who was faithful.

This last requirement was probably more important than all the rest together. Oliver van der Kleve had a horror of unchastity, a deep-rooted repugnance of it which amounted almost to obsession. To his mind, what in a husband might be forgiven as a natural and, indeed, healthy release of the sexual urge, should be regarded in a wife as something unclean and very far from natural, and those women who forsook the marital bed in search of casual and adulterous liaisons were in Oliver's opinion little better than whores and should be treated as such.

It would never have occurred to him to consider the possibility of an obverse side to this coin: that it was just as reprehensible an act for a father and husband to desecrate the vows of marriage as it was for a wife; and that for society to damn a woman for adultery whilst condoning the same offence in a man was nothing less than hypocrisy.

Indeed, Oliver himself had taken a mistress during his first marriage, and saw nothing wrong in doing so.

He had met the young woman in the autumn of 1858 when his wife Maria was carrying their second child. As one who held frequent sexual exercise as not only normal but necessary for his good health, he was finding the restrictions of pregnancy irksome, and happened to remark as much to a close acquaintance while both were dining together one evening at their City club, Gresham's in Abchurch Lane. Being upon the point of taking a position with a merchant bank in Edinburgh, the acquaintance generously offered Oliver the use of his own young mistress whom he'd set up in rooms near St Paul's. There was the small matter of providing for her keep, of course, but other than that he was free to borrow her services for as long as required.

This transaction was not an unusual one between gentlemen. Whereas the less fastidious might avail themselves for under a shilling of any of the cheap little dollymops cluttering the pavements after dark, a more discerning type of man invested his money in one particular 'magdalen' in return for her undivided attention, discretion and exclusiveness; and like any other investment, provided the terms were mutually agreeable and the lady herself raised no great objection, she could be treated as a marketable commodity.

Sadie Collins had offered no objection at all. A sensible young woman, she was quick to see the advantage to herself of having a 'regular' while her own gentleman was absent, for the pimps and ponces would soon sniff out a girl who'd lost her protector and wasn't pulling in trade. And she hadn't risen from the alleys of Whitechapel at fourteen to put herself back there again at twenty.

Besides, having once set eyes upon Oliver van der Kleve,

she told herself she'd be a fool not to oblige him in every way she could. He was a good-looking man, real quality; well-mannered, too, which made a change. Her regular gentle man – the one who'd been keeping her this past half-year – he was all right, but a bit on the stout side and wore stays, and drank too much on occasion and knocked her about. Still, she wasn't complaining. There were worse ways for a girl to earn a living in London.

Sadie was of a philosophical turn of mind. When her stout lover suffered an apoplexy in Edinburgh and died within the month, it seemed no more than proper that her new gentleman, Mr van der Kleve, should assume full proprietorial rights to her services. And when *his* wife died, in childbirth in 1858, he did the handsome thing and moved her from the rooms near St Paul's to set her up in something altogether finer, a place not far from his club where he was handy to visit her two or three times a week.

Life fell into a very comfortable pattern during the course of the next few years. She wouldn't say she got to know him well – he wasn't that sort, being the private kind who never had much to say for himself – but she could always anticipate his requirements and even add a few bizarre touches of her own which she knew he'd appreciate. Physically, he was quite predictable. They all were, men. And so she had known at once that there was something up with his love life when, early in 1862, he'd started wanting her to dye her dark hair blonde and dress herself in white and behave – God help her – as though she'd never had a man in her life before.

It was a request with which Sadie Collins, true professional that she was, complied; and throughout Oliver's somewhat bloodless courtship of Catherine March, she who was his kept mistress had played the role of proxy for the virginal young woman who was to be his second wife. It was a curious arrangement, and in time an empty one, for Sadie had seen her protector alter from a man whose sexual ability had never previously failed to one who more and more often left her bed dissatisfied, without having touched her. There was no love involved between them, so it was not the lack of attention which hurt. It was the fact that she was no longer any use to him, that after – what was it, seven years nearly? – he'd grown bored with her.

When, at the start of this new year, 1865, he informed her he was to be married, she'd hardly been surprised. What *had* astonished her was that he should continue to pay her rent and send a monthly allowance, even though she was no longer providing the service for which she'd been kept.

And indeed, Oliver had fully intended ending their liaison and pensioning his mistress off to the safe distance of some place or other in Highgate. The irony of the situation now was that his new wife's quite obvious revulsion at the physical side of their union had put him into two minds on the matter. Sadie was a most undemanding creature – not blessed with any great intelligence, but an inventive and generous woman who knew how to satisfy his wants. Perhaps it would not hurt to keep her where she was for a while longer, so conveniently near to his club . . . at least, until Catherine proved less fearfully and frigidly unresponsive to his demands as husband.

5

"I have had a discussion with Beatrice," Oliver van der Kleve announced peremptorily, coming upon his wife in the conservatory at Sion Place. The couple had been back in Tunbridge Wells from their wedding tour almost a fortnight now, and Kitty was discovering the conservatory to be the only place to which she might escape alone in search of solitude.

Informed by the butler, Nicholls, where Madam would be found, Oliver had been on the point of requesting her presence in the library; but then changed his mind, deciding to seek her out for himself. This was the third time in as many days that he'd been told she was in the conservatory and he was curious to know what it was that attracted her there.

"I have had a discussion with Beatrice, concerning the running of the house. I thought I should tell you myself what has been decided."

His sudden intrusion shattered the stillness of the secluded garden room. Kitty remained as she was, seated in a wicker chair among the green shadows of ferns, her only acknowledgment being to lay down in her lap the book she'd been reading.

Accustomed to her silences, Oliver went on, "As you know, Catherine, this visit I am about to make on the bank's behalf to Amsterdam may mean an absence of some duration. A week, at the least. And in view of that, I think it might be best if Beatrice were to assume charge of the household whilst I'm away."

His wife marked her place in the book and closed it carefully before putting it aside.

"Beatrice will have charge of the household." She repeated his words expressionlessly.

"Yes. It is her opinion that you have not yet acquired sufficient practical experience to take the responsibility entirely upon yourself. I am inclined to agree. A few days away might

43

not matter, but if I am to be detained any length of time abroad I will feel more at ease knowing that the routine of my house is being capably maintained."

There was a brief pause.

"Am I expected to give up the keys?" Kitty touched the chatelaine hanging from the belt at her slender waist, symbol of her position as mistress of Sion Place.

"Naturally. Though only until my return."

"I see." The feeling of relief with which she had received the news of her husband's departure was now suddenly shattered cruelly into pieces. Her domestic responsibilities were the one pleasure she had as his wife, the one absorbing interest which enabled her to tolerate all else in their marriage. By taking away the authority of her position he robbed her of the only happiness she'd ever known from him, and by reinstating Beatrice in her stead, he delivered her into the power of a woman whose hatred was growing daily more and more obvious.

A wave of utter desolation swept over her. Bleakly, she said, "But won't the servants think it rather strange?"

"The servants are not employed to hold opinions. I have already instructed Nicholls he is to take his orders from Beatrice during my absence." Oliver was unnecessarily terse. He had not been entirely comfortable with this decision, arguing that Catherine would be able to manage the household perfectly well, given assistance if needed; but Beatrice had been most emphatic that were something to occur which demanded attention, his young wife would be insufficiently capable of dealing with it properly. Far better, she'd said, that she assume total control herself, as before. That way there would be no cause for confusion amongst the staff.

He cast a critical glance around the conservatory. It was a place he scarcely ever set foot in, being no great lover of green growing things, and in the sunny warmth of the afternoon he found its atmosphere oppressively close.

"Why do you come here, Catherine?" he wanted to know, seeing her hand stray once more towards her book. "Surely somewhere indoors would be more agreeable if you wish to read?"

"I find it perfectly agreeable here."

"It cannot be healthy. The plants take up so much of the air."

44

"I had not noticed. Besides, there is a window kept open –"
She indicated the sloping glass roof, half obscured by the
creeping tendrils of a vine. "The gardener assures me the
seedlings will take no harm from any draught provided
the weather stays warm."

"But *why* do you come here?" he asked again, more aggressively.

Kitty bowed her head. How should she answer – that she
found privacy, and quietude, somewhere to be alone, where
Beatrice's resentment and Angelina's spite were not continu-
ally thrust upon her, where she was not made to feel that
everything she did was watched and noted and criticised?

"It is . . . very peaceful," she responded after a moment,
carefully. "And I enjoy looking out upon the view."

"You may do that from the terrace room, or the morning
room."

"There is no seclusion there."

"Seclusion? Why should you wish to be secluded? Who is
there to interrupt you? The staff have their duties, Beatrice
attends to personal business, Angelina is out of the house each
morning at her lessons, and I am away in the City on four
days a week. There is only Mr Rivers who could possibly
disturb you –" Mr Rivers was Angelina's private drawing
master – "and I cannot imagine that he would wish to be the
cause of any distraction."

Kitty said nothing. She had yet to meet this tutor, but
imagined him as the dry, chalky kind of old fellow whom she
had known at Miss Meyrick's, eking out a living teaching
indifferent pupils the art of applying pencil and paint to
paper.

"Then I may not use the conservatory, sir?" she asked at
last, quietly and without looking up.

Something in her subdued tone touched upon Oliver's feelings of conscience at having earlier given way to Beatrice, and
with an ill grace he answered, "I do not wish to seem harsh.
I cannot forbid you to come here, I suppose, when clearly your
mind is set upon it."

He threw another glance around. The conservatory was
built against the south wall of the house and from its many
paned windows looked out across the sloping lawns towards a
distant vista of wooded countryside, where Broadwater Forest

45

rose upon the horizon. In the spring sunlight the pale tender green of newly opened leaves showed as a haze of fresh colour against a washed blue sky, and for a moment he was touched by something of the beauty of the scene as though seeing it for the first time through another's eyes. Then the sensation flickered away, leaving behind only a vague sense of loss that he had not been able to share that instant of appreciation with his wife.

He looked down at her again. She had taken up her book once more and seemed to be waiting for him to leave, that she might resume her reading. For some reason this irritated Oliver. In almost every way she was proving herself the compliant and dutiful model of womanhood he had expected, and not even her cold and unresponsive submission to his nightly love-making concerned him unduly, since that was no more than inexperience and would mend itself in time; but he had discovered one flaw he had not thought to find, that there was something in his wife's manner which made him feel . . . well, he could not quite put a finger upon it. It was something very small, and yet significant, as in this instance of the book . . . something which gave an impression of her complete indifference.

Breaking the silence, he asked brusquely, "What is that you are reading? May I see?"

Obediently Kitty held up the slim volume. He took it from her, glancing at the title on the spine, and a frown of displeasure immediately creased his brow.

"*Hints to Young Women in Domestic Service?* What can possibly be of enlightenment to you there? It's a manual for servants!" He threw the book aside on a shelf. "Small wonder you feel the need to hide yourself from view if that is the type of thing which takes your interest."

Stung by the contempt in her husband's voice, Kitty plucked up courage to explain herself. "It is not for my own benefit I am reading it, sir."

"No? Then for whose?"

"Rosie Maguire."

"Rose Maguire?"

"Yes."

"The under-housemaid?"

"Yes."

46

"Why on earth should you wish to concern yourself on Maguire's behalf? She's of no consequence."

"With your permission, I wish that she might become my lady's maid."

"What – !" Oliver appeared quite genuinely astonished at such a naïve suggestion. He stared at his wife for a moment, nonplussed; then recovered himself. "Lady's maid? What nonsense is this? I trust you have considered the girl's qualifications. She would be useless to you."

"That is why I am making a study of the book, sir. So that she may know where to begin in her duties, and what to do."

The astonishment changed to sarcasm. "Is she not able to study that for herself?"

"I thought . . . I thought it would be simpler for me to follow the instructions and then explain them to her."

"You mean, she does not know her alphabet well enough to be trusted to understand."

There was no answer.

Oliver made a sound of exasperation. "Since it is I who pay the girl's wage, I think I have a right to demand some explanation of your reason for this preposterous notion."

His wife looked down at her hands, twining them in her lap. "I do not wish to have Jane Perrins wait upon me, sir. She is Beatrice's maid. And with respect, you said yourself only the other day that I should have my own woman to attend me."

"I did. I also said that I would arrange the matter upon my return from Amsterdam."

"Then can I not spare you that trouble?" She raised her face to him again in quick appeal, quite unconscious of the effect her loveliness created among the soft-lit shadows, the curve of cheek and chin rimmed with an opalescent light from the sun's rays overhead. "If I were allowed Rosie, there would be no need for you to have to concern yourself with the bother of agencies and interviews."

"The idea is preposterous." Oliver repeated himself, but with less vehemence. The intimate closeness of the air within the conservatory held the smell of his wife's fragrance, the palma violet scent of her skin and hair, and this combined with her nearness was having the effect upon him of arousing his deep dark hunger for her, a hunger which he'd lately come to realise would never be sated no matter how many nights he availed himself of her tantalising beauty in the lamplit privacy of their bedchamber.

He gave no sign at all of his feelings, though, but continued instead with a consummate self-control practised over many years, "I cannot understand why you should want some ignorant, unlettered girl for a lady's maid when it is far more sensible and practical to employ a properly trained woman. Someone after the character of Miss Dobby."

The look of appeal faded in Kitty's eyes.

"You liked Miss Dobby, did you not?" her husband persisted.

She nodded.

"And you found her capable and trustworthy?"

"Yes, sir. But if I may say, so is Rosie Maguire. Please do not think me forward if I speak in her defence. She has worked in this house long enough, surely, for her honesty and willingness to be known. If you were to advertise or apply to an agency for someone as satisfactory as Miss Dobby, there is no guarantee of being sent one."

"Agreed. You should bear in mind, however, Catherine, that the rest of the staff might not take at all kindly to Rose Maguire's swift promotion. There is a world of difference in status between an ordinary house servant and a lady's maid, as I would have expected you to know. Rank and precedence count quite as much amongst the domestic class as they do amongst Society. You cannot take a girl from an inferior position and set her up above her own superiors. It causes ill feeling, and where there is ill feeling there is very often bad service."

"Then I may not have Rosie." There was nothing in Kitty's tone to betray her bitter disappointment, only a dutiful acceptance of her husband's decision. After all, she herself had been raised from an inferior position and she knew the feelings that had aroused in some quarters.

"Well –"

About to say no, Oliver hesitated. Rose Maguire had been in his employment almost two years, and as far as he could recall there had been no complaint against her from Nicholls, who was a good butler and kept a firm hand on affairs belowstairs. Indeed, had she proved a poor servant, Beatrice would have had her dismissed months ago. The only black mark against Maguire's character was the possibility of clumsiness, of which Jane Perrins had accused her on the day of the wedding; but that had been looked in to, and no proof of it found.

He reached across to the shelf and took up his wife's book, flicking through the pages.

"Well —" he said again, "I do not hold out any promise, but there is no harm I suppose in my speaking to Nicholls on the matter. It will have to wait until my return, though."

There was a quick, tight smile.

"You see, Catherine, I am not dismissing your wishes out of hand. I am a generous man, and a fair one. I trust you will remember that tonight and return me some small appreciation of your gratitude."

Rose Maguire was almost eighteen years old, the third daughter of a family of nine living at the top end of Tunbridge Wells, in one of the little rows of back-to-back terraces. Her father had a coal business here which he ran with the help of his two older sons, fetching the coal from the Medway wharf at Tonbridge and delivering it round the streets to his customers on a brightly painted dray. He was a well-known character in the area, fond of his beer, his horses and his ferrets; a brawny, jovial man whose only failing was a quick temper.

This he had inherited from his own father, an Irish mercenary during the time of the Napoleonic Wars at the beginning of the century. Selling his services to the French, the senior Maguire had been captured after Wellington's victory at Toulouse in 1814, and together with hundreds of fellow prisoners of war brought to England for incarceration. He was fortunate not to be held in one of the hellholes of rotting galley hulks moored in the Thames and Medway estuaries, where so many were to die from dysentery and typhoid fever. Instead, he was brought to a camp in Kent, and after the general release following Waterloo, elected to stay here and try his fortune in the hopfields of the Weald.

Rosie was secretly rather proud of her old reprobate grandfather. To him she owed the dash of Irish blood which had given her her deep blue eyes and dark, curling hair. In all else she was a true Maid of Kent, her mother's people coming from

49

Paddock Wood, where they had kept an alehouse on the edge of the village green for years.

The girl had come to work at Sion Place shortly after her sixteenth birthday, in 1863. This was her second position in domestic service. The first had been as a maid-of-all-work for a couple on the London Road, where apart from the cook she'd been the only servant; but the hours were long and arduous and the pay very poor, and after eighteen months her mother had taken her away from there and found her a better position in the van der Kleve residence in the superior area of Mount Sion.

This was a different world altogether. There was a staff of nine – a butler, manservant and cook, two housemaids, two kitchen maids, a groom and a gardener. And that was not including Miss Perrins, and a laundry woman who came in once a week.

Rosie had very soon discovered whom she might trust and whom she must fear; and among the latter had been Perrins and Miss Beatrice. Of the others, she had made a friend of Mary Ellen Martin, the older housemaid, and acquired an admirer in Mr van der Kleve's manservant, James Randall.

When it was learned that the Master intended marrying again there had been a good deal of hushed speculation below-stairs as to how this would affect Miss Beatrice's authority, and no one was better relieved than Rosie when it was made known that the new Mrs van der Kleve would in future be mistress of the house. As she said to her mother on her half day off, Miss Beatrice had been like a scalded cat about the place, but it served her right to be brought down a peg. She'd ruled them all with the rod of her tongue long enough, her *and* that Perrins.

Her duties as under-housemaid included cleaning and tidying Mrs van der Kleve's dressing room, and it was here that she'd encountered the new Mistress on several occasions since the wedding tour. Their conversation had naturally been limited to a few sentences, but – as she said again to her mother – Madam had such an agreeable manner, so quiet and kind, it was a pleasure to be of service. Her and Miss Beatrice, they were as different as chalk was from cheese.

For her own part, Kitty van der Kleve had taken to young Rose Maguire from the day of her marriage, when she had experienced such a strong sense of fellow-feeling for the girl over the incident of Mr Terris's crystal fruit bowl. Prudently, she had made no mention as yet about having her as lady's maid, deeming it better she should first approach her husband for his permission before raising hopes; and though he had certainly not said yes, she believed he would give the request his consideration, as he'd promised.

One morning just a few days after Oliver had left on his business in Amsterdam, Kitty rang down to the servants' basement, wanting Rosie to put some stitches in the whalebone hoop of a crinoline petticoat.

It was the other housemaid, Mary Ellen, who answered her bell.

"I'm sorry, ma'am," the girl said awkwardly, "but Rosie's not here."

"Well, it isn't important. Will she be long on her errand?"

"Beg pardon, ma'am, but she hasn't gone on any errand."

"Oh? Then where is she? It's not her day off – I thought that was Tuesday?"

"It is, ma'am. I mean, it was." Mary Ellen was looking uncomfortable. "I think you'd best speak to Mr Nicholls, ma'am."

"Nicholls? Why? What for?"

"That's not really for me to say, ma'am."

"Very well." Sensing there was something wrong here, Kitty rose from her chair. "Then I shall go down to the morning room, and perhaps you would ask Nicholls to come to me there."

"Yes, ma'am."

The morning room was already occupied when Kitty went in. Her sister-in-law Beatrice was seated at the bureau, writing a letter, and cast a sour look across her shoulder as she saw who it was disturbing her. Since her brother's departure, the older woman had missed little opportunity in reasserting herself in what she considered her place as rightful mistress, and the atmosphere of the house reflected that fact.

"You wished to see me, madam?" The butler knocked at the door and entered, addressing himself deferentially to Kitty.

It was Beatrice, however, who answered. "What is this, Nicholls?"

"I beg your pardon, Miss Beatrice, it was Mrs van der Kleve who sent for me."

There was another look, sharply impatient this time. "Well, Catherine? Make haste and say what you want. I have a further three letters to write here this morning and would be very much obliged if I might be allowed the room to myself."

Kitty's cheeks coloured slightly at such unnecessary rudeness in front of one of the staff.

"It is about Rose Maguire, Nicholls," she said quietly. "I sent for her to my dressing room, but it appears she is not in the house."

"No, madam." The butler's stout features retained their impassive expression.

"Then may I know when she's expected to return?"

"She will not be returning, madam."

"Not returning?"

"No, madam. Miss Beatrice asked me to dismiss the girl."

"*Dismiss* her? May I know why? What has she done?"

It was Beatrice again who interrupted to answer this question. "She was an unsatisfactory employee. Too forward and familiar in her manner. A bad influence upon the others."

"But – why was I not told?" Kitty stared dismayed at her sister-in-law.

"Why should you be told, Catherine? It is I who am responsible for the household during my brother's absence. I thought you understood that."

"Yes. But if I'd known in time, at least I could have provided the girl with a reference."

"*I* provided the reference. Dismissal without notice." There was a certain smug satisfaction in the voice. "It was all she deserved, and will teach her in future to put a curb upon her pertness."

But it was not pertness which had brought about Rosie Maguire's dismissal, and Kitty knew that. The real cause was the personal favour she herself had shown to the girl.

6

Young Angelina van der Kleve hummed contentedly beneath her breath, a sly smile curling the corners of her mouth, concentration given entirely to what she was doing. Above her, the delicate pink blossom of a cherry tree trembled in the slight breeze, its paper-thin petals drifting down to lie beside scattered shreds of torn lace blown away across the grass. In her lap, waiting the attention of her busily destructive fingers, were the last few of a dozen Swiss lawn handkerchiefs which had been part of her father's wedding gift to her stepmother, Catherine.

The tuneless humming stopped for a moment, and the smile became a smirk. This was becoming good sport for Angelina, this creeping into the hated stepmama's room and stealing something. It was a way of getting her own back; and if she were discovered there, why, she could always pretend Aunt Beatrice had sent her on an errand. Aunt Beatrice wouldn't tell on her. She detested the stepmama quite as much as did Angelina.

The child took up another flimsy handkerchief and began methodically ripping off the embroidered lace border. In her mind she was envisaging the scene when Papa should enquire why his wife was not making use of the gift he had given; and how stupid and silly she would appear when she had to confess to mislaying the box. Papa would then become angry, as he always did, and blame the stepmama for her negligence, saying it showed how little she cared. Then she would fall into one of her long boring silences and sit like a wooden doll in her chair without moving, so that Papa grew even more vexed and left her there to sulk alone while he took himself off to the library.

The humming began again. The last of the lace was shredded into pieces and cast away on the grass. For a while Angelina regarded her handiwork with considerable satisfaction; then screwing up the tattered squares of material left from her destruction, got to her feet and went across to the low ha-ha edging the lawn to thrust them out of sight between the stones. Returning to her place by the cherry tree, she knelt down again among its scattered petals, crinoline-hooped skirts swaying up behind to reveal frilled pantalettes and a pair of high-buttoned boots.

This was the picture which presented itself to Jonathan Rivers as he came down the sweep of stone terrace steps in search of his pupil, and to his artist's eye it created quite a charming little cameo – the splash of ivory-pink cherry blossom against a hazed green background, and the child in blue and cream kneeling alone. The charm was promptly ruined, however, by the sullen expression which Angelina turned upon him at his approach.

"It's ten minutes after three," he said pointedly, knowing that the niceties of conversation were entirely wasted upon this badly mannered girl. "You were supposed to be in the terrace room, working upon the sketch I set you."

"*You're* late. You should have been here earlier," retorted Angelina rudely. "Anyway, the sketch is boring. I want to do something else."

Her tutor regarded her with stoicism. Were it not for the fact that he needed the regular income in order to live, he would prefer to be almost anywhere than here each week, attempting to teach this intolerable young person the basic rules of line and perspective. But her father paid him well, and being loth to lose the money, Mr Rivers was obliged to do what he could to turn her sow's ear talent into something more like a silken purse.

"You will finish the sketch. You cannot progress to something else until you've had sufficient practice in composition."

Angelina wrinkled her nose; then, gracelessly, got to her feet again. Despite her insolence, she was at that age when she was beginning to feel the first clumsy stirrings of calf love, and was secretly just a little attracted to her drawing master. He was far older than she, of course – twenty-five at least, which made him almost twice her age – but rather good-looking, with his velvet jacket and bow-tied silk cravat, and his thick brown hair worn romantically long at the collar. Aunt Beatrice said he smelled of turpentine and oil paint, and his boots needed mending.

Tossing back the ringlets from her face, Angelina announced in a sudden know-all manner, "I've got a secret, but I'm not telling you."

"Then don't, I've really no wish to hear it." Jonathan Rivers took her by the arm and turned her in the direction of the terrace. "Come along, you have until four o'clock to work upon your drawing –"

"*Why* don't you wish to hear it?"

He ignored the interruption. "And we've lost sufficient time already this afternoon. Your father doesn't pay me for wasted tuition."

"I shall tell you anyway." The child twisted herself out of his grip and danced a few steps ahead. "It's about my stepmama. I know something no one else does –"

"Angelina –"

"She destroys all the presents my papa gives her. She does! She spoils them and then hides them away where she thinks no one will see. But *I* know. I've watched her. And that's not all, either. Why, she's ripped up the things Papa bought for her trousseau –"

"*Angelina.*" The young tutor tried again. "Don't you listen? I am not interested in hearing any of this."

His pupil made a face, contorting her pudgy, pimpled features into an ugly expression. "Why not? It's true! I suppose you're sweet on her."

"That is being impertinent." Something in his tone gave a warning not to try his patience further. Angelina sneaked a sidelong glance. The blue-grey eyes returned the glance with distaste.

"It *is* true," she said sullenly, turning her back and hunching up her shoulders, high-buttoned boots scuffing against the gravelled path. Now Mr Rivers was annoyed with her, and all because she'd wanted him to pay her some proper attention. That was why she said the things she did – the bigger the lie, the more notice she received. Anyway, it was all that detestable stepmama's fault, she should never have married Papa and come to live here. It wasn't wrong to tell lies about *her*, in fact it served her right, and Angelina hated, hated her. She wished Perrins would put poison on her hairbrush so that all her hair dropped out, and fill her scent bottle with privy water to make her stink.

She cast another glance at her tutor's face. He was looking towards the end of the terrace where something had caught his eye. Angelina followed the look, and the childish malevolence of her thoughts showed for a second in her expression as she recognised the slender figure outside the terrace room door.

"Now I shan't be able to work at my drawing," she said pettishly. "*She's* there. She'll keep interrupting, and spoil the lesson."

Jonathan Rivers did not answer immediately. He had met his employer's new wife for the first time only last week, since Mrs van der Kleve had been either out or occupied elsewhere indoors each time he'd come to the house. The meeting had been no more than a brief self-introduction as she went through the hall to the morning room, but he had been struck at once by her air of stillness, and the total absence of expression in the carved marble beauty of her features. How cold she was, he'd thought – cold and remote.

"Of course your stepmother won't spoil the lesson," he replied, starting to mount the terrace steps. "Don't make excuses. There, see – she's going back inside."

"Good!"

"Why do you dislike her so much?" The sudden, unexpected question was not one he had meant to ask – it was the sort of familiarity which he'd always been at pains to avoid with his pupils. But it had been out of his mouth before he could stop it.

"I hate her, that's all." Angelina was unengagingly frank. "She's horrid. She's always causing trouble and displeasing Papa. *And* she interferes in everything. Aunt Beatrice hates her, too, and so does Perrins."

Aunt, niece and lady's maid – what an unholy trinity! The young man felt a quick sympathy for the new mistress of Sion Place if she had these three already turned against her; but then, women were all the same, never content unless they were at odds with one another over something and happiest when they'd succeeded in making everyone else as miserable as sin. The sympathy receded.

He ushered his reluctant pupil along the terrace and in at the open door.

"Good afternoon, Mrs van der Kleve –"

She was standing inside by the easel looking at her stepdaughter's work and did not turn to acknowledge him as he entered. The clear cool light from the windows fell upon her profile, giving the skin an almost translucent sheen with just the faintest warm blush of colour at cheek and temple and earlobe.

Her voice, when she spoke, was quiet and steady.

"Angelina is doing well, I hope, Mr Rivers?"

"She would do better with more application to what I am trying to teach her."

He had not meant to sound abrupt, but that was how it came; and before he was able to soften the words with something lighter, Angelina had burst in rudely – "You're not to look at my drawing. It isn't finished. Papa said you weren't to see it until it was done."

"Did he? I'm sorry. I didn't know that." There was no change in tone. She might have been speaking to anyone, not to a wretchedly odious child who addressed her as though she were one of the scullery maids. "Then I'll leave you alone to get on."

For the first time, she glanced across at Jonathan Rivers; and giving him a small, grave smile, turned away again without another word and went through the inner door into the house.

About half an hour later, Kitty left Sion Place on her way to meet Harriet Seymour at the tea room on the Parade. Had she wished, she was quite at liberty to invite her friend to the house, but it was a blessing to get out for a while on to neutral ground, away from that forbiddingly pursed-lipped, disapproving atmosphere.

Her route led her steeply downhill, past the elegant façades of Georgian town houses which within the last century had replaced the earlier, smaller buildings erected to accommodate visitors during the Season. At the foot of Mount Sion, at its junction with the High Street, she turned left into the narrow cobbled lane leading along the back of the Royal Kentish Hotel, past a huddle of small shops towards the chapel of King Charles the Martyr. Here, on the opposite side of the road, was the entrance to a double row of tree-lined arcades which were the heart of the Wells and site of the iron-rich chalybeate springs which had brought about the town's existence as a health resort some two hundred years earlier.

Avoiding the horse traffic, she crossed over into the upper Parade and made her way along the pantile-paved colonnade of shops almost to the further end where, facing the bandstand, a narrow little half-timbered building boasted a popular tea room on its ground floor.

Harriet Seymour was already there when she arrived. The two friends had hardly seen each other since Kitty's marriage – Harriet had been at Broadstairs with her mother – and consequently there was much to talk about. Having no one else in whom she might confide, it was a relief to be able at last to air her feelings about Rose Maguire's dismissal almost a month earlier.

"I went to see her, of course," Kitty said, nearing the end of the story. "I had her address from Randall, the manservant. She lives at the top end of town, in Holly Bank Terrace. Do you know it at all? Behind Crescent Road?"

Harriet shook her head and took a sip of tea without replying.

"I must admit, I wouldn't have known where to find it myself if Randall hadn't accompanied me. He was quite as stung as I at the heartless, cruel way in which Beatrice got rid of the girl, and seemed anxious to do what he could to help."

"I hope, my dear, the dreaded Bea didn't discover where you'd gone."

"Oh, no. We took care to leave the house separately, and meet by the Five Ways emporium. Then it would look as though I'd done some personal shopping and he were there to carry my parcels."

Harriet took another sip, holding saucer close beneath teacup. "So what was the outcome? You saw Rose Maguire and – ?"

"Well, I told her how sorry I was to lose her . . . that I'd had no say in the matter, and wasn't aware even that she'd been dismissed –"

"You didn't mention the post of lady's maid?"

There was a shrug. "What would have been the point? It was too late then, and might only have upset the girl to know."

"Quite right."

Kitty took up her own cup and saucer. "It cheered me to see how pleased she was with the reference I'd written. At least she'll have no trouble now in finding herself some other position."

She had spoken about Rose to Oliver van der Kleve when he returned from Amsterdam, drawing his attention to the gross unfairness of the girl's treatment; but he'd scarcely even listened, saying Beatrice had already told him of the matter and he was quite satisfied that she had acted correctly.

"Well, my dear, you did what you could to make amends," Harriet said consolingly, "and Rose Maguire should think herself lucky. But it still leaves you without a maid of your own to attend you, so what is The Husband proposing to do about that? Has he said?"

"Only that he'll see to it when he has time."

"But didn't he give his promise before he went abroad?"

"Yes. But now the excuse is business. It's something to do with this ending of the war between the American States. Don't ask me to explain. The Stock Market has gone up, or perhaps down, and so he must be in the City throughout the week attending the bank's affairs."

"Well, *that* can't be causing you any great heartache –" Harriet helped herself to a wafer-thin slice of bread and butter. "You'd prefer him to be out of the Wells, surely."

"I don't know that it makes much difference. At least while he's here playing the martinet that dreadful child of his is somewhat better behaved, and Beatrice takes more care to hide her animosity. Whenever we're in company together she has a way of freezing a smile on to her face, as though she were suffering an attack of rigor mortis."

Kitty held out a hand for Harriet's cup and refilled it from the nickel-silver teapot at her elbow.

"My one pleasure is hoping she may stick like that if the wind changes."

She passed the teacup back again.

Watching her expression, her friend observed the slightly wicked humour at the corners of the generous mouth turn into a grimace.

"The one advantage of having a husband who works in the City, Harriet, is that he must occasionally spend the night away from home."

The import of this particular remark was not lost upon the other; and after a moment she responded gently, "You're still very unhappy, aren't you, dear."

There was a nod.

"Perhaps you'll grow used to it."

"What – my unhappiness, or my husband's attentions?" Kitty's voice was low and she cast a glance around the nearby tables as she spoke, not wishing to be overheard. "Unhappiness is a thing I learned as a child to accept, and tolerate. But the other – no, Harriet, never. There's nothing on earth can make me accept such degrading behaviour."

"Is it so bad, then – after all?"

"Yes. I'm afraid it is."

Through the tea room windows, the scarlet and white uniforms of the town band showed vividly against the sunlit green of lime trees behind the bandstand, and the strains of a medley of light operetta drifted in through the open doorway over the hum of conversation.

Kitty picked up her teaspoon and toyed with it for a minute before adding milk to her cup and stirring it round. Then, leaning forward a little, she said, "He brought me back a gift from Amsterdam . . . he said I should wear it to please him."

There was a pause. She replaced her spoon in the saucer.

"What was it?" prompted Harriet, curious to know.

"A white silk nightgown. A most expensively beautiful thing. I'd never seen anything so lovely. It seemed a sacrilege, almost, to put it on for no other purpose than to sleep in it. Indeed, I said as much – but he insisted. And now I can never wear it again without remembering how he managed to sully whatever feeling of pleasure and gratitude his gift had given me."

Kitty stopped abruptly, biting her lip.

"I will tell you the truth," she continued again after a moment. "I have seriously considered leaving Mr van der Kleve . . . separating from him."

"But Kitty, dearest –" Harriet was somewhat taken aback – "if you did that, where would you go? What would you do?"

"I'd thought of placing an advertisement in one of the newspapers, offering myself as a private governess. After all, I am qualified. I have my diploma from the Academy."

"But no reference." A quick note of caution sounded.

"The diploma might have been sufficient." Another pause; then, almost desperately – "I *would* have found a post, Harriet. If not by advertising, then through an agency. *Something* would have turned up, I know."

"So many 'woulds' and 'hads'. It all sounds rather in the

past tense to me. As though you've already abandoned the idea?"

"I've had to. There was no choice."

"Very sensible. Can you imagine the scandal! My dear, just think – Beatrice would have gone about like a cat with two tails, telling everyone 'there, I told you so'. Would you allow her that satisfaction?"

"Yes, I would."

Harriet shot a quizzical look over the rim of her teacup. "Now you're being perverse."

"I don't care! Oh, surely you must understand? I simply wanted to escape . . . to get away from it – them – everything. And now . . . I can't."

"But why can't you? What has changed?"

"What do you suppose –" The band music outside swelled into the finale, forcing Kitty to raise her voice against its sound. "I think I may be pregnant, Harriet. I think I may be carrying Mr van der Kleve's child. So you see, he has me trapped . . . there's no escape for me . . . no escape now, anywhere."

Kitty's pregnancy was officially confirmed in mid-July by the family physician, Dr Adeney. Her child could be expected about the third week in January, almost exactly nine months after her marriage to Oliver van der Kleve.

The news had a mixed reception at Sion Place. Oliver himself expressed a happy satisfaction that their union had proved so quickly fruitful and trusted the infant would be a lusty boy – the son and heir denied him by his first wife's death in childbirth.

This insensitive reminder of her predecessor's fate, coming at a time when Kitty was suffering the onset of queasy sickness, offered nothing in the way of reassurance. Beginning already to feel like death herself, she hardly needed the late departed Maria van der Kleve held up as a cautionary example. Neither did it help her confidence that Oliver decided as a safeguard to her health that Beatrice should continue to have the responsibility of managing the household's affairs.

Predictably, young Angelina viewed the expected arrival of a half-brother or sister with resentful jealousy. A 'little stranger' in the nursery was a cuckoo in the nest of her father's affections, pushing her further into the background, perhaps displacing her entirely – a suspicion fostered by her aunt, whose own reaction of grim approval that Oliver had done his duty by the family name was matched by the opinion that this child should be reared as far as possible without its mother's participation or interference.

"But my dear Beatrice – you cannot simply deny the infant its mother's existence!" the Reverend Mr Edward Terris exclaimed, having listened with strained politeness to a defence of this view. The Sunday morning service at St Bride's had taken rather longer than usual, due to the over-zealous preaching of a visiting missionary clergyman, and he was anxious to get away. Unfortunately, Beatrice van der Kleve had chosen this moment to capture him as he was locking the vestry door.

"Are you suggesting that Oliver's wife is not fit to rear the child herself? Is that your argument?" He pocketed the key and looked round the empty pews in an abstracted manner, wondering whether his verger had remembered the baptism here this afternoon at half past three.

"I would not venture so far as to say she's unfit," Beatrice replied, "but there is a possibility that her influence upon the young infant might not be a beneficial one."

"I think you are allowing natural concern to sway your judgement. Let me counsel you to be guided by your dear brother, and I am sure that upon reflection you will find your fears unfounded —" The minister began moving down along the side aisle in the direction of the porch. If he hurried, there might just be time for a glass or two of something before luncheon.

Beatrice followed. "But would you not agree, Edward, that Catherine's background makes her quite unsuited to have care and control of this child? She was a foundling. And what is in the blood will show itself in the flesh. Who knows what kind of unstable tendencies there might not be at work within her."

Mr Terris's hand was now grasping the iron ring of the porch door.

"Dear lady, as Christians we can only judge upon the evidence we have. Your brother's wife has always conducted herself in a quiet and seemly manner, and I very much doubt that Oliver would have married her had he had reason to suspect any flaw or impediment in her nature."

The handle was turned and the door swung back, letting in light and air and sound from the Sunday street. Below, at the foot of the steps, Jane Perrins was standing waiting for her mistress.

"Be guided by your brother," Mr Terris said again, ushering Beatrice out and closing the door behind them both, "and trust in the Lord's goodness that all will be well. Now I must ask you, please, to forgive me, but, alas, duty tears me from the further pleasure of your company —"

He gestured vaguely towards the vicarage across the street, and setting his low-crowned black felt hat upon his head, hurried away down the steps in search of escape.

A look of mingled pique and frustration flickered for a

moment in Beatrice's eyes as she followed this hasty departure. She had deliberately stayed behind after morning service to speak to Edward Terris in confidence, and it had been a long and somewhat chilly wait in the draughty, stone-floored church. To be honest, this matter of her sister-in-law was not as pressing as she'd made it sound: the real reason for her waylaying Mr Terris went rather deeper and was of a more personal nature. For some weeks now, she had felt that the minister was avoiding her, and as is so often the case with those who harbour secret emotional attachments which cannot find open expression, her imagination had been at work upon this supposed neglect, fretting away at it until she'd convinced herself that she was being deliberately slighted.

The Reverend Mr Edward Terris had been her brother's friend for more than a dozen years, and Beatrice had always lived in hope that one day he might regard her with new eyes – not as Oliver's sister, but as the wife of his bosom, to be the helpmate and confidante of his ministry and recipient of his lonely heart's devotion. As long as he remained a bachelor, this hope could be nurtured in countless imagined little ways – the lingering glance, the casual touch of the hand, the ready smile and complimentary word, so much to be remembered in the dark hours of the night and interpreted as tokens of a covert affection bestowed so very discreetly upon Beatrice herself.

Now, though, he quite appeared to be avoiding her. The last time he had taken a meal with them at Sion Place, his conversation was noticeably strained, and only showed its usual wit and warmth when addressed to her sister-in-law Catherine. With *her* he had been most affable, behaving in his normal manner, all smiles and joviality, so that it had made Beatrice grind her teeth to have to sit and witness it, waiting for the few small crumbs of notice he occasionally threw in her own direction.

Could it be, she wondered, that Edward's susceptible nature was being seduced by that artful creature's behaviour – his attentions distracted by the way in which she seemed to hang upon his every word, gazing at him under her eyelashes with that false and fawning expression so that the poor dear man had been quite taken in by her guile? Yes, surely that must be it! And all a pretence, of course, like so much else with the former Catherine March, for did he but know it, behind that too-perfect beauty lay a selfish, greedy, grasping little mind which manipulated men entirely for its own ends. How else could Oliver have been persuaded to take her as his second wife had she not practised her clever wiles upon him, leading him to believe her the tractable young innocent that he did? And now Edward Terris, likewise a victim –

Beatrice clasped her prayerbook to her box-pleated bosom and descended the church steps to the waiting Jane Perrins.

Aloud she said, "I think we might return home by Grove Hill. The walk will benefit us both", and left it at that.

Perrins pursed her lips a little thinner and dutifully fell into step a pace behind her mistress. Loyal as she was to Miss Beatrice, there were times when that loyalty could be stretched a trifle, especially when she was made to remain standing so long in the street, to be gawked at by every passing male. It was one thing to be requested to wait while Miss Beatrice had 'a few words' with Mr Terris, but quite another when those few words stretched into twenty minutes.

Her ladyship wouldn't get anywhere with him, of course. Perrins could have told her that six years or more ago, when first she'd entered service at Sion Place and saw what was what. Miss Beatrice was a fine-looking woman, but not what you might call an oil painting. She had a strong face – like her brother the Master's, very striking and well-boned – but what was handsome in a man was not generally quite so pleasing in a female. Mr Terris now, *he* had an eye for something softer and sweeter altogether. He liked his ladies young and pretty, and it was Perrins's opinion, having watched him at his ways, that the younger and prettier they were, the more the minister buttered them up with his flattery. If Miss Beatrice was hoping to marry him, then she hoped in vain. The only thing she had in her favour, poor woman, was money – and Perrins had a suspicion it wasn't money Mr Terris was wanting to tickle his fancy between the bedsheets of a night.

Not that she didn't have a certain amount of sympathy for her mistress. She knew what it was herself to admire a man and have to stand by and see him mopping and mowing round another female's skirts. In her own case, though, there was the added torment of sharing the same roof together, for it was the Master's own valet, James Randall, who was her secret love – as nice and neat a young man as was to be found, but a dreamer. Perrins had done her best to show a discreet interest, hoping he'd take the hint and invite her along on his day off – a jaunt out to Knole, perhaps, or a row on the Medway. But no, Jem Randall only had eyes for the under-housemaid, Rose Maguire, following her about belowstairs like a puppy dog on a leash and billing and cooing in her ear whenever he'd half a chance.

Knowing the cruel jibes the other servants would poke if they knew, Perrins had kept her feelings to herself, pretending she didn't care – none of them liked her much, anyway, and she wasn't about to give them all the satisfaction of seeing how much it hurt to watch her Jem making cow's eyes at Maguire. When the sly little madam finally got her come-uppance from Miss Beatrice, in May, there was a chance he might put her from his mind now, not seeing her under his nose all the while; but it was only a faint chance, and fading, for Perrins had recently learnèd from Mrs Reynolds the Cook that the two were keeping company still about the town, and Mrs van der Kleve was encouraging it.

For her own reasons, Jane Perrins shared her mistress's opinion of the Master's new wife. Not quite the same reasons, perhaps, but equal in the depth and compass of their resentment. As she and Beatrice paused at the top of Grove Hill for a moment's breath, she said carefully, in the refined tone of voice she always used, "Mrs van der Kleve will be concerned, won't she, madam, that we're so long returning from church?"

And was gratified to hear the other answer – "Let her wait, Perrins. There's no harm done if she's inconvenienced. She'll have plenty more to fret her, *plenty* more, if I can help it."

The dead mouse, neatly placed in the centre of her pillow, was blamed as the work of one of the kitchen cats, but Kitty knew otherwise. She was beginning to recognise the certain smirking satisfaction upon her stepdaughter's face whenever the child had been up to mischief, and that smirk had been there this evening when Angelina passed her on the stairs to the first-floor landing.

Droplets of blood had spotted the white pillow case, and even after the mouse was removed and a clean cover fitted, Kitty could see the little creature there still just as she had found it, stretched in its final death throe, its head broken in and its grey fur matted with its gore.

She had been very sick.

"But it's gone now – look, there's nothing there at all." Oliver van der Kleve was starting to lose patience. He had prepared himself for bed and come into their room expecting to find his wife already retired, only to be greeted by the sight of her huddled in a chair, legs drawn up beneath her nightgown, hugging her arms about herself and looking as bleached as death.

"Now please don't be foolish, Catherine. You cannot spend the entire night like this. Come along –" He held out a hand. "It was only a mouse, for heaven's sake, and the thing was quite dead."

No. It had been moving when Kitty found it. She gave an involuntary shudder and clasped herself still tighter, fighting down the nausea threatening to overwhelm her again.

"Come to bed!" Her husband bent forward and took her by the arms, drawing her from the chair. "You need to rest properly. You heard what Dr Adeney said."

The doctor had told her she must expect to suffer a few months' queasiness in the early stage of her pregnancy, and had counselled plenty of sleep and light, milky meals. But the vomiting was constant, and the slightest thing seemed to turn her stomach the sight of uncooked meat, the taste of wine, the smell of Beatrice's hair pomade, tobacco smoke, poached fish, even the scent of the lavender bags used to sweeten the bed linen. At the same time she had found herself with a perverse craving for certain foods, especially burnt toasted bread and oranges, which she would happily have eaten for every meal if she could.

Dr Adeney, a caring and kindly man, had assured her that all this was perfectly natural, and had prescribed a general tonic for her sickness, suggesting several short walks each day by way of exercise. No mention was made of more intimate matters. Kitty had lacked the courage to ask, but had supposed that now she was pregnant her husband would refrain from sexual intercourse; and was therefore uneasy as well as repulsed when he seemed to wish to persist in his attentions. Surely this could not be right – it would harm the child, she thought. But in the absence of professional advice, not knowing what to do, she had continued to submit herself to the nightly ordeal of being his wife.

"Oliver –" She pulled back from his arms, the nausea pearling her brow with perspiration. "Don't make me come to bed. I can't . . . I'm not well."

"Nonsense, it will make you more comfortable to lie down."

"No . . . please!"

"Now stop this, Catherine. You were perfectly all right this afternoon at the Broadwoods. In fact, Henry remarked to me how fit and healthy you were looking."

Kitty put a hand to her throat, fighting down the desire to be sick again. It was true, she had felt quite recovered for a while today and had enjoyed taking tea with their neighbours the Broadwoods, who lived just down the hill at Bowling Green House with two young children, Mary and Alfred. But hardly had she been back at Sion Place than this dreadful queasiness gripped her once more and it was as much as she could manage later on to eat supper. Finding the mouse there on her pillow had proved a little too much for her stomach.

She sat down again, heavily, and leaned her head against the chair wing, eyes closed, wishing that Oliver would go away and leave her alone with her misery.

"Shall I ring down to the kitchen and ask Mrs Reynolds to make you an infusion? That seemed to give you some relief the other morning, did it not?" There was sudden solicitude in his voice. He disliked illness, and it vexed him to see how easily his wife allowed herself to succumb to what was, after all, a minor discomfort expected of her condition; but by the same token he did not wish to appear uncaring.

"Catherine?"

Slowly she opened her eyes once more and looked up at him.

"Do you wish me to ring down?"

There was a slight shake of the head. "Thank you . . . no . . . I want nothing."

"Then I insist that you come to bed –" Again he raised her out of the chair, and this time swung her effortlessly into his arms and carried her across to the mahogany four-poster. The covers were already thrown back. Carefully, mindful for once of her state, he laid her against the pillows and seated himself at her side, pushing back the rose-damask bed curtains which his first wife Maria had sewn during the waiting months of her own ill-fated pregnancy.

The oil lamp on the table cast a shadow over Kitty's face, emphasising the ghost grey pallor of those lovely features; and touched by some slight prick of pity, Oliver leaned forward and brushed back the tumbled hair from her forehead.

She gave a little start and flinched away.

"Don't worry, I won't bother you tonight," he said harshly, the pity instantly replaced by sharp irritation at that unconscious rejection of him. Getting to his feet again, he moved away to take up the lamp, the pale yellow light throwing his broad-shouldered figure in silhouette against the wall, and cupping a hand round the top of the glass chimney, blew out its flame and came back round to his own side of the bed, dragging the curtains shut as he climbed in so that the two of them lay enclosed in darkness.

After a time he said testily, his head turned away, "I wonder sometimes, Catherine, whether I would have married you had I known how cold a wife you would be. I do not ask for affection, but surely I have a right to expect you to be a trifle more accommodating of my needs."

There was silence; and thinking he would get no response, he was on the point of turning over to sleep when Kitty said, in a whisper almost, "I am sorry if you find me unsatisfactory. I have done my best always to oblige you . . . performed all the duties required of me."

"It is not your obedience that is at fault. It is the manner in which you comply – your reluctance, your lack of response, your unwilling attitude. I am not forcing you to do anything contrary to the obligations of marriage. I merely ask that you not make your distaste for the natural act quite so painfully evident."

There was another silence. Outside below in the street the sound of a passing horse cab carried clearly as it rounded the corner and picked up pace again down Mount Sion.

"I know that you are disappointed in me . . . and I have tried, truly I have, but I cannot help myself."

Her words fell between them both in the darkness; and the strength of her unhappiness lent her a sudden courage. She had to tell him now – now, before her heart failed her; while the frail straw of her dreams was still there to be clutched.

"If you wish . . . if you wish, I will go away."

He gave a violent start. "Go away – ?"

"Yes. Surely it would be for the best if I went, if I left this house –"

"Don't *dare* to speak of such a thing! I'll not hear another word of it! You are my wife – my *wife*. You carry my child. You will stay."

Beneath the outrage in her husband's voice, Kitty might have caught an edge of bewilderment and pain had not her own wretchedness so deafened her to it. What had she expected – that he would agree to what she'd asked? That he would allow her the freedom to make a new life elsewhere for herself? What a futile hope!

A kind of dumb fury born of despair seized upon her and she made to get up, but anticipating her movement, Oliver reached over and grasped her roughly by the shoulder, pulling her back.

"So now we have the truth. Is this how you would repay me for all my efforts? I have given you everything – rank, wealth, education, even my name – and what have I ever received of you in return but coldness and aversion. You lack for nothing in this house. Your every need and comfort is attended to. You are clothed and fed and entertained at my expense. I do you the signal honour of taking you in marriage and giving you my child – and what is your response? You threaten to abandon our union. You threaten you will leave me –!"

He dragged her against him among the mound of pillows, crushing her in the strength of his arms, the force of his reaction astonishing even himself. Thrust away in the deepest recess of half-remembered memories there was an echo here of old pain, old hurt, a buried nerve of childhood lying forgotten all these years under layers of an adult's self-protection.

"Don't –" he said thickly, his mouth against the soft, warm curve of her throat. "Don't ever say that to me again. You are mine, Catherine, *mine*, every part of you. I will never let you free of me, I swear it, never – never."

8

As Kitty's pregnancy advanced into its fifth month, Oliver decided to have a portrait done of her for the drawing room, to hang with those of other members of the van der Kleve family. Jonathan Rivers was invited to submit preliminary sketches for the work: several of his oil paintings had been much admired the previous year when they were exhibited at the Assembly Rooms, and his obvious talent and reasonable fees impressed Oliver sufficiently to give him the commission.

The first sitting was arranged for the morning of Monday, the fourth of September, when the art master would not be engaged with private pupils. Though the actual portrait itself would be done at his cottage studio off Hungershall Park, the initial drawings were to be made in the terrace room at Sion Place, thus dispensing with any immediate need of a chaperone.

Kitty could not make up her mind whether she was looking forward to these sittings or not. While she supposed it might be interesting to see herself depicted as the subject of a painting, the idea of being scrutinised in detail by a person she hardly knew was just a little daunting, and she hoped that Mr Rivers would excuse her if she seemed at all apprehensive.

"I've never sat for anyone before, you see," she admitted to him on that first morning, standing awkwardly watching while the young man moved a chair into one of the window bays to catch the cool, clear light. "Does it take very long?"

"Well, that depends –" He stood back and examined the chair's position, head tilted at a slight angle, his normally humorous mouth set in concentration. "Depends upon the subject, ma'am. Some sitters are less difficult than others. Would you –" he indicated the seat politely – "would you sit there for a moment, please? I'd like to get a rough idea of composition."

Kitty complied, folding her hands at her waist to hide the

tell-tale swell of pregnancy. Oliver had decided she should wear a muslin chemisette, lace-trimmed and threaded with lavender ribbons, together with a high-belted silk overskirt in a darker shade of the same colour. He had also proposed the way her hair should be dressed; but not liking the fussily ringleted style which Jane Perrins had done, she'd brushed it out and re-arranged it herself in a simple chignon, tying it back from her face with more of the lavender ribbon.

Jonathan Rivers examined his subject critically. The clothing was far too staid and unimaginative – what was needed was something which revealed the shoulders to show off those lovely flesh tones and good bone structure. It would also distract the viewer's eye from the thickening waistline, although a little judicious artist's licence could be used there for the finished picture.

He took a few steps to the left, framing his sitter from a different angle and visualising the effect of the light's direction on her face.

"No doubt your husband's already discussed with you how he wishes the portrait to be done."

"He hasn't, no." Kitty kept her eyes fixed straight ahead, her lips barely parting to answer.

"It's all right, you may move if you wish, ma'am. You won't blur the picture." Jonathan tried to put her at her ease. One of the earliest things he'd learned about portraiture was that the best results were got from making the sitter relaxed and comfortable: unconscious tension showed itself in the muscles of the face, distorting the features very slightly so that what the artist captured was not a natural likeness but a mask.

He went on, "Mr van der Kleve's instructions were that you should be shown seated, three-quarter face, with a background view of the garden through the window behind. This is only my fourth commission, but I must say, none of the others have been quite as specific."

"Is that a help or a hindrance?" She watched him go over to his satchel on the table and take out a pad of cartridge paper.

"Generally a hindrance. You'd be surprised, ma'am, at the number of people one hears of who expect their portraits done in the style of Rembrandt or Gainsborough or Van Dyck, and all for the price of ten guineas. I must confess, though, what your husband proposes is more or less what I think I'd have decided upon myself had the choice been mine. Something light and uncluttered and airy."

While he spoke Jonathan Rivers selected several soft-lead pencils from a box and stuck them into the breast pocket of his velvet jacket.

"When I do a portrait, Mrs van der Kleve, I like to develop a theme, a motif. Let me explain – but please, there's really no need to keep so still, I'm just going to make a few rough sketches to start with –"

He drew up a chair for himself a few feet away and sat down, one leg across the other to rest the drawing pad, his eyes concentrating on Kitty's features as he continued with what he was saying.

"My last commission was a Tonbridge magistrate. After discussing the gentleman's wishes, I decided we should emphasise a certain solidness and weight in the portrait – the gravity of judgment, the heavy hand of the Law, you follow the sort of thing I mean. And therefore I tried to introduce that feeling of solidness by painting him against two large pieces of furniture, his library desk in the right foreground with the subject standing at centre resting his hand upon an open volume, and in the background, a neo-classic bookcase. To counter the monotony of too many brown tones, I reflected a certain amount of light from the glass of the bookcase doors, and balanced that with the illumination of a reading lamp on the desk."

There was nothing pretentious or boastful in the way the young artist described his work, simply a quiet confidence that what he did was what he was best at doing, had been trained to do competently, and took pride in doing well to the satisfaction of those who commissioned him.

"It was that portrait which Mr van der Kleve saw exhibited last summer," he went on after a moment or so, pausing to consider the progress of his sketch of Kitty's head. "He was kind enough to admire it."

Having been so stiff and self-conscious at the start of this sitting, the object of his concentration was now beginning to feel slightly less awkward, and ventured to ask, "And what will be your theme for my portrait? Have you decided?"

"Not yet . . . not quite. I will first need to know you rather better, ma'am."

"Oh?"

"Does that sound presumptuous? It wasn't intended. What I meant was, the artist doesn't simply make a copy of what he sees, like a photographic image. There's a great deal more involved. What he's attempting to do is produce an interpretation, an appraisal, of his subject – their character and temperament – the essence of their nature, if you like. It's amazing how much there is to be read in the human face and attitude if only one chooses to look closely enough – but most of us are really quite blind to the inner aspects and features of those around us. It's not until we see things through someone else's eyes that we realise how much more there is than mere appearance. I hope I'm not boring you?"

"No, not at all! Do please go on." Kitty was fascinated. She had never before been in the company of a man who spoke so easily, cutting across the division of sex and class to converse with her as an intelligent equal.

Jonathan gave her a half-smile, and getting up, moved his chair round to a different angle to start a fresh drawing.

After a pause he continued, "Portrait painting has been called the materialisation of an individual soul. A little high-flown, perhaps, but near enough the truth to be a good description. When I was studying in Paris –"

"You were in Paris?" The interruption came quickly, almost eagerly, halting him in mid-sentence.

"Yes."

"Do you know the Rue Quincompoix?"

"Quincompoix?" He repeated the name with faultless intonation.

"In Les Halles."

There was a moment's thought, and then a shake of the head. "No, I don't believe so. I'm familiar with Les Halles, of course. The Rue Quincompoix must be one of those small cobbled streets in the area?"

Kitty nodded. "It was my home for almost two years. I attended a ladies' finishing school there – L'École Rambouillet, owned by two English sisters."

"Did you, indeed?" A pause. "I wonder, ma'am, could you turn your head a little more to the right? Thank you." Another pause; then – "Well, this is a happy coincidence. Myself, I was in Paris for eighteen months, at an *atelier* on the Île de la Cité, less than a stone's throw from the Conciergerie –"

"Oh, I know where that is! We were taken there quite often to visit Notre Dame Cathedral. I remember the Conciergerie being pointed out to us as one of the prisons used during the Revolution. It was where Marie Antoinette was kept before her execution."

Jonathan smiled again. "I see you know your French history."

"Yes – history was always one of my favourite subjects." Kitty's enthusiasm got the better of her natural reticence. "The house containing L'École Rambouillet had a story which used to intrigue me. It was once the property of a Scotsman named John Law, who ran a private bank there at the beginning of last century – a *banque générale*, issuing its own notes. He was so successful he was able to found several commercial companies dealing in the French American colonies – something to do with a tobacco monopoly. But then he over-reached himself, and in 1720 his 'Mississippi Scheme' as it was known suddenly collapsed, like the South Sea Bubble, and he was forced to leave the country in rather a hurry. While I was living there in his house, I often used to imagine him and his wife and children, wondering what their lives must have been like –"

She stopped abruptly, colour rushing into her face as she realised how she'd been allowing her tongue to run away with her. Then, starting to laugh, she said, "Dear me, now it's *my* turn to be boring."

"Not at all." Jonathan Rivers put down his sketch to regard her, making a mental note of the loveliness of her face when she smiled, that slight confusion in her expression adding a delightful touch of innocence. "Not at all. I have just learned something about you, Mrs van der Kleve. You see? Already I feel I'm starting to know you better."

She laughed again. It was the first time she had done that in all the months she'd been at Sion Place.

The mellow light of a westering sun came in at the low windows, patterning the floor with golden rectangles and winking in the reflection of brass and copper and the ruby-red

75

of wine bottles. One of these, half empty, stood on the table beside its partnering glass amid an orderly clutter of cartridge paper, pencils, charcoal sticks, oil tubes and brushes – the tools of the trade of Art. An easel leaned in one corner of the small cottage room, a cupboard occupied another; while the end wall was taken up by a deep inglenook fireplace, framed by a lintel of black oak, the gaping mouth of its hearth filled with apple logs.

There was a scullery beyond, served by a pump outside the door; and up the narrow flight of stairs, a bedroom beneath the low-raftered roof, looking out from its single eye across fields of barley and wheat towards Broadwater Forest. There were no rear windows to Beckets Cottage: it had been built snugly against a rocky outcrop, so that its back walls were formed entirely of natural sandstone, roughly plastered over with lime.

When first he had come across the place three years ago in 1862, Jonathan Rivers had known at once it was where he wanted to live: though it had been uninhabited for a time and its rooms were damp and the windows filmed with dirt, he'd experienced a sense of belonging, of home-coming, the moment he ducked his head to go in at the door. Within a week, Beckets Cottage had been his for a rent of three guineas each Quarter Day.

He reached out a hand now and picked up the half empty bottle, filling his glass again, hardly taking his eyes from the pages of drawings spread out before him on the table. These were the fruit of three sittings Catherine van der Kleve had given so far, and technically competent as they were, not a single one of them satisfied him.

Swallowing a mouthful of wine, the young man sat back in his chair and took up one of the drawings to study it. This was the final sketch he'd done, and showed his sitter as he intended she would be seen in the finished portrait: exactly as her husband wanted, three-quarter face so that she looked away to the right, the windowed garden filling the background behind her.

But it was wrong. All wrong. Everything about it – the pose, the setting, the negative content – was wrong. Painted as it was, it would be the portrait of a vapid young woman placed among the symbols of middle-class conformity, an empty-headed marionette with a pretty face . . . a hollow shell.

And Catherine van der Kleve was none of these things.

He threw the drawing down again and sat for a while staring moodily in front of him at the lime-washed wall. Glowing shafts of light crept imperceptibly across its uneven surface as the autumn sun sank lower in the trees outside, sending the first wavering shadows of evening into the room. There was something about this time of day, as twilight approached and colours began to fade, that always struck Jonathan as mysterious and elusive, neither one thing nor another, neither light nor shade. As a child he had secretly feared the falling of dusk because it changed the familiar world to a place of invisible terrors; but as a man, an artist, he had come to love its strange ethereal beauty and its solitude.

His eyes dropped again to the scattered drawings. Catherine van der Kleve . . . who was she . . . *what* was she. Discover that, and he had the key to her portrait. For several minutes he sat glass in hand, concentration creasing his brow as he looked the sketches over yet again, an association of images running through his mind.

And suddenly the idea was there.

Light and shade . . . light and shade. Yes, that was it! Light and shade – that would be his theme!

He threw back his head, draining the wine at a gulp, and pulled a fresh sheet of paper towards him. Supposing he were to show her seated as required, but looking out of the canvas directly at the viewer – thus – illumination coming from somewhere to the left so that only half her face was lit, the rest obscured in shadow. Yes – and the background, the garden through the terrace room window – that could be painted as seen at twilight, hazy soft outlines and colours, everything muted to emphasise a feeling of ambiguity about the portrait.

Jonathan worked quickly, using bold, economical strokes. The idea of having his sitter looking out and not to the side transformed the expression of her features wonderfully and made the whole picture come to life. Mrs van her Kleve had a manner of bending her head slightly and directing her glance from under her lashes in a way that was both shy and enigmatic: it was this that he would capture, for it seemed to sum up everything about her, the 'otherness' of her personality, the light and shade . . . the illusion.

He had spent some six or seven hours in her company over the past few weeks, yet scarcely knew her any better now than at the beginning. Like still waters, she changed her reflection according to the weather of her mood, sometimes bright and cheerful and quick to smile, at other times grave, withdrawn, hardly speaking. She presented such a contrast of character, almost as though she were masking her true self behind a façade: on the surface a cool and self-possessed young woman isolated within the rigid social structure of her husband's class, yet showing – like chinks of light through a curtain – occasional tantalising glimpses of a young girl, uncertain, naïve, defensive.

He had to admit it, Catherine van der Kleve was starting to intrigue him.

Her conduct in the presence of other members of the family was most revealing. At their second sitting, young Angelina had come bursting into the terrace room demanding to be allowed to stay and watch; and although Mrs van der Kleve had addressed the child pleasantly, asking about her lessons that morning, Jonathan's trained eye had noted immediate signs of agitation, small things, unimportant in themselves, but together indicative of tension and underlying stress. With her sister-in-law Beatrice, the signs had been more obvious, betraying a certain amount of uneasy fear in the widening pupils of the eyes, the slight flare of the delicate nostrils, the bone-white knuckles of the hands clasped in the lap.

But by far the most telling had been the way in which she'd reacted to her husband.

Mr van der Kleve had been present during the latter part of the third and final sitting at Sion Place, having arrived back from London in time to discuss the progress of the preliminary work. Jonathan had ventured to suggest that his wife's portrait would gain considerably were she to wear something more suited to the mood of the painting; and he had described the style of gown which, in his opinion as an artist, would show to best advantage.

Clearly, this did not go down at all well.

"Mr Rivers, you may be aware of a popular saying, to the effect that 'he who pays the piper calls the tune'," had been the terse response. "It is I who decide in what manner of dress my wife shall be painted, and if it does not happen to suit the 'mood' of your work, why then, sir, that is your misfortune and not mine."

The hectoring tone had annoyed Jonathan quite as much as the refusal; but he could ill afford to antagonise a patron, especially one of Oliver van der Kleve's standing and influence, and therefore he'd answered with a smile of deference, "As you say, sir, the decision is yours."

Mrs van der Kleve had sat in silence throughout this brief exchange – indeed, apart from responding to her husband's greeting when he first came into the room, she had neither stirred nor spoken. Jonathan threw a quick glance towards her. In the four or five minutes since their sitting was interrupted, she had turned into a frozen statue, as stiff and tense as if she were in the presence of something which quite terrified her.

The thought had struck him at once that there were undercurrents here which ran deep, for such a marked reaction hinted at a darker, less attractive side to a marriage which on the surface appeared unruffled by any discord.

Attempting to draw some response from her to melt that icy fear, he'd started putting away his work, thanking her for being such an exemplary sitter, and mentioning the fact that if required he'd be able to provide a chaperone when she attended his cottage studio the following week.

"Thank you, sir, but my wife has a chaperone already," Mr van der Kleve interrupted. "She will be accompanied by her sister-in-law."

As he said this, his attention had been given to a page of drawings, and he did not see the sudden swift look his young wife gave him at this piece of news. Jonathan Rivers saw it, however; and it told him a great deal.

It was not fear Catherine van der Kleve felt for her husband. It was utter loathing.

9

Sion Place, Mount Sion,
Tunbridge Wells.
Sunday, the 29th October, 1865

My dear Harriet,
Yesterday's post brought me your letter from Abroad –
and oh! I was so pleased to receive it and learn all your
news. From your description of the town of Baden-Baden,
what an admirable place it must be, with its *old* Roman
Baths and its *new* Castle, and *twenty-nine* hot springs, no less;
and how glad I am to know that your dear Mama has
benefited so from your sojourn there together these past
weeks. The rheumatism can be most painful, I believe, and
therefore what a blessing to her to be somewhat relieved of
its discomfort.

You must not poke such fun at yourself – altho' I must
admit, it made me smile to read of your adventure with the
dashing Herr Doktor. It may be as you say, that no amount
of hot spring water will straighten your leg, however often
a day you are told to dip it, and I am sure the young man's
fascination was with your Company and Conversation, for
think, my dear, how many limbs he must see in the course
of a Season, and in what variety.

You write that he scarcely glanced at your face; well,
Harriet, that may have spared your blushes, for when I am
sitting for Mr Rivers (as I told you) he regards me with such
an intensity of gaze that I feel myself colour to the ears and
know not where to look.

Do thank your Mama for her kind enquiry after my
health. It is very much improved this past month and the
nausea is by no means as severe as before; however, I still
have this *sentiment* that all is not well with me, despite Dr

Adeney's assurance that it is my fancy. I am growing quite stout now, and require the waists of my gowns let out to accommodate the increase. What a fright I look, and how I do hate it. Beatrice tells me I should keep more indoors – it is not *nice* for a female in my Condition to be seen too much in public, she says, it draws attention. And indeed, there is something a little shameful to my mind in going about loose-corseted; tho' Mr Rivers has several times declared that it lends itself wonderfully to the classical style of art.

What do you think, my dear – you will never guess! I have my *own maid* at last, and who do you suppose it to be, but Miss Dobby who attended me during the Wedding Tour. I will tell you how it came about, for no one could be more surprised than myself. Mr van der Kleve again applied to the agency in Town (it being convenient to the Bank's chambers), and seeing his name, Miss Dobby wrote straightway to inform us that her Mother was now passed on (a merciful release for *all*), thereby freeing her of her obligation. I cannot tell you what a satisfaction it is to me to have her here: she is like a breath of sweet air in the oppressive confines of this house. And oh, what joy! – she is allowed to accompany me to Mr Rivers's studio in place of Beatrice, whose presence, I will confess, made me so wretched on that first occasion, it was as though I had turned to stone. Indeed, I believe Mr Rivers thought so, too, for his manner was most abrupt, and he curtailed our sitting after no more than *half an hour*.

Dear friend, I can hear you ask – but what of Rose Maguire? Now that I have Miss Dobby, have I put the Other entirely from my mind? My answer is no, for I have occupied myself on her behalf wih some success, as I will tell you.

You will know that Mr van der Kleve and myself have several times been favoured by the social invitation of a gentleman and his wife in the Neighbourhood. (I say *wife*, but must confide to you, Harriet, that when first we were introduced, I thought the lady to be his daughter, for she is a considerable number of years his junior.) They reside at Bowling Green House, which is named for the old pleasure ground upon Mount Sion; they have two young children, Alfred and Mary; and Mr Broadwood served as a Member of Parliament at one time, but is now retired from all occupation. There, now you have made their acquaintance!

That is all very well, you will say, but what has it to do with Rose Maguire? Patience, and your curiosity shall be satisfied.

On Tuesday last, I went to take tea with Mrs Frances Broadwood at her kind invitation, and found her somewhat out of countenance, for Mr Broadwood had only that morning dismissed one of the housemaids for dishonesty; and, as I learned, this was the third girl in as many months who had left their service *under a cloud*. Mrs Broadwood told me that she quite despaired of finding one to suit and would be much obliged for any recommendation. Well, of course, I seized upon this chance, and confided to her Rose Maguire's unhappy story – and now, my dear, what do you think but that Rosie is housemaid at Bowling Green House!

I will own, it has pleased me greatly to render this assistance, for three people have profited thereby: Rose herself, her young man James Randall (that is, Mr v–d–K's servant, as you know), and her friend who is our maid Mary Ellen Martin. They are able to meet with one another when their duties permit of the time, for the back yard of Bowling Green House lies at the end of the alley behind Sion Place.

I should say, perhaps, that *four* persons have profited by my providential action, since Mrs Broadwood, also, expresses herself vastly satisfied with the turn of events, and, as she says, is beholden to me for relieving her of the *worry*. She is a most amiable young woman, and solicitous of my well-being, for I am able to confide in her my fears for my Condition, and she answers me very sensibly and with much reassurance.

You will understand, Harriet, what a consolation it is to have someone near to whom I can turn and in whom I feel I may safely put my trust. But do not, dearest and best of friends, think for a moment that you are replaced in my affections! Never a day passes but that I think of you, and wish with all my heart for the comfort of your presence.

Let me tell you of Mr Rivers's studio, for it is exactly the place I would desire for myself had I the choice. I did not know what to expect, for a *studio* sounds very grand; and Hungershall Park is one of the most fashionably select areas of The Wells. Imagine, then, my pleasure and my astonishment when I discovered a mouse-hole of a cottage, buried away in a lane behind the Park, and as pretty a country spot as one could wish for. Beatrice, of course, turned up her nose in scorn and was very *dainty* about entering what she declared was hardly better than a labourer's hovel; and indeed, the place was built for such, for Mr Rivers told me himself it belonged to Beckets Farm.

At our last sitting, he showed Miss Dobby and me the lane, and the water splash at the end, and the farm beyond upon a hill; and oh, Harriet! if you could but see it, it would steal your heart, I know, for it is quite everything which you and I used once to talk of together at Miss Meyrick's. Do you remember? Our games of Fancy and Pretend? Where we would live, and in what manner of place? Well, then, I will tell you, that had I but one wish to be granted, I would choose Beckets Cottage to share with you, my best and truest friend.

Mr Rivers appears greatly complimented by my interest in his rustic abode, and has promised to make a painting of it in the Spring, to give to me. How strange it is to reflect, by then I shall have borne a Child; altho' to tell truth, I do not care to think upon that.

You have heard the news, of course – concerning the death last Wednesday week of Lord Palmerston, the Prime Minister? Lord Russell was appointed in his place the next day, as you will doubtless have read in the English newspapers. I believe he is not so opinionated as the Other.

Well, my dear, when I turn to *politics* to fill out the lines of my page, you may be sure that I have nothing more to write! So therefore I will bid you a fond adieu, and hope to have more from you by this next week's post.

Kitty

Harriet Seymour removed her steel-rimmed reading spectacles, letting the hand which held her friend's letter fall to her side. She had read it through twice since it was brought to her by the hotel *dienst*, the first time quickly to learn the gist of its news, the second time with greater care and interest. Judging by its buoyant tone, Kitty seemed less unhappy now than before: clearly, she had started to weigh the advantages of her life against the disagreeableness, and was learning to count each small blessing as it came, for there was an optimism in her news which had been lacking in previous letters.

It did so help, of course, having a person like this Mrs Frances Broadwood close by – more than any doctor, what Kitty needed was another young mother to counsel her, someone to lend an ear of sympathy and offer guidance and common sense, someone who'd gone ahead of her along the path of matrimony and already encountered its sudden twists and turns, its hidden obstacles. Doctors were all very well, but being men they tended to see things unimaginatively in stark black and white, and for all their professional expertise had little understanding of a woman's mind.

Harriet gave an unconscious sigh and glanced away through the hotel window, the neatly written pages quivering very slightly between her fingers. She was feeling really quite vexed just now upon the subject of men in general, and doctors in particular, having much against her better judgment fallen a little in love with one who was both. She broke her own rules by doing so, for being of a stoical turn of mind, she had long ago forced herself to face the fact that there were few men in the world likely to entertain any great passion for a plain-featured female with a crooked leg.

"Harriet?"

Her mother's voice behind her in the doorway broke into her reverie.

"Harriet – what are you doing there at the window? You said you were going to rest this morning. I looked for you in your room."

"A letter has arrived, Mama –" Kitty's epistle was held up in evidence. "And I wanted to read it before we went down to luncheon."

"A letter? Oh, is it to do with your treatment, dear? Has Dr Hoffmann made his decision?"

"No, Mama. It is not from the good Herr Doktor." Harriet's tone gave a hint of dry humour. Her mother was inclined to make Peter Hoffmann the sole topic of every conversation if allowed. "It's from England. From Kitty."

"Mrs van der Kleve? Ah, well, I expect Dr Hoffmann will be writing tomorrow."

"No doubt he will." The humour took on a note of subtle

irony. "It is always tomorrow that holds our best expectations. Would you care to hear what Kitty has to say?"

Mrs Seymour inclined her head, and closing the door behind, moved stiffly across to a chair, walking with the support of a stick.

Her daughter replaced the steel-rimmed spectacles.

"She says . . . ah, yes, here – she thanks you for your enquiry after her health, and wishes you to know that it is much improved now, and the nausea is not as severe as it was. She also writes . . . let me see, I had the passage somewhere –"

"Do you not think, my dear, that I might read for myself?" A net-mittened hand was held out in a somewhat impatient gesture.

"As you wish, Mama."

Leaving the window, Harriet took a few clumsy steps towards the small stout woman in morning dress whose autocratic features bore more than a fleeting resemblance to those of Her Majesty Queen Victoria.

"But do sit yourself down, won't you? You know it does your rheumatism no good at all if you stand too long."

"Yes, yes, I know what Dr Hoffmann advised, dear." Mrs Seymour allowed herself to be assisted into the Hotel Adler's tapestry-covered chair, fussing with the ribbon of her lorgnette to untangle it from the black jet beads upon her bosom.

While she commenced a thorough perusal of Kitty's letter, her daughter glanced away again out of the window. Their hotel stood on a flank of the rocky spur crowned by the ruins of the Alte Schloss – the old castle of Baden-Baden – and was built in the style of a medieval fairy-tale fortress with turrets and towers and crenellated balconies. The private suite taken by the two Seymour ladies during their month-long stay occupied one of the corner towers, and looked out across a gabled roofscape towards the black pine forests which had given this southern part of Germany its name.

Somewhere down below among the sternly elegant buildings of the new town which had risen here since the turn of the century, was the clinic of Herr Doktor Peter Hoffmann, *Beinarzt*, where the halt and crippled of limb sought to be healed of their lameness; and where Harriet Seymour was in peril of losing her heart.

She had encountered him on the second morning here, at

the hydropathic baths. Her mother had gone to the steam vapour room to be treated for the good or otherwise of her rheumatism, leaving Harriet to wait in the marble-tiled foyer; and this being her first visit to the establishment, she'd been curious to go inside to observe the public bathing area from the balcony provided for that purpose.

The heat had been quite overwhelming – notices advised that the spring water gushing from the natural rock exceeded 150° Fahrenheit – and the clouds of steam which billowed across the surface of the baths lent the scene a curiously dreamlike aspect, enveloping the white-swathed forms of those in the water so that they appeared indistinct and ghostly, their voices echoing in the cavernous space like disembodied souls.

Feeling herself turn suddenly faint, Harriet hastened to leave the balcony; but lameness and vertigo together caused her to stumble, and the next thing she knew was a man's arms catching her up in the very nick of time.

"Was ist los, gnädiges Fräulein? Sie sind krank?" said a voice at her ear. And then, as she muttered a confused reply – "Ach, forgive me, please. You are, English, yes? Allow me to be of service. You are perhaps unwell, I think?"

She'd looked up into a pair of dark eyes in a thin, clever face, and made some self-deprecating answer about her clumsiness, saying thank you, but she was perfectly all right now. Her Good Samaritan was not to be persuaded of this, however, and had insisted upon leading her courteously by the elbow to one of the benches in the foyer and seating himself at her side. By the time her mother's steam vapour treatment was completed, Harriet had learned his name, his profession, and the address of his clinic; and had made her first appointment for a consultation.

Since then, life and Baden-Baden had taken on an entirely different aspect.

"Well, my dear, I must say –" Mrs Seymour let her lorgnette fall on its watered silk ribbon and laid aside Kitty's letter to address her daughter. "I must say, it seems to me there is a certain somewhat headstrong attitude to be read between the lines of your friend's correspondence."

"Headstrong, Mama?" The other's attention was still half-given to the vista of the new town below, and the thread of green which marked the tree-lined *strasse* wherein stood the Hoffmann Clinic. "Headstrong in what way?"

"She writes amusingly. But her letter is full of the type of incautious observation which one might expect of a giddy unwed girl – most certainly not of any respectable married woman. Why, there is hardly a mention of her husband, yet the name of some person called Rivers occurs in almost every paragraph."

"And is that something we should criticise?" Hearing a slight note of disapprobation, Harriet came loyally to the defence. "Mr Rivers is engaged in painting Kitty's portrait, therefore the two are naturally obliged to spend a certain time in each other's company. How else is the work to be achieved? He cannot paint from memory."

"But to refer to the man as she does, and so often –"

"Oh, Mama, you read too much in too little! Were she *not* to refer to him, then I'd suspect something to hide. As it is, the poor dear has so few amusements to distract her, a novel diversion of this kind is bound to occupy her mind and be a feature of her letters."

Mrs Seymour gave the point her consideration.

"Besides, Mama, we must bear in mind that she and Mr Rivers are drawn together by the interests they have in common. Both have resided in Paris, and you'll recall that Kitty confessed in her last letter the pleasure it gives her to speak of her memories with someone able to share them. Now is that being headstrong?"

One eyebrow was raised a fraction. "It might be construed as a great deal more unless Catherine expresses herself more carefully and learns to govern herself with the restraint and discernment due to her position. I know what a warm and affectionate creature she is, but one does not become familiar with *artists*, nor evince a desire to reside in any *mouse-hole* of a cottage."

Mrs Seymour said this with some emphasis, as though artists were a breed rather beyond the pale of decency, and their choice of residence open to questionable doubt.

"Furthermore, I cannot understand all this fuss about finding a housemaid a new position, and being concerned that the girl should have time and liberty to meet her acquaintances in some back alley. Why, what on earth are things coming to when the mistress of a house occupies herself with such vulgar arrangements!"

"Oh, I don't think Kitty meant –" began Harriet.

Her attempt at interruption went ignored.

"I regret to say, my dear, that fond as I am of her, your friend still has a great deal to learn about the distinction of class in our society. That she prefers the company of employees to that of her sister-in-law or husband, I fear betrays a certain lack of breeding in her background. She has much for which to be grateful to Mr van der Kleve. And it is my opinion that she should show that gratitude properly, by conducting herself with better dignity and decorum."

"But Mama, you are judging Kitty too harshly. You do not know the half of what she's been made to suffer."

"Fiddlesticks! The circumstances of her origins were unfortunate, I know, but providence has given her everything – education, upbringing, and an excellent marriage. Yet upon each occasion that she has been a guest in our house – where, I will add, she has always been most welcome – I have yet to hear a gracious word spoken of the orphanage which raised her, or the charity of those who saw to her instruction."

Harriet was not going to let this pass without challenge. "She was the so-called workhouse girl at Miss Meyrick's Academy, and treated worse than any servant. I know, Mama. I was there, and witnessed for myself what poor Kitty had to endure for the sake of 'charity'."

"She was fortunate to gain a place at all in such a highly reputable establishment!" There was a sharp rap of Mrs Seymour's lorgnette upon the arm of her chair to stress the fact. "Catherine is a sweet and amiable young woman, and I hope for her sake that she will not become of that kind which are never content with what they are given, but expect constantly to receive more. This marriage to Mr van der Kleve, for instance – a most advantageous match, yet she appears far from happy –"

"If I might interrupt again, Mama, Kitty's unhappiness has much to do with the lack of affection and love."

"Love? Love? What is love in a marriage? Respect is all that counts, my dear. Respect and moral duty. Love is a sentiment for the lower classes."

Harriet shook her head. She had heard these views upon

rank and obligation aired too often in the past to be surprised now at their repetition; but that Kitty should have provoked quite so much warmth was a cause for some perplexity. What could her mother have read in that letter which she herself had overlooked?

"Now that is enough on the matter." Mrs Seymour put out a hand, signifying her wish to be assisted to her feet. "It is time we were going downstairs to luncheon. And afterwards, Harriet dear, a short promenade upon the terrace, I think. We must not neglect the exercise which Dr Hoffmann has so kindly prescribed for you."

What *was* in that letter? She would read it through again. And perhaps somewhere between the lines she might find the clue to what Kitty hadn't written . . .

10

As Christmas approached at Sion Place, plans to celebrate the festive season were becoming the main focus of everyone's attention, both upstairs and below. Because of her child, due in four weeks, Kitty herself was unable to play much part in these preparations, spending much of her time with her feet up on a *chaise-longue* beside the drawing room fire, occupying the idle hours with sewing or crochet to make little gowns and bonnets for the baby's layette.

Perhaps to compensate for this enforced exclusion from all the activity, Oliver van der Kleve had taken her up to London at the start of December to see a performance of *The Bohemian Girl* at Covent Garden, which she enjoyed greatly. He had also arranged for them both to view an exhibition of the works of a group calling itself the Pre-Raphaelite Brotherhood, whose paintings had been exciting great controversy during the past decade for their startlingly ambitious approach to romantic theme and technique.

Though criticised still in some quarters, the group had prevailed upon popular taste sufficiently to become well established, and were now considered acceptably fashionable by the middle classes; enough, at any rate, to attract gentlemen to bring their wives and families to this exhibition.

Kitty had been utterly captivated by it. Several times she'd heard Jonathan Rivers mention the Pre-Raphaelites, speaking of his admiration for their work, and so she was interested to see for herself what it was that so influenced his opinion. She had not been disappointed, for the glowing stained-glass colours of each canvas, and the marvellous realism of detail, were quite extraordinarily evocative.

She reminded herself she must remember to comment upon it when she and Mr Rivers met at the Christmas Eve dinner party which Oliver was having at Sion Place. It was planned to use this social occasion to give the first showing of her portrait – now finished and ready to hang and courtesy naturally dictated that the young artist be invited to attend.

The twenty-fourth of December would be a day Kitty was not to forget. By mid-morning the entire house had undergone a quite astonishing transformation, for Oliver wanted everything to be exactly right for his guests, and had spared no expense. In the entrance hall, enclosed in the curve of the staircase, stood an eight-foot spruce very handsomely decorated with scarlet streamers and tinsel, and hung from every bough with candles and coloured glass baubles – the custom of the Christmas Tree had been introduced by the late Prince Consort from his native Germany, and it was now becoming all the fashion to have one, even though the needles did shed everywhere and cause the servants extra work. More traditionally English was the Bough or Bunch hanging up in the hall inside the front door: two hoops fastened together and twined with red ribbon and plenty of holly and mistletoe, beneath which the guests might exchange seasonal kisses at the end of the evening.

The gardener, assisted by his boy, had already brought indoors the yule log of seasoned applewood, to burn on the drawing room hearth through the night until Christmas Morn; and a housemaid was busy putting up sprigs of bright berried holly along the picture rails. Every one of the servants had been afoot since long before dawn and would not see their beds again until the early hours of tomorrow, but their reward would come on St Stephen's Day when Oliver distributed the Christmas boxes and gave them all the afternoon off to visit their families.

By seven o'clock when the first of the guests were arriving, Sion Place was ablaze with a glow of lamplight and candles, and its usually cold, austere atmosphere for once mellow with a welcoming warm smell of festive cheer.

The Broadwoods, making their way through a light fall of snow from Bowling Green House, were most impressed.

"My dear sir –" Henry Broadwood announced, taking Oliver's hand to shake it, and at the same time throwing an appreciative eye towards the tantalus of filled decanters on the drawing room sideboard. "My dear sir, I must say this is all very splendid! Eh? What?"

His young wife smiled across at Kitty, seated at the fireside on the *chaise-longue*, and going over to sit beside her, added prettily, "How invitingly charming the house does look from the street. If this snow settles, it will make *such* a picture."

"Best it doesn't settle, Fanny m'dear," Mr Broadwood rejoined. "Should we have a freeze tonight there'll be the very deuce of a business getting the carriages up and down the hill. Mount Sion's steep enough in the best of weather, Lord knows, but with a surface of ice –"

He made a face, promptly altering the expression to a smile as he saw the van der Kleves' butler moving in the direction of the decanters.

A short while later, glass comfortably in hand and several more guests to add their company to the congenial scene, he observed to his host, "I was thinking t'other day it was time I took young Mary away from her governess and put her into school. Now this ladies' academy on the London Road – you sit on the Board, do you not, sir? What d'you say to it being the right place for my daughter? Eh?"

"Mr Broadwood, I can pay it no higher recommendation than to send my own daughter there –"

While Oliver extolled the merits of Miss Meyrick and her establishment, his wife and Frances Broadwood had been joined upon the *chaise-longue* by Mrs Adeney, here with her husband the doctor, and the three were now discussing together the benefits of peppermint as a remedy against chills of the stomach. By the time their conversation had moved to the newly fashionable 'Princess' style of gown, the arrival of more guests had claimed Oliver's attention, leaving Henry Broadwood to wander with his glass over to the ladies.

"Well, when do we see this portrait of yours, m'dear?" he boomed at Kitty, ignoring the fact that his wife had already been speaking. "Like it, do you, eh? Made a good job of it, has he, this young artist chappie?"

"Now Henry, which question do you wish answered?" countered Frances Broadwood, glancing sidelong at Kitty with one of her teasing smiles. "The first, or the last? Or the one in between?"

"Perhaps I should take them each in order," Kitty responded for herself, sharing the smile. "Firstly, the company will see the portrait when we're all assembled here after dinner.

Secondly, do I like it? Yes, very much, very much indeed. Which I think also answers your third question, sir."

"And does Mr van der Kleve admire it also, pray?"

"Henry, that is enough!" his wife interrupted again. "You are not on the back benches now." The affectionate raillery of her tone revealed great pride in her husband's former position as a Member of Parliament. "If you wish to join us ladies in our conversation, we were in the throes of discussing the new waistless style of gown and whether it will lead to a demise of the crinoline."

"And how am I expected to contribute to such a topic, m'dear, when the only thing I know of gowns is the length of your dressmaker's bill!" Mr Broadwood emptied his glass and looked round to take a fresh one from the tray being carried among the guests by a maid.

It was at that moment that Kitty saw Jonathan Rivers standing alone in the doorway, obviously waiting to present his card to Nicholls. She started up at once with a quick half-wave of the hand; but someone moved in between, blocking the view, and he failed to notice her.

"Would you please forgive me –?" she apologised to the Broadwoods and Mrs Adeney. "There is someone here I must welcome."

Getting up from the *chaise-longue* she crossed the room, her pregnant body forcing her to excuse herself several times to pass between the groups of guests.

"Mr Jonathan Rivers," the butler announced in polished tones, and there was a moment's hush while heads turned towards the door for a cursory examination of the latest arrival. Then, as the buzz of conversation started up once more, Kitty approached, hand held out in greeting, saying, "How good it is to see you again, Mr Rivers. I'm so pleased you were able to come this evening."

The warmth in her voice and the quick, childlike clasp of her fingers on his were entirely unconscious.

"Would you care for a glass of mulled wine to take off the chill?"

"Thank you, that would be most acceptable." Jonathan's eyes did not leave her face. The last time he'd seen her, at the end of November for the final sitting at Beckets Cottage, she had looked tired, as though her condition were sapping her of strength; but tonight her features had a luminous freshness, the creamy bloom of her skin burnished by the glow of candlelight, and those wonderful violet eyes sparkling with her smile. There was something magical about impending motherhood, he thought, the way it bestowed a special beauty upon a woman; and to a woman already as beautiful as Catherine van der Kleve, it had the effect of quite taking a man's breath away.

"I see you've chosen to wear the dress tonight," he said, indicating the *décolleté* evening gown of raspberry crushed velvet in which Kitty had sat for the finishing stages of her portrait. "Good. I'm pleased. Your husband's guests will be able to judge for themselves the accuracy of my work by comparing it with the original."

"And comparing it very favourably, I'm sure," she told him. "I hope, Mr Rivers, my picture is going to bring you many more commissions."

"A sentiment I echo entirely, ma'am. Ah –" He looked quickly away from her, seeing Oliver approach. "Mr van der Kleve. Good evening, sir."

There was just the right amount of deference in his tone and manner as he reached to shake the older man by the hand, at the same time giving a slight bow in acknowledgment of the fact that his host was also his employer and patron.

"I was making the comment to Mrs van der Kleve, sir, that by wearing this gown tonight, your guests will be able to appreciate how faithfully I've reproduced its –"

"Quite so, Mr Rivers, quite so." Oliver's expression tightened into instant irritation. He had not wished his wife to be painted attired thus, but in the end was forced to allow it since his own choice of dress had started to give at the seams with the advance of her pregnancy. Even then, he had not wanted her in anything too revealing of neck and shoulders; but again his wishes were set aside, for as Catherine had ventured to suggest, it was only fitting she should be shown wearing the van der Kleve pearls, and for that a *décolletage* was most certainly needed.

This affair of the gown had been his first vexation. His second was with the finished painting itself which, though he acknowledged it to be a remarkably fine work of art, had a curiously disturbing effect upon him each time he looked at it.

Somehow young Rivers had captured the essence of Catherine, that elusive other-worldliness about her that made her always so remote and unreachable to him; and to see it there caught so perfectly at another's hand served only to increase his own vague sense of loss and longing for something he knew not what.

The third cause of Oliver's vexation had arisen only a few minutes since, watching his wife make her way across to greet Rivers at the door, and noting how her face so transparently reflected her pleasure at the fellow's arrival. In all the time he'd known her, she had never once looked at him in that manner, and it irked him considerably that she should save her smiles for others whilst denying them to her own husband.

He made no effort to master his annoyance, and seeing the maid carrying in a replenished tray, summoned her with a peremptory gesture. "A glass here for this gentleman —" adding somewhat tersely, "I have arranged that the portrait be brought in from the morning room while dinner is in progress. It will hang over there —"

He indicated a blank space on the window wall, between the swag of crimson velour drapes.

Jonathan nodded politely, and his eyes went to the wide chimney breast above the elegantly fluted marble fireplace. *That* was where he had always envisaged the work would be displayed: the focal point of attention as one entered the room, not cramped away between a pair of fussy drapes whose colour clashed abominably with the subtle tones of his painting.

He said nothing, however. It was not his place to do so.

"If you would be good enough to make yourself available immediately after dinner, sir," his host concluded, beginning to move towards a more welcome guest just then being announced at the door by Nicholls, "I shall expect you to wait upon me in my study to receive the balance of your fee before you leave."

"But Mr Rivers may stay to see the portrait hung, surely?" Kitty came in impulsively before she could stop herself. "That was the purpose of his invitation."

Her words were either not heard, or else ignored. Her husband's attention was now elsewhere.

Jonathan took a long drink of his mulled wine.

"It doesn't matter," he said quietly, putting the glass aside.

"I should hate to abuse the hospitality of the house by remaining longer than I'm welcome, Mrs van der Kleve."

"But this is so silly! The high point of the evening comes after dinner is finished, and if you have gone, it will be spoiled. They will all want to discuss the portrait."

She threw a glance over her shoulder towards the crowd of guests, and he noted how she seemed to cut herself off by the use of that 'they' rather than 'we'.

"It doesn't matter," he said again. "Truly, ma'am. Besides, I'd prefer not to see my work hung upon that particular wall."

She looked back at him quickly. "No? Why not?"

"It isn't the right place. Over there would be better –" he nodded towards the fireplace, dominated by an over-florid oil painting of Oliver's father, Cornelius van der Kleve. "And even that's not the ideal position. If I were to choose where to hang it myself, I think I'd select the terrace room."

"But then no one would see it!"

Jonathan smiled, and took up his glass again. "That's true. I forget, in order to eat one's cake one must first have to earn one's daily bread. Or to put it more simply, beggars can't be choosers. To your good health, Mrs van der Kleve." He saluted her and drained the wine at a gulp. "I must confess, I shall miss your company now that our sittings are over."

"Oh –" Kitty's cheeks coloured at such frankness, and not knowing how to answer, she turned her head and pretended to give her attention to a bowl of winter-flowering cherry on the low table beside her.

Without glancing up she said after a moment, in a voice so soft he had to lean forward to catch the words, "I believe I shall miss you, too, Mr Rivers. It has been very pleasant . . . making your acquaintance."

"Don't call it acquaintance. Say, rather, friendship."

To that there came no response, beyond a reluctant shake of the head as she put out her fingers to touch the pale, fragile blossom.

"Oh, I'm sorry! I'm presuming too much, am I, ma'am? Perhaps you'd rather I tug my forelock and thank you for condescending to honour me with your notice?"

The suddenly savage, cynical note in his voice made Kitty bite her lip.

"I'm sorry –" he repeated himself, instantly contrite, before

96

she could say anything. "Forgive me, please. I don't know why I spoke like that. It was wrong. I hope you'll excuse me."

"Of course."

There was an awkward little pause.

"And now *you* must excuse *me*." She looked up at him again, but behind her attempt at a smile lay a troubled expression clouding her beautiful face. "I really must go and greet some of the other guests."

Jonathan stood aside and made a somewhat theatrical bow and sweep of the arm; then, as Kitty moved away among the crowd, he looked round him for another drink, anything to blunt the suddenly painful bite of self-anger.

What the devil was he doing here tonight, he asked himself – dressed up in a hired suit and mismatched shoes so as not to offend against the hallowed rules of etiquette. He wasn't one of them, one of these upright pillars of Tunbridge Wells society gathered here to massage one another's sense of middle class superiority. He was an artist, an outsider – damn it, he didn't belong in their hierarchy of rank; and yet they represented the host body upon which he and his fellows, like parasites, clung in order to live – it was their prosperity and privileged status that paid his rent and put food upon his table.

With a nod of thanks to the attentive maid, the young man helped himself to more wine, his blue-grey eyes following Kitty across the room. How long had he known Mrs van der Kleve? Three months? Four? Such a very short time. And how *well* did he know her? Ah, that was a question not so easily answered. How well was it possible ever to know an enigma.

The only thing that Jonathan Rivers could state with any certainty was that she was quite extraordinarily lovely, and very, very desirable; and if he wasn't careful, he might find himself forgetting that she was another man's wife.

Kitty, too, was troubled this evening. As a Christmas gift, Oliver had presented her with an expensive item of jewellery – a matched three-piece set of necklace, ear-drops and bracelet all of chased gold, set with opals. She did not like opals. They were beautiful gemstones, but there was something about them, something arcane and malevolent, that made her very uneasy at having to wear them. She had managed to persuade her husband to allow her to put on the van der Kleve pearls for this dinner party, to mirror the image of her portrait; but the opals were waiting upstairs in their oyster velvet case, ready to be displayed on Christmas Day; and it was no use her trying to tell Oliver that she'd rather he took his gift back and exchanged it for some other – he would only be annoyed and accuse her of superstitious nonsense.

It wasn't nonsense, though. By wearing those opals, Kitty had the strongest misgiving she would be drawing down ill-fortune upon herself and her unborn child.

Despite the sociable face she wore for her husband's guests, she had been feeling inwardly low and lacklustre until that moment earlier when Jonathan Rivers arrived. The sight of him there had seemed to give her sudden strength, as though she'd been no more than half-alive before, and if her heart beat faster, surely that was in pleasure at seeing a familiar countenance among such a largely anonymous crowd of her husband's acquaintances.

Oliver had been really most rude, she thought, to invite him here and then treat him as dismissively as he had, like a servant or tradesman. Even more unforgivable, Mr Rivers had been placed in quite the worst position at dinner, seated between the open door and the lift hatch serving the kitchen two floors below, so that there was a continuous draught blowing upon him from both sides. To make sure at least that he did not lack for conversation, she directed the comments of other guests towards him by mentioning his work and his commissions and how well young Angelina was progressing under his teaching; and though she was too far along the table to speak to him herself, she compensated for this by smiling often in his direction.

At the end of dinner, when the ladies withdrew again to the drawing room leaving the gentlemen to their spirits and cigars, Kitty noticed that Oliver had not even done Mr Rivers the courtesy of remaining at table, but excused himself immediately to go to his study.

She made some apology of her own to the others and went downstairs alone to the entrance hall, intending to show some manners by bidding their guest goodnight as he left the house.

There was no one else about down here, and without the gas lamps the only illumination came from the candles among the branches of the Christmas tree, filling the hall with a lambent flicker of light.

When several minutes had gone by, there came the sound of a footfall on the half landing, and Jonathan Rivers thanking Nicholls for bringing his hat and cloak. After that, silence; and then a single set of footsteps continuing on down the stairs.

"What's this –?" He had drunk rather more than was good for him, but it did not show. "Waiting to see me off the premises, Mrs van der Kleve?"

For the second time that evening his tone stung her, and she dropped the hand held out in farewell.

"I wanted no more than to wish you a happy Christmas season before you went."

"How kind." It was difficult in that dim light to see his face, only that he was looking at her, cloak flung over a shoulder, silk top hat in hand, one white glove pulled on but left unbuttoned, telling of a hasty wish to be gone.

Above them both, hanging on its cord of plaited ribbons, the Kissing Bough turned very slightly in the draught from the porch door.

The young man hesitated a fraction, then moved closer. Had he not had quite so much wine to drink, he would never have dared to presume as far upon his host's hospitality as he was about to do.

"Since it *is* Christmas, may I salute you in the time-honoured way, ma'am?" And before Kitty could reply – before she even realised what he intended – he had taken her fingertips in his and raising them, bent his head to kiss them; then, straightening, made to turn away towards the door.

What happened next she hardly knew, only that their hands seemed suddenly to cling together, refusing to be parted, pulling them towards each other. For a moment they looked into one another's eyes as though astonished; and then Mr Rivers bent again towards her, shutting out the candlelight, and before either of them thought of the precipice brink they were treading upon, his mouth had brushed her cheek and very gently touched her trembling lips.

11

"Well, I don't know what to say of it, I'm sure. But you may take it from me, Miss Dobby, there's worse to come. That there's a snake, unless I'm much mistook."

Mrs Reynolds, Cook at Sion Place, held the china cup closer to the oil lamp at her elbow, the better to inspect the pattern of tea leaves around its bowl.

"Yes – a snake," she repeated herself lugubriously. "Mind you, Miss Dobby, I'm not a-saying it's an altogether reliable way o' reading the leaves, this. It's the person whose fortune is being told what should rightly be the one to turn the cup."

She looked across the top of her spectacles at the lady's maid opposite. A short while ago Dobby had brought down Mrs van der Kleve's afternoon tea tray, and while sitting to enjoy a cup of her own, had asked as a matter of idle interest whether Mrs Reynolds was able to read the Mistress's fortune.

Cook had agreed to try, priding herself on her ability to foresee the future by this method, and taking the delicate china cup, had held it over the saucer in her left hand and swirled its dregs round three times before turning it smartly upside down.

"A snake *and* a pair o' scissors." She examined her findings again, her double chins squeezed into plump rolls against the starched white pinafore bib. "And both lying so close to the rim, an' all. Deary me."

"What does it mean, Mrs Reynolds?" asked little Susan Smith, the scullery maid, craning her mob-capped head to peer over the other's shoulder. "Does it matter, then, where you see the signs?"

"O' course it matters, my wench. The closer they fall to the rim, the quicker and sooner what they foretell is a-going to happen. Now the snake – d'you see it, just there? – that means the Mistress must be careful who it is she confides in, for there's somebody secretly a-scheming to make trouble for her.

And the pair o' scissors, why, that's a sure and certain warning she'll be parted from them she loves afore long."

Mrs Reynold gave the cup another turn between the dimpled palms of her hands.

"Down here 'tis even worse. Look, see that? That there's a bed plain enough, but broke apart in the middle. A bad sign – oh, very bad."

"Why? What does it mean?" young Susan asked again, pressing closer.

"It means that Mrs Reynolds takes a scattering of tea leaves and lets her fancy read into them whatever she feels will fit," interrupted Jane Perrins, seated at the other end of the kitchen table with a piece of sewing in her lap. "If you ask my opinion, it's all a lot of foolish nonsense."

"Beg pardon, but there's nobody asking your opinion." Cook removed her spectacles and eyed her critic belligerently. "I went and read *your* leaves aright, didn't I? There was a face there plain as could be in your cup last week, and that always means trouble wi' teeth. And where was you Monday morning, Miss Perrins? Having a tooth pulled, didn't you tell me?"

"That tooth had been paining me for some time, as it happens." As always when she was annoyed, Perrins's daintily refined speech grew more exaggerated. "I must say, I'm surprised at *you*, Miss Dobby, for encouraging such silliness. I judged you for a person of rather more intelligence."

Amelia Dobby did not rise to the bait. She and Perrins had crossed swords already in the two months she'd been here as lady's maid to Mrs van der Kleve; but being a quiet, self-effacing woman, she would prefer to turn aside trouble with a smile rather than answer it with a quarrel.

"I value your good opinion of me, Miss Perrins," she said, courteously inclining her head. "But since your judgment errs upon the side of generosity, I may be allowed a fault or two, I hope."

Not knowing quite what she should make of this remark, the other pursed up her lips and in silence fell to her sewing again. Usually she kept to her own room, disdaining the company of the kitchen, but the January weather was so bitter cold that despite a small fire in her grate to take the frost from the air, her fingers had been too numbed to hold a needle and she was forced to descend to the warmth of the basement to do her work.

"What *does* a broken bed mean, Mrs Reynolds?" young Susan persisted, still twisting her head to see for herself what the leaves foretold. As she spoke there came a noisy clatter of boots outside the window as someone ran down the iron steps into the yard, and then a moment later the sound of the back door opening.

"Here's Jem back at last." Cook ignored the girl's question to rise ponderously to her feet. "Come along now, Susan, get these tea things washed and put away and let's have the table cleared –" And as a fair-haired young man came through into the kitchen unwinding his muffler from round his neck – "Took your time, didn't you, my lad? Ten minutes you'd be gone, you said."

"Brookses hadn't got what you wanted, Mrs Reynolds. I had to go all the way down to Champions on the Parade." Jem Randall produced the object of his errand, a drum of pickling spice, and put it on the table. He winked at Susan. "And there was a queue o' folk there waiting to be served."

"At Champions?" Mrs Reynolds didn't believe a word of it. "Go on wi' you! You've been down the alley a-talking to Rose Maguire, that's where you've been."

"Well . . . all right, but it was only a minute or two."

"You'll catch your death, standing about in the cold this weather. A good job Mr Nicholls ain't here. He wouldn't half ha' given you what for, being gone so long."

"Ah, well I'm back now so there's no harm done." Jem favoured the company with one of his engaging grins, including everyone except Jane Perrins: since entering the kitchen he'd hardly spared a single glance in her direction.

Taking off his coat, he went and hung it with his muffler in the scullery passage; then, standing himself in front of the range fire to warm the backs of his legs, he announced, "What d'you think I've just heard from Rosie –" and paused, savouring the drama of the moment. "Madam's opals have been found."

"*Found?*" Miss Dobby was first to react to this news; and Cook wasn't slow to follow.

"Found where?"

"You'll never guess –" He looked round the expectant faces.

Even Perrins was watching him now, out of the corner of her eye, waiting. "In Broadwoods' yard."

"Broadwoods' yard – ?"

"Aye, Mrs Reynolds. That's where they were. Still in their case, thrown over the wall into the flower patch. It was Rosie who discovered 'em lying there."

"Well I never! And in Broadwoods' yard of all places!"

Susan Smith poked her head through the scullery hatch. "And there's none o' the jewels a-missing?"

"No, not one. Ear-bobs, bracelet and necklace, it's all there safe."

"Thank the good Lord for that." Amelia Dobby's relief spoke for everyone. Those opals of Mrs van der Kleve's had put the household in an uproar two days ago when they vanished into thin air from Madam's dressing room. A good thing the Master was away in Birmingham on business, or there'd have been an even worse to do when the jewellery couldn't be found: Nicholls had had the whole place turned upside down, and would have notified the constabulary if Beatrice hadn't stopped him.

"So it *was* a thief as got in." Mrs Reynolds had to sit down again, her legs failing her at the thought of some prowler creeping about the house at dead of night. "Lawks a' mercy! What a thing!"

"Mrs van der Kleve has been told, I hope?" came in Dobby again, sensibly. "She knows the jewels are recovered?"

Jem Randall nodded. "Mrs Broadwood brought 'em round herself this morning when she called. What strikes me as rum is that nobody's seen fit to say aught to us – I mean, we were the ones as came most under suspicion. You'd ha' thought Miss Beatrice might've mentioned some'at to Mr Nicholls."

"Who is to say that she hasn't?" Perrins objected. "You know Miss Beatrice particularly wished the whole business to be kept as quiet as possible."

"Aye. And why, that's what I'd like to know." Jem shot her a quick look before glancing away again. "She'd ha' shouted loud enough from the rooftop if she thought my Rosie had anything to do wi' it."

Perrins hated to hear him speak of Rose Maguire in that possessive fashion. Her sallow complexion took on a mottled hue and she lowered her eyes again to her needlework.

"It's my belief she's known all along who it was took those opals," he went on, rubbing the backs of his thighs where the fire was starting to burn. "And I'll tell you who *I* think it is, an' all. Young Miss Angelina."

There was a moment's silence; and then an exclamation of disbelief from Cook. "Go on wi' you! Miss Angelina? She'd never do a thing like that, not take what she shouldn't, not Miss Angelina. Why, that's – that's pilfering, is that."

"And if one of us had done it, it'd be called thieving or worse." Now that he'd shot his bolt, the young valet had nothing to lose by passing on something else he'd learned. "She's been taking things from the Mistress's room for months. Rosie told me so. But Miss Beatrice has always been careful to cover up for her –"

"That's not true," Jane Perrins cut in coldly. "I could have you dismissed for saying that."

"Ah, but you won't. We all know what's going on up there. And if you want to know what I think –" Jem looked round him again, thumbs thrust importantly into his striped waistcoat pockets – "I think it's high time the Master put his foot down. Miss Angelina would soon behave herself if she was better controlled. The trouble is, there's one too many mistresses in this house, and if Miss Beatrice won't oblige by stepping down out o' the way, then it's the Master's job to see to it she's made to."

In the pallid wintry sunlight filtering into the dressing room through the net lace curtains, the opals seemed to burn with a secret fire of their own, their milky surface skimmed with iridescent colours like an alchemist's flame. They were beautiful . . . and horrible. And Kitty wished with all her heart that it was a thief indeed who'd taken them, to spare her the trial of having ever to wear them again. As soon as she'd discovered the stones were missing, however, she had known where to lay the blame, for any thief worth his salt would have taken the rest of her jewellery, too, and not been so maliciously selective.

The tooled leather case lay open on the table before her now, its contents expensively displayed against the oyster velvet lining. Opposite, biting her sulky lip and looking down at the carpet, Angelina van der Kleve stood in rebellious silence.

"Well – ?" her young stepmother asked her again. "What have you to say for yourself? It *was* you who took this jewellery, wasn't it?"

The silence was maintained. Only the slightest shrug of one shoulder gave an indication of any response.

"If you don't answer me truthfully, Angelina, I shall be forced to tell your papa when he returns from Birmingham."

"You wouldn't dare! He'd never believe you." This, at least, provoked some sort of reaction.

"My dear, he would believe me. Why should I deceive him by fabricating such a tale?" Kitty tried to keep her voice quietly reasonable. "All I am asking is that you admit your guilt and apologise for it, and make me a promise that you'll do nothing like this again."

The sullen face contorted itself into scowling anger. "I won't. You can't *make* me do anything – so there."

"As you wish. But this isn't the first time you've stolen from my room, I know. I may have turned a blind eye in the past to your wrongdoing, but that was because I hoped it might stop of its own accord, and spare us both a painful interview. Obviously my hope was misfounded. I'm sorry I must speak like this, but you leave me no choice. Handkerchiefs and books and other personal items that you've taken – that I can forgive, but the jewellery is quite another matter."

There was a pause. The scowl on Angelina's face grew darker and she lapsed once more into a stubborn, surly silence.

After several moments her stepmother tried again. "*Why* did you take these jewels? You knew that what you were doing was inexcusable. What did you hope to achieve?"

No answer.

Kitty gave a sigh. "Very well. When your father returns home tomorrow evening I shall tell him the whole story, from first to last, and leave it to him how best to deal with your misconduct."

"You won't! You won't!" The shout was accompanied by a stamping of the foot.

"Excuse me, my dear, I *will*."

"I'll call you a liar."

"Oh? And how do you think Papa will respond – do you expect to win his support by contradicting me so? He will hardly regard you as a very pleasant child to use such words."

"I am not a child." Realising that her insolence could be reported, Angelina tried to pick upon this as a devious means of wriggling out of trouble. "I shall be fifteen next month –"

"All the more reason to appreciate right from wrong."

"And when I'm *sixteen*, I shall be old enough to elope to Paris with Mr Rivers."

The mention of the name was so totally unexpected that Kitty's heart gave a jump. She had not seen Jonathan Rivers since the dinner party on Christmas Eve, but he had been constantly on her mind. It had been such a little thing, that kiss they'd shared – a touch of the lips in innocent farewell – yet she had lain awake all night burning with its memory. Jonathan was an artist, she'd told herself repeatedly, and artists, like actors, not tied down by social inhibition, behaved in a different manner from everyone else: a kiss to them was nothing, given and forgotten in a moment like a clasp of the hand in greeting or goodbye.

Why, then, could she not rid herself of this feeling of guilt, that what had happened between them both was wrong? Wrong not because they might so easily have been witnessed, not because they were committing any offence and breaking the laws of propriety, but wrong because the touch of Jonathan's mouth upon hers for that fleeting moment had awoken something within her which she'd never known before, nor even suspected was there . . . a chord of response so tender that it made her tremble still to remember it.

"Didn't you hear what I said?" Angelina's aggressive tone brought her back from her thoughts. "Aren't you listening? I'm going to elope to Paris –"

"Yes, I heard you."

"Well – ?"

"Well . . . I trust you have asked Mr Rivers's permission."

"Oh, *he* will ask *mine*. He's spoony about me already." The plump adolescent features took on a look of smugness. "I can tell that by the silly way he stares at me. All my friends at Miss Meyrick's know."

Kitty regarded the smirking expression with veiled distaste. She could imagine the ready audience there would be to listen to such nonsense and encourage it.

"And do your friends also know what a dishonest little girl you are?"

The smirk vanished.

"Do they know that you creep about in other people's rooms to steal belongings? Do they know that you took some valuable jewellery which your father had given as a gift, and threw it away in an alley?"

The scowl was back, this time made uglier by a narrowed look of hatred. "You can't prove it. You can't prove it was me."

"Oh, so you do admit that it was?"

"No!"

"Then we must leave your Papa to decide the truth for himself."

Kitty turned from that vindictively hostile face, suddenly wearying of a scene which was leading neither of them anywhere but deeper into mutual aversion.

"Go along now," she said dismissively, closing the lid of the jewel case. "I've nothing more to say to you. Words are obviously wasted."

There was a taut silence; and then a shout of "I hate you! I *hate* you!" as Angelina stamped her foot again, indulging herself in a tantrum of rage. When Kitty chose to ignore this, she went on in a viciously spiteful manner, "It's *you* who should go away. I hope you die when your baby's born. Yes, I do. I hope you die just like my Mama did. It will serve you right for taking her place. You don't belong here, you belong in the workhouse where you came from –"

"Angelina –" Her stepmother tried to stem this flow of virulence, hearing in it an echo of Beatrice van der Kleve speaking. She moved round the table towards the girl, intending to show her the door if she would not control herself, but hardly had she taken more than half a dozen steps when Angelina snatched up a small china ornament and held it clenched in her hand as though threatening to throw it.

"Keep away from me!"

"Now don't be foolish. Put that down before you break it."

"Keep away –" The hand went back to hurl the ornament, and Kitty shied from it involuntarily, her arm up to protect herself.

As she did so, her foot caught against a ruck in the carpet causing her to stumble, thrown off-balance by the cumbersome weight of her pregnancy. She put out a hand towards the table to save herself, but missed, and as she went down sideways she caught herself a terrific crack on the temple from the carved wooden corner.

For several moments the pain almost blinded her, and she could only lie where she'd fallen, half-stunned, her head spinning with stars. Then, as she tried to push herself up, groping for the table leg as support, she felt a sudden hot wetness come gushing from her, soaking her petticoats; and another pain – a knife-thrust sharpness this time – pierced her through the body.

Crouched on all fours, Kitty reached out a hand towards her stepdaughter for help. But there was no one there. The door stood ajar. Angelina had already gone.

12

By the time Oliver van der Kleve arrived back in Tunbridge Wells early the following evening, his wife had been in childbirth for more than twelve hours. Dr Adeney was in attendance – and his news was not entirely reassuring.

"I'm afraid this is going to be a protracted labour," he warned Oliver, his voice low as the two men stood together near the bedroom door. "The waters broke late yesterday, and I would have expected her contractions to start almost immediately and get stronger as the night wore on. But they've been very slow, and very weak."

"Is there nothing you can do to hasten things?"

"Unfortunately not at this stage. Once the birth channel is properly dilated –" Dr Adeney made a gesture. "Well, then I shall use forceps if necessary, but until then it's a matter of hoping and waiting."

Oliver glanced over his shoulder into the room. Several more oil lamps had been brought in as darkness fell and placed where their light would shed the most effective illumination; and in the unpitying brightness Catherine looked so slight and vulnerable lying there against the pillows, her hair done up in braids like a child's to keep it from her face. She was almost unnaturally still, and for a moment the fancy crossed Oliver's mind that the bed had already become a bier – the bier which had borne his late wife Maria, surrounded in a blaze of candlelight among the shadows of this same room six years ago.

He turned back again to Dr Adeney and said harshly, "She's not in any danger, is she? Catherine's not going to die?"

"Now, now, Oliver, we don't want talk like that. Your wife's a healthy young woman –"

"So was Maria."

"But Maria was never very strong. And her baby was a breech birth." The elderly doctor glanced in turn towards the bed. He had fought hard and long to save the first Mrs van der Kleve; and he would fight even harder and longer if necessary before he allowed this second likewise to slip away from him to a premature grave.

"Be assured, Catherine is in no immediate danger."

"And the child?"

There was a little hesitation. "I shall do all in my power to see there's a safe delivery. But you must bear in mind, Oliver, the pregnancy has not been an easy one – the nausea and debilitation which your wife suffered may have had a weakening effect upon the infant's development, and – well, labour has started earlier than it should. We can be certain of nothing until the birth is over. I am sorry that I can give you no better comfort than that."

A shadow of despair crossed Oliver's features. More than almost anything else in the world he wanted a son, a healthy young son, to bear his name into a third generation of the van der Kleve banking concern. He was well aware of the risk attendant upon childbirth; but he had already lost one wife to that grim reaper of mortality, and it was unthinkable that another should be taken from him in like fashion. Surely, by Maria's death he'd already paid the ransom for Catherine's life.

Seeing his drawn expression, Dr Adeney gripped his arm in reassurance.

"You've had a long journey home from the Midlands. You look tired. Why not take some rest while you can?"

Oliver nodded. "Perhaps you're right. One of the servants can make me up a cot in the dressing room. I'll stay with her a little longer, though . . . just for a few minutes more."

Going back into the room, he went and sat quietly beside the bed, leaning forward towards his wife, elbows upon knees, hands clasped tightly together.

Sensing his presence, Kitty opened her eyes. The dull, leaden ache of the contractions had receded a little for the moment, taking with it some of the fear and pain of the past hours, and she felt heavy and lethargic as though even to think demanded too much effort.

Seeing her look towards him, Oliver said softly, "Catherine . . . Catherine, dearest . . . be strong. It will all soon be over."

He had never called her dearest before; and the way he

spoke the word . . . Kitty tried to concentrate her thoughts, but somehow they eluded her. She was aware of the touch of her husband's hand on her forehead, and his question, "What's this? How did you come by such a bruise to your temple?" – and then the pain was back again, mounting slowly and slyly within, nudging its red-hot way along each separate nerve of her body.

She held her breath, waiting for it to slacken; but this time, suddenly, it was stronger than before and seemed to go on swelling inside her, raking deeper and harder until she thought she would scream. Gasping, she dragged at the bedsheets, twisting her head from side to side, her face crumpled into a mask of suffering; and Oliver's arms were round her, holding her tight, cradling her to his chest.

"There now, there . . . there now, my dearest." He tried to comfort her, his mouth against her burning cheek; and in her anguish she clung to him, crying, "Stay with me! Oh, don't let me go!" as though he were a lover.

Pain wiped the past from her mind. Aversion, disgust, apprehension – every emotion harboured against this man was swept away, and the only thing she knew was the strength of his arms and the gentling sound of his voice easing her body little by little from its rack of torment. When the contraction had passed she lay exhausted against him, as though sated, breath ragged between her parted lips; and then a voice – was it the doctor? – said, "You must leave her now, Oliver," and she felt the arms withdrawn.

After that there was nothing but pain – hot, fierce, brutalising pain, shot through with searing streaks of agony. Just before the forceps were applied she was given some chloroform, and as the merciful drops soaked into the cloth covering her face, she felt herself begin drifting away into a grey-fogged wasteland of unconsciousness that was filled with the distant echoes of Dr Adeney's voice.

And then, for a while . . . nothing.

In the early hours of next morning, Saturday the thirteenth of January, Kitty was delivered of her baby. Not the robust and lusty son the father wanted, but a sickly little scrap of a daughter clinging to life by the barest thread.

Against all expectation, the tiny creature survived the first critical twenty-four hours, and by Monday her thin, mewing cries had started turning to wails of hunger. Kitty herself was still far too weak to try to feed her, and on Dr Adeney's advice Oliver hired a wet-nurse, an ample-breasted young woman with a recent baby of her own who came up Mount Sion through the snow four times a day to suckle both infants together. By the end of the first week when the small wrinkled body had gained a few ounces of plumpness and the yellowed waxy skin showed a better colour, the doctor expressed cautious optimism that the mite would survive; and in view of the fact that its mother had such a scant flow of milk and needed to conserve her strength to make a good recovery, he suggested the wet-nurse's services be continued until weaning.

Nothing could have suited Beatrice van der Kleve better. A pity the ugly little thing had not been a boy, but never mind, it was Oliver's flesh and blood and he'd already chosen the name of Henrietta for it, after their paternal grandmother Hendrickje van der Kleve. Ten days after the birth, Kitty woke to find her baby's silk-draped cradle missing from beside the bed; and frantically ringing to ask what had happened, she was told that Miss Beatrice had ordered both baby and cradle's removal to a small room next to her own, which would henceforth serve as the nursery.

"Oh, yes, I'm allowed to see her. They bring her in to me, place her in my arms for five minutes, and then remove her again."

Kitty spoke in a level voice, but watching her face, Harriet Seymour caught the little tremor of the chin which told of inner heartache.

"So Beatrice has taken charge?" she said.

"Yes."

"And having given birth, your services are now dispensed with."

"It would appear so. I'm not able to feed Henrietta . . . and until I'm permitted out of bed, I can't dress her or bathe her, not even rock her. There's a nurse maid now, I understand, to see to all that."

"Well, first things first. You must think of yourself, my dear, and build up your health and strength." Harriet, as usual, applied practical shrewdness to the situation. "Beatrice is quite right – you're no use to Baby as you are. But once you're up and about again, *then* will be the time to assume your proper role of Mama and retrieve your tender chick from Aunt Bea's nest."

"If only it were that simple!"

"Isn't it?"

"I don't know. Dr Adeney came to see me yesterday. He said she'd had some kind of convulsion . . . a fit. Nothing very serious, but he's suggested she has a little fresh air each day. Beatrice keeps the nursery fire stoked like a furnace, Dobby informs me."

There was a pause. Kitty looked down at her hands, pale against the coverlet.

"Oh – did I tell you the Broadwoods called to visit?" she began again suddenly in a forced rush of brightness. "They looked in at Baby and declared her the dearest wee thing, and said I really wasn't to worry that her hair is falling out for it will all grow back again . . . at least, it was Frances Broadwood told me that. I doubt her husband knows about such matters."

"No more do I." Harriet smiled, observing her friend's expression and not for an instant taken in by this feigned show of cheeriness. Kitty was trying hard to put on a brave face for the world, but to one who knew her well and loved her, the long and distressing ordeal of bearing a child only to be denied the rights and rewards of motherhood, told a revealing story: somewhere during the past weeks she had lost that innocent freshness which had made her look younger than her twenty years, and the beautiful features now bore a subtly vulnerable maturity.

Harriet uncrossed her legs. On Dr Peter Hoffmann's advice she had taken to wearing a built-up shoe to correct her lameness, and though it helped her to walk more evenly, the crippled limb had developed a most persistent nagging ache as muscles and joints adapted themselves to the change.

"By the by –" she went on, shifting to a more comfortable position in her chair, "what came of the affair of Angelina and the opals? You've said not a word about Oliver's reaction."

"That's because no one's mentioned anything of it to him. Baby's arrival rather pushed the whole thing into the background."

"But you are going to tell him, I trust?"

Kitty pulled at the blue silk ribbon threaded through the

camisole lace at her breast. "I don't know. It depends upon Angelina. Perhaps I really should allow her one final chance to redeem herself. She seemed quite sorry I'd hurt my head falling against the table."

"But it was she who caused that to happen!"

There was another brief hesitation. "Well . . . not on purpose, I'm sure. To be honest, Harriet, it seems somehow rather pointless raking the matter up again. Informing Oliver will only result in a lot of unpleasantness and set the girl against me further."

"My dear, you'd be wiser to suffer the unpleasantness now than to store up future trouble and worse for yourself. Angelina and Beatrice together are two heads on the same neck. Deal with the one while you can, and you'll be drawing the sting of the other."

"The sting of the Bea?" Kitty laughed softly at her friend's unintentional pun. "Do you think it can hurt me more than it has already?"

"I do. And I advise you strongly to throw yourself upon your husband's protection and give him your confidence. He's no fool, Kitty dear. He knows his daughter's character. He'll take your part, I'm sure."

"You think so? Then why does he permit his sister a free hand here in everything she wishes? I may be called mistress in this house, but it's she who's in charge of the staff – and I may be the mother of Henrietta, but it's Beatrice who decides who shall have care of her."

"This is true, and I share your grievance, believe me. But, as I've said, once you've regained your health you can match Beatrice at her own game – and for that you'll need Oliver. Oh, I know what you're going to say –" as Kitty made to interrupt – "that you have no role in your marriage other than that of decoration and plaything. But I think you're mistaken. I think you underestimate your own worth in your husband's eyes. You must take a leaf from Bea's book, my dear, and practise a little more guile and cunning. Men are susceptible creatures, and a loving word whispered in the ear works miracles of persuasion."

Kitty left off pulling at her ribbon and leaned forward, legs drawn up, bunching the bedclothes to herself. For several days following 'Etta's birth she'd thought she must surely have imagined the gentleness she'd received from Oliver, the consoling comfort of his arms helping her through her pain – it was so unlike the man she knew to behave in such a tender manner. Now, though, she had come to realise that memory wasn't playing her false: she'd been shown a side of his character she never guessed existed, and it was something to hold on to, some little happiness to lay by for the future of their marriage.

"Perhaps you're right, Harriet," she said, resting herself back again amongst the mound of pillows. "Perhaps I've allowed too much fear and ignorance of the facts of life to blind me to reality. There are many lessons I've yet to learn . . . and bedroom diplomacy is one of them. But if that's the way to be mistress in my husband's house and mother to my child, then it's a lesson that may well repay my study."

Among those calling at Sion Place to pay their good wishes upon the birth of a daughter, was Jonathan Rivers. In truth, this courtesy was no more than incidental to the young man's purpose in waiting upon Oliver van der Kleve, for though he was genuinely pleased to learn of Kitty's safe and successful delivery, there were two matters of rather more urgency to be discussed with his employer.

The first was his forthcoming absence from Tunbridge Wells, made necessary by his father's grave illness at the family home in Shropshire: it would mean, of course, that he was unable to give Angelina any further drawing lessons for the time being, as he trusted Mr van der Kleve would understand.

The second was a request to be allowed to show Mrs van der Kleve's portrait at a Spring exhibition in Sevenoaks; and to justify his asking, he took trouble to explain that it was viewings of this kind which enabled artists to advertise their work and talent to the public and thus hopefully attract further commissions.

Having heard him out, Oliver's response was a terse, point-blank refusal. His wife's portrait was now private property, he said, and not something to be gawked at by a lot of tom noddies as though it were a billboard poster on a street hoarding.

The blunt rejection rankled considerably, for that picture – undoubtedly the best he'd ever painted – was to have been the centrepiece of Jonathan's display of work. Argument, however, would be a waste of breath: one did not quarrel with the likes of Mr van der Kleve if one wished to stay employed. Obviously the gentleman preferred to forget that had he not himself been one of those 'tom noddies' he so contemptuously dismissed, the portrait of Catherine would not have been commissioned in the first place.

Catherine . . .

Oh, but it was dangerous to think of her as that. Far better to refer to her mentally as Mrs van der Kleve, and let the formality of title act as curb to his growing admiration. Since that extraordinary moment on Christmas Eve when wine had made him bolder than was sensible or wise and he'd kissed her soft, moist, yielding mouth, he'd thought of Catherine van der Kleve with increasing frequency and – he had to admit it – with deepening desire.

On the very verge of motherhood she might be, but nothing could detract from the aura of feminine sexuality which clung about her, the more potent for being so entirely innocent.

Robbed of his hopes for her portrait, Jonathan left the next morning for Shropshire, quite unaware that the reason behind the refusal was a jealousy for the work amounting almost to neurosis – a neurosis induced by the uncannily perceptive accuracy of his own artistic talent. Ironically, had he been less gifted, possessed of less intuitive insight into the truth concealed by the façade which Kitty showed the world, her husband might perhaps have been more willing to comply with his request.

Travelling by third-class railway coach via Birmingham to Wellington, the journey was a long and wearying one, as well as dirty; and the unheated wooden carriage in the frosty cold of January allowed blasts of icy air to swirl about the shoulders of its passengers. Hardly had he arrived at his parents' home in the uplands of the Wrekin north of Coalbrookdale, than the young man succumbed to a severe chill, giving his mother and sisters two patients now to nurse instead of one.

Fortunately the elder Mr Rivers's condition had been temporarily arrested in its downward course, so that the family's spirits were less heavy with the gloom of impending death that had filled them of late. Once his own health was upon the road to recovery, Jonathan took to spending much of his day seated at the window of his father's bedchamber with easel and oils, keeping the older man quiet company while he painted the winter landscape of snow-smooth dales dominated on an iron grey skyline by the long whaleback swell of the Wrekin.

It was his mother who suggested that he make a copy of Catherine van der Kleve's portrait to show at the exhibition in place of the original. There was no law against it, surely, and he'd brought the sketches of the work with him to show his sisters. A pity not to use them . . .

The winter landscape was abandoned. For the next fortnight, until his father's death, Jonathan Rivers worked hour upon hour with a fever born not of January cold now, but of impatience. The second portrait – exact in almost every detail to the first – was completed two days after the funeral.

At its lower edge it bore the legend *La Belle Dame aux Ombres* – 'The Lady of Shadows'.

13

"Dearly beloved, forasmuch as all men are conceived and born in sin; and that our Saviour Christ saith, none can enter into the Kingdom of God except he be regenerate and born anew of Water and the Holy Ghost; I beseech you to call upon God the Father, through our Lord Jesus Christ, that of his bounteous mercy he will grant to this Child that thing which by nature she cannot have; that she may be baptized with Water and the Holy Ghost, and received into Christ's holy Church, and be made a lively member of the same."

The Reverend Mr Edward Terris was forced to raise his voice a little on the final line to make himself heard above the squalling screams of the infant about to be christened.

Now two months old, Henrietta Sophia van der Kleve was still a tiny underweight creature, but what she lacked in size was more than made up by the continuous noise of her crying, as though in fretful protest at having been hurried so inconveniently into life. She hardly seemed to sleep at all, and when she did, the sudden silence in the house was quite startling. The original nursemaid had been dismissed when found trying to lull the babe with drops of gin to get some respite; and it was by sheer providence that among those interviewed as her successor had been a young woman so hard of hearing as to be virtually deaf. Being bright in all other ways, and an excellent reader of lips, she was ideally suited for the work and promptly engaged upon the spot.

Mr Terris cleared his throat and cast an unhappy look towards Beatrice van der Kleve.

"Let us pray . . ."

Misinterpreting the glance, Beatrice returned him a private smile and held her wailing god-daughter closer to her bosom in what might appear like fond devotion. The infant was as tightly swaddled as a flannel parcel inside the white lace christening gown and shawl, so there was no risk of any dampness seeping through to leave stains upon the mauve silk of her bodice.

"Almighty and everlasting God, who of thy great mercy didst save Noah and his family in the ark from perishing by water . . ."

The minister launched himself into a monotone delivery of prayer, his baritone vowels rounding out the words in almost theatrically exaggerated manner. Out of the corner of his eye he could see the baptismal guests seated in the nearer pews and he made a mental note of one or two of the more affluently dressed whom he must seek out later at the reception. It was wonderful how efficaciously a well-conducted service drew guineas from the purses of the wealthy, in response to a discreetly mentioned need for new altar cloths or such.

"Dearly beloved, ye have brought this Child here to be baptized –" Having concluded that part of the liturgy with a short reading, Mr Terris now held out his hands in a gesture inviting the godparents to step forward to the font. There were five of them to make the appropriate vows on the infant's behalf: Beatrice van der Kleve, Harriet Seymour, Mr and Mrs Henry Broadwood, and Humphrey Jaggers, senior partner in a firm of City solicitors.

"Dost thou, in the name of this Child, renounce the devil and all his works," the five were invited collectively, "the vain pomp and glory of the world, with all covetous desires of the same, and the carnal desires of the flesh, so that thou wilt not follow, nor be led by them?"

There was a well modulated chorus of "I renounce them all", followed by a further procedural exchange of question and response, somewhat drowned by the protesting screams of the object of this solemn exercise.

Receiving the infant into his arms, and careful not to trail the shawl into the font, Mr Terris intoned, "Name this Child –" at the same time baring the tiny head to receive a trickle of holy water from the scallop-shaped dish in his right hand. It was a more general practice at baptism to immerse the infant entirely naked, but Dr Adeney had advised against it in this case since the sudden shock to such a delicate constitution might well bring on a fit.

"The child is to be named Henrietta Sophia," Humphrey Jaggers, as principal sponsor, responded for the others.

"Henrietta Sophia –" The water fell in a dribble over the downy head. "I baptize thee in the name of the Father, and of the Son, and of the Holy Ghost. Amen." The symbol of faith was traced with a thumb lightly upon the forehead.

Unaware and uncaring of anything but her own angry discomfort, the baby continued to express a profound lack of appreciation for all this rite and rigmarole, adding her piercing little screams to the concluding prayer. Handed back across the font to Beatrice, who in turn surrendered her to the nursemaid behind, she was forthwith carried away to a rear pew of the echoing church where her noise was less disruptive.

"Amiss – ? Of course there's nothing amiss with the child." Beatrice was quite curt with Harriet Seymour outside on the steps at the end of the service. "And no, Miss Seymour, I do not think that a second medical opinion would be advisable. My brother and I have every confidence in Dr Adeney's course of treatment."

Harriet would have liked to suggest that little 'Etta might thrive more readily if she were allowed a mother's natural love; but the carriages were drawing up to convey the party to Sion Place and the moment for such observation was lost. Watching Beatrice move away to attach herself to Mr Terris, she resisted a mischievous urge to play gooseberry and follow the pair into the front carriage, and instead accepted Mr Jaggers's arm to the landau behind.

It had been decided to hold the christening reception in the terrace room, to take advantage of a mild spell of late March sunshine which had arrived to brighten the tail end days of winter. Harriet had not been in this room since the van der Kleve wedding breakfast a year ago, and could not help but cast her mind back to that earlier occasion as she seated herself beside a large conservatory palm in one corner to observe the rest of the gathering. What was remarkable was that so little on the surface appeared to have changed in those past twelve months. Perhaps there was a touch more grey showing at Oliver's temples, but his manner was still as icily reserved as on his wedding day; and his sister had clearly advanced no further in her dogged pursuit of Mr Terris, to judge by the way that reverend gentleman was trying to avoid her limpet-like attentions. The ghastly Angelina had grown up somewhat and was beginning to look buxom, though burgeoning young womanhood went ill with the childishly surly cast of her features. As for Kitty – well, Kitty had lost her innocence and matured visibly in a year, but seemed as alone and withdrawn and isolated now as she had on the day she'd been a bride.

So much water flowing under the bridge in a twelvemonth, yet hardly a ripple to show for it . . .

Harriet accepted a glass of champagne.

Henry Broadwood and Mr Jaggers wandered past, the wine already audible in their braying tones as they discussed the effect bound to be felt upon British trade as a result of the recent abolition of American slavery.

Then Angelina came by, stopping to toss her corkscrew ringlets and exclaim rudely, "I don't know why they invited *you*, Miss Seymour. No one knows you except my stepmama. *I* should have been one of the godmothers, not you – Aunt Beatrice promised. You went and took my place, and I think you're hateful."

"The feeling, my dear, is entirely reciprocated." Harriet smiled sweetly; and when Angelina crossed her eyes and poked out her tongue, did not hesitate to respond in like fashion.

Mr Broadwood and Mr Jaggers were moving back now, this time with Oliver van der Kleve, the glasses of all three replenished, their discussion shifted to the newly started North Sea–Amsterdam Canal which the merchant bank of van der Kleve Lindemanns was helping to finance.

Seeing his daughter go flouncing past towards the terrace door, Oliver interrupted the talk a moment to call out, "Ah – Angelina. Mrs Adeney is asking to speak to you –" and then, with a slight acknowledgment of Harriet as he went by, continued his conversation.

Through the sheltering green fronds of the potted palm it was possible to see, without being seen, Beatrice van der Kleve stalking Mr Terris down the room from one knot of guests to another, a performance which afforded Harriet Seymour much amusement while she waited till Kitty was free of her social duties to join her. It was obvious that the clergyman wished to ingratiate himself with those of Mr Jaggers's party who'd travelled down from London to spend the weekend here; and equally obvious that he was finding Beatrice's hovering presence at his elbow a nuisance.

"If Mr Terris were not a gentleman of the cloth, I'd say he

was trying to cadge something, the way he's mopping and mowing, and wringing his hands," she remarked a short time after.

"He is." Kitty van der Kleve threw a dismissive glance over her shoulder as she seated herself beside her friend. "Contributions to St Bride's Church funds."

"And Bea keeps ruining his flow of verbosity?"

"I rather gather she'd prefer he gave her a solo performance in the garden."

The two exchanged dry looks.

"Do you know –" Kitty sipped a mouthful of champagne from her glass – "Dobby tells me she religiously saves all the hair caught in her hairbrush at night and keeps it in a bag. Apparently she intends using it as stuffing for a cushion, to give to Mr Terris as some grisly kind of keepsake."

"Lord above – what a notion! Will he accept it, d'you suppose?"

"Who can say? If he doesn't, she will be mightily offended."

"Even so . . ." Harriet gave a little shudder. Then, looking up, her sharp mouse features hastily transformed themselves into a sudden brightness. "Why, Mr Terris –! Kitty and I were just this instant speaking of you, sir." Nothing in her voice indicated the start he'd given them both by his silent appearance from the other side of the palm. "Won't you care to join us?"

Whether he had heard their conversation or not, neither could tell. The plumply elegant face wore its usual unctuous smile and the pale eyes fixed themselves blandly upon Kitty as he acknowledged the invitation with a bow.

"Indeed, dear ladies, you flatter me! That I should be the topic of interest to two such charming creatures is compliment enough without the added pleasure of a request of my company." The smile turned into a smirk and Edward Terris folded his hands together upon his comfortably rounded stomach. "Alas, however, I must refuse you. I merely came, dear Mrs van der Kleve, to thank you for the kindness of your munificent hospitality, and bid you my reluctant adieu. Evensong, you understand . . . one must not neglect one's duties to one's faithful flock."

"Oh – oh, no. Of course not, Mr Terris." Kitty tried to fit her expression into a suitably serious cast and hunted round for some word or other to give him in parting appreciation of her daughter's christening.

Harriet saved her the trouble. "May I say, sir, before you leave us, how very dignified I found the service today at St Bride's. I have often remarked to Kitty that this parish is to be envied in the inspiring qualities of its spiritual observance."

The clergyman's smirk became a positive simper. "*Too* kind of you, too kind, ma'am. One does one's humble and unworthy best as steward of the Lord's house, and St Bride's has a very generous patronage —"

At that moment Mr Terris's attention was distracted by the sight of Beatrice van der Kleve bearing down upon him from the left, and cutting himself off in mid-sentence, with as much clerical dignity as he could muster, contrived with a hasty farewell to make his escape in the opposite direction.

Kitty and Harriet looked at one another, and had trouble concealing their laughter until Beatrice had gone by.

"If ever a pair deserved each other, they do," Harriet declared, biting her lip to control her unseemly mirth. "What a pompous ass the fellow is —" she parodied the minister's plum-voiced tones — "'one does one's humble and unworthy best' —"

"You shouldn't have encouraged him." Kitty's mouth twitched at the memory. "What was all that about St Bride's inspiring qualities? Really, Harriet! How you can say such things and yet keep a perfectly straight face —"

"Practice, my dear. That's all it is. Practice. It's astonishing what people will believe if it's what they want to hear. Perhaps you should try a little of such subterfuge on Oliver."

The smile died away in Kitty's lovely eyes.

Pretending not to notice, her friend went on, "Tell me to mind my own business if you wish, but do I detect a slight melting of the iceberg between you and The Husband? Or is it imagination?"

"I . . . I'm not sure I know what you mean."

"Oh yes you do. I saw Oliver glancing towards you several times in the church, and with what looked suspiciously like fond attention, too."

"Fond attention?" Kitty began to laugh again, but this time there was no humour in the sound. "Is that what you call it?"

"Well — a certain warmth of regard, then. These things are

difficult to tell with Oliver, I admit, since he always appears so poker-faced, but there *was* something there, Kitty. I'm sure of it. And I rather hoped, after what you'd told me a while ago, that your relationship might be improving."

The other emptied her glass of champagne. For a second or two she remained silent, her gaze fixed upon a pool of spring sunlight spilt from a window across the floor.

Then quietly, almost tonelessly, she answered, "There was a moment, Harriet, when I was in labour with 'Etta, that I thought I glimpsed a more tender and caring side to my husband's nature. He was gentle with me . . . gentle and considerate . . . and I told myself afterwards that perhaps I'd misjudged him all these months and that his . . . attentions were not as loveless and selfish as I'd imagined. But I was wrong. I was bearing what he fondly hoped was his son and heir, that was the reason for his solicitude. That, and his concern not to lose another wife in childbirth, having gone to all the expense and effort of replacing the first."

The look upon Kitty's beautiful face was one which her friend, in all the years she'd known her, had never seen there before; and it was frightening. Only a few minutes ago the two of them had been laughing together at Mr Terris like a pair of giddy young girls; and now it was as though a different person had suddenly taken her place – someone stony-eyed and older, with a mouth downturned in bitterness and the tight, pinched whiteness of anger round the small nostrils.

"But, my dear –" Harriet began.

"No – let me finish. Had I been one of his mares in foal, my husband would not have shown me any less than the same amount of consideration and care. I'm an investment, you see – an investment for his future as well as a pastime and amusement for his present. He calls me his wife –"

Kitty's voice broke on the word and she averted her head. Then, recovering herself after a moment, she went on, "Since the baby's birth I have tried to be what he wants – I have tried to oblige him – but he makes me feel like . . . well, I must say it – like a slut."

She twisted the stem of the champagne glass back and forth between her slender fingers in an agitated manner; and when she spoke again there was a sudden sadness, a bewilderment, in her voice which tore at the other's heart.

"Oh, Harriet, if only he'd left me those foolish illusions . . ."

Those illusions, created on the night of Henrietta's birth, had been a buoy of hope for Kitty, carrying her through the wearing, wearying days which followed. Deprived of her baby's care, and forced to keep to her bed till her body mended, she'd allowed herself to indulge in a fantasy that behind that tight-reined façade her husband hid a gentle and loving part of himself which no one but she had glimpsed; and that if she could but find the key she could unlock his complex nature and discover what he seemed at such pains to conceal from the world.

But what was the key? – Love? Obedience? Submission? Her own womanly weakness and need? Harriet had advised her to take a leaf from Beatrice's book and practise a little deception; but in what way? All she had to hold on to was that single strand of memory – Oliver's arms giving her strength, his quiet voice easing her down from the plateau of her agony.

That strand indeed was all she had, and she clung to it for comfort, feeding her own illusions on the repetition of remembrance. Until one evening just a week or two ago when the hope, the dream, of a kinder future had seemed cruelly shattered.

She and Oliver had gone with the Broadwoods to see a play performed at the Assembly Rooms on the Lower Parade, and as this was the first social event which Kitty had attended since her confinement, she was determined to make the evening a success. She'd been especially attentive to her husband, smiling at him frequently and joining in the lively conversation at the interval; but it was Henry Broadwood rather than Oliver who'd seemed most appreciative of her efforts, for he was constantly interrupting to pay her silly compliments and draw her aside to murmur things which, for the noise, she could not hear.

Try as she might, she could hardly avoid his attentions without appearing rude, and so she pretended to laugh – and was absolutely mortified when, at the end of the evening as she and her husband were bidding the Broadwoods goodnight, Henry had taken her hand and kissed it in a most embarrassingly fulsome manner.

Mr Broadwood may have been just a trifle tipsy on the

brandy he'd drunk with Oliver; even so, his gesture was uncalled-for and in the light of what followed, had the most painful repercussion for Kitty – a repercussion which not only ruined her evening but flung her once again into total despair at the callous and cruel insensibility of her husband's behaviour.

He had not previously approached her for any resumption of sexual contact since Henrietta's birth – indeed, had been advised by Dr Adeney to abstain from any such activity until Kitty's body, painfully torn by the use of the forceps during her delivery, should be fully healed.

It was clear that Henry Broadwood's conduct had irritated Oliver tonight, however, and his irritation showed. Without acknowledging Kitty's words of gratitude for a pleasant evening, he went directly to his study once they were home and stayed there for some time, so that she was already asleep when finally he came up to their bedchamber.

The first she knew of his presence was the sudden coldness of having the coverlets dragged from her.

Shaking her roughly into wakefulness he'd said harshly, "You were very attentive to me earlier, my dear. Quite the little tease, in fact. Or was that all for Henry's benefit?" And when, half-dazed still with sleep she struggled to gather her wits to reply, he gave her no chance but launched instead into a most extraordinary tirade, accusing her of being no better than some common cheap coquette in her behaviour, and swearing he'd teach her better.

What followed then could only be described as a most violent assault. Unprepared, unguarded, Kitty tried to resist, to defend herself; but this seemed to provoke her husband even further, and pushing her face-down into the pillows he'd kept her pinned there by the shoulders, crushing her with the full force of his weight, while he used her little better than if she'd been a dog.

Her tender flesh, newly knitted from her baby's birth, was on fire with the excruciating pain of what he was doing; and though she screamed at him, wept, pleaded with him to stop, he continued to ride her until jealousy and rage and lust were finally sated.

Almost fainting with the agony of her throbbing body, her mouth filled with the iron taste of blood where she'd bitten into her lips, she'd felt him rolling from on top of her to lie exhausted on the bed, the sound of his laboured breathing gradually growing quieter in the stillness of the night.

For long minutes neither of them moved. Then he had said at last, in a curiously humble, almost entreating, tone, "Don't hate me, Catherine. Please . . . say you don't hate me for this."

She turned her head, pushing aside the tangle of hair from her face, intending to tell him precisely that with all the strength she had left in her. But the words died on her lips. Oliver was weeping, silently and desolately, tears running unchecked across the angular planes of cheek and temple into his darkened hair.

And Kitty had turned her face away again, her own tears falling, weeping for herself and her broken dreams.

14

Oliver van der Kleve generally travelled up to the City twice a week, making the journey on a first-class ticket which ensured an adequate amount of privacy and comfort. It was a routine he had kept to throughout his years as a widower, varying it only upon his second marriage when he'd started spending each night of the week at Sion Place. So much daily travel up and down the South Eastern Railway had proved wasteful of time and business, however, and since the New Year he'd reverted to his former practice, using rooms at his club, Gresham's, for midweek accommodation.

On his way up to Town shortly after little Henrietta's christening, Oliver happened to share a carriage from Sevenoaks with a regular fellow-traveller, and observing that gentleman glancing through an art catalogue, he had asked – *The Times* being dull fare that morning – if he might see it for himself when the other was finished.

The catalogue proved to be of the works of local artists being shown at Bligh's Rooms in Sevenoaks until the coming Saturday, the fourteenth of April. Remarking upon the high standard of amateur work these days, Oliver had been about to add that he might well go along to view – when his eye was caught by the name of Jonathan Rivers, recalling at once to mind the young fellow's insulting gall in wanting to show Catherine's portrait at some spring exhibition or other.

No sooner was he reminded of that than he'd felt a hot flush of anger burn his face as he turned the page and found himself looking at a printed reproduction of that very picture.

"What the –!" he had exclaimed aloud, startling his carriage companion by his vehemence. "By God, there'd better be an explanation for this!"

The explanation was uncovered that same afternoon when, at some considerable inconvenience to himself and his bank's business, Oliver had travelled back again to Sevenoaks. There upon a wall of Bligh's Rooms, for all the world to gawp at, hung *La Belle Dame aux Ombres*, so faithful a copy of the original that one might almost suppose them to be one and the same work of art.

Even though the portrait was exorbitantly priced in his opinion, he had not hesitated to buy it; and upon returning to Tunbridge Wells, sent a note to Jonathan Rivers by one of the servants requesting an interview with him that same evening.

The interview opened without any pretence at courtesy.

"I make no apology for having you summoned here," began Oliver bluntly, standing to face the younger man across his study desk. "Indeed, I will not even thank you for obliging me with your presence."

"I was unengaged this evening, as it happened, sir." The truculent way in which he was addressed warned Jonathan that his employer had not invited him here to exchange pleasantries. Nevertheless he'd be wise to respond in a civil and mannerly fashion if he knew what was good for him. "It was no inconvenience to comply with your request."

"Whether it was inconvenient or not is neither here nor there to me. In fact, the inconvenience is mine, Mr Rivers, in that I have been obliged to waste an afternoon's business on your account."

"Indeed? I am sorry to learn that –"

"Oh, but you will be sorrier yet before you leave, you may depend upon it!"

The words came aggressively. Oliver van der Kleve leaned forward on his fists, knuckles white against the polished oak surface of his desk.

"While you are in my employment, sir, I expect you to conduct yourself in an open, honest and entirely trustworthy manner. It has come to my notice, however, that your behaviour has been quite to the contrary and that not only have you shown yourself to be unprincipled, but also devious and deceitful – an opportunist who will not let such small considerations as honour or duty lie in the way of his own contemptible ambition. No – you will hear me out, sir –" as the other made to protest his bewilderment at this attack – "you will cast your mind back, if you please, to a previous interview here between us, sought at your request to ask that you might have the loan of my wife's portrait for an exhibition of art. And it might further please you to recall that I refused – most emphatically so."

"If I may be permitted to speak, Mr van der Kleve –" Jonathan tried again. He was suddenly beginning to see what this extraordinary outburst was about. "If it concerns a copy which I made of Mrs van der Kleve's portrait –"

He got no further.

"Indeed it concerns such a copy, Mr Rivers. A copy which you did without my permission, knowing that I had expressly stated my opposition to any public showing of the original. A copy made in the deliberate awareness that you were defying my wishes."

There was an angry pause.

"I speak of *this* copy, sir!"

Bending behind his desk, Oliver seized up the gilt-framed painting bought at Bligh's Rooms and rested it in front of him.

"There is only one thing I wish to ask of you before I proceed further with this distasteful business," he went on savagely, "and that is to know whether there are yet more duplications of this picture."

Jonathan shook his head, not a little unnerved by the disconcerting surprise of being confronted quite so dramatically with his own work.

"No?"

"No, Mr van der Kleve. That is the only copy I made. You have my word on it."

"A somewhat worthless assurance, I think." The unmistakable sneer brought colour to the young man's face. "Your word, sir, appears to mean very much less to you than the sum of guineas you anticipated receiving from the sale of this – reproduction. You will understand, of course, that as its purchaser I expect to be fully recompensed for the price I paid."

"Certainly you'll be recompensed, sir." Jonathan came forward a step and put out a hand towards the picture as though with the intention of taking it. "And in return, I trust you'll allow me to have the portrait back. Not for re-sale, naturally –"

"By God, I'll see you damned first! D'you think I'll permit you to walk from my house carrying this picture beneath your arm as though the matter amounted to nothing more than a simple *quid pro quo*?"

"But surely, if the money is repaid the work reverts to being mine again – at least, that is how I understand the Law."

"Don't you quote the Law at me, sir!" An ugly flush suffused Oliver's features. His grip upon the frame tightened. "This copy, being an unauthorised and illicitly made duplicate, *in Law* becomes and remains my property by virtue of the fact that the original already belongs to me."

"Mr van der Kleve, if you will but listen a moment –" The other stuck doggedly to his argument. "That painting is not an exact copy. There are various differences, as you must surely have noticed. And the title – your wife's portrait bore no title, whereas this is called –"

"I know what it is called. If you must plagiarise your own work, Mr Rivers, you might at least do it in honest English fashion as hide your deceit behind fancy French. *La Belle Dame aux Ombres*. The Lady in Shadow. Is that how you perceive my wife? Overshadowed by marriage, perhaps? Living some twilight existence?" He gave away more than he realised.

"No, sir. The title merely alluded to the play of light and shade which I used as a theme for the work."

"Indeed." There was a tight smile. "Well now, since we cannot agree upon either the provenance or purpose of this – allegory in oils, there seems only one course of action left to take to resolve the matter."

Something in his employer's attitude warned Jonathan of his intention. He opened his mouth to protest . . . then closed it again. A sudden fear of this bitter and implacably obsessive man seized him and he stood irresolute, his eyes fixed upon Catherine van der Kleve's portrait, waiting in mounting apprehension for what might be about to follow.

"Come, sir –" the sneer was back in Oliver's voice – "what a dull imagination you possess. Surely you can hazard a guess at my solution?" And not waiting for any answer "No? Then permit me to show you."

Holding the gilt frame in both hands, he raised it to shoulder height and quite deliberately smashed it down across a corner of his desk. There was an ugly ripping sound as the canvas gave under the force of the impact; and when he raised the picture again Catherine's face had gone. Calmly, yet with a methodical violence which shocked Jonathan to see it, he proceeded to tear the canvas in two from top to bottom, leaving it hanging from its frame.

"Yours, did you say, Mr Rivers?" Satisfied with his destruction, he held out the shattered picture.

Words choked in the other's throat. What he had just witnessed was an act of total and unjustifiable vandalism, made even more obscene by the fact that it was his own wife's lovely form and features that the man had despoiled.

"Oh, by the way, before you leave –" Oliver van der Kleve's tone reflected a sudden contrived boredom. "You do appreciate, of course, that I no longer consider you suitable for employment in my house. A week's notice, I believe, were the terms of your contract? You need not trouble yourself to serve it, Mr Rivers. And kindly do not expect me to furnish you with any reference."

He glanced down at the broken frame in his hand, and tossed it contemptuously aside to the floor.

"You can find your own way out."

It was the housemaid Mary Ellen Martin who found the remains of the picture. Needing some strong brown paper to send a parcel to her widowed mother, she'd been searching through a pile of stuff put out in the yard for the rag-and-bone cart and discovered exactly what she wanted – even to a decent length of string – wrapped around some rubbish from the Master's study.

It was against household rules, of course, but nobody would know she'd opened it, and she could always bundle it up again in a couple of pages of the *Courier*.

What she uncovered inside the brown paper caused her to widen her eyes in astonishment, for she'd only that morning seen Madam's portrait hanging in its usual place in the drawing room – indeed, had whisked it over with her duster. To find it here now, like this, was almost as bad as that time she and Rosie Maguire had come across a dead baby in the wash-house and hadn't known whom to tell for fear they'd get the blame.

Curiosity won over hesitation, however, and Mary Ellen smuggled the battered canvas indoors to show to Miss Dobby (who, being a reliable sort, might be trusted with these things) to see what she thought.

The upshot of the discovery was that Kitty van der Kleve learned for the first time of the existence of a second portrait of herself – though how it had come into her husband's possession, and why it should have been destroyed, was a total mystery. She could go to Oliver and ask, of course; but the manner in which the painting had been deliberately damaged and bundled up as rubbish for the rag-and-bone man, put her on her guard. And besides, it would only mean trouble for Mary Ellen for breaking rules and finding the picture in the first place.

The alternative was to speak to Jonathan Rivers, since this was obviously a copy of his work. But then, to add to the mystery, Mr Rivers failed for several weeks to come to the house to give lessons; and when Kitty finally dared – with carefully feigned indifference – to enquire the reason why, she was astounded to be told of the young drawing master's dismissal. The fellow's services were no longer required, Oliver said tersely in reply to her question. Angelina was getting sufficiently adequate tuition in art at Miss Meyrick's Academy.

Something told her there must be more to the matter than this. And such are the little twists and turns of Fate which are called coincidence, that it was only a day or two after that she happened to meet Jonathan Rivers himself, and learn something of the truth.

She'd been out with Amelia Dobby, enjoying a leisurely afternoon walk through Mount Sion Grove into the pleasantly rural neighbourhood of Calverley Park, and back again by way of the Broadway and railway bridge into the High Street. The two of them had stopped for a short while at Mr Colbran's Library to peruse the new novels, and were just turning the corner into Little Mount Sion when Dobby remarked, "Why – isn't that Mr Rivers there, ma'am? Up ahead on the right?"

Kitty paused to look in the direction her maid was pointing.

"Yes, I believe it is. Oh, wave to him, Dobby! He hasn't seen us, I don't think."

And then –"Ah, he has. Look. He's turning back in our direction."

They continued on their way up the steep incline of the cobbled street until near enough for greeting, stopping to speak to the young man by the steps of the Wesleyan meeting-house. It was not a long conversation. As he explained, Jonathan had come into the Wells to see a colleague, Mark Saltmarsh, gilder and artists' colourman, whose premises were below in the High Street.

"I've been fortunate enough to be commissioned to do several more portraits, you see, and need to order the frames made up in good time." He looked at Kitty. "I hope you're keeping well, Mrs van der Kleve? And the baby?"

"Thank you, yes." She smiled. "I'm pleased to hear the news about your work, Mr Rivers. How heartening to find yourself in such demand! It could hardly have come at a better time."

His look sharpened into a small frown; and she went on quickly, "I mean, to be freed at last of Angelina."

"Oh, that. Yes. I'm only sorry that I had to – well, abandon your stepdaughter's tuition in quite the manner forced upon me."

Now it was Kitty's turn to frown. Something in the way he'd said that made his dismissal sound a rather less straightforward affair than Oliver had described it.

There was a moment's pause; and then, just a trifle awkwardly, glancing down at her gloves, she said, "To be honest, I must confess to my surprise upon learning you'd gone . . ." Should she mention anything to him of that other portrait? "But of course, now that Angelina is receiving lessons at Miss Meyrick's, I quite understand your reason for agreeing to leave us."

"Agreeing to leave, ma'am?" Jonathan's questioning tone seemed to pounce upon the words. "*Agreeing* – ? I assure you, there was nothing in the nature of agreement about it! Your husband sent me packing without reference –"

He caught himself up, checked by the sudden startled expression in her face. As though she had no idea what he was talking about.

"Oh, but I thought you knew – ? No? Indeed, then I'm sorry . . . forgive me. I seem to have spoken out of turn."

A brewer's dray turned into the narrow side-street at that moment, making a delivery of barrels to the public house just below them on the left, the clatter of hoofs and iron cart-wheels on the cobbles drowning out whatever it was he said next.

Raising his voice above the racket, the young man repeated himself – "I'd like you to hear the truth, Mrs van der Kleve.

About a second portrait I did. Can we meet again somewhere?"

Kitty sensed, rather than saw, the quick look she was given by Dobby at her side. In the circumstances, such a request was most irregular; and if not improper, then very nearly so, coming as it did from a dismissed employee to a married woman. But the temptation to accept was strong. Jonathan Rivers had been a friend, almost a confidant, and for that – for those hours the two of them had shared together while he painted her, and for the memory of a brief, sweet moment last Christmas Eve – Kitty told herself she owed him this favour.

Caution, however, sounded its small warning.

"I – I don't know," she answered uncertainly, her own voice raised a little against the noise. "It might prove difficult. To leave the house, I mean. My absences are always questioned."

"Please try."

"But how – ?"

"I'll arrange something. Leave it to me. I'll send a message."

He pressed her hand for a moment; then, not waiting for any response, swung round on his heel and went off down the middle of the street past the loaded dray, leaving Kitty to stand, her head half-turned to look after him, wondering at the sudden deliciously fearful feeling of anticipation she felt at his going.

15

It was Amelia Dobby who acted as go-between. Not that the lady's maid altogether approved of her young mistress receiving clandestine messages, but she approved even less of the peremptory manner in which Jonathan Rivers had been dismissed, and – feeling for her own neck, perhaps – had a certain amount of fellow-servant sympathy for him. Added to which, there was something in the situation which appealed strongly to the streak of middle-aged romanticism in her nature.

Mr Rivers had somehow learned that Thursday was her half-day off and that she generally spent it taking a horse-bus ride to one of the villages in the area, because the Thursday after their meeting in the Wells, she'd found him waiting for her at the ticket office next to Osborne's Omnibus stand, hanging about pretending to read the timetable on the wall.

"Off somewhere pleasant today, Miss Dobby?" he asked, cool as you like, when he saw her. And when she said Groombridge, he'd recommended The Crown there as a good place for refreshment, adding casually, "Would you give your Mistress this from me when you get back –" producing an envelope from his pocket.

It had 'Private' penned across it in printed copperplate, and all afternoon Dobby's fingers had itched to lift the gummed flap and read what was inside. She contained her curiosity, however. Somewhere in her own background there lay an affaire with a married gentleman which had taught her the importance of prudence and discretion. If Madam wished her to know what was in the note, she'd acquaint her with its contents all in good time.

As it happened, Jonathan's message was brief and to the point; and carefully mentioned nothing to identify either sender or recipient, merely asking – "Are you able to take tea with me here on Monday?"

Kitty van der Kleve read it through twice, before tearing envelope and page lengthways into strips and setting light to them on the flame of her dressing-room oil lamp. 'Here' was presumably Beckets Cottage where he lived, and 'take tea' was meant for four o'clock. And Monday, as he knew, was the day on which Oliver always travelled up to London. It would be no hard matter, therefore, to inform Beatrice that she'd be out for an hour or so that afternoon – walking on the Common if it were fine – and that Dobby would accompany her. This was something she did quite regularly for exercise, at Dr Adeney's suggestion following her baby's birth, so should give no cause for suspicion.

It was glorious May weather. The hedges were white with hawthorn blossom filling the warm air with a scent of sweet almond, and cow parsley foamed in the ditches on either side of the lane; but Kitty had no eyes for any of it. The closer she and her maid drew to Beckets Cottage, the more apprehensive she felt that someone might pass by and see them there, and that somehow Oliver would come to hear of it. It was a totally irrational anxiety, for she was doing nothing that was wrong; and besides, the only people using the lane were more likely than not from Beckets Farm beyond the water splash. Even so, the uneasiness preyed on Kitty's nerves, and she was more than relieved to see Jonathan's porch door standing ajar as she and Dobby turned the bend towards the cottage.

He was waiting inside, standing where he could see them both through the pebble-glass panes of a window. Sunlight shafted in at the open doorway, and as Kitty came up the path and paused hesitantly for a second on the threshold, her shadow was thrown across the red-tiled floor and against the further wall.

"Come in," he said, "please –" and stepping forward to greet them, closed the door behind Dobby as she followed her mistress inside.

Kitty gave a quick glance round. Nothing had changed here since she was last in the place in the autumn, for her portrait sittings. Jonathan had set a corner of the table with a white cloth, she noticed, and there were cups and saucers ready on a tray with a milk jug and sugar basin which didn't quite match. The room smelled faintly of wood-smoke.

"Thank you for coming," he said; and indicating a chair –

"Won't you sit down? You've had a warm walk. And Miss Dobby —? You'll join us in a cup of tea, too, won't you?"

"No thank you." Dobby folded her hands primly on her reticule and stood where she was just within the door. It was one thing to chaperone her mistress, but quite another to be invited to sit at the same table and drink from the selfsame pot. A person of her years' service knew better than to be so familiar, whatever the situation. "I'm quite content to wait."

"Then take a seat, at least."

She acquiesced, placing herself on an upright wooden chair between the windows, thinking that young Mr Rivers had gone to a great deal of trouble over something which could have been told in two minutes in the street.

"If you'll excuse me a moment, I'll just go and put on the kettle." He addressed himself awkwardly to Kitty, moving past her towards the scullery off one end of the room; and there followed the sounds of water being pumped and then the rattle of a poker between the bars of a hob-grate as he stirred up the wood fire.

"It's very good of you to consent to my request," he went on again, returning to seat himself opposite at the table; and an edge of strain was now more noticeable in his voice. "I hope it's not put you to any great trouble?"

"You wanted me to hear the truth," she said simply, by way of answer.

"Yes, I did. I do."

She looked at him across the mismatched crockery. "One of the housemaids found a second portrait of me in the yard. It was badly damaged and put out for rubbish. I'm curious to know why, Mr Rivers. Why you painted it, why it was destroyed."

"And why I was dismissed quite so peremptorily from my post?"

"That too." She paused, and then added quietly, "That most of all."

"It's kind of you to show concern. The plain fact of the matter is that I did something which caused your husband to demonstrate his excessive displeasure — and for that I was discharged."

"Without any reference, you said."

He grimaced. "Without any reference."

"That seems . . . rather harsh."

"Your husband is a harsh man, as I've found to my considerable cost."

Kitty wondered whether she ought not to defend Oliver against this indictment of his character. Any other wife would, perhaps. Since she could only agree with it, however, she decided to say nothing, her gaze shifting from Jonathan's face towards the cupboard-top clutter of brushes and paint tubes behind his shoulder.

In the moment's silence which followed, the kettle could be heard beginning its throaty bubble out in the scullery.

"Excuse me –" He made to jump up again, as though too edgy to stay still for long.

"Shall I see to it for you, Mr Rivers?" Dobby came in on a tactful note, rising with him. If she had to play gooseberry to these two, she thought, she might as well do it from the scullery as sit twiddling her thumbs in the living room.

"Oh – would you mind?" He glanced across at her, his good-looking features tense and unsmiling despite the apparent lightness of his words. "I'm rather out of practice at brewing a decent pot of tea for visitors."

So I see, Dobby told herself, eyeing a number of wine bottles, some of them empty, catching the dusty sunlight in a corner of the chimney ingle.

She went out, pulling the door to behind her, hearing him say to her mistress, "How much time do you have before they expect you back?" and wondered why he couldn't give her the courtesy at least of calling her ma'am or Mrs van der Kleve.

"I've an hour, that's all," Kitty responded. "I told Beatrice we'd walk across the Common as far as Major York's Road, so it's not too much of a deception. This portrait –" she switched the conversation adroitly back again – "you promised you'd tell me about it?"

"Yes. The portrait. A copy I made of the original – but then, you know that, of course, having seen it – or rather, the ruin of what was left of it. I approached your husband early in the year to ask his permission to show the first one in an exhibition at Sevenoaks. He refused."

"So you did another."

Jonathan gave a terse nod. "I painted it from the sketches

139

while I was away in Shropshire, at my parents' house. Actually, it brought me a great deal of consolation. My father was dying at the time, you see."

"Oh. Oh, I'm sorry."

There was a pause.

"Pardon me, ma'am –" Dobby put her head in at the door. "Should I pour out the tea?"

Kitty glanced at their host. He made a little gesture of the hand indicating an invitation to do whatever was wished.

"The Spanish have a saying," he said. "*Mi casa es tu casa.* My house is your house."

There was a look in his blue-grey eyes which lent an intensity to the words, filling them with deeper meaning, and for several moments he kept his gaze fixed upon Kitty, as though in contemplation of that beauty which he'd seen so grossly violated at her husband's hands.

"The portrait copy –" he began again when Dobby had finished their serving. "I'd no idea Mr van der Kleve might be in Sevenoaks to see it exhibited. Even less that he might want to buy it."

"Oh, it was offered for sale, then?"

"At a price. Deliberately fixed too high to attract a purchaser."

"But Oliver acquired it, nonetheless."

"Yes, and demanded his money back when I was summoned for interview to explain myself."

"How typical." The comment was out before Kitty could stop herself. And immediately regretted. It made her sound disloyal and lacking in duty to her husband, and was not the kind of remark a married woman ought properly to make in front of others. "I mean . . . being a banker, he dislikes taking a loss where he might make a gain. And if the portrait was damaged –"

"But *he* was the one who damaged it!" Jonathan interrupted to exclaim. "I was made to stand and watch while Mr van der Kleve deliberately destroyed my work in front of me."

There was a moment's incredulous silence.

"He did that? But – *why?*"

"Because he didn't want the copy for himself, and was damned if anyone else should have it." And seeing the look on her face – "It's true, believe me. I had the temerity to suggest I'd reimburse him his cost if he returned me my picture."

Kitty put down her cup in its saucer without tasting the tea. "So having ensured he'd not be out of pocket, he saw to it that *you* were left with nothing, neither painting, nor post, nor reference."

A note of bitterness crept into her tone.

"As you remarked some minutes ago, Mr Rivers, my husband is a harsh man."

She could say that now without the pricking of a disloyal conscience. That Oliver should have conducted himself in such a manner – wreaking his senseless violence upon her image much in the way he liked to abuse her body, and then venting himself upon Jonathan Rivers for daring to trespass upon the hallowed ground of his authority – this filled her with a sudden terrible, scalding resentment.

She threw a quick glance over her shoulder towards her maid. Dobby could be trusted not to breathe a word of any of this, she knew.

"I'm sorry –" She turned her eyes again to Jonathan. "Truly, I am. Please will you accept my apologies for my husband's behaviour."

"*You* don't need to apologise. None of it was your fault."

"Even so, I feel . . . horribly guilty."

"Don't."

He leaned forward towards her across the table, his hand resting on its surface only inches from her own, as though he would have reached out to touch her if he could.

"I can paint you again, and better. And as for the lack of a reference – damn it, my work is my reference! I don't need pieces of paper to prove I'm an artist."

Kitty returned his look; and after a moment lowered her gaze, unable to meet the pain and the anger she read in his expression. This conversation between them had been stilted by tensions on both sides, and she wished they'd been able to relax with one another, as they used to during the sittings. She had enjoyed those times so much, looked forward to each one with a pleasure she never knew in her married life, nor indeed in her life before that; and she felt that she couldn't bear to leave Jonathan today on this difficult note of strain which had scarred their meeting.

Taking up her cup she drank from it, as much to ease the dryness of her throat as anything; then, replacing cup and saucer on the tray, said awkwardly, "I'm afraid it's time we were starting back now," and made to rise from her chair.

"Oh – must you? Already?" His expression changed, betraying instant disappointed regret; and Kitty knew instinctively that there was so much he wanted to say to her still, and could not because of Dobby's presence there, like a barrier between them both.

She stood up, drawing on a French-grey kid leather glove which matched the colour of her small, smart hat.

"Dobby –" she said quickly, before the impulse passed and propriety put a stop upon her words – "would you walk ahead along the lane, please? To see whether there's anyone about? I'll catch up with you in a short while."

"As you wish, ma'am."

Not so much as a flicker of the eye showed that there might be anything in this request which broke the rules of decorous conduct. Quitting her seat, the maid gave a small nod of leave-taking to Jonathan Rivers, warmed by the merest suspicion of a smile, and directed herself to the porch door. A few moments later her steps were heard receding down the path, and a click of the gate latch as she went out into the lane.

Jonathan had already risen to his feet to face Kitty. Now that they were alone, the young woman felt a sudden reticence come over her, and instead of looking up at him, kept her gaze fixed upon the table. She sensed him move, and then he was standing beside her, so close that she could smell the faint aroma of the Imperial macassar oil he used to subdue his thick, unruly hair.

"Catherine . . ." he said intently, "Catherine, I must see you again. Soon. Please . . ."

For a moment she could not answer, wanting to say yes and yet fearful of what might become of her if she did.

"*Please*," he urged again, his hand upon her arm drawing her round towards him.

She raised her head, feeling the rush of blood warm her cheek and throat as she met his eyes and saw what was now so plainly written there – desire, and admiration, and longing.

"How can we meet again," she heard herself murmur. "If

142

Oliver were ever to learn of it . . . No, no – we can't. We mustn't."

"He won't learn of it. We'll be careful. Oh, Catherine, if only you knew how much I miss you!"

He held her closer, pulling her against him and folding her into his arms. Without knowing it, she had dreamed of this moment for so long, all through those empty, aching months since Christmas Eve when he'd kissed her, and by that kiss had awakened something for him in her heart.

"Jonathan . . ." she murmured again; and it was the first time she had ever spoken his name aloud. "Jonathan . . ."

He tilted her small chin upwards with a forefinger, kissing her upon the brow, his lips warm against the creamy smoothness of her skin. Then, growing bolder, his mouth moved down to hers and found it ready for him, half-open, yielding, so moistly fragrant that to kiss it was like tasting honey. He felt her tremble against him, a shudder that seemed to run through her whole body and made her lips quiver beneath his; and then she was pushing him away, twisting her head aside and crying out softly, "No – no, we mustn't. We mustn't. This is wrong. Oh, please – let me go!"

Desire for her made him want to refuse, made him want to press her to him again and sate his senses with that marvellous mouth; but faced with her resistance he forced himself to move back a step, his arms falling to his sides, hands clenched into fists to stop himself from touching her.

Thickly he said, "I can't let you leave, not like this. I can't let you simply walk out through that door and not know when I'll see you again."

And when she made no answer –

"Say you'll come back! Catherine – promise you will!"

"If only I could." The words were barely more than a whisper spoken to herself.

She took up her other glove and her reticule from the table; and after a moment continued in a calmer manner, "We both know we are playing with fire. I can't pretend that I'm not attracted to you . . . but what future is there for us in pursuing a friendship which can only bring us pain, and for me at least, disgrace. I am married to Mr van der Kleve, and not all the wishful thinking in the world can ever alter that. So please – Jonathan, please – help me to do what is right and sensible?"

This little speech was made without looking at him, as though to say it to his face might have robbed her of all willpower.

"Will that make you happy?" He stretched out his hands in a gesture of appeal. "Will it make you happy, if we do what's right and sensible? Is that what you want for us both?"

"We have no choice!"

"But will it make you *happy*?"

"You know it won't. Oh, why are you so cruel? I have taught myself to accept my burden of misery . . . all the hurt, and the heartache . . . but when I'm with you I begin to realise what happiness truly is – and it makes me twice as sad. Can't you understand that? I'd rather have nothing at all than half a dream."

She turned away and took a few quick steps across the room to the door, and Jonathan had to force himself to remain where he was and not go after her, though he felt his whole being crying out with desire for this extraordinary woman. To him, she seemed a prisoner; a prisoner not only of a loveless marriage but of the standards and obligations of her husband's class, and of a society which judged its wives as hardly more than chattels. Would that he could give her a taste of freedom!

"Forgive me, but I mustn't stay any longer," she said, looking back for a second, her hand already on the knob to turn it. "Dobby will be waiting –"

His despair cut short her words.

"You'll come back to me, Catherine? Won't you? No matter how you try to forget me, you can't push aside what we feel for one another."

"I must go –" she repeated blindly. And then – "Don't call me Catherine. I hate that name. I'm Kitty –"

The door opened; and he heard her light little step hurrying her away towards husband and home and child, and the suffocating emptiness of genteel respectability.

16

During the early part of June 1866 Harriet Seymour was once again with her mother in Baden-Baden to take the waters, and to receive further hydropathic treatment from Dr Peter Hoffmann. In the second week a letter had arrived for her at the Hotel Adler. It was from Kitty, and its contents spoke of a heart and conscience being pulled apart by the twin demons of self-doubt and temptation.

Dearest Friend,
   I have taken up my pen on several occasions since your departure Abroad, but my thoughts are so distracted, that any letter which I attempted was very soon abandoned for want of sense and clarity. So that you will not wonder at my silence, I have this Morning purposed myself to write down all that is in my heart, in order that you may judge of my situation at this present time, and advise me if you will.
   When I saw you here last, I confided in you the meeting which I had had with Mr Rivers at his cottage, and the confusion into which I was thrown by his demonstration of affection. You counselled me against further such meetings, rightly warning of the consequences should it be discovered that I had allowed myself to be alone in his company; and further, that my behaviour would but appear to encourage an intimacy between us.
   I resolved to follow the wisdom of your advice, and harden my heart against any further pleading of his that we should meet again; and indeed, tho' several *billets* came to me by Dobby's hand, I destroyed them unopened, lest by reading them I might be moved to act upon their message. But then – oh, Harriet, I am ashamed to relate it! – I encountered Mr Rivers whilst walking in Mount Sion Grove with Baby in her carriage, and such was my weakness at seeing him

again, that I pretended to the nursemaid that I had dropped my glove behind upon the path, and must go back to look for it.

He – that is to say, Mr Rivers – declared himself fully sensible of his folly in seeking me out in so public a place, but my coldness had driven him to this desperate measure, he said, and he would not hesitate to do so yet again, unless I agreed to our meeting elsewhere. What could I do – ? I will confess to you, dear Friend, that my head and my heart both were in a *whirl of anguish*, for fear that we should be observed there together; but his pleading was so eloquent that my resolve never to see him more was swept aside – and in a moment I had yielded and given him the assurance for which he pressed me. I could not help myself, for surely he is the most amiable – nay, the most *wonderful* man in all the world.

Now I know not whether I am in Heaven or in Hell. On Monday last I kept a rendezvous with Mr Rivers which has left me in such a state of joy, and fear, and confusion, that it is beyond my power to describe it. He swore that he cared for me, that I was more to him than very life itself, that his existence was an emptiness without me – and many more such similar sweet sentiments; and when I struggled to remind him of my circumstances, he answered me in so tender and fond a manner that had I but needed proof of his affections, I could not have doubted his sincerity.

"Do as you will," he said upon our parting – "whatever your determination may be, I must consent to it, and by so doing resign my eternal happiness to your care."

Oh, Harriet, what am I to think? – how am I to act? – for it would seem that a choice which is scarce any choice at all is laid upon me – whether to yield to the natural impulse of my heart and allow myself to taste of the deliciously Forbidden Fruit which is offered – or whether I should attend upon the urgings of my conscience, and remind myself that it is the duty of every wife to remain contented with her lot in life, in that station wherein Providence has placed her.

I am so distracted that I start at almost every sound, and cannot hold a conversation without I must weigh each word and set a guard upon my tongue. At the same time, I have an unreasonable desire to smile which comes upon me at sudden intervals, together with a feeling of utter blissful happiness. *Thank Heaven* at least that Oliver has ceased his inquisition of my daily business, for he would surely suspect these inconsistencies, and quiz me for their cause. However, since that dreadful occasion of which I told you, when he attacked me in so rough and violent a manner as to render me almost senseless, he has been forced to heed Dr Adeney's stricture, and has desisted from troubling me since with his attentions; indeed, he chooses to remain in the City from a Monday to the week's end, so that we live almost as strangers to one another.

Ah, dearest Harriet, what should I do? I have by me at this moment a letter from Mr Rivers in which he writes such tender and devoted lines in praise of me that the blushes upon my face are sufficient proof of how agreeable I find it to be thus addressed. I cannot disguise from you with what a yearning heart I think of him; tho' doubtless you will tell me to call in the assistance of Reason, and seriously to reflect upon the perils which are like to attend our folly and consign us both to ruin.

I have seldom lamented upon the lack of a Mother's guidance in my life; but believe me when I tell you that I am at such *sixes and sevens* with myself at this present time that the wise direction of a Parent would be of the most desirable benefit. Alas, there is only you to whom I may unburden myself; and so, trusting in the mutual bonds of amity, I will conclude this letter with an appeal to your dear Affection to counsel and advise me, and remain yours in sincere friendship –

Kitty

Between the hopeless joy, the pain, and the appeal in these lines there were to be read signs of a mind already closing itself to the voice of common sense and sanity. She did not know it – how could she? – but Kitty was falling in love for the first time in her life; and under the spell of such blind enchantment, judgment and its attendant reasonings are very often flawed.

Had the situation been reversed, had it been Harriet Seymour writing to Kitty to confess a deepening attachment to a young man whose company she preferred above that of her own husband – and knowing that such a liaison was forbidden, still courted the risk of discovery which would ruin her in the eyes of Society and seriously damage her character and good standing – in such a case, Kitty's concern for her friend would have left her in no doubt but that this dangerous fondness must be nipped in the bud of its growth. And would have advised accordingly – which is what Harriet Seymour did in her response to the letter.

She wasted time and ink in doing so. Kitty had pleaded for her friend's good counsel; but what she really sought was justification for her own conduct, encouragement which would give her the excuse to continue it; a *carte blanche* to ease her conscience so that each time the angel of caution upon one shoulder whispered 'this is wrong', the demon of temptation seated on the other countered with, 'ah, but *Harriet* said it was not wrong! *Harriet* said you must follow your heart!'

So it was, that when Harriet actually wrote advising Kitty to break off her friendship with Jonathan Rivers, and not give him further opportunity to 'press his suit' (as she put it), Kitty was loth to accept this clearsighted argument, and spent a night in a flood of tears over what she saw as her friend's perfidy. That she was able to weep unwitnessed in the privacy of her bedchamber made her unhappiness twice as self-indulgent, for had Oliver been sleeping at her side, the mask she always wore to conceal and shield herself from the world would have placed its own restraint upon her anguish.

As she had written in her letter, however, her husband now left her alone, not having approached her for any resumption of sexual relations since that evening of his violent assault almost three months earlier. The hurt she had sustained then had left her in such pain and discomfort that she was forced to seek medical help; and having examined her, and prised from her the cause of her injury, Dr Adeney had made no bones about telling Oliver van der Kleve what he thought of such brutish mistreatment of a young mother hardly yet recovered from the rigours of a difficult labour. Being a man of enlightened views for his time, the doctor had stressed that the best way in his opinion to ensure the conception of a healthy son was to allow a period of total continence, so that Mrs van der Kleve's system might be thoroughly rested and her body healed.

Oliver had obviously taken these words to heart. The stricture upon continence applied only to Kitty, however, and not to himself; and since it was considered unhealthy and likely to lead to nervous disorders if a gentleman did not practise regular sexual relief, he had accordingly resumed physical intimacy with his London 'magdalen' Sadie Collins.

This was a side of his life which he'd always been at pains to keep completely separate from his role as *pater familias* and member of Tunbridge Wells society; indeed, it is doubtful even whether his friend the Reverend Mr Edward Terris was aware of Sadie Collins's existence. Mr Terris, being of the 'broad and hazy' variety of Anglican cleric, may have suspected Oliver of resorting on occasion to some discreet little *maison d'assignation* of the kind frequented by gentlemen of taste and delicacy, but he would have baulked at the idea of a kept mistress in a private suite of rooms. The only ones of Oliver's acquaintance who knew about Sadie were fellow City financiers and company chairmen each of whom had similar arrangements of their own.

One of these, like Oliver a member of Gresham's, had in his employment as lady's maid to his dear wife in Chiswick a long-standing crony of Amelia Dobby's. The two domestic servants had met years earlier as under-housemaids together, and striking up an intimacy, had remained on hobnobbing terms ever since, for both of them – Cockney born and bred, though no one would ever guess it from Dobby's refined tones – had always worked in and around the London area. Since her removal to the more genteel purlieus of Tunbridge Wells, however, Dobby had perforce been seeing less of her friend than previously; and so it was that when the pair met again, an interval of several months had elapsed, with a consequent accumulation of gossip's debris to be picked over.

There are generally two sorts of women into a friendship: one talkative, lively, dominating the conversation with tittle-tattle; the other more passive, more circumspect, saying little while listening much.

Dobby was of the latter kind. Kitty van der Kleve was right to trust her, for though the maid enjoyed a chat she never repeated confidences, and though she might be the receptacle of the most diverse and illuminating information about her employers, she was careful never to divulge anything of a private or personal nature. Thus her acquaintances might learn almost everything worth knowing about those working belowstairs at Sion Place, but remained only vaguely informed about the family they served above.

During the course of the afternoon's reunion at a tea-shop off Leicester Square, Dobby was required to sit listening with rather more patience than usual, for – as her friend declared more than once over the next hour – "there was such a lot had been going on in Chiswick between the Master and Missus as would take a week or more in the telling were every detail added."

The gist of the story was that Missus had suspected for some little time that Master had been squandering money and attention on some fancy piece in Town, and to satisfy her mind, had set a private detection agent upon his tail. The suspicion being confirmed, she'd determined to catch out Master at his nasty tricks (as she said) and embarrass him in such a manner as would teach the old fool to know better next time.

Taking her maid with her, she'd journeyed into the City to the address given to her by the agent, a couple of rooms near St Paul's, and not finding anyone at home to her knocking had set herself to wait upon the stairs. Eventually a young rust-haired woman appeared from the street below, and being challenged by Missus whether or not she was Mr ——'s dollymop who lived here, had answered very pertly that no, she was Mr van der Kleve's, and merely come a-calling.

It was at this point in the narrative that Amelia Dobby sat up a little straighter in her seat.

"Mr van der Kleve? Was that the name she said?"

Her friend nodded vigorously. "That was the name she said, the baggage."

"Are you sure?"

"No mistaking it. There can't be two alike in the City o' London, surely. It's not like a Smith nor a Jones. And when I asked her 'Mr van der Kleve?' she turned and looked at me all sly like – such a look it was! – as though she could've bitten her tongue for saying it. After that – well, after that, Missus set on to her about this fancy piece o' the Master's and kicked up a right ol' shindy, I tell you, when t'other claimed as how she hardly knew her at all except to speak wiv."

"And she didn't mention Mr van der Kleve again, I don't suppose," Dobby said thoughtfully.

"Not her! She'd said too much already. What a thing, though, eh?" The friend rolled her eyes in mock disgust and helped herself to another chocolate éclair. "*Masters!* You can't tell wiv 'em these days. And yours married not hardly above a year, an' all. They need a reg'lar dosing wiv salts, if you ask me, the perishin' lot of 'em."

A view with which Dobby was inclined to agree.

For over a week now she'd kept her dangerous knowledge to herself, weighing up in her mind whether she should tell her mistress what she'd heard or whether it might not be better to keep a still tongue and say nothing. After all, what was there to be gained but unpleasantness and further misery for Mrs van der Kleve – and even like as not her own dismissal for carrying tales. No, best to let sleeping dogs lie, thought Dobby.

"With all the exercise she has been taking of late, I wonder that she isn't in the very bloom of health." There was just the slightest touch of sarcasm in Beatrice's tone. "Yet to look at her, so peaky and pale, one would think that she never set a foot out of doors."

About to enter the drawing room at Sion Place, Kitty paused, recognising herself as the subject of her sister-in-law's conversation. She heard the chink of china cup in saucer, and then the Reverend Mr Terris's voice responded with its usual velveteen blandness, "But might it not be some lingering frailty which keeps the colour from her cheeks? I refer to the – ah – the happy arrival of little Henrietta."

"Nonsense, Edward. Catherine was brought to bed six months ago, time and enough for any young woman to recover. If you wish to hear my opinion –"

Kitty pushed open the door and entered the room.

"Good morning, Beatrice." She directed a tight smile. "Mr Terris." And crossing to the silver tea service on the occasional table – "I hope I don't interrupt?"

"Dear lady, not at all!" Mr Terris sprang to his feet in greeting; and then, reseating himself, "Your name was but at this moment upon our lips. Beatrice was telling me of the commendable care which you take of your health by regular exercise."

His mild eyes lingered upon Kitty's profile as she poured herself a cup of tea from the pot. Far from appearing peaky and pale, he thought the young creature had a most becoming flush to her face.

"How kind of Beatrice." She added milk to her tea and stirred it slowly, hoping that the tremor of her hand would not be noticed. It was silly of her to feel so guilty; and yet she could not help it. Mr Terris had requested a word with her here in the drawing room, and her mind had instantly flown in a dozen different directions, wondering what it could be he wanted, whether it might have anything to do with Jonathan . . .

She forced herself to turn, to smile again, to say, "I believe there was something you wished to tell me, Mr Terris?"

"Indeed, my dear, indeed." He paused to sip his own tea, taking an irritating time about it, little finger of his right hand cocked in fussily affected manner. "I shall be absent from the Wells on Saturday next." The cup was replaced in saucer. "A visit to an acquaintance in Chichester – a canon of the cathedral there. Splendid fellow, he will be celebrating the fortieth anniversary of his ordination, and there is to be a special service of Thanksgiving to which I have been most kindly invited." Another pause, another sip of tea. "And so, dear lady, I have come to make my apologies in advance. And to offer you every felicitation."

"I'm obliged to you for your trouble," said Kitty faintly.

Something in the vagueness of her response caught Beatrice's attention, for she came in sharply, "You cannot have forgotten, surely, Catherine?" And with a softening glance towards the minister – "Mr Terris was to have been one of the principal guests at this dinner of yours on Saturday."

"Yes. Of course." It was Kitty's birthday on the twenty-third of June. Her 'official' birthday, that is: as a foundling, no one knew the exact day, so the orphanage, as was common practice, had used the date of her baptism. To celebrate the event, Oliver had suddenly announced that they should give a dinner party at the house. The twenty-third was this coming Saturday, but the fact had somehow slipped her mind. There had been so much else to occupy her thoughts in recent weeks.

A little of the tea in her cup slopped into the saucer and she put both hurriedly down again on the table, folding her hands under her arms, pressing them against her body. Why did she shake so much?

"I'm sorry you are not able to attend, Mr Terris. But I quite understand."

"I shall pray for you, naturally, my dear." He bestowed one of his pious smiles upon her. "Have no doubt of it, you will be remembered among the petitions which I offer up in the cathedral."

What would he pray for, she wondered. Her happiness? Her future? Her role as wife and mother? If so, what a waste of his breath! God was on the side of the angels, not the sinners.

"I trust you will remember me also, Edward," Beatrice observed, a trifle archly. "I should take it as most remiss were you to neglect those of us who are truly your friends."

The piety of the smile slipped a fraction, to be replaced by smooth professional affability. "Perfection needs no prayer, my dear Beatrice! But if any word of mine, however poor, can sway the mercy of the Almighty, then be assured that I shall not omit my fond duty to all beneath this roof."

Beatrice folded her thin lips into a line and shot an acid look at her sister-in-law as if to say – there, see how he favours you above me!

"Mindful of the fact that I shall not be present with you to celebrate your day," Mr Terris went on suavely, turning his full attention once more to Kitty, "I have brought with me here a small token of my respectful esteem which I hope you will accept as a salutation upon your anniversary."

He reached a hand into the capacious pocket of his black serge frock coat and produced a small wrapped packet which he held out, adding somewhat playfully, "Mind now, Catherine, it must not be opened before the day!"

"No, of course. Thank you, Mr Terris."

She took it from him, turning it over and over in an agitated manner, wanting only to be gone from the room, away from the censure in Beatrice's eyes, back to the privacy of being alone with her thoughts and her dreams, and the soaring secret happiness of her love for Jonathan.

"If it is fine this afternoon," she said, forcing herself to speak as naturally as she could and addressing herself to her sister-in-law, "I should like to take an hour's walk upon the Common . . . with your permission."

Mr Terris appeared to find something droll in this simple request, for he gave a bray of laughter and before Beatrice could answer, had interrupted her with – "Dear lady, since when has the Mistress required permission to walk abroad beyond her own doorstep?"

"It is my brother Oliver's rule. While he is absent from the house, I, as senior member of the family, am the one responsible here," Beatrice informed him in a tone which took some of the amusement from his face. "And no, Catherine, I do not think it would be wise of you to venture out today. You were gone far too long on Monday, after losing your way, you said. It may rain this afternoon. Indeed –" glancing towards the window, which showed a sky innocent of any cloud – "it looks very much as though we shall have a summer shower. I would prefer you to remain indoors and occupy yourself with a little reading or needlework."

Kitty's features were bleached of expression. After the merest ghost of a pause she responded with a grave little nod, keeping her eyes lowered lest the sudden angry brightness of tears betrayed her.

"Very well."

Dobby would have to go to Beckets Cottage with a message; and she herself must go on enduring this aching, longing pain for another day, another two days – who knew how long – before she was back in Jonathan's arms again.

17

It was Jonathan who had suggested the High Rocks. Growing increasingly impatient of the snatched half-hours which he and Kitty shared together in secluded wooded byways of Tunbridge Wells Common, he had cast about for a place where they might go which was both local and fairly anonymous – somewhere they could escape the shadow of furtive, hole-and-corner secrecy which dogged their meetings, and had Kitty constantly looking over her shoulder, listening for footsteps.

She refused to come to Beckets Cottage, knowing that once alone behind closed doors there would be nothing to check the runaway wheels of their intimacy and propel them both into an act of love from which there was no turning back again to friendship. Instead, they made their rendezvous the old race-course which had served Tunbridge Wells in its Georgian heyday, but was now fallen into disuse and become overgrown with bracken and birch, a haunt of rabbits. Few people ever came to this part of the Common, preferring the open areas near the cricket ground where there were views of the town to be enjoyed from well-kept paths and benches.

For several weeks now Jonathan had been racking his mind to find some way in which he and Kitty might spend a longer time alone together. What had begun for him as an artist's appreciation of classic beauty had over the past months advanced through the various stages of attraction until it presently became the exclusive emotion of his life; and his craving to possess that beauty for himself and unlock the physical passion which he sensed lay dormant and unrealised within her still – for all that she was a married woman – was starting to drive him wellnigh mad with frustration.

At first the whole idea of an afternoon together had seemed impossible, a dream for his midsummer nights of wakeful, restless desire. But then, early in July, opportunity presented itself.

It was the custom of St Bride's Church each year to take the Sunday School children on a day's excursion to the sea, an outing which the Reverend Mr Terris – as shepherd of these little lambs – regarded as his bounden duty personally to supervise. There was no lack of helpers; and among those ladies of the parish volunteering assistance, the name of Beatrice van der Kleve was noticeably to the fore: indeed, the Sunday School outing was a peak among the troughs of her existence, providing as it did an opportunity to impress her company for twelve unbroken hours upon the Beloved's notice.

This year the excursion was to be made on a Thursday, to avoid the unseemly rush of folk who descended upon the coast of a week's end; and since Thursday was also Dobby's half-day off, with Oliver in the City and Angelina at school, Kitty for once would be entirely alone at Sion Place, able to come or go as she wished without question or supervision.

The temptation to fall in with Jonathan's proposal, that they escape for the afternoon to the High Rocks at Eridge, was too excitingly strong to resist. Baby would be safe enough left with her nursemaid; and for a few hours Kitty could slip away from reality into a world of make-believe in which husband, marriage, duty, had no place – a world where she was free to be with Jonathan as she so longed always to be, enjoying the forbidden affection for which she yearned.

The adventure had its risks – what if she were recognised, for instance? – how would she explain herself to Beatrice and Oliver? – but they were risks she was quite prepared to chance. As Jonathan said, where was the crime in going to visit a place of local interest on a summer's day?

The pair of them laid their plans carefully, like eager conspirators. Kitty was to travel by one of the horse-drawn wagonettes charging a sixpenny fare to carry visitors out to the Rocks, and departing from a stand conveniently close to Mount Sion in the London Road. Jonathan would make his way separately, on foot, since it was no great distance from his cottage to walk across the fields behind Beckets Farm into High Rocks Lane. Once there, to avoid the problem of waiting where someone might notice, they arranged to meet on the path beyond the entrance turnstile, since the area outside was used as a carriage stand not only by those coming to see the sights, but by others using the Cape of Good Hope inn opposite.

The High Rocks had been a popular feature of the neighbourhood since their discovery by patrons of 'the Wells at Tunbridge' in the seventeenth century. The place had an instant fascination for romantic Restoration tastes, being a spectacular outcrop of sandstone heights riven and fissured by chasms, and grown over with pendulous swags of creeper and ivy. Within the next hundred years, as London Society flocked to the Wells and extended its influence upon the district, enterprising proprietors spanned the gorges with rustic wooden bridges, cut steep flights of steps into the stone and laid out bosky glades where visitors might disport themselves. By the 1850s the place had been transformed into a Gothic pleasure ground, with coloured lanterns lighting winding paths, several small summer-houses and chalets, a high-hedged maze, and a lake afloat with water lilies where folk might boat or skate according to the season of the year.

Kitty had been here twice, once before her marriage when Oliver brought her during his courtship, and once since in company with their neighbours the Broadwoods. Jonathan, on the other hand, knew the place well from the many times he'd come to paint the scenery, especially in spring when the bowers of rhododendrons were a blaze of stained-glass colour reflected in the margins of the lake, and the red-grey rocks soared against a sky of sun-stippled cloud.

The sky today looked sultry, a deep enamel blue, and the air was very still and humid. Kitty was glad she'd decided to wear something light, a day dress of slate-coloured silk under a lace mantle, and a small straw hat trimmed with a veil. What a good thing veils were so fashionable just now, for they hid the features admirably.

Jonathan was already at their rendezvous, leaning a shoulder against a spur of sandstone, legs crossed, hands thrust into pockets, whistling quietly to himself, a young man apparently without a worry in the world, until one noticed his expression. Seeing Kitty approach along the path, he pushed himself upright and took a few casual steps into her way, even though there was no one near to observe this little piece of play acting.

"Any difficulty?"

"None." She smiled up into his eyes, the warm blush of happiness suffusing her cheeks as she took his arm. "I told

Nicholls I was going out and wouldn't be requiring tea. And Angelina won't be home before half past six – I made doubly sure of that by asking Mary Ellen."

"So we have at least four hours to ourselves."

There was no disguising his own pleasure. He gave the hand on his arm a squeeze. "But I must warn you, my darling, I intend to be very strict with you. Certain words are forbidden this afternoon."

"Indeed? And which are they?" She threw him an impish glance through the patterned lace veil.

"The disagreeable ones."

"And what are the penalties if I happen to forget?"

Jonathan paused on the path. An angle of rock concealed them from anyone who might be following. Raising Kitty's gloved hand to his lips, he answered, "You must say a hundred times 'I love you, Jonathan'."

The blush deepened in her cheeks. So far in their courtship she had not ventured to put into words the sentiments which she harboured for this wonderful man. Admiration and regard, yes, and expressions of affection; but these had been only the first tentative, tremulous essays of a heart just awakening to the power and passion of love. The deeper intimacies of emotional feeling had yet to be confessed by either of them, as though both were aware that any such admission would remove the last delicately balanced restraint upon their relationship and plunge them down the slope towards that bitter-sweet blindness which society calls adultery.

Releasing her companion's arm a moment, Kitty made a play of shaking out her silk parasol and raising it above her head.

"I see I must choose my conversation carefully," she said with a little laugh; then, taking his elbow once more, the parasol held at a slant across her shoulder, "May we go into the maze? It's the perfect place to avoid meeting others."

"D'you think you can trust me to lose us both in there?"

"I rather hope you might." She laughed again. "I should like to be lost with you . . . for a while, at least."

"Then your wish, madam, is granted –"

Turning into a side path which led down towards the right, Jonathan directed their way between walls of smooth-faced rock which here and there rose to a height of some seventy feet above them. Carved into the sandstone like a frieze were innumerable names, initials and dates, many now weathered by time and faded to shallow blurs, others fresh-cut in deep, raw gouges scoring the walls like wounds.

"Shall I carve our names before we leave?" he suggested. "As a memento?"

"Oh, best not. Someone might recognise."

"Our initials, then. J. R. and –" A sudden thought occurred to him, and he paused. "That's strange! How odd – the fact's not struck me till now. Your name – your father's, I mean. You don't know what it is."

"No. No, I never have. My name before –" Kitty almost said marriage, one of this afternoon's taboo words. "My name was March. But that was given to me by the orphanage."

"March . . . Mm, well, it's as good as any other. Names are only labels, after all, stuck upon us for convenient identity."

He pressed her hand again.

"I shall carve J. R. and K. M. And in years to come, when I'm a venerable old gentleman, I'll be able to look at those letters, and remember."

"Remember what?"

"Remember you . . . my sweet, my incomparably lovely Kitty."

She felt a glow of pleasure at his compliment; but then a sudden unwelcome touch of melancholy crept in. The future for them both was so uncertain, so filled with the unpredictable capriciousness of Fate. Who could say what tomorrow might not bring in its wake to make their memories better unremembered?

"Was there nothing ever discovered about your background?" Jonathan went on lightly. "Your parents, your origins?"

She shook her head. "Nothing at all. Oh, the orphanage authorities made enquiries, of course. Mothers who abandon their babies are generally unmarried, or in some other trouble, and so might be known to the local constabulary, the parson perhaps, the workhouse. But no one was ever found for me . . . whoever she was, she'd vanished without trace."

"And left you alone in life to fend for yourself."

"Yes."

"Well, whatever her reason, she must have been a remark-ably beautiful woman." Once more, that complimentary note. "Do you never wonder what became of her?"

There was a note of reluctance in Kitty's answer. On such a happy day as this, she hardly wished to be reminded of the past.

"Occasionally. There've been times when the notion's come into my head that I might have passed her as a stranger on the street, and not known her. But it opens too many questions, so . . ." She gave a little shrug. "There's no point to it."

"That's true. Look —"

Sensing her unwillingness to pursue the subject of her parentage further, Jonathan indicated a handrail beside the path ahead, and a flight of steps descending through a break in the rocks to a lower level. "Here's where we turn off to the maze."

Another young couple were just coming up, the woman holding an infant and grumbling at the steepness of the climb; and though they scarcely glanced at Jonathan and his com-panion as they passed, Kitty averted her head, tilting the parasol forward to conceal her features.

At the foot of the steps the path widened to join a well-used thoroughfare, with a glimpse of the sunlit waters of the lake away through the trees to their left, the shouts and laughter of boaters carrying to them on the still, warm air. There were rather more folk about here, in couples or family groups, wandering along from the entrance turnstile, some of them making for the lake, others towards the children's garden with its painted seesaws and swings; not many, Kitty was relieved to see, going off in the direction of the maze.

As the two of them passed inside the wicket-gate, Jonathan remarked on the afternoon heat, saying how close it was starting to feel, and hoping she wasn't uncomfortable; and indeed, once within the maze itself, the air did seem much heavier, trapped between the narrow high-hedged passage-ways of privet. This oppressive atmosphere added in Kitty's mind to an almost dreamlike impression, the smooth-turfed corridors leading from one into another, then another, like reflections of a mirror's image, each one identical to the last; and though there were people there, they never appeared in view but moved invisibly on parallel paths, their disembodied voices coming always from somewhere else along the never-ending hedges.

Once away from the entrance, Jonathan had slipped an arm about her slender waist to draw her close against his side, pausing every dozen or so steps to steal a kiss. Neither spoke much, for this was one of those timeless moments precious to any relationship, when merely to be together is utter bliss. It was only after several false turnings and re-traced routes that they eventually reached the heart of the maze, and discovered they'd taken over half an hour to do so, so absorbed had they been in each other.

It was very still here. There was not a breath of wind to stir the sluggish heat, and now that the voices had died away the only sound was a drone of bees among the privet flowers. All other noise – the boaters on the lake, the children, the click of the turnstile gates – was deadened by the high green walls which surrounded them, enclosing them both in this little circle of silence.

Overhead, the sky had taken on a sullen, sultry look and the brassy glare of the sun was beginning to tarnish to a sickly orange.

"I suppose we should be thinking about going back," Jonathan said after a while, unwillingly, his mouth against Kitty's cheek, breathing in the fragrance of her skin. She was cradled upon his knee, on the decorative cast-iron bench put here to refresh the weary, her hat and parasol laid on the seat beside them.

"Oh – must we?" She ran the tip of a finger down his profile, tracing its outline and lingering a moment on the warm, firm lips whose kisses had just given her such pleasure. "I could stay with you here for ever and always . . ."

Putting up her hand again she started to play with his hair, gently twisting one of the strands above his ear into a curl. She could never do this with Oliver, she thought; but with Jonathan – dearest, *dearest* Jonathan – the barriers were down, and there was no holding back, no embarrassment, no feelings of awkwardness.

He caught her hand in his and kissed it. "I could stay here for ever, too. But we really ought to go now, my darling."

Kitty sighed, and withdrew her arm reluctantly from round his neck; and slipping from his embrace, got to her feet to shake out the creased silk of her skirts. At that moment there came a low, faint, rumbling reverberation, like far-off cannonfire, and both felt the air quiver about them as though something had shaken the atmosphere.

"That sounded like thunder," Jonathan observed. And when Kitty had put on her hat and adjusted the veil – "Come on, best we're out of here if there's a storm brewing up. We'll go and find somewhere to shelter."

By the time they'd made their way back again through the maze, the sky had darkened considerably and the first distant flash of sheet lightning lit the horizon beyond the lake, engraving the landscape in a split second of silver. Within almost the same space of minutes the breeze which had started as hardly more than a breath now seemed to strengthen itself, blowing the heat of the summer day along the narrow pathways and pushing at the skirts and hats of women as they herded their families back towards the turnstiles, to the haven of the Cape of Good Hope across the lane.

Knowing Kitty's fear of being recognised if they followed after the rest, Jonathan took a different direction, leading his companion on a path upward through the rocks and over one of the rustic little bridges which at this point spanned a deep cleft. Here, built into an angle of the sandstone face, was a chalet overlooking the lake below, a small timbered building with thatched roof and leaded window furnished plainly with a couple of benches.

He closed the door behind them both and slipped the latch firmly into place. The view from up here was quite dramatic – it was one he knew well, having painted it several times – and its drama was now intensified by the sulphurous yellow light. Even as they watched together from the window, a peal of thunder filled the sky and was followed four or five seconds later by another lightning flash and the first large, fat drops of rain spattering the dust of the rocks.

"Will it last long, do you think?" Kitty asked nervously. "I must be home by six o'clock or there'll be all kinds of questions asked."

Jonathan took her into his arms and hugged her against him, his cheek on hers through the patterned lace.

"Don't worry. These summer storms never last long. It'll blow itself out inside half an hour."

"I do hope so! Supposing I were late returning and Oliver –"

"*Oliver?*" He pounced on the forbidden name with something very like a boy's glee. "Ah, but we agreed not to mention Oliver, remember? You owe me a forfeit for that, my darling."

"Oh . . . oh, so I do."

Kitty shifted her head to look up into his eyes, the light from the window throwing a faint shadow of lace across her features.

"Well?" He grinned down at her.

"Well . . ."

She hesitated; then, with a poor effort at pretence and a mischievous smile in return – "I've forgotten what the forfeit was."

"No excuses. It was to say a hundred times 'I love you, Jonathan'."

"But that would take too long!"

"Then say it once."

Suddenly the humour was gone. Lifting her veil, he folded it back over the brim of her hat; and then held her by the shoulders away from him at arm's length, his expression as serious as she'd ever seen it.

"Say it, Kitty. Say you love me."

"I don't know –"

"*Say it.* Please. I want to hear you tell me. Surely you must know already that it's love I feel for you – that I'd do anything – anything – to have you for my own. Is it so much to ask, three simple little words?"

Without waiting for her answer, he pulled her against him and bent his head to kiss her, his lips caressing hers until they parted for him.

"Say it," he whispered.

"Oh, Jonathan . . ." Kitty felt herself begin to tremble, as she always did when he kissed her in this way – not with the rough insistence of her husband, but slowly and sensuously, tasting the sweetness of her mouth.

Her body betrayed her. Not even to herself had she dared to admit it before, fearing perhaps that the confession of love would carry her into a world of emotions of which she knew nothing; but her self-restraint was melting. She was aware of his hand moving from her waist, his fingertips tracing the outline of her breast beneath the smooth silk sheath of her gown; and again she murmured, "Oh, Jonathan . . ." and then, with a soft cry that was like a surrender, "Oh . . . I love you!"

He kissed her once more, less tenderly, his desire fed by the exultation of knowing now that she was his and his alone – not Oliver van der Kleve's – but *his*.

"My sweetest angel," he whispered against her mouth, "I want you so. Let me – please – let me . . ."

She offered no resistance as he started undoing the tiny pearl-buttoned fastenings of her bodice. It was only when his warm hand slipped inside and cupped her nakedness that she moved, and that was to press herself to him with a sigh that was almost a groan.

Lightning flickered again, but neither saw it; and the rain upon the rocks added its drumbeat to the roll of thunder. But neither heard. After a while Jonathan drew her down to lie beside him on the dusty boards, cushioning her bared head upon his arm, kissing her eyes, her throat, her lips; then, emboldened by her response, he raised her skirts and began stroking the long smooth line of stockinged leg beneath.

As was the custom with most young women for the sake of comfort and hygiene, Kitty never wore drawers in summer, and the touch of Jonathan's fingers stealing to the soft naked flesh exposed above her garters sent a throbbing surge of sweetness coursing through her body. It was a feeling entirely new to her, almost frightening in its delicious intensity – she had never known, never even dreamt, that her own body could give so much enjoyment – and she heard herself moaning aloud as each touch and caress intensified her pleasure.

Oblivious now to time or place, she parted her legs in an invitation to love; and when Jonathan took her, she reacted with an abandonment to natural passion which shocked even him.

18

There were no questions, and no suspicions. By the time the three van der Kleves, husband, sister and daughter, each arrived home at Sion Place from their separate day's pursuits, Kitty had already bathed herself and changed into another gown and was seated alone with her thoughts upon the terrace, an unread book opened beside her. The only sign of anything unusual was a deep flush in her cheeks and a reddened swelling of her lips where Jonathan's kisses had bruised them; but to the casual eye, these merely looked like the result of sitting too long without a bonnet in the sun.

"I hear there was a storm in the district this afternoon," Oliver observed at dinner. And that was all.

In the days which followed, if Kitty appeared rather more withdrawn than usual, frequently smiling to herself as though absorbed in some private daydream, it was dismissed as another of her strange moods, and ignored. There was too much else to occupy attention just now: Oliver preparing for a fresh business trip to the Continent, Beatrice feverishly helping to organise St Bride's Summer Fête, and Angelina only this last month advanced to Miss Meyrick's own class at the Academy and made Head Monitor, which placed her in a position of power over the younger pupils.

For almost a fortnight Kitty held out against the urge to see Jonathan Rivers again. She wanted to be with him more than anything in this world, loving him as she now did; and there were days when she had to struggle against the overwhelming temptation to snatch up her baby and go running from Sion Place, abandon everything and make a new life at Beckets Cottage with her lover.

What held her back was a peculiar sense of modesty. To tell the truth, she felt not a little troubled at the way she'd allowed him – almost encouraged him – to seduce her that afternoon, and the utter abandoned manner of her behaviour whilst they'd been making love. How shameful it seemed to her now; and yet how darkly, achingly, hauntingly exciting.

Her attitude to the sexual intimacies of life had been irreversibly altered. She knew she would never again be able to feel the same about her own body; and more important, she realised now what it was that drove her husband in his desire to possess her. It was about this time that Oliver had decided to resume conjugal relations between them, and having known a lover's tenderness and skill, Kitty was made all the more aware of his thoughtless, selfish indifference to her own needs. When he touched her body, it was to rouse himself, not her, and when he took her, it was only to satisfy his own hungry passion.

Yet even so, in spite of the way she despised him for this self-absorption, she could not help but experience some re-awakening of sexual feeling during their intercourse, and find herself fighting to suppress it for fear that her pleasure might betray her adultery. It was one thing to respond dutifully to a husband's needs, but quite another to surrender oneself to that delicious intoxication of the senses she'd known with Jonathan; and for that reason, she never pretended it was her lover who held her in his arms during those nights when Oliver sated himself of her beauty in the darkness of their bed.

She started meeting Jonathan again while Oliver was away in Amsterdam, slipping from the house in the afternoons whenever she could snatch a fleeting hour among the concealing summer greenery of the old racecourse. The more he made love to her, the more responsive grew her body, like an untuned instrument brought to perfect pitch. And if they spoke at all, it was of love, not of the future . . . as if both of them realised that time was all too short and precious to waste on dreams.

For this autumn evening's dinner party at the Broadwoods, Angelina had been allowed to wear her hair 'up' for the first time. The occasion seemed to go quite literally to her head, for Kitty could not recall her stepdaughter being quite so obnoxiously pert and demanding of attention. The gentlemen appeared to find such behaviour amusing, especially their host Henry Broadwood, who encouraged it all the more by telling Angelina what a 'deuced fine gel' she was growing into and what devastation she must be causing already to the hearts of the 'young shavers' of her acquaintance. The smirking

Angelina responded to this compliment with such conceited silliness that Kitty noticed several eyebrows being raised behind ostrich-plume fans.

"What an inveterate philanderer I married," Frances Broadwood murmured to her across the chair of the guest seated between them at dinner. "And what a mercy it is he's too long in the tooth to act upon his imagination."

It was unusual for the normally doting Frances to speak of her husband in such an acerbic fashion. She interrupted herself for a moment to respond to some query from the gentleman seated on her other side; then turning again to Kitty, went on, "It's all flattery to his own vanity, of course. He's really quite harmless, the lamb – for were the object of his evening's flirt to show signs of taking him seriously, he'd retrace his steps a mile!"

Her glance shifted across the table to a youngish woman opposite, a Mrs Russell, introduced to Kitty at the start of the evening as being two years widowed, and only recently come out of black crape into lavender mourning. Beside her, staring glumly into space, was her son, a gingery-fair youth with the downy fluff of a first moustache upon his lip and a gutta-percha collar forcing up his chin into a stranglehold of discomfort. Kitty had earlier noticed Henry Broadwood dancing attendance upon this Mrs Russell, and might have suspected that here lay the cause of Frances's pique had she not been informed that the widow's late husband was a close kinsman of the family.

As though becoming aware of her scrutiny, young Arthur Russell's eyes suddenly focused themselves upon Kitty's face across the table, and a painfully tight smile struggled to manifest itself. He was no more than twenty, if that, and the boyish fuzz upon his lip made him look still less; but there was no mistaking the warmth of a man's admiration in the quick exchange of glances between them. Unusual for his colouring, he had blue-grey eyes like Jonathan Rivers, with a faint line of concentration between the brows and the same way of dropping his gaze from Kitty's eyes to her lips and back again in a way that was unconsciously attractive.

To be reminded so of her lover caught her off guard. She looked down hastily, but not before a tell-tale flush of colour had stained her cheeks. Ever since that day at the High Rocks it was as though she had been divided into two separate identities – one, the obedient and dutiful wife suffering in silent patience the strictures of a loveless marriage, the other, a woman who had broken the bonds and discovered what it was to be truly alive, to be truly herself. Yet with that knowledge had come such a burden of guilt and fear and – yes, shame, that sometimes Kitty felt as though she bore the mark of her adultery stamped upon her face for all to see, like a stigma.

She loved Jonathan with all the passion of a heart just woken to the mystery of that self-surrender which binds a woman to a man; and at the same time she had learned what it felt like to be vulnerable to hurt, to swing between a heaven and hell of emotion, to be plunged into the darkest depths of despair whilst paradoxically touching the very heights of happiness.

Her glance returned again to young Arthur Russell. He had been seated next at table to Angelina and was now attempting a somewhat awkward conversation which, to judge by the fiery colour of his ears, was proving a difficult social exercise.

"I wonder whether Mr van der Kleve has considered the advantages of an alliance with the Russells," Frances Broadwood observed in an aside to Kitty, slipping into the now vacant chair between them while the fish course was being removed to make way for the salmi of game.

A little motion of the head indicated the direction of her comment. "As you know, my dear, my husband Henry sits on the board of Faber and Russell, and since poor George's death – George was his cousin, Mrs Russell's late husband – he has cast himself in the role of mentor to young Arthur until the boy comes of age."

Kitty's mind was only half upon what was being said, the other half was still miles away in a dream of its own.

"And of course," Frances continued, blithely regardless, "he would like to see his nephew properly settled into the right connection as much for the company's benefit as for the boy's own. So there you are, my dear. As Henry said to me only last evening, it would not surprise him in the least if Mr van der Kleve were not considering Arthur as a suitable match for his daughter's hand."

This time Kitty had grasped the import of her neighbour's confidence.

"But Angelina's not yet sixteen," she responded, slightly

taken aback by the notion of her obnoxiously childish step-daughter being a candidate for such mature considerations. "She's hardly more than a schoolgirl still."

"Ah, but one has to plan these matters in advance, Catherine! It does no good to leave them until the last moment. When does her birthday fall?"

"Next month. November the tenth."

"There you are! Why, in another year she will be seventeen, which puts a different complexion upon it. I was scarce more than that myself when darling Henry commenced his courtship. Oh, admittedly I was a little more . . . shall we say *mature* in my outlook than Angelina. But there's time yet for improvement. It's astonishing how young girls these days seem to grow up so very suddenly."

At this point in the discussion the gentleman placed between Kitty and Frances returned from his absence from table, obliging the latter to remove herself back to her own seat, and thus putting an end to her talk.

Kitty looked again at Angelina. The girl had been dressed by her Aunt Beatrice in a flounced satinette gown decorated with clumps of ribbon, and in a shade of moss green which gave the muddy skin an unbecoming tone. Her hair – probably her finest point – had been swept into a half-chignon and held in place with a beaded net, a style which at least lent a little maturity to the plump, stolid features. The girl's conduct, however, was far from what one might expect of someone being viewed as prospective wife to the young man seated beside her, and it amazed Kitty that Arthur Russell should be managing his embarrassment quite so well against the silly display of exhibitionism which his attempt at conversation had provoked.

Kitty's eyes moved on down the table, past the decorations of coloured autumn foliage and berberis, to where her husband was sitting between the two Misses Daukins. Oliver was leaning back in his chair, arms folded across his double-breasted dress coat, his brooding gaze fixed upon the cloth before him in sightless abstraction. Impossible to guess what it was that so preoccupied his thoughts: he had seemed very morose of late, but Kitty had not enquired the reason and he had not volunteered one. Doubtless it was business, for she'd gathered from their occasional conversation together that the bank of van der Kleve Lindemanns was involved in the financing of

169

the Atlantic Telegraph Company, whose attempts to lay a deep sea cable across the Atlantic Ocean earlier this year had met with costly failure.

There were times when she'd thought Oliver must surely guess that she was pursuing a love-affair with some other man, especially at the beginning, in the summer, when she'd reached that secret crossroad in her life and chosen to follow her heart, and not her head. But as the weeks passed by and he'd shown no sign of aroused suspicions, her terror of discovery had eased a little; until recently . . .

The gentleman on Kitty's left, proprietor of Colbran's Library in the High Street, chose the moment to address a remark, distracting her from her reverie.

Yes, indeed, she agreed with him, this *was* a most pleasant social occasion, and yes, the dinner was excellent. And yes, indeed again, Mr and Mrs Broadwood were the most delightful of hosts and their house oh, quite, quite charming.

Having thus discharged himself socially, the gentleman returned once more to the enjoyment of his salmi of game which, to judge by the way he applied knife and fork, was like all else this evening, agreeably to his taste.

Kitty picked around the edges of her own plate. She had already eaten sufficient to satisfy her small hunger, and hoped that no one would be noticing the amounts she left untouched of the courses still to follow. Beatrice had commented only the previous week that her appetite would not satisfy a bird; and she knew from the evidence of her looking-glass that her face was paler of late, and thinner, emphasising the porcelain translucence of her skin.

The last time they had made love together, within the green curtain bower of a willow's branches on the Common, Jonathan himself had remarked on Kitty's increasing fragility and chided her for it, saying she must take more care of herself and not neglect her proper nourishment. She was reluctant to explain to him that the very notion of food made her ill, and that this, like the cold perspiration which often dewed her body, and the rapid feverish beating of her heart in the sleepless hours of the night, were but a part of the symptoms affecting her physical well-being since committing herself to this affair with him. Now that she knew her lover better, she was starting to learn his dislike of morbidity and illness, and what he called the silly dramatics of hysterical females, and fearing to lose any part of his affection, she'd hid her secret from him.

Was love always so painful, she wondered? Was it the same for all who'd been wounded by its barb – this terrible endless deep yearning, this emptiness of life when apart, this clinging on to dreams of sweetest piercing happiness when together? Or had she herself alone been singled out to suffer because what she was doing now was wrong, no matter how sincere her love for Jonathan, no matter how unhappy her marriage to Oliver . . . it was still adultery, however one chose to view it.

The plate, with its picked-over serving of salmi, was removed from in front of her by a maid, and another set in its place for the saddle of mutton. The meat was being carved at the sideboard opposite, and as Kitty watched the knife slicing through the roasted flesh, releasing droplets of pink blood to dribble down its surface, she experienced a sudden queasy sensation in the pit of her stomach. Averting her eyes, she pretended to occupy her attention with the table displays of foliage, but the queasiness persisted for several minutes and was not improved by the appearance of a helping of underdone mutton upon her dinner plate.

"Stewed celery, ma'am?"

The maid held a serving dish between Kitty and the gentleman to the left.

"No . . . no, thank you." She shook her head hastily, and tried not to look as the pulped white vegetable under its coating of sauce was spooned out for her more appreciative neighbour.

"A little gravy for your meat?"

Again she was forced to decline, accepting only a small helping of steamed potato for appearance's sake to lie beside the untouched mutton.

"Catherine?" Frances Broadwood's voice held a note of veiled curiosity. "You are not eating, my dear?"

Excusing herself to the guest between them, she leaned forward, her eyes flicking back and forth across Kitty's face as though something there had revealed itself suddenly to her notice. "Is the meat perhaps not to your liking? Would you prefer a slice better done?"

Hardly had she opened her mouth to refuse than Kitty felt her queasiness increase to a sudden sharp nausea and the acid

171

taste of bile sting the back of her throat. Fearing she was about to disgrace herself in front of the assembly, she pushed aside her chair with a muttered apology and got to her feet before the Broadwoods' butler could motion one of the servants to assist.

"Excuse me –"

Frances rose with her, adducing the situation at a glance; and moving away from the table, she took Kitty discreetly by the elbow to go with her from the dining room into the cooler air of the main staircase landing.

"Would you care to lie down a little while? Shall I ring for my maid to attend you?"

"No – Thank you, Frances. I'll be recovered in a moment." Kitty leaned on the supporting arm, the nausea passing to leave a curious tired weakness in its wake.

"What is it?" Oliver's voice sounded behind them. "What's wrong, Catherine?" He had seen his wife's exit, and realising that something was amiss, had followed at once from the dining room.

"Are you not well, my dear?" he enquired of her, coming to her side.

"I think, Mr van der Kleve," said Frances Broadwood, her eyes again examining Kitty's pale face in that knowing fashion and a little smile curling the corners of her mouth, "I think that your wife's indisposition may possibly have its cause in some future happy event. I hope I am right, Catherine? Is that not so?"

Kitty felt the sudden warm pressure of her husband's hand upon her arm, and the constrained eagerness of his manner as he perceived to what it was their hostess referred. Only recently, he had been speaking of his desire that there should be another child, a brother for little Henrietta.

He was pleased, Kitty could sense that. And it frightened her. She had so dreaded that she might become pregnant. For the past two months she'd had no menstrual course; and now this evening's sickness . . . her body's betrayal of its condition seemed all too clearly confirmed.

19

She was carrying either Jonathan's child, or Oliver's. She so wanted it to be Jonathan's, the fruit of their love for each other; yet against every inclination and instinct she must pray that for the sake of that love and to protect it from discovery, the father was Oliver van der Kleve.

He was delighted by the new pregnancy. This time it would be a son, he said, an heir; and to show his satisfaction he took Kitty for a week's holiday in Paris just after the opening of the New Year of 1867. This manner of rewarding his young wife's fruitfulness occasioned a great deal of resentment at Sion Place, for only a month or so earlier he'd been promising Angelina a visit to Paris, and now, by taking Kitty in her place, he not only broke that promise to his daughter but added considerably to the girl's animosity towards her stepmother.

The response was the usual silly, spoilt display of sulking and flouncing about which, together with rudeness and incivility, so taxed Kitty's patience that this time she made a complaint of it, with the result that Angelina spent a very uncomfortable half-hour in her father's study. In a tantrum of tears she fled to her aunt, and Beatrice – taking her niece's side as she inevitably would – in turn conveyed her own reproach to Oliver so that the whole thing degenerated into a vicious household circle of grudges and grievance, with Kitty made the innocent scapegoat at its centre.

She was heartily glad to escape from it all for a while to the polished, glittering elegance of the French capital. Here, re-visiting her old haunts around the Rue Quincompoix, and kindling memories of those two years spent here being 'finished' at L'École Rambouillet, she was able to feel herself a million miles removed from the petty jealousies of Sion Place, and the tensions weighing upon her from her relationship with Jonathan Rivers. She had told Jonathan of the baby, of course, expecting his reaction to be one of deep disquiet that she should have been thus compromised by their affair; but he had appeared quite strangely unconcerned by her news, telling her only that she must under no circumstances give her husband cause to suspect that this child might not be his.

Oliver was very attentive. Kitty had only to express the merest whim and it was indulged, or the slightest wish and it was granted her. They spent a day at Versailles, another at Choisy le Roi, an evening at the Opéra; he bought her new gowns in the fashionable shops along the Rue St Honoré, escorted her up to the cobbled heights of Montmartre to explore the warren of medieval streets around the famous Red Mill landmark there, and hired a cabriolet to drive them into the Bois de Boulogne where the trees in the January sunlight sparkled under wraps of fresh-fallen snow.

Such generosity and consideration touched Kitty where she felt it most keenly – upon her conscience. And the more that conscience smarted, the greater grew her feelings of guilt; so much so, in fact, that in reparation for the deceit she was practising upon him, she tried to compensate Oliver for his husbandly indulgence by being rather warmer and softer towards him, more giving of herself. The guilt even extended in some curious fashion to the awful Angelina, as though distance had lent a kind of distorted enchantment to the household scene, and in a moment's rush of charity she asked Oliver for a little money that she might buy the girl a gift as a memento of their holiday.

A short way along the street from their hotel was a high-class *confiserie* or confectioner's shop, selling all manner of chocolate and sugared delights to tempt the sweet of tooth. Knowing her stepdaughter's fondness for such things, Kitty decided upon a selection of little hand-made bonbons which were a speciality, and had them arranged in a box bearing upon its lid a rural view of St Germain des Prés.

. Tied in its satin ribbon, this peace-offering was, alas, received with less than gratitude by its recipient once they were back again in Tunbridge Wells. Upon learning from her father that it was Kitty herself who'd decided on this gift, Angelina promptly threw the box aside, declaring that she *loathed* French confectionery; and it was only after a sharp paternal rebuke and demand for immediate apology that she could be persuaded to conduct herself with a better grace and thank her stepmother for her thoughtfulness.

Whether or not this second pregnancy was beginning to effect a subtle change in Kitty's general mood, making her inwardly calmer and more passive, she could not tell; but it was about this time that despite all the provocations offered, she started to feel the first small kindling of sympathy towards young Angelina. The girl was her Aunt Beatrice's creation, encouraged from earliest age to be sly and spiteful, filling the gap of love left by her mother's premature death and her father's indifference with a noisy petulant selfishness which fed upon its own attention-seeking. The destructive instincts which lie as seeds within all children had in Angelina's case been encouraged to grow into the objectionable traits which isolated her from friendship and affection, so that she was driven more and more to turn to her aunt as her only ally and confidante.

Why Beatrice van der Kleve should deliberately have worked to twist a shallow nature into something so utterly unattractive, Kitty could scarce imagine; but knowing her sister-in-law as she now did, she suspected that the reason lay in the older woman's need to see herself self-mirrored through another – that lacking husband, child or any close relationship, she had used Angelina as a substitute for what her spinster's life and her own unfortunate temperament had denied her.

"No one could have spent a more unhappy childhood than I," Kitty said one day in conversation with Frances Broadwood when the subject of her stepdaughter arose. "Whilst I don't wish to appear ungrateful for the charity of those who raised me, there was never any affection or warmth or fondness shown – and yet a child needs these things just as surely as it requires nourishment and discipline. So you see, though I certainly do not condone Angelina's behaviour, I'm beginning to recognise that she, too, in her own way has suffered unhappiness. And I sympathise with her."

The admission caused genuine astonishment.

"But how can you say that, Catherine? She's a positive little trouble-maker! My own daughter Mary carries home the most dreadful tales from the Academy – hardly to be believed, some of them. Angelina assuredly does no credit to herself by the way she conducts her duties as Monitor."

"I agree. But caught between the influence of Beatrice and the indulgence shown her by Miss Meyrick – well, really, Frances, what else can one expect?"

And it was left at that.

There was, however, to be a sequel; and a most unlooked-for one, as it proved.

At the beginning of February the hitherto mild winter weather suddenly changed, and those who had been congratulating themselves upon escaping the worst of January's icy rigours now found they must pay dearly for their premature optimism. Instead of rain, there came sleet, carried on the back of a bitter north wind that sent freezing gusts whistling round street corners to howl in the chimneys and batter at every door-crack and draught-hole.

After several days of this blustering cold there was a three-inch fall of snow, followed by nights of hard frost which iced everything to a treacherously smooth surface and made progress through the streets of Tunbridge Wells a most hazardous exercise. The bottom end of the High Street near its junction with Mount Sion was one of the worst places for spills and accidents. Here, because of the steepness of the incline, rows of steps edged the raised pavements down to the road, with here and there a handrail for convenience; but what in all other weathers had been of helpful service to those wishing to cross to the further side, now proved quite otherwise, for these same steps became ledges of impacted ice on which many a boot heel and walking cane slipped, depositing the unfortunate pedestrian into the gutter.

Salt was put down, and ashes from the shop grates, soiling the grey-white streets with dirty smudges; and the hackney carriage company in Grove Hill Road arranged for straw to be spread to give some purchase for horse hoofs on the cobbles. Even with such precautions as these, though, there were still mishaps, including one poor gentleman who tumbled the length of the steps into the road by Noakes the draper's and cracked himself so severely upon the head that he died the next day of his injury.

While the weather remained at its worst Kitty had stayed indoors at Sion Place – not necessarily because she disliked the bleak cold (wrapped up snugly enough she would have

176

welcomed the exercise, in fact) but because her husband forbade her to go out, and himself chose to keep to the house rather than risk a journey into Town which might have left him stranded there. The enforced inactivity of sitting day after day in a chilly room beside a fire whose efforts at warmth were no match for the draughts, after a time proved sorely wearisome; and when young Angelina mentioned at dinner one evening that there was a book she required for her English grammar, Kitty seized upon this with an offer to go down into the High Street the next morning to ask whether there might be a copy to be had from the bookseller's there.

Had Oliver been present at table he would have refused to countenance such an excursion, being most particular that his wife must take every care of her health in her present delicate state; but it so happened that he was dining out with Mr Molineux, of the firm of bankers upon the parade, and so remained in ignorance of her intention, since no one thought later to inform him.

The morning was fine enough: the wind had shifted a little and felt less piercing, and the pewter-grey sky was broken here and there with ribbons of silver through which the fitful glimmer of a pale sun brought some light to the streets.

Well protected against the cold in a fur-lined mantle, Kitty left the house while her husband was busy attending to his correspondence in the study. She did not trouble to take Dobby with her, not thinking it worthwhile since she was only going down the hill and a short way into the High Street, and would hardly be out above half an hour.

It was more slippery underfoot than she'd realised, however, and the passage of folk along the pavements had worn the ice to a glassy sheet so that she was obliged to hold on to the iron railings of house fronts as she began her descent. Halfway down, where a modern-minded property owner had removed his railings in favour of a decorative brick wall, she found even greater difficulty in negotiating her way and was on the point of admitting defeat and turning back again, when just then a baker's delivery man came along and very courteously offered her his arm as support for a few yards.

Reaching the level foot of the hill at length, where Mr Lawrence's photographic studio formed the corner with the High Street, Kitty was able to relinquish her hold on the railings and move with better ease on the ash-strewn pavement outside the shopfronts; and in another few minutes had almost reached her destination when – quite suddenly, and without any warning – an avalanche of frozen snow started to fall from the roof slope directly above.

The first she knew of her predicament was a low rumble which made her glance up, and then a *whoosh* as the weight of the snow cascaded down towards the ground; and springing back to avoid being caught, her foot slipped at the edge of the icy pavement steps and she went over sideways.

There was a moment's terrible shock of pain – and then blackness.

"Catherine?"

Someone was calling to her from a long way off.

"Catherine – dearest?"

The voice sounded muffled, but she recognised it. She opened her eyes; and immediately experienced a blinding thrust of light which felt as though it stabbed right through her.

"Lie still, now! Don't try to move." Oliver's tone was sharp and yet concerned, and with an underlying note that was almost one of anger. "Lie still, Catherine."

She wondered why he should sound so strange. What had happened? Why did her head pound so dreadfully? Why – And then she remembered . . . the ice on Mount Sion, the snowfall . . .

"Angelina's book." Her words came out thickly, in a whisper. It seemed suddenly the most important thing in the world that Oliver should know about his daughter's book, the reason for her errand. She had hoped that little gesture of help might enable her to win something of the girl's confidence, weaken the animosity, reduce the barrier of ill will between them both.

Her thoughts wavered and drifted; when she opened her eyes again she felt the same stab but not so painful this time. Above her was a high white ceiling lit by gas jets within opaque globes, and in front . . . in front, beyond the foot of the bed she was lying upon . . . a sash window, framed by shutters, looking out on an oblong of slate-coloured sky.

Someone took her hand and held it; and she heard Oliver saying, "Yes, she's awakened at last" – still with that curiously

178

angry edge to his words – before her hand was released and a shadow fell across her face, obscuring the too-fierce light.

"Now, Mrs van der Kleve –" A woman's voice this time, soft and patient and caring like a mother's. "How are we feeling, my dear? A little weak, perhaps?"

"Yes . . ." The response was a faint one. She did feel weak, weak and drained, as though she'd been ill. "Where . . . am I?"

"You're in the hospital, my dear. You took a very nasty tumble yesterday and hurt yourself."

"What she was doing out of doors at all, I cannot think," Oliver came in. "In such conditions – to put herself in jeopardy – and the child –"

"Yes, yes, Mr van der Kleve, I do appreciate your concern. But this is not the moment . . ." There was a warning there in the quiet, kind voice. Kitty caught it.

"All for a book!" Oliver sounded almost disgusted. "As though it could not have waited a few days until the streets were safer."

But I *wanted* to go out, Kitty answered him in silent defence; I was so bored, being alone . . . you were occupied, Beatrice ignored me . . . there was only Dobby. I *needed* to go out.

"When shall my wife be allowed to return home?"

"When the doctor sees fit to discharge her, sir."

"And how long is that? Do you know? Can you tell me?"

"No. I'm sorry . . . there may yet be complications."

Complications. Kitty wondered about that word. It sounded – foreboding. Then the notion crossed her mind that she might have broken a limb in the fall – a leg, perhaps, or it may be a rib or two. Now that she was coming more to her senses, the various units of her body were beginning to signal their separate messages of hurt: a hot throbbing ache in her left shoulder and hip, that stabbing pain whenever she opened her eyes, and a discomfort like a heavy, dragging cramp in the lower part of her abdomen.

The shadow which had been shielding her from the brightness of the gas jets moved away again.

"I'll leave you for a little while to rest, Mrs van der Kleve. Just you lie still now, and I'll be back shortly to see how you are."

The owner of the mother's voice touched her hand once

more, and then was gone. And for a while there was nothing . . . somewhere in the background, footfalls and murmurs, like a sigh of sound, but between Kitty and her husband only silence.

The minutes stretched out; and then Oliver gave a sudden awkward cough, a clearing of the throat, as though there were a lump in it.

"*Why* did you have to go from the house, Catherine?" he asked in a tone of quiet reproach. "Why did you disobey me, dearest? I was only thinking of your good. And our child's."

She turned her head very slightly on the flat pillow. Someone had braided up her hair into tight plaits, and the movement caused a little tugging pinprick of fresh hurt.

"If only you had informed me first of your intention," he went on, leaning forward to look down at her from his chair at the bedside. "If only you had come to me! There has been far too much of this going out alone of late, without a word to anyone of where you are. It must stop now. I shall see that it does. I should have acted sooner, when Beatrice first told me of it."

His eyes never left Kitty's face, but moved back and forth across her features in an agitated manner.

"Do you know what you have done by your wilfulness? They said I was not to tell you, but I must. You have caused yourself to miscarry –"

That dull cramp in her body . . . oh God, her baby . . . she had lost her baby . . .

"– but mercifully the doctor here is of the opinion that it should not have any ill effect upon your future duties of motherhood."

Her baby . . .

She had longed for it, feared for it, to be Jonathan's child; and now there was nothing at all, its brief four months' existence brought to a sudden end in the expulsion of a miscarriage.

Tears gathered at the corners of her eyes.

"I'm sorry . . ." she whispered. But whether the apology was to Oliver for her adultery, to Jonathan for her failure, or to her own self for the child she had lost, not even Kitty really knew.

20

One person at least was relieved to learn of Kitty's miscarriage. When she had confided her condition to Jonathan Rivers, he had pretended to share her happiness that the baby might be theirs; but privately the possibility had appalled him. They had taken great care to keep their liaison a secret, and the last thing Jonathan wanted was for it to be blazoned abroad in the features of any child of his appearing like a cuckoo in the van der Kleve nest.

He loved Kitty, adored her; but in the somewhat narcissistic, shallow-rooted way which many artists feel towards their models. From the first, he'd been infatuated by her beauty, and as the sexual attraction grew, his desire for her had become a permanent hunger which could only be sated by possession. Since that day in July when they'd first made love together during the storm at High Rocks, he was a man obsessed with the gratification she brought him: never had he known a woman so apt for pleasure.

At the same time, he was sensitive enough to care for her feelings; and balancing his own urgent want against her present state of health and mind, he had taken up his pen to send her the following letter.

Thursday noon, the 14th February

My darling Kitty – sweetest Valentine – I do not have the words to write sufficient to give you comfort, but know that my every moment's thought is with you, dearest one. When I learned from Miss Dobby of the hurt you had taken, you may imagine my agitation and concern; – indeed, so great was both that I would have rushed forth there and then to be at your side, had not the voice of prudence constrained me.

Beloved, I share your sorrow at the loss of the child you

carried; but think of this: – it may well be that Fate has seemed cruel in order to be kind, for any revelation that your Husband might not have sired the infant would have caused you a far, far greater sorrow had it exposed our love to the judgment of Society. I only write this in order to convince you how deeply I am concerned in your welfare and happiness, you must believe me.

My darling sweet heart, all eternity has passed since our last embrace together, and I cannot tell you with what an ardent longing I yearn once more to hold you near. This cruel separation which has been enforced upon us has led me to consider, dearest one, that were it possible, I should like you to come with me upon a brief visit to Shropshire which I must shortly undertake, that I might show you something of that District's beauty whilst selfishly enjoying a few days of your company for myself alone.

Will you at least consider this suggestion? I am sure that between us we may contrive some plausible excuse to explain your absence. Meanwhile, I implore you to have a care for yourself in order that your recovery might be the sooner achieved; and remain your most devoted lover –

Jonathan

The letter, delivered by the invaluable Dobby some days after her mistress's discharge from hospital, was burnt almost as soon as read; but its contents remained fixed indelibly upon Kitty's mind. The possibility of going away to Shropshire with her beloved, for however short a time, seemed so extremely remote that she forced herself to dismiss it – only to find her thoughts constantly drifting back to the idea in a wishful wondering fashion.

"It's out of the question, of course," she told Harriet Seymour, having decided – if only to hear a second opinion – that she must confide in her friend. "I mean, just suppose . . . well, just suppose that there *were* a chance, what on earth could I tell Oliver?"

"Precisely. You can hardly go to him and say 'Oliver, dear, Mr Rivers has invited me to spend a few days alone in his company, therefore would you mind awfully if I accepted?' I can well imagine the furore that would cause!" Harriet raised a cynical eyebrow. "Mind you, if it were Peter Hoffmann making *me* a similar invitation, I should be tempted to accept like the proverbial shot."

"Oh –? Would you?"

"Yes. But he won't. The dear Herr Doktor has no romance in his soul, unlike your drawing master."

"What you mean is, Harriet, that he has made no attempt to compromise you."

"Unfortunately, no."

For the first time in recent weeks, Kitty managed to laugh.

"Oh, but it's not amusing!" her friend protested wryly. "When Mama and I were last in Baden-Baden, Peter was so attentive to me that I could scarce believe my own good fortune. Yet since our return, I've heard not a word from him, despite having written two rather affectionate letters. My pride is in danger of being hurt, Kitty. I knew it was a mistake, to fall in love."

The laughter died in Kitty's eyes. Leaning back among the pillows of her bed, she turned her face away to look towards the rain-smeared window, and after a moment said quietly, "Yes . . . falling in love does have its price to pay."

She had not told Harriet that the child she'd been expecting might be Jonathan's; in fact, she had not told Harriet that she and he were lovers, though she very much suspected that her friend had already gathered for herself that the relationship was such. One of the admirable things about Harriet was that she never condemned, never judged; she merely accepted that everyone had their own standards and principles by which they lived, and if those standards and principles fell below hers, why, so long as they did no harm, what hurt was caused – it would be a dull world indeed if each man behaved exactly like the next.

Yet in the situation which existed between Kitty and Jonathan Rivers, hurt *had* been caused, and she felt a moment's quick shame that her friend might have guessed that. A woman could be in love whilst remaining innocent of any wrongdoing: it was only when that love was allowed to develop to physical passion that the stain of misconduct smirched her integrity, and as a counterbalance to the stolen happiness, reduced her self-respect and pride accordingly.

"If you were not married to Oliver," Harriet said perceptively, "would you care to be the wife of Mr Rivers?"

"Why . . . why, what a thing to ask –" Kitty looked round again, a quick blush of colour in her face.

"I only enquire because it might put a different complexion upon my advice. You see, if you did *not* care for the gentleman, there would be no point in entertaining his friendship. But were your affections to be so strong as to consider marriage – always supposing you were free to do so – then I cast no blame upon you, Kitty, for wishing to steal a few days alone with him."

"You – would not blame me?"

Harriet shook her head. "In your place, my dear, I would do the same. All *I* lack is the opportunity."

"Ah, but your situation is rather different. You're not bound by obligations and duties to a husband and child."

"Would that I were! But I very much fear that any fond hope I've entertained of becoming Frau Hoffmann is starting to wilt through neglect." The little plain mouse face put on an expression of stoicism. "What a good thing it is, my dear, that I learned early in life never to expect too much of anything, and thereby spared myself the pain of disappointment."

This observation was followed by a pause for pensive reflection. The rain outside spattered in sharp gusts against the bedroom windows, and an occasional flurry of drops found their way into the chimney and trickled down to fall hissing among the glowing coals in the grate. Noticing the fire starting to burn low, Harriet got up to attend to it herself; and then, settling her small, slight form once more in the bedside chair and dusting a few specks of ash from the cuff of her balloon sleeve, she picked up the conversation again.

"I have had a thought. When you've quite recovered your strength, Kitty dear, you might like to consider a short holiday of convalescence – in fact, I'm sure that your doctor can be persuaded to prescribe one. Therefore it seems to me that your few days in Shropshire may very well be accommodated without arousing much suspicion – if your heart were indeed set upon such a venture, and I hasten to add that I'm neither condoning nor condemning the escapade."

"Escapade –!" Kitty uttered a short, dry sound in a poor attempt at humour. "Yes, I suppose that's how it must appear to you, Harriet . . . a foolish escapade." She gave her friend a troubled glance. "Tell me – what *do* you think? Are we being reckless . . . irresponsible . . . Jonathan and I? Two people flying in the face of all that's moral and decent –"

"I've already told you my opinion. Love has its own laws. The only thing which concerns me, Kitty, is that you are not about to jump from one frying pan into another, and create even further heartache for yourself."

Yet that was precisely what she *had* done. Since losing the child, she had felt as though she were living again in some dark dream, for Oliver held her to blame for that loss, and his disappointment and displeasure had served to underscore her failure to fulfil the role expected of her. Those days they'd had together in Paris had brought them just a little closer; and now it was spoiled, and the old reserved, withdrawn attitudes were back again, the emotional guards put up as barriers from which they each conducted the silent hostilities of two people set poles apart from one another.

A house without happiness was one of the saddest places on earth, Kitty had learned; its rooms empty of laughter, no warmth, no colour anywhere; no peace . . . However unwise the decision might prove, whatever the cost to pay, if there were the smallest chance of going away with Jonathan she would take it, if only to know what sweet promise her life might have held had she met and married him instead of Oliver van der Kleve.

"Let us suppose for a moment –" she said cautiously, testing the possibilities of the situation, "let us suppose, Harriet, that Dr Adeney advises a short holiday in the countryside for my convalescence, as you say – how would you suggest we so arranged matters that I shared it with Jonathan? I can hardly imagine Oliver would allow me to convalesce in Shropshire, when there's not a soul there with whom either of us is acquainted. Besides, have you considered that he might wish to accompany me?"

"Not if he were led to believe that you were going no further afield than Frant." Harriet's expression appeared totally innocent of guile.

"*Frant* – ?"

"Yes. The scheme merely requires a little imagination. Oliver could surely raise no objection if I were to invite you as a guest to Frant for a week, for no one could be more in the depths of the country than there, yet remain quite conveniently close to the Wells."

Kitty felt her heart begin to beat a little faster.

"But if I were staying with *you*, then how –"

"No, no, but you wouldn't be! Don't you see? That, my dear, is the point. We would merely be practising a slight deception, leading the Husband to *suppose* you were in Frant, when in actual fact you'd be miles away elsewhere."

"Oh . . ." There was a long pause. "You mean, you would provide the pretext for my absence."

"Exactly. I would be your alibi."

In the midst of Kitty's growing excitement, a touch of doubt intruded itself. "Would that not involve the connivance of your family, though? Your mother, at least, would have to be told."

"Not at all. There'd be no need. You see how my mind is working on your behalf! The matter simply requires a certain amount of careful planning. You will tell Oliver that you're to spend a week at Frant as my guest – I will confirm that – you travel instead to Shropshire – and should he require news of the progress of your convalescence, why, then I shall supply it!" Harriet was positively enjoying this embroidery of her scheme.

"Ah, but supposing he were to take it into his head to visit?"

"What – visit Frant? Now, tell me, dear, is that likely? He spends his week in London. And besides, he has scarce little fondness for *me*, and no acquaintance at all with my family. So wherein would lie his reason?"

Kitty's answer was a shrug; and then, on a sudden little laugh of nerves – "We should have to make Dobby a party to this, of course."

"Of course! She's to be trusted, is she not?"

"Oh, implicitly. She's – well, she's played the go-between for Jonathan and me since the beginning. To be frank, Harriet, I·often wonder what she must make of it all . . . she never offers her opinion, merely says 'yes, ma'am' and 'no, ma'am' to whatever I ask of her."

"Then she's a pearl of great price, my dear. And obviously has a shrewd head upon her shoulders. There are not so very many positions open to a lady's maid where she would be treated as generously as she is here, and have you thought that she may well be relishing the intrigue of the situation?"

"I believe you're right. Beneath that quiet façade she hides a very romantic turn to her nature. The books she chooses to read are proof enough of that."

Kitty's elation caused her to smile at the memory. Several times she had asked Amelia Dobby to read aloud to her of an evening to pass the hours till bedtime, and the selection had invariably been from the poems of Christina Rossetti, or else the works of the Brontë sisters or Mrs Gaskell.

"So – that's that!" Harriet clapped her hands upon her knees in a satisfied manner, and rose to her feet. "The next time I call on you, my dear, I trust to see you not only recovered but in far better spirits. What is life, after all, if not an adventure – so take my advice, seize what it offers whilst you can! All too soon it passes by and steals our youth from us, and there is little that is emptier than an old age without memories."

Kitty astonished herself at the ease with which she was able to put Harriet's stratagem into effect. Dr Adeney thought her suggestion a most sensible one, that she complete her recovery from the miscarriage by spending some days in the country air, and he advised Oliver accordingly. The middle of March would be an excellent time, and it was most kind of the Seymours to offer Mrs van der Kleve the hospitality of their house at Frant. His only slight concern was that baby Henrietta, now a year old, was not thriving as well as she might; but the nursery was Beatrice's domain, and under her direction the child could not be more capably supervised, Dr Adeney felt sure.

In the weeks before the date of her departure from Tunbridge Wells, a series of notes passed between Kitty and Jonathan Rivers, discreetly exchanged via the indispensable Dobby, whose only response to her mistress's disclosure that they'd be travelling rather further afield than supposed, had been a murmured "You may rely upon me entirely, ma'am."

The plan devised between the lovers was that they should meet beyond Frant on the second day. This would serve to allay any possible suspicions, for Kitty was to be driven down to the Seymours in her husband's carriage, and it would look odd indeed, as Harriet said, if she were immediately to depart again elsewhere the moment she arrived. The same stratagem would need to be adopted for the homeward journey, Kitty returning from Shropshire to spend a final night at Frant in readiness for Oliver's carriage calling the following morning to convey her again to Sion Place. And if the Seymours should think all this going and coming rather strange, Harriet had no doubt but that she could contrive some convincing explanation, as she assured her friend.

The arrangements went without a hitch. Jonathan was waiting with a hired vehicle a short distance outside Frant village, and by late morning they were in London to catch the Chester train from Euston Station. Kitty had packed as little as possible by way of personal baggage: any excess would have to go with her maid to a hotel in the Bayswater Road, where Dobby was staying while mistress and lover were together in Shropshire. (It would hardly do, as Jonathan pointed out, for them all to sleep three to a room in the small cottage he'd taken, and Kitty was quite used to attending to her own dress and toilette.)

"You're not regretting coming away with me, are you, my darling?" he asked her in the draughty second-class railway carriage taking them both on the last leg of their journey to Wellington. She had seemed unusually quiet all day, but he tended to put this down to the fatigue of travel.

"Of course I'm not. Why on earth should I feel regret?" She smiled at him warmly, then glanced away again through the night-darkened window, her reflection mirrored there upon the glass. The same reflection showed her Jonathan's face, the handsome, almost boyish face she loved and knew so well; and without turning to look back at him, she held out her hand.

"We're here . . . we're together. It's what we've both wanted for so long."

"If you're worried –" he began, taking the hand in his own and lacing their fingers so that they rested entwined on his knee – "remember, we're going where not a soul will know you. Let's look upon these few days ahead as our reward to ourselves for all the times of separation we've had to endure. Why not!"

Those final two words echoed her own thoughts, but in a different key. How could she explain to him? She needed him so much, wanted to stay with him always and never have to be apart again. With Jonathan she felt more fulfilled as a person, as a woman, than she could ever say. He had brought her alive with happiness. Once they had returned to Tunbridge Wells, how was she to bear to have to start living once more the lie that was her life at Sion Place?

"I love you, Jonathan." She moved her head on the uncomfortable horsehair padding of the carriage seat and gave him another smile.

He squeezed her hand. "I love you, too. Trust me and believe that."

"I do."

Kitty looked through the window again. Outside, the anonymous countryside flowed by unseen in the darkness of the spring night. She had no idea where they were, in what county; and after a while her eyelids began to droop as the heaviness of an exhausted sleep crept over her.

She awoke with a sudden start.

"Oh – where are we? Is this Wellington?"

"No, no. Wolverhampton. We've a little further to go yet." Jonathan had been asleep, too, cradling her head upon his shoulder. He sat up now, peering out into the gas-flare of the station, porters running up and down outside their carriage window to attend to the luggage of disembarking passengers.

"Try to sleep again."

Obediently she closed her eyes; but her limbs felt stiff and cold from the inactivity of slumber, and after a few moments she roused herself up, chafing her hands together.

"What is the time? It must be very late."

Jonathan took his silver repeater from the fob pocket of his waistcoat and flicked open the lid. "Almost ten o'clock."

He replaced the timepiece. "You're shivering. Here – a sip of this will warm you –" taking out a small leather-covered flask. "It won't do for you to catch a chill, my darling."

The fiery heat of the brandy struck Kitty's throat, making her cough as she swallowed. Her lover gulped a mouthful for himself, wiping his lips on the back of his hand before offering her the flask again.

After several minutes she could feel her body begin to glow inside from the spirit's warmth, and a pleasantly euphoric giddiness lightened her head just a little. Jonathan drew her grey travelling cloak further round her; and before she slept once more, she remembered telling herself how wonderful these next few days were going to be.

After all, every contingency had been anticipated and planned for, so what was there to worry about – what could possibly go wrong?

21

Between the Shropshire market town of Wellington and the deep gorge of the River Severn some miles to its south, there lay an area of small villages clustered along the surface seams of coal which provided their livelihood. Opencast mining had been carried on here in the shadow of the Wrekin hill for centuries, and the rolling landscape was pitted with the honey-comb pock-marks of shallow craters. Where seams had been worked out, woodland had grown back again to cover these scars with the green flush of birch and holly and bracken, isolating into rural pockets the tiny hamlets whose three or four cottages had housed the miners' families before they moved away.

It was to one of these hamlets, along the Dawley road, that Jonathan Rivers brought Kitty, to a small white cottage perched on the slope of a hill with the Wrekin brooding black against the skyline behind it. The place had been built in the mid-seventeenth century, and had thick stone walls and a lichen-grey roof pulled snugly down over its dormer-eyebrowed windows.

After a sound night's sleep Kitty was ready to pronounce it the dearest little cottage imaginable, with its single bedroom tucked beneath the eaves and a dog's-leg staircase leading to the stone-flagged living room below. The only water was to be had from a pump across the lane, and the only heat from the wood which Jonathan cut down to burn in the wide-mouthed hearth; but spartan as these conditions were, Kitty would not for the world have exchanged them for all the comfort and warmth and domestic convenience which Sion Place could offer.

"Home is where the heart is," she told her lover as they lay together at the end of that first day, their arms around each other on the pegged-rag rug, watching the flames lick up into the chimney mouth, with the sough of the night wind whispering across the darkened fields outside.

They made love there on the unyielding floor, and the firelight threw their shadows in sudden leaps and jumps against the plain, homely, whitewashed walls which had witnessed so much of life and death here down the years of occupation. Afterwards they climbed the stairs to the box-bed with its lumpy feather mattress and slept in one another's embrace until the birdsong of a new day roused them.

Kitty lay curled on her side, feeling her lover's warmth against her naked body. The pale half-light of morning touched his features, pearling the sheen of sleep on his skin, and gently she reached to stroke his cheek, delighting in the sensation of waking to find him there beside her. She had fantasised about this in the early dawn of so many other mornings, her empty arms conjuring the remembrance of his strength, his smell, his voice; and now the fantasy was realised. It was the happiest moment of her life.

Jonathan yawned and stretched himself, then pulled her into his arms and kissed her forehead.

"You were crying in your sleep," he said thickly.

"Was I?"

"Mm."

"I must have been dreaming. Did I wake you?"

He grunted and kissed her again, then turned his head on the pillow to look over to the uncurtained window.

"Why should I be sad?" she asked with a little smile, snuggling against his shoulder. "This is such heaven, being here with you. It's the only place on earth where I belong."

There was another yawn. He passed a hand over his face, wiping away the tiredness, setting his mind into shape for the day. "No more unhappy dreams, then." He turned back to her.

"No more unhappy dreams, I promise. We have only these few days to share together – perhaps it was that."

·"Mm . . . ?"

"Perhaps the thought of having to part again. Oh, Jonathan –" Kitty hugged herself to him – "why can't it always be like this for us? Why can't we stay here for ever?"

"And live on love? That won't pay the rent." He softened the words with another kiss.

"No, but I've been thinking . . . wouldn't it be wonderful?

Simply to be together all the time, and never have to say goodbye."

"Yes. Wonderful."

The smile on her lips widened artlessly as her daydream drew her towards even sweeter possibilities. This romantic invitation of her lover's to be with him here in Shropshire was, she believed, the prelude to a shared life for them both, a foretaste of what he intended for their future.

"When we return to Tunbridge Wells –" she went on, caressing his cheek again, loving the masculine roughness of its morning stubble, "I won't stay at Sion Place. After this it would be impossible, and I couldn't bear it. I'll ask Oliver to let me go. Yes, that's what I must do – I'll ask him to release me from our marriage. Then baby Henrietta and I will be free to come and live with you at Beckets Cottage." She ran her fingertips over his mouth. "You'd like that, wouldn't you, Jonathan?"

There was a long, long moment of silence.

"Wouldn't you – ?" she prompted, raising her head to look into his face, expectant of seeing her own happiness mirrored there.

Instead, she found his expression for some reason tightened into a small frown; and before she could speak to ask what was wrong, he answered a fraction off-handedly, "I don't think that would be very wise. Telling your husband about us."

"But – why not? We love one another!"

"My darling, think of the scandal there'd be."

"What do I care about scandal. I *need* you – I want to be with you, live with you as your wife. Oh, I know what public opinion will say. But dearest, I also know that nothing in this world can keep me apart from you now."

"Kitty, listen –" Jonathan pulled his arm from round her and half sat up, leaning one elbow on the pillow to look down at her. "We mustn't do anything hasty which we'll regret. Let's leave things as they are for a while. Why spoil what we have."

He smoothed back the hair from her face, seeing reflected there a sudden suspicion of hurt in her eyes. How was he to tell her? How could he explain? Apart from the damage any scandal would do to his career, it had never been his intention that their relationship should develop into a permanent one. And despite the strongly physical desire he felt for her – call it love – he was in no position to have Kitty living with him openly at Beckets Cottage. In fact, the last thing he wanted was a dependent mistress and her child clinging to his shirt-tails for support, just at a time when he was struggling to establish himself as a society artist.

The unwelcome thought rose in his mind that now she'd got this notion of leaving her husband, once back in the Wells she'd be pestering him with it on every occasion they met, and putting him under considerable pressure to make a decision.

What a pity . . .

He bent to kiss the downturned lips, coaxing them to open for him; and when he felt Kitty start to respond, took her into his arms again and began making love to her in a somewhat casual and self-indulgent fashion.

As if by tacit consent, nothing more was mentioned of their early morning conversation, and the two of them spent this next day together in Shrewsbury, a short distance by railway from Wellington.

Catching her first glimpse of the sun-tipped spires and castle towers in the distance across the water meadows of the Severn, Kitty was ready to recapture a lighthearted mood, declaring the scene enchantingly like a medieval fairy-tale. With its Welsh Bridge to one side and its English Bridge to the other, and almost encircled by a broad loop of the river, the town stood at the historical crossroads of two cultures, Jonathan explained as they descended from their carriage.

Kitty gave his little lecture fond attention; but found rather more to take her interest once they were in the narrow climbing streets, where timber-and-lath houses crowded out the light on either side. In places the upper galleries leaned drunkenly together overhead, gables almost meeting, as though to hold one another up from collapse, while below them a warren of passages burrowed between shopfronts, bearing quaintly curious names such as Murivance, Mardol and Dogpole.

As a boy, Jonathan had attended the old grammar school here, boarding with an aunt in St Mary's Water Lane: his cousins lived at the house still, and he proposed calling upon them this afternoon to visit. Kitty would not be able to accompany him, of course (how should he introduce her, after all?) but there was plenty to occupy her attention along by the river for an hour or so until his return.

Though his reluctance to speak of their living together still pricked her a little, she did not allow herself to fret too much at her lover's temporary desertion; but the following day, when she was left all alone at the cottage from morning till early evening, the loneliness and unfamiliarity of the place proved rather more difficult to endure and made her feel quite home-sick. This time Jonathan had gone to see his mother and sisters some miles away at Little Wenlock, and though he promised he'd only be gone a few hours, in fact it was almost dark when he returned.

Instead of the expected apology, however, his first remark as he came in at the door was one of criticism.

"My goodness, it's almost as cold in here as outside! What's the matter with the fire, Kitty?"

"It's gone out," she answered distractedly; and then – "Oh, Jonathan, where have you been? I was so worried that something had happened."

The reply seemed dismissive. "I wasn't far away. I suppose you've been sitting here all afternoon imagining the worst."

"I didn't know what to think – you said you wouldn't be many hours –"

"Now I hope you're not going to chide me," he interrupted her, perhaps a little too sharply. "I'm sorry you've been left longer than intended, but I could hardly rush away from the family home the moment I'd arrived. Besides, my mother wished me to stay and eat with them – how could I refuse?"

Moving past, he went across to the table by the wall and put down the cloth-wrapped bundle he'd been carrying, and at the same time cast a glance towards the fireless hearth.

"You've burnt all the wood I brought in?"

"Yes. There wasn't much. You said you'd –"

"I know what I said! I said I'd chop some more when I returned." Again, that little note of sharpness. "I'll attend to it now."

He came by her again to go out at the door, his handsome features set and unsmiling; and Kitty wondered what it was could have happened today to so sour his mood.

In a while she could hear the sound of his axe strokes ringing in the stillness of the evening air. She crossed to the window and looked out. There was enough light left in the sky to see to the trees where he was working, but dusk had drained all colour from the scene and made it murky and drab, edging in black the outline of naked branches against wind-shredded layers of cloud. Despondently she pulled the shutters together and latched them, plunging the interior of the room into shadow with only the soft yellow glimmer of an oil lamp for illumination.

Night had fallen completely by the time Jonathan was finished. His exertions had warmed him to a sweat, and he'd stripped off waistcoat and shirt to rinse himself down at the pump across the way, running back into the cottage to dry himself by a fire of fresh kindling ablaze on the hearth.

"There's some food there in that bundle," he said, jerking his chin in the direction of the table. "Have some if you're hungry. It's game pie, I believe. My mother insisted I take it to bring away with me."

Kitty had eaten little all day, apart from some bread and cheese left over from the previous evening's meal. She had never had an especially good appetite – a legacy from the semi-starved days as a charity girl at Miss Meyrick's Academy – but the country air seemed to have whetted the edge of her hunger, and she could feel her mouth watering in anticipation as she went to untie the cloth around the pie.

"Oh – will you have some too?" she paused, turning to ask.

"I wouldn't mind a piece in a minute." Jonathan dragged his shirt back on over his head, tucking in the tails inside his trousers and pulling up his braces. "But you help yourself to whatever you want. I've already eaten a good meal today."

The pie was delicious, a thick buttery golden pastry lid with a deep layer of pressed meat beneath. Kitty needed no second bidding to take a piece.

After a while, when the pangs of her hunger had been somewhat satisfied, she commented out of curiosity, "I suppose your family must have wondered where you were staying."

"They asked, yes."

"And what did you tell them?"

Jonathan took a bite of the slice he'd just cut himself. "That I was here at the cottage, of course. It's a place I've taken several times before in the past."

"Oh."

Kitty turned this over in her mind. Then, before she could stop herself, remembering how he'd dismissed her earlier talk of their being together – "Have you ever brought anyone else – another woman – here?"

The question hung in the air like an accusation while he slowly finished chewing.

"How d'you hope I'll answer that, I wonder," he said at last.

"With the truth."

"The truth can be a hurtful thing if told at the wrong time."

"Then you *have* brought someone else here."

There was an off-hand gesture. "Well . . . yes, yes, I have. You didn't imagine I'd lived entirely without experience before I met you, surely?"

He said that as though he didn't care whether he wounded Kitty or not, she thought. Not once had she tried to pretend to herself that she was the first female Jonathan had ever lain with – he was too skilful a lover – but she had never enquired into his past, never wanted to know. Perhaps the sudden difference now was that they were together in a place where he'd shared himself with another, held a different woman in his arms in this very room; yes, and in the bed upstairs where they'd been sleeping in such close and tender intimacy these last two nights.

Disillusionment began to spread its insidious grey web of joylessness over all the hopes she had cherished. She pushed her plate away, her appetite gone.

"I'm sorry. You were right, I shouldn't ask questions if I didn't want the truth."

"And I'm sorry that I couldn't be kinder, and lie." Jonathan gave her a crooked smile.

"Did you . . . did you love her as much as me . . . this other woman?" It was like having an aching tooth, asking these things: knowing the pain of probing at it, yet unable to resist.

"D'you really wish to discuss the subject, Kitty?"

She wanted to shake her head, but found herself nodding. "*Did* you love her as much as me?"

There was a shrug. He got up from his chair and went to throw a fresh log on the fire, sending showers of sparks flying up into the chimney.

"Who can say? Love's different every time."

"Is it? I've never been in love before . . . I don't know much about it, so I can't judge."

"Oh –" suddenly he was impatient. "This is a silly conversation! Let's stop it. We came away to be happy, not to bicker and find fault with each other. I've said I was sorry for leaving you alone today –"

"That has nothing to do with it."

"Yes, it has. You've worked yourself into an ill humour, and now you're looking for some excuse to vent it upon me. I'm beginning to wish I hadn't brought you with me on this visit."

"And I'm beginning to wish I hadn't come!"

Tears of anger, as well as hurt, welled in Kitty's eyes. This had been such a weary, dreary day, with only her own thoughts for company; and now, to make things worse, it was ending up in argument and rancour.

"You came back here snapping at me as though *I* was the one who'd done wrong," she went on. "After I'd spent hour upon hour cold and hungry, wondering that something might have happened to you."

"Well, something *did* happen, as a matter of fact," Jonathan broke in tersely, giving her a look. "You may as well know about it, I suppose. We've always said we'd have no secrets from one another."

He thrust his hands into his trouser band and hunched his shoulders; then, turning from the fire to sit down again – "It's my cousins' fault. They shouldn't have interfered. But how were they to know – I mean, they had no idea. I've never once mentioned your name, never revealed our relationship. They believed I was here alone, otherwise I'm sure they'd not have taken it upon themselves to act as they did."

Kitty watched his face. "Are these the cousins you visited in Shrewsbury yesterday?"

He gave a nod. "I haven't told you this before. Well, it didn't seem relevant. But some years ago, soon after I'd returned from France, it was expected that I'd marry a young woman of good family. We had known each other since childhood – her people were well acquainted with mine, and all that. However, the time I'd spent in Paris had altered me a good deal – opened my mind, matured my outlook – and, well, to cut the story short, Susanna and I quarrelled and we parted."

There was a pause in Jonathan's narrative. Kitty waited in silence, motionless, her eyes still fixed upon him.

After a moment he went on awkwardly, "She went abroad and we didn't meet again . . . until today. My cousins knew that she'd returned to live in the district this last month, that she was still unwed, and they wrote at once to tell her – they've always been very close, you see – they wrote to tell her I'd be at Little Wenlock, should she wish to renew our . . . acquaintance."

"And did she? Wish to renew the – acquaintance?" Kitty marvelled at the levelness of her tone.

Another pause; another nod of the head.

"And you? What are your own feelings, Jonathan?"

This time he responded again with a shrug, wanting to cause the least hurt and yet knowing that the quickest cut was probably the kindest.

"How can I say? Seeing Susanna today – oh, I don't know! It aroused such pleasant memories. I must be honest with you, Kitty. When you spoke the other morning of leaving your husband to live with me, it came as quite a bit of a shock. I mean, the whole thing's out of the question – you do realise that, don't you? No, wait a minute, let me finish –" as she made a sudden stricken movement – "it's best we have this out now, don't you see? Whether or not I'd met Susanna again, the situation between you and me would have needed an airing any way before too much longer. The plain truth of the matter is, I never intended this relationship to be a permanent one, with us living together, and I'm sorry if anything I said or did ever gave you that impression."

Without looking at Kitty, he leaned forward, elbows on knees, his fingers buried in his thick hair.

There was a long silence. The firelight touched the welling tears in her eyes, making them glint like sparks as they fell.

"Then you've never loved me at all," she said at last in a whisper.

"Of course I've loved you! But I'm in no position to have a scandal round my neck. Your husband is a very influential man."

"So . . . it would seem your choice is made –" Kitty's voice broke on a quiver of pain. She bent her head and looked down, the tears splashing the whitened knuckles of her folded hands.

For a moment or so she was unable to go on; and when she raised her head again, Jonathan was staring at her, and even the shadows of firelight could not hide the guilt there in his eyes.

"Perhaps it would be best if we left tomorrow," she said, a little breathlessly. "Tomorrow, instead of Thursday."

"If that's what you wish."

Oh, it's not what I wish! she cried back at him in mute anguish. But what can I do? Why did you bring me here, only to shatter my dreams into pieces? I trusted you – wanted you – needed you so much . . . too much, perhaps . . . and now there's no future for us to share, no more joy, no more hope; only memories.

God help me, how am I ever going to bear it.

They left for the south early next morning, changing at Wolverhampton and again at Birmingham for the train to London. Arriving at Euston late that afternoon, the first priority was to go to the Bayswater Road to collect Miss Dobby from the private hotel where she'd been temporarily deposited. Unfortunately, she'd gone out – the porter could not say where – and several hours were wasted waiting for her.

Jonathan suggested that Kitty ought to go on alone; but the convolutions of their original plan worked against this, for it would have entailed hiring a vehicle to drive her into the country to the Seymours at Frant, and she could hardly take one from Tunbridge Wells station in case she were recognised there.

Dobby did not return until late evening – she'd been to the Music Hall with a friend, she explained apologetically – so it was that they were forced to stay overnight in separate rooms at the hotel, and start off again on their journey at first light the following day.

Neither Kitty nor Jonathan Rivers had much to say to one another. Both accepted that this might well be the last time they would spend together, and it created an almost insupportable tension between them, a tension compounded of guilt, regret, and on Kitty's side at least, the terrible leaden ache of wounded emotion.

The French had a saying: 'Love makes time pass; time makes love pass.' Though it broke her heart in two, she was beginning to realise that she'd been living in a fool's world, for Jonathan had obviously never felt for her in the same deep, self-sacrificing way in which she felt for him. However intense his passion had been, it was bound by its very nature to burn itself out eventually.

They made their farewells to one another on the lane from Frant. Jonathan had halted the pony and trap hired in Buckfield, and walked a short way along with Kitty and her maid until the barley-twist chimneys and red roof tiles of the Seymours' house could be seen through the trees. Before turning back, he took Kitty's hand and raised it to his lips, saying quietly, "God bless you, my dear –" and then he was gone, walking quickly away up the lane, while she stood there in the pale spring sunlight, the warm impress of his mouth growing cold on her hand; as cold as the tears on her cheek.

He did not look round again.

She remained without movement until his trap had passed completely out of sight; then, rousing herself with an effort, turned and compelled her sorrowing steps to take her in the opposite direction.

Within another ten minutes she and Dobby were at the drive of the house, and just approaching the carriage turn in front of the main door when a window above was thrown open and a face appeared, leaning forward in a strained attitude to look out towards them.

It was Harriet Seymour.

She waved, and called out a few words which neither woman below was able to catch, then vanished again; and several moments later, while they were standing there still wondering what was to do, the porch door opened and Harriet came limping out to meet them. From her expression and hurried gait it was obvious there was something amiss.

"Oh, Lord, Kitty – thank heavens you're here!" she gasped, coming down the steps to her friend. "The most *awful* thing has occurred. I scarcely know how to tell you!"

She reached out to seize the other's hand.

"Your husband's been here to fetch you home to Sion Place. When he discovered you'd stayed but the one night – oh, Kitty, I fear he's quite demented! You must return to him at once, my dear. It's your baby – your poor baby. Something has happened – something terrible – and Oliver has been searching for you everywhere!"

22

They faced her across the room like judges – her husband Oliver, Beatrice his sister, and Dr Adeney. The face of each reflected the same censure, the same rejection; in the doctor's eyes perhaps some slight touch of pity; but in Oliver's nothing but blazing anger, and in Beatrice's the sneer of triumph.

On the drawing-room mantelpiece behind, the tick of the ornate bracket clock was the only sound, ponderously keeping time in the lengthening evening silence. Its gilded fingers stood at nine o'clock, but for Kitty an eternity had passed since the Seymours' carriage brought her home to Sion Place five hours ago.

Her child was dead – little Henrietta, the baby she had scarcely known. They had told her so. Henrietta was dead, that sickly, squalling, under-sized little thing they'd never allowed her to love. Baby had suffered a further convulsion – a teething fit, said Dr Adeney – and choked to death in her perambulator carriage in the Grove park.

Henrietta Sophia van der Kleve, aged fourteen months . . .

Her nursemaid – the same whose deafness had recommended her so well to Beatrice – because of that very deafness had heard nothing. Ah, but what tragic irony . . . the park full of spring sunlight, the trees bursting with new life, the nursemaid in her silent world, and the child being rocked in her pretty carriage, choking, dying . . .

And the mother, where was the mother? Climbing the cobbled streets of Shrewsbury on her lover's arm and stealing a little time of happiness in the company of strangers. It didn't make sense. But then, for Kitty nothing made sense any more. Her child was dead; and her lover, too, bidding her farewell, preferring some other . . .

"Would you leave us, please?" Oliver's voice broke the stillness of the room. "I wish to speak to my wife, alone. Would you mind – Beatrice? Dr Adeney?"

Kitty raised her head. They were looking at her still, even as they went through the door, looking at her out of the sides of their eyes; and then the door was closed again behind them and there was no one there but Oliver.

At times like this the mind skipped across the surface like a flat stone on water, refusing – unable – to face the yawning depths of darkness threatening to suck it down into near insanity. Her child was dead, and her adultery common knowledge; but to Kitty, just now it seemed of greater importance that she had left her reticule in the Seymours' carriage, that Beatrice had forbidden Harriet ever to enter the house again, that Angelina had been sent to stay with Mrs Russell and the eligible young Arthur (what diplomacy, what tact, what an eye to future advantage!)

"Well, madam – ?" Oliver's voice cut like steel across the space between them, and Kitty flinched a little. "What have you to say for yourself?"

What had she to say for herself. She gave the question her consideration. What was she expected to say? That she was sorry? That she regretted her actions? That she hoped for forgiveness?

"Come, you will make me an answer!" Even in anger his words were cold.

She twisted her fingers together and examined them with studied care. Yes, she ought to answer, she supposed; and she would, too, if only she could think of something to reply. He had tried to make her into the perfect wife, and she had proved herself imperfect; and at Miss Meyrick's Academy imperfection was a punishable offence for it showed the want of attention to duty. Ten strokes of the cane and a diet of bread and water . . . What punishment would Oliver exact?

"Tell me what response you require, sir." She kept her eyes lowered, her fingers entwined, her voice at the subservient level of tone which Miss Meyrick demanded. "Tell me, and I will oblige you."

This little show of what he took for insolence in the face of such monumental guilt excited his anger even further.

"Do not delude me with your play acting, madam – you can no longer come the innocent with me! I may have been blind in the past to your devious nature, but the scales have

dropped from my eyes now and I see you in the light of truth
exposed for what you are – a liar and a Jezebel."

Liar and Jezebel . . .

"You are not fit for decent society, madam. Not fit to
be under this roof. By your flagrant misconduct you have
besmirched the name of my family, exposed my household to
public ridicule and called into question my own personal
reputation and integrity. I am ashamed to own you as wife."

To own you as wife . . .

Oliver flung his words as though each were a separate shaft
of hurt calculated to cause Kitty the greatest wound he could
manage.

"I should have heeded Beatrice!" he continued, swinging
away in disgust. "By God, I wish now that I had! She warned
me against you from the start, counselled me to exercise some
caution before honouring you with my attention. I took you
from nothing – from the gutter and worse – I educated you at
my own expense and effort – and this is how you repay me,
by betraying every principle of honour and virtue with your
harlotry –"

Harlotry . . .

"You are the perfect example that one cannot make a silken
purse from a sow's ear. As my sister says, no doubt but that
you take after your mother, and I would have done you a
greater service had I had you trained for the profession of
whore."

Whore . . .

The blow to his pride, to his manhood, suffered by Oliver
through his young wife's adultery drove him on remorselessly,
bitterness and resentment pouring from him in an unleashed
torrent, as though by ridding himself of this poison which
cankered his system he might find some healing, some peace.

"How I can bring myself even to look upon you, God alone
in his mercy knows. You should be thankful indeed that you
have this chance to make your apology for what you have done
to my name and to my family. Therefore I ask you again,
madam – what have you to say in defence of yourself?"

He glanced across, his features rigid; and despite – perhaps
even because of – an anger which was divided by a hair's
breadth from some deeper emotion, he thought he had never
seen his wife appear more lovely, more desirable . . . a

Messalina, exposed now in her infamy and yet with the power to arouse a lust for possession that weakened a man into wanting her more than his very honour.

"Well – ? I am waiting. *What have you to say?*" The demand came again, emphatically. "Some word of repentance, surely? Some sign of contrition?"

"Is that what you wish, sir?"

"It is!"

"Then, indeed . . . indeed, I am sorry." Still that subservient tone, and still the eyes downcast, the hands clasped, just as Miss Meyrick had taught.

Oliver stared. "And what else? Or is that all?"

"What more do you want of me? I have said I am sorry. Is that not enough?"

"No, by the Lord, it is not! You think that one small word, so reluctantly uttered, can atone for the enormity of your abhorrent behaviour? You think a mere 'sorry' can wipe clean the slate of your conscience and restore you to my affections?"

"Nothing can wipe clean my conscience, sir. That has been my cross and my burden from the beginning."

"There, at least, is some small admission of guilt!"

"I should add also my apology, sir. My apology for being unable ever to love you. In that I have failed you as a wife." She might have been passing an observation upon the weather for all the expression there was in her voice.

This admission of her inability to care for him, in some strange way caused Oliver a greater anguish even than the knowledge of her adultery. She had given her love to Jonathan Rivers – thrown away upon that thief something which should have been kept sacrosanct within marriage for her husband. That was a betrayal for which he could never forgive her.

"And I am sorry, too . . . sorry . . . for Henrietta."

For a second the dreamlike monotony of Kitty's speech faltered; and sensing a chance to offer hurt for hurt, Oliver flung back quickly, viciously, "Sorry for a child you never wanted? Oh, spare me your hypocrisy! In view of all I have learned today, perhaps it's as well she's dead. Who knows what tainted bastard blood she may have inherited – like that other, yes, the one you miscarried, the one it was doubtless your intention to foist upon me as a legitimate heir, knowing well it could be some Rivers cuckoo in the family nest. Ah,

206

you need not deny it, madam –" as Kitty raised her head to look at him – "I have had the story in its entirety from your Miss Dobby, who thought that a full recitation of the details might procure her a reference before she handed in her notice."

Dobby? What, the indispensable, painstaking, circumspect Dobby? Kitty's mind skipped again across the surface, then shied away, refusing to accept the implications.

"It was a mistake, of course. The woman should have known better than try bargaining her own skin for yours." Oliver sounded a note of grim satisfaction. "The only reference she had from me once she'd finished her Judas account was an order to Nicholls to eject her on to the street – and with not even thirty pieces of silver in lieu of notice."

There was a moment's drawn-out, disbelieving silence.

"Dobby's – gone," Kitty said at last, more in the manner of statement than question.

"She has." As he spoke, Oliver turned and went to the bell-pull, and while waiting for his ring to be answered, continued, "But her loss should not discommode you unduly. You appear able to manage well enough without a maid's attendance – and facilities here are, shall we say, somewhat less primitive than in Shropshire."

Then, as the door opened – "Ah, Nicholls. Will you tell Miss Beatrice that Mrs van der Kleve is about to go up to her room, and would she request Perrins to ensure that Madam remains there until I order otherwise."

In an age when wives were regarded as their husbands' possessions, and women generally as having been created by the Almighty only slightly superior to dogs and horses, infidelity was viewed as not only shockingly wrong but downright wicked – an offence representing the betrayal of both Family and Religion, those twin pillars of respectability upon which Victorian society was built.

Even against such a moral climate, the discovery of his wife's adultery hit Oliver van der Kleve rather harder than it might many another husband. It was not only that she had allowed herself to be seduced by someone he'd employed in his own house, but that having shown herself so cold and unresponsive in their marriage bed, she had actually preferred to give herself – her body – her affection – to another man. It never occurred to him that his wife might have appreciated his own attentions better had he shown her some occasional expression of love and consideration. To a man like Oliver, consideration meant only weakness, and love was something he had taught himself long ago to forget.

All that concerned him was that Kitty had been unfaithful in heart and spirit as well as in the flesh; and in this rejection of himself, he suffered the reopening of a terrible wound, a wound received in childhood through an event which had happened in his sixth year and which had affected the young boy so badly as to mark the grown man for life.

Oliver van der Kleve had idolised his mother. To him she was a paragon among her sex. Tall and exquisitely stylish, with her classic features and curling chestnut hair she had been one of the leading beauties of Regency London, and in her son's adoring eyes the most wonderful woman alive. No social event of the Season was judged a success without her; her witty repartee and sharp-humoured intelligence made her the darling of the salons; and as a patroness of the Arts her circle of friends was both wide and extraordinarily varied.

From the day of his birth in 1825, Oliver's whole world had been centred upon this astonishing creature. Then, shortly before his sixth birthday, something occurred which would overturn that world entirely, destroying his trust and leaving him with an emotional hurt too deep ever to heal.

During her husband's periodic visits on business to the Continent, Georgiana van der Kleve had been in the habit during the Season of entertaining privately at their Chelsea house. In the early hours of one morning, awakened by unfamiliar sounds from her room below, young Oliver had gone down; and discovered his mother upon the great canopied bed, naked in the arms of one of her guests. The sight had frightened the child considerably. Afterwards he retained only a confused image of candlelight and shadow, white limbs gleaming, his mother's mewing cries, and the man hairy and dark like some savage animal upon her; but at the time he had thought she was being attacked, and rushed to pull her assailant from her.

What happened next was the recurrent nightmare which would stay to haunt his dreams. Like some goatish satyr the man leaped up and thrust him away; and to his consternation, instead of making her escape, his beloved mother turned upon him, her face ugly with anger – anger and something more, contorting her features into the frightening mask of a stranger. Oliver had never seen her thus before, and had stood uncertain, torn between the conflicting emotions of fear *for* her, and fear *of* her.

"Mama – ?" he cried out; and she had answered with words which seared themselves into his heart and mind for ever, words which were cruel and harsh and hurtful, telling him that he was a bad, naughty, wicked child to come sneaking into Mama's bedchamber, and that if he should tell Papa, something dreadful would happen – Mama would no longer love him and it would be all his own fault, for being such a nasty little boy.

He had gone back alone to the nursery, and wept.

In the days which followed, his mother behaved outwardly much as before, but young Oliver had the strangest, most terrible feeling that she had ceased to care for him; and this sudden exclusion from all he held most precious became twisted up in his mind with the nightmare scene in her room – as though love meant rejection, and man and woman's nakedness was all of a piece with punishment and pain.

Not long afterwards – a month, perhaps – Georgiana van der Kleve set London society by its ears when she eloped to Italy with her lover. Their affair, common knowledge within her own circle, had finally been discovered by her husband – though the identity of the informant remained conjecture. In his bewilderment Oliver was convinced she'd gone away because it was *he* she held to blame. Certainly, he never saw her again: his father, angry and extremely bitter at being exposed to the public odium of cuckoldry, told his young son the brutal facts – that his mother was a jade, a trollop, who'd abandoned home and family for the dubious charms of a second-rate opera singer. She would not be coming back; and her name was never to be mentioned beneath his roof again.

Nor was it. There was an acrimonious divorce, and Oliver and his sister Beatrice were removed from London to the house of a relative in Tunbridge Wells, to be reared by a succession of tutors and governesses. Much later, when he was twenty or so, he learned in a roundabout fashion that his mother had married her Italian lover and was now the Comtessa di something or other, with another son to pamper and pet.

But by that time, Oliver van der Kleve had hardened himself against hurt.

The Reverend Mr Edward Terris rested his elbows on the arms of the morning room chair and placed his plump fingers neatly together. Opposite, looking very tired and pale, he thought, Kitty van der Kleve waited in silence, her tension betraying itself in the upright way she sat on the edge of her seat.

"Well now, my dear," he began, clearing his throat unnecessarily and giving her one of his patronising little smiles, "this is an unpleasant duty I am called upon to perform. You may wonder why I am here in your husband's stead, but the fact of the matter is that Oliver – Mr van der Kleve – has asked me to discharge this task on his behalf – as his spiritual director, you understand – and therefore I feel that in these – ah, very painful and distressing circumstances, I can do no less than oblige."

It was really most tiresome of Oliver to expect the Church to do his dirty washing for him, the minister thought privately, examining Kitty in a speculative manner over the top of his pince-nez spectacles. But he could hardly refuse so generous a friend and patron of St Bride's . . .

"You do appreciate, I trust, my dear, the very unfortunate position in which you have placed yourself by your – ah, lamentable conduct?"

Kitty's eyes, dark-shadowed from the past two sleepless nights at Sion Place, regarded him with a kind of watchful, waiting defensiveness.

"I do appreciate my position, sir, yes."

"I am gratified to hear it. The acceptance of one's wrong-doing is the first step towards repentance of one's sins."

Mr Terris played a rapid tattoo with his fingertips and gave another, slightly more indulgent smile.

"Mr van der Kleve informs me that you have already sought forgiveness for your behaviour."

"I have said that I am sorry –"

"Exactly so! The fact that he feels disinclined at present to accept your apology is due to a belief that your appeal to him was motivated by a sense of guilt and not by any true sincerity. I must say, I have attempted to persuade him to show clemency

– as pastor I can do no less, indeed – but I recognise the strength of righteous anger which compels him to disregard my counsel at this time."

His listener made a slight inclination of the head, although whether it was in agreement, or whether simply in ac- knowledgment, Mr Terris could not say. Such a pity the silly girl had been tempted to misbehave as she had! The scandal it would cause once the affair became public knowledge could only redound to the bad odour and discredit of St Bride's where she was a regular parishioner. Why could she not have come to him, her spiritual adviser, for guidance when the itch of impurity first began to manifest itself in her tender flesh?

He cleared his throat again.

"No doubt you will wish to be informed, my dear, of your husband's intentions for your future –"

This was the distasteful part of the interview. Mr Terris laced his fingers together in an attitude of prayer and pursed his moist pink lips for a moment; then, drawing breath, launched himself upon the sentence.

"He desires you to know that his house is no longer your home, and that he expects you to be removed from it before his return tomorrow. You are to take with you nothing except a change of wardrobe and any personal effects which you brought with you at the time of your marriage. You are permitted to keep your wedding ring, but no other items of jewellery which Mr van der Kleve has bestowed upon you."

The recital was made in the minister's most dignified pulpit manner, as though to disassociate himself from too close an involvement in this act of banishment.

"Further, my dear, it is my painful duty to tell you that your husband intends at the earliest opportunity to consult his solicitor, with a view to bringing a suit for divorce on the grounds of your adultery, and citing Mr – ah, Mr Rivers as co-respondent."

The Reverend Mr Edward Terris's pink lips quivered a fraction. The shame, the disgrace of it all to St Bride's. *Such* a pity . . .

23

"I'd never ha' believed it of her, not Mrs van der Kleve. She was always such a quiet, mimsy-mannered sort o' lady."

Mrs Reynolds, Cook at Sion Place, put out a floury hand and scooped up water from a bowl on the table before her, dashing it with a flick of the fingers over the pastry she was kneading.

"But then they do say often as not it's the quiet 'uns as wants the watching. I mean, look at that Dobby – who'd ha' thought it, eh! Sitting here wi' us of an evening, full well knowing what was a-going on, yet never so much as a word of it slipping her lips. Unnatural, I call that."

Mrs Reynolds sounded quite aggrieved at this failure of Miss Dobby to acquaint the household staff with details of their mistress's 'gadding', as she called it.

"I dunno, I still think it's *ever* so romantic." Mary Ellen Martin, senior housemaid, looked up from mending the torn lace border of a white linen tray cloth. "I'd ha' fallen in love wi' Mr Rivers myself, given half a chance. Ooh, he was that handsome!"

"You mind your tongue, or the devil might have it." Cook threw a sharp eye round from the table. "It was him being so handsome as caused the trouble. She'd never ha' looked at him twice if there'd been nothing there to tickle her fancy. Aye, and I dare say he was bold wi' it, an' all. She should ha' known better, her a married woman not above a year wed."

"It was discontent that did it," put in Jem Randall. Unlike the others in the servants' kitchen, he had nothing to occupy him but sat lolling at his ease in Mr Nicholls's chair by the range fire, hands behind his head, feet up on the polished brass fender. Being Friday, it was Mr Nicholls's afternoon off, and in the butler's absence the young manservant was inclined to take liberties.

"If you ask my opinion, the fact o' the matter is that Mrs

van der Kleve wasn't happy – anybody wi' sense in their head could see that. She was the Master's wife but she wasn't allowed to be Missus here, and that was the cause of it all."

"Says you." Mrs Reynolds lifted the ball of dough and slapped it down again on the table, puffing out a fine dust of flour across the surface. "She should ha' kept to her place when she come here first and recognised Miss Beatrice was in charge."

"But Missus was given the keys –" Mary Ellen started to argue.

"Oh, aye, I'll grant you Missus was given the keys – and look what happened –" there was another slap of the dough. "In no time at all she'd made Rosie Maguire her personal maid, and who knows but what she mightn't ha' promoted the gardener's lad to footman if Miss Beatrice hadn't gone to see Master demanding to have them keys back for herself."

"It was a mistake, was that. He should never ha' let her have her way," was Jem's response. "The Master would ha' done better to leave things as they were 'stead o' chopping and changing around. It put Mrs van der Kleve in a bad position, as though she weren't to be trusted."

"And the same thing happened wi' Baby, an' all," Mary Ellen came in again. "Why, no sooner was the poor little mite born than Miss Beatrice went and took over. It's as though she can't a-bear the young Missus to have anything of her own."

"Aye. You're probably right there," agreed Jem. "I don't wonder things have turned out as they have."

Mrs Reynolds failed to share this point of view.

"Two wrongs never did make a right, and you can't tell me otherwise," she declared flatly. "There's a deal o' difference atween suffering spite and worse, and going making up lies and a-carrying on wi' another man. Mrs van der Kleve should ha' held her tongue and minded her place, and not put herself in the path o' being tempted. No decent young married woman would do what she went and did, gallivanting off to foreign parts wi' a drawing master."

This was said as though a drawing master's profession somehow worsened the offence considerably.

"To think of it! The very thing! And getting that Miss Seymour involved in her misdeedious ways, putting her up to telling such downright falsehoods. Master's well rid o' such a baggage if that's how she's a-going to carry on."

"*Has* he got rid of her, d'you reckon, Mrs Reynolds?" This came from little Susan Smith, the scullery maid, who had been all this time standing ready with the flour dredger and listening open-mouthed to the conversation.

"That's none o' your business, my wench." With a sharp jerk of the head, Cook indicated an earthenware crock on the table, and when it was passed to her, lifted the kneaded dough and put it within, covering it with a cloth.

"Now set this aside by the oven to rise. And you, Jem Randall, get your boots off my fender! I don't polish them bars for you to rub blacking all over."

"But *has* he got rid o' Missus, Mrs Reynolds?" young Susan persisted, her curiosity risking a cuff round the ear. "Won't she come back again, d'you think?"

It was Jem who answered that. Removing his feet to the floor, he crossed one leg over the other. "She's gone off wi' Miss Seymour. Abroad somewhere."

"Oh? Who told you that?" Mary Ellen was ahead of Cook in getting the question in first.

"The Seymours' groom."

"She's off abroad? Are you sure? I mean, she took no more'n a change o' clothing wi' her when she left here Sunday. All the rest of her things are still hanging up in the wardrobes."

Jem shrugged. "I'm only repeating what I heard."

"Abroad, eh." Mrs Reynolds wiped her hands on her pinafore skirt, and there was a peculiarly knowing expression on her plump, lardy face. "And no clothes nor nothing wi' her. Now what does that suggest, I ask." And without waiting for response – "I'll tell you. Sounds to me as though Mrs van der Kleve's been told to swing her hook elsewhere. Aye. She come here to this house wi' hardly a stitch on her back, and that's how she's a-gone. Master's shown her the doorstep."

"Which should satisfy Miss Beatrice nicely." Jem Randall got up from the butler's chair and straightened his striped waistcoat with a little tug. "Well, good luck to her an' all, says I –"

"You'd best not let Miss Beatrice hear you a-speaking like that. Nor Jane Perrins, neither!"

"Oh, I don't intend to, Mrs Reynolds. But there's no rules

against thinking, and what I think is that the Missus is better off out of it. God knows, she had little enough here to bring her much happiness, so mebbe it's high time things started looking up for her elsewhere."

If Harriet had acted a little more prudently, if she hadn't encouraged Kitty to go off with Jonathan Rivers – and not only encouraged her, but actually *persuaded* her, provided her with the *means* – then dear Kitty wouldn't have been in the scrape she was now. And what a scrape! It couldn't possibly be worse, Harriet told herself. If one were to write the whole thing down, it would read so much like a Greek tragedy that no one would ever believe such a tale to be true. Thank heavens Dr Adeney had had the good sense to see what a state Kitty was in and offer to take her into his own home, dear man; and when Oliver van der Kleve made that impossible, at least the doctor had the further good sense to acquaint Harriet herself of the situation and solicit her assistance.

But *of course* she wanted to help! Dear Lord, the whole unhappy episode was all her fault entirely, for if she hadn't interfered as she had (albeit much against her better judgment) Kitty would not have had the excuse to go off to Shropshire. And who knows but that if she'd remained at Sion Place, and instead of some deaf nursemaid, been herself the one to take Henrietta into the park – why, that poor wretched little baby might never have choked to death! So there, as well, was a further blame to lay at Harriet's door – little wonder, she told herself, that she felt so terribly, *terribly* guilty about it all.

She was in hot water with her parents, too, for the way she'd misled everyone; and being on bad terms at home was what had decided her finally to make the decision she had: that she should take both Kitty and herself together out of the way for a while, abroad somewhere; yes, abroad – to Baden-Baden. What an excellent idea. If Kitty were about to suffer a nervous collapse, as Dr Adeney feared, then what better place to have one; and it would make Harriet feel *so* much easier in her own conscience to see that her friend received the very best treatment available . . .

"Kitty dear, if I've told you this once, I've told you a dozen times. You are *not* beholden to me!"

Harriet was prepared to get quite cross. Tilting her parasol against the sharp bright April sunlight, she threw a glance of annoyance at her friend beside her on the terrace bench.

"I appreciate your feelings about accepting charity, but this is *not* charity. Odd though it may seem, you are here as my chaperone, and I wish you would learn to be a little more gracious about accepting what it's my pleasure to give you. Now if I hear one word more about debt or repayment, I warn you, I shall be mightily offended."

Then, as though to soften the sternness of her words, she reached across and adjusted the plaid blanket covering Kitty's knees, tucking it closer around.

The pair had been staying as guests at Baden's Hotel Adler for almost a fortnight now, and the fact that Harriet was bearing all the expense had become a bone of some contention between them. That Harriet was well able to afford it, having at twenty-one inherited a private income of her own from her grandfather's estate, was not the point: Kitty had not a penny-piece to contribute, and therefore felt herself a burden, a state of mind which tended to aggravate the low spirits in which nervous exhaustion had left her.

Thanks to the excellent medical treatment she'd received here in Baden-Baden, the threatened collapse which Dr Adeney feared had been avoided, but only narrowly, and at some cost to Kitty's physical well-being. That healthy and wholesome young creature who had entered upon marriage two years earlier was now almost as pale and delicate looking as any of the tubercular invalids coughing their lives away in the spa's sanatorium; but the young Herr Doktor attending Kitty was satisfied with her progress, as he informed Harriet, and the prescribed rest cure, together with peace of mind, should complete her healing – given time.

In view of Harriet's adopted role as her friend's nurse-companion and benefactress, there was a touch of irony in the fact that being the married woman of the two, it should be Kitty who was chaperone (for of course, the laws of society dictated that no single lady might travel unaccompanied, but required the 'protection' of a male relative or married person of her own sex). This reversal of their roles had occasioned some weak humour of late, since Harriet invariably went out alone, not caring – as she said – two pins whether her reputation was ruined or no.

Having despatched herself with what some might consider unmaidenly haste to renew acquaintance with Peter Hoffmann, she had dined with him twice at the Adler so far, and attended the Stadtopera as his guest to see Wagner's *Lohengrin* (currently much in vogue here).

"If anyone should feel guilty, it's I," she said now, continuing the theme of her conversation. "I leave you alone evening after boring evening whilst I'm out enjoying myself, and I don't believe you've complained once."

"Of what should I complain?" Kitty responded with something like her old spirit. "It would be a poor friend who'd begrudge you this new-found happiness."

"A poor friend, indeed! If Mama were here to chaperone me, I know how it would be – she'd insist on keeping to me like a shadow wherever I went, and weighing up every word and gesture of Peter's to be picked over anon. Why, he admitted to me recently that his reason for not responding to my letters was knowing Mama would expect to be shown everything he wrote. So you see what a priceless service you are rendering me, Kitty dear!"

She gave the other's hand a quick squeeze.

"Now let us not quarrel any more over pounds and pence. The little I've done for you is being repaid in kind with something of far, far greater worth – so the debt is mine, not yours."

There was a gusty sigh and she looked away, her thoughts full of her Beloved, her gaze ignoring the splendid vista from the hotel terrace and searching out instead that part of the New Town below where he would be busy at this hour of the afternoon in his clinic.

"Has Dr Hoffmann passed any comment upon my – my situation?" asked Kitty after a time, interrupting.

"Medically, do you mean?"

"No. I referred to my personal situation. My plight, I suppose."

Harriet's expressive face screwed itself into a look of instant hurt. "You surely don't think I've been making it my business to discuss a thing like that with him?"

"You may have mentioned it, I thought . . . in passing."

"Well, if I did, it *was* only in passing."

"And what was his observation?"

Harriet became slightly evasive. "He knows that you're here for treatment, of course."

"Of course. And – ?"

"Oh, very well! If you wish to have his exact words, they were this – 'in love, as in all other matters, experience is a doctor who comes too late.' It's a quotation from somewhere or other."

The silk-fringed parasol was given an agitated twirl. In Harriet's opinon, Kitty should let bygones remain bygones: in her state it was not at all healthy to hark back too much to the recent past, and she oughtn't to be encouraged.

"'Experience is a doctor who comes too late' . . ." Her words were repeated slowly, almost pensively. Then – "What did he mean by that, do you suppose?"

"Why, I hardly know. Have you had enough of the terrace now, dear? Shall we go inside before the air begins to cool?"

"No, let's stay just a while longer, please. The view is so beautiful, and the sun is quite warm still. Did he . . . did he say anything more, your Herr Doktor?"

"Upon what subject?"

"Oh, Harriet, don't be so stuffy! I know you consider it morbid of me to keep dwelling upon what's gone, but I'm not going to pretend none of it ever happened. That would be self-deceiving. It simply isn't possible to wipe away two whole years from one's mind and wish oneself back in the past again, to start at the beginning and put right all the wrong –"

"Kitty –" The parasol was snapped shut with a decisive click. "Kitty, you are allowing yourself to become agitated, and that really will not do. Now I agree that you cannot forget. But as Peter observed, it's difficult to heal a wounded heart if you will insist on breaking it afresh with memories. *Das Grund des Morgens legen wir heute –*" Harriet quoted again. "We lay tomorrow's foundations today."

"Is there one word of his that you *don't* recall?" asked the other, prepared to smile at such a display of adulation.

"Hardly a one. But then, he speaks such great sense. He tells me, by the by, that he would like to meet you."

"Indeed? As an interesting study in pernicious melancholia?"

"Of course not. The interest is purely social. After all, my dear, you are the nearest thing I have to a sister."

Kitty was immensely touched by this unprompted statement. Reaching over, she took her friend's hand in both hers and held it tightly.

"Oh, Harriet – I am the most undeserving of creatures to have a friendship as generous and loving as yours."

"Fiddlesticks. Don't you remember, at Miss Meyrick's awful academy, when you were the charity child and I was poor pitied 'Peg Leg', how we always had each other to offer some small crumb of comfort? We swore we would be friends for ever, whatever betide us – and so we are."

They smiled at one another.

"You will like Peter, I know," Harriet continued. "And more importantly, I want you to heed his advice. He has a most astute mind and will give you his impartial opinion, so I hope you will feel able to speak to him in full confidence about your domestic situation . . . and what action you should take to defend yourself."

Kitty knew to what this referred. Since arriving in Baden-Baden there had been a letter from Jaggers & Youngman, the London solicitors with whom her husband Oliver dealt. It had been sent by Mr Humphrey Jaggers, senior partner – and, ironically in the circumstances, one of baby Henrietta's godparents – to inform her that his firm had been instructed by their client to proceed with the gathering of preliminary evidence, and suggesting that Mrs van der Kleve might wish to take legal advice and seek proper representation for herself.

When she had been told, that dreadful day at Sion Place, that her husband wished for a divorce, Kitty had wanted only to oblige. What did it matter that she would be disgraced, publicly shamed as an adulteress, the fault – the guilt – was hers; and at the time she'd had no thought for anything beyond that, certainly not for her own future, or the possibility of defending herself against Oliver's action.

Like a sleep-walker almost, dazed by grief and shock and bodily weariness, she had gone upstairs to start packing the few things allowed her; and there, tucked beneath the embroidered cover of her Bible, she'd come upon a note.

It was from Amelia Dobby, obviously scribbled in haste and

left behind the previous day, after the woman's peremptory dismissal from service.

"Madam –" it read – "you know what has happened. He is a harsh man and he will have his pound of flesh. Well, here is something that will interest you. Mr van der Kleve is keeping a woman in London. Her name is Sadie Collins, at rooms near St Paul's, and I know this to be the truth. – A. D."

Kitty had been in no state of mind just then to take in the full import of this information; but – *keeping a woman* – ? Surely that could mean only one thing. If Oliver indeed had a mistress, then the fact cast a very different interpretation upon her own position: he meant to divorce her for adultery, when he himself had apparently been committing the selfsame transgression. The hypocrisy of it did not bear thinking about.

Dobby's revenge in return for being dismissed (for that was what this was) had presented Kitty with a trump card. Oliver was threatening to name Jonathan Rivers in his lawsuit. Very well. In her own defence she could threaten in turn to bring a counter suit, citing the unknown Sadie Collins as co-respondent.

But did she dare?

Perhaps more to the point – did she *want* to?

24

A few miles to the south of Frant village, amid a rolling counterpane countryside of fields and copses and little brooks, lay Loxley Wood. It was a farming community composed mainly of labourers and their families, and was one of those hamlets still common in mid-Victorian England where change had come but slowly over the centuries and the Industrial Revolution gone almost unnoticed. Everyone worked on the land, from childhood to bent old age, the daily rate of pay being so low that death itself alone was regarded as being sufficient good reason to stay home abed.

Several of the farms had originally belonged to the Stillborne estate, but that had been sold off piecemeal over the years and by the time of Mr Reuben Stillborne's decease in 1853 there remained here only one farm and a row of dwellings known as Agricola Cottages to be inherited by his grandchildren, Harriet Seymour and her brother William. During young Will's absence abroad in the American States, the farm was managed by an agent, and Agricola Cottages rented to tenant workers. And it was to one of these, number three, that Kitty van der Kleve came to live at the end of April 1867 upon her return from Baden-Baden.

Until a month or so previously, number three had been occupied by an elderly labourer, a widower. Unhappily for him, the old chap had had the ill-luck to lose a leg to gangrene and was carted off to the workhouse infirmary, where he'd not lingered long before following after his wife into the grave.

Harriet had felt most awkward about offering Kitty such lowly accommodation, but as Kitty herself pointed out, it was a matter of Hobson's Choice: being both penniless and homeless, she'd be more than grateful for any kind of a roof above her head, no matter how humble. Her only concern was that she might be depriving some labourer's family of house-room; but number three Agricola Cottages had something of an odd history, and the Stillborne agent reported to Harriet that his farm people had in the past appeared disinclined to live there.

Harriet had made some enquiry into this, and uncovered the fact that the place was thought to be haunted, though how and by what, no one could tell her. The only thing of any relevance to come to light was the suicide of a young woman in the 1830s, an event still fairly fresh in the memories of older folk living in Loxley Wood at that time. It was a tragedy common enough in rural areas: the girl had been seduced by a faithless lover, and having borne his bastard child, smothered the babe and then hanged herself from the hearth beam.

Kitty, when told, thought this story a sad one rather than sinister. What she found a little more disquieting was not the cottage's reputation so much as the attitude of her new neighbours, for none of them knew quite what to think of the lovely and ladylike creature residing at number three, with neither husband to bed nor work to hand, and they tended to treat such a misfit among them with open suspicion. Nor did the fact that she was visited so often by Miss Seymour and shown such deference by the agent, Mr Dutton, lessen their distrust. She was plainly one of 'them' – (them being any class above their own) – and it didn't seem right she should be living here among folk who weren't of her kind. That someone should want to better themself in life and move up a rung of the social ladder, this they could understand; but that someone of superior class should choose to lower themself to the level of common labourers, was felt to be an unnatural betrayal of the proper order of things, and generated uneasiness.

Consequently, Kitty's first weeks at Agricola Cottages might have been passed in friendless ostracism had she not had Harriet there so frequently with food and company, and Mr Dutton's man to replenish her woodstore. There were other matters, too, to occupy her mind: acting upon the advice of Dr Peter Hoffmann, she had approached a solicitor upon her return to the area to request legal representation; and from the evidence of Amelia Dobby's letter it appeared she'd be able to show good cause to the courts for her action in bringing a counter suit for adultery against her husband.

As Messrs Alleyne Walker explained, there would be little difficulty in verifying the existence of Sadie Collins: a few discreet enquiries through an agency was all that was required. The problem might possibly arise that Miss Collins refused to co-operate in providing statements regarding the exact nature of her relationship with Mr van der Kleve; in which case it might become necessary to pursue other channels of investigation. In their experience, however, these matters were soon resolved.

Thus, Kitty's original decision not to contest Oliver's action for divorce was now set aside; and Messrs Alleyne Walker had written on the last day of April to Jaggers & Youngman in the City, informing them accordingly and naming a Miss Sadie Collins, of Gloucester Buildings, Cloak Lane off Cannon Street, as co-respondent in their client's counter suit.

Maytime in the Sussex countryside was beautiful this year. Each day held a balmy mildness that made work in the fields a pleasure instead of a penance, and the nights were soft and warm, and so still that the air was like velvet to the cheek.

Kitty walked a good deal, taking the paths from Loxley Wood into the country roundabout, for the first time in her life truly alone and, except in matters financial, her own mistress. These pleasant hours of solitude completed the healing of a bruised and battered spirit: there was something in the burgeoning woods and spring-fresh fields that communicated itself, something in the reflection of sunlight on leaves and the scent of bluebells flowering in a haze-drift of colour that took away the dull smart of her unhappiness, and replaced it with peace.

She would return to Agricola Cottages of an evening tired out but content, often to find Harriet there, or Mr Dutton the agent, to share a half-hour's company and conversation; and had it not been for the forthcoming legal action hanging its fire above her head, these days at Loxley Wood might have been the most tranquil Kitty had ever known.

Coming back one Sunday from a walk as far afield as Shatterford which had kept her out since midmorning, she had prepared herself something for a meal, and afterwards taken her rush-seat chair to sit in the open doorway and enjoy the evening's sunset. A group of women were gathered round the pump on the village green across the way, standing with their

223

water pails beside them, arms crossed, heads together in conversation; and though they looked over their shoulders in Kitty's direction from time to time, not one called out to acknowledge her.

After a while she went back inside the cottage and lit the oil lamps, intending to read for an hour or so before she went to bed. The people here would warm to her eventually, she told herself: hers was a strange face in a place unused to strangers, and she did not hold them to blame for their unfriendliness.

It was very quiet indoors, very still. The lamp flames swayed to and fro, casting a pattern of shadows against the walls. Dusk crept slowly in at the unshuttered window, and across the green she could see faint squares appearing as one by one other lamps were lit in other windows, spilling their homely light into the gloom.

Whether it was her imagination or not, Kitty could not say, but there seemed an unfamiliar atmosphere within the cottage this evening – a listening, waiting, watchfulness that disturbed her very slightly. Several times she glanced round as though half-expecting to see something behind her in the room; but there was nothing except the shadows, no sound except the whispering flicker of flame tongues.

She rested her book on her lap, her attention wandering to the age-blackened beams overhead in the low ceiling. One of them, near the open hearth, was fitted with a bacon hook for smoking sides of ham. Kitty stared at it for several minutes, and the thought came upon her that it must have been from this very hook that the girl in the story hanged herself. The notion caused a tiny shiver of apprehension to run down her spine: how easy it was to frighten oneself! She picked up her book again and tried to immerse her mind in Mrs Gaskell's *Lizzie Leigh*, but the sensation of being watched grew stronger little by little, and in her imagination she began to see the shape of a body suspended in the lamplight's glimmer – an outline, nothing more, but swinging very slowly from the bacon hook.

Come, this will never do, she told herself sharply – she was allowing her fancy to play tricks with shadows – and getting up, she moved one of the lamps to the hearth where its comforting reflection on the empty beam quietened her fear.

There was no clock in the room by which to tell the time,

so it might have been ten or even twenty minutes later that Kitty became aware of a new disturbance. At first she imagined there must be a child crying somewhere outside in the darkness; but then it seemed to come nearer, yet oddly growing no louder, until it was just beyond her in the little scullery, not a child's cry but a woman's, low and plaintive, and so full of a dreadful sadness that Kitty's heart faltered at the sound.

"Who's there?" she called out, jumping to her feet and snatching up a lamp from the table. "Who's there? Who is it?"

Going to the scullery door she pushed it ajar. The place stood empty – empty and now eerily silent. For a moment she stood there uncertain, the muffled beat of her blood loud in her ears, nervousness making the lamp tremble in her hand; and then the sobbing seemed to break out once more, but behind her in the other room, as though there were someone there where she herself had been but a second before.

"Who is it?" she cried out again, not daring to turn for fear of what she might see. "What do you want?"

The echo of her words came back as if from far away in the long and drawn-out whisper of a sigh; then the sigh itself faded upon the air into stillness. Almost in the very next moment, or so it seemed, there was someone knocking at the outer door and a voice – a man's voice – calling, "It's only me, ma'am. Michael Dutton. Can I trouble you just a minute?"

Kitty ran from the scullery to fling the door open, panic lending speed to her heels; never more glad in her life to see a friendly face there upon the step.

"Oh, Mr Dutton – Mr Dutton – please come in, do!"

The farm agent was taken aback by this welcome. "Hey up, what's wrong?" he asked, following her back inside and shutting the door. "You look as though you've taken fright at some'at."

He was a short stocky man with avuncular features set in a jovial, weather-reddened countenance, but just now his expression betrayed honest concern.

"Are you all right, ma'am?"

"Oh, Mr Dutton –" she turned and clung to his arm. "There's something here – I heard it only a minute ago – a woman weeping – oh, how it alarmed me!"

"Now then, now then –" he patted her hand in a kindly

manner. "No need to take on. I'll soon have it rooted out, don't you worry, whatever it is."

Taking the lamp she was still holding, he gave a quick glance around.

"It seemed to be in the scullery," Kitty said breathlessly, keeping close beside him as he started to move.

"The scullery, eh? Right –"

The lamplight outlined his comfortable broad shape against the wall as he went across and made a cursory examination of the inner room.

"No, there's nothing to see there," he said, coming out again. "Might it have been upstairs, mebbe?"

"I heard it here, I'm certain." She shook her head in emphasis. "It was someone weeping – sobbing – I *know* it was."

Mr Dutton gave her a searching look. "I'll go up and make sure anyway, ma'am. Just to set your mind at rest."

Kitty forced herself to sit down at the table, hands clenched in her lap, listening to his reassuring footsteps on the narrow stairs, and then moving overhead, across the bedroom and back.

"Belikes it was an owl," he said, when he'd rejoined her once more. "Perched on your chimney, mebbe. The sound 'ld carry down."

Setting the lamp on the table, he pulled out a chair, and at her little nod of invitation seated himself opposite.

"I think I know the difference between an owl and a woman in distress, Mr Dutton," Kitty said defensively. "I'm told . . . I'm told this cottage is haunted –"

"Oh, you don't want to listen to village tales, ma'am. It's old wives' gossip, that's what. I'm sorry Miss Harriet thought fit to mention it to you, you here alone at night, an' all."

"But someone hanged themself . . . a young woman."

"Aye. A time back, they did. Meself, I don't believe in ghosts." The agent stretched his leather-gaitered legs out before him and tucked his thumbs into his waistcoat pockets, the picture of stolid reality.

After a moment he went on, "It's you being all on your own that's brought me round this evening, as it happens. I was up at the farm earlier, and a gentleman come by asking for you by name, wanting to know where it was he could find you."

"A gentleman – ? Did he say what his business was?"

Mr Dutton shook his head. "It was Izzard spoke to him, and he never thought to enquire till t'other had gone."

"Oh." Kitty gave a small frown. "Then I wonder who it could be?"

"That's what I thought, meself. You're not expecting any visitors, ma'am?"

"No."

"Ah. Then it's a good thing I thought to warn you. Now he knows where you're living, this gentleman might be back. Best you lock your doors, if you'll take my advice."

The thought of being locked inside with the disembodied spirit of a suicide frightened Kitty rather more than some flesh and blood stranger seeking her whereabouts.

"It may only have been a person calling on behalf of my solicitor," she ventured.

"Solicitors nor their clerks work of a Sunday, ma'am," Mr Dutton reminded her practically. "Leastways, none that I know of." He gave her another of his looks. "Don't mind me asking, but you're not a-feared to be left here, are you?"

And before she could answer – "If there's anything untoward happens, just you slip round to next door and get 'em to send their lad up to the farm after me."

"Thank you. I will."

"Aye, well don't forget."

Mr Dutton set his hands on his knees and rose heavily to his feet. "Folk round here might seem a bit sidy and suspicious, but they'll not deny their help where it's needed."

Kitty rose in turn to see him to the door.

"It was good of you to call," she said, raising the latch. "I hope I didn't appear too foolish . . . alarming myself as I did."

The agent began a reply; but whatever it was as he went through the open door died in the saying. Something beyond in the moonlit darkness had claimed his sudden attention. Raising herself to look past his shoulder, Kitty saw the outline of a man standing there a short way along the path.

"Now then –" Mr Dutton called out angrily, squaring himself to take a pace forward down the step, "so you're back again, are you? Mebbe you won't mind stating what your business is at this hour?"

The figure came forward into the ring of light shed by the

cottage lamps. As she recognised the features, Kitty's hand went to her throat; and then she said as calmly as she could, "It's quite all right, Mr Dutton. This gentleman happens to be my husband —"

25

Oliver van der Kleve's presence in that small cottage room was almost overpowering. Refusing Kitty's polite invitation to be seated, he stood in front of the fireless hearth, his riding crop still tucked beneath one arm, hands thrust into his breeches' pockets. The only concession he had made to courtesy was to remove his curly-brimmed hat and toss it aside on the table.

"So –" he said, looking about him in a scornful fashion, "this is what you have come to. No doubt it suits you better to live as one of the labouring class."

"At least the way I live is of my own choosing," Kitty answered bravely, determined that her husband should not see into what a state of nerves she had been thrown by his startling and totally unexpected appearance out of the night.

He gestured with his head towards the door. "I observe that your choice of male company grows no better –"

"If you are referring to Mr Dutton, he is the farm agent here, and has been kind enough to render me service."

"Indeed. Which is why, doubtless, he was in your bed-chamber but a short while ago."

Kitty's face flushed red at the insinuation. "He was there at my request –" she began.

"Oh, I'm sure! Had I arrived a little sooner, I might even have caught the gentleman *in flagrante delicto*."

"Had you arrived a little sooner, sir, you would have found me here alone. Mr Dutton preceded you by fifteen minutes at the most."

This suggestion that there might be anything improper between herself and the agent roused Kitty to a spirited display of self-defence. Her chin went up.

"If you have come here to sneer and jeer and draw base assumptions from a perfectly blameless circumstance, then I hope that at least you will have the good manners to leave again immediately and trouble me no further. Mr Dutton has a care for my welfare and safety, and that is all."

"So I noticed when he bristled up at me just now." Oliver's scornful tone was tinged with a note of cynicism. "What a good thing, my dear Catherine, that you drew him off when you did, or there might have been blood shed. I was so very touched to hear you acknowledge me still as your husband."

"Whilst you remain my husband, sir, how else should I acknowledge you?"

"My, my, we have grown little claws that scratch! It is remarkable what a metamorphosis may be effected by the continental air. And I had supposed that you were travelling abroad for the sake of your health – ah well."

"It pleases you to mock me. Is that why you troubled to seek me here in person – so that you could make my situation a butt for your ill-humour?" Kitty's generous mouth was drawn white with defiance. She had no idea what had brought her husband to Loxley Wood – and at such an uncivil hour – but she refused to give him the satisfaction of knowing how greatly his presence intimidated her.

"I really think you should go," she went on. "No purpose can be served by our conversation. If there is anything you wish to discuss, then perhaps it would be better to do so through my solicitors."

"'My solicitors' –" Oliver mocked her words. "How very high and haughty we have grown. As a matter of fact, my dear, it is solicitors which have brought me on this little social errand."

He reached a hand inside his riding-coat pocket and produced a flat envelope, which he threw down on to the table. "From Humphrey Jaggers," he said briefly.

"So? What has any communication from Mr Jaggers to do with me?" Kitty made no attempt to take it up but remained seated where she was at the other side of the table.

"Oh, but it has a great deal to do with you. I understand from this letter that you intend to bring a counter suit for divorce on the grounds of my own adultery."

"Yes. That is so."

"And citing Miss Collins as the co-respondent."

"Yes."

"Damn it –" Oliver snatched the crop from under his arm

and brought it down in sudden anger against the side of his leather knee-boot. "Damn it, Catherine, have you not considered the consequences? Would you ruin my professional reputation by having my name dragged through the gutter press?"

"*Your* reputation? *Your* name?" For a moment Kitty was speechless. Then, recovering herself, she flung back – "It seems to me, sir, that you take a very blinkered view of this divorce. You are as much guilty of the act of adultery as I am. At least I admitted my own involvement, while you – you kept silent, hoping no doubt to appear the injured party even though yours was the graver offence."

"*Mine* was the graver –?" He took a step forward, his shadow in the lamplight spilling across the wall behind her.

"Yes! My affair with Jonathan Rivers lasted but so many months, whereas you had been keeping this – this Miss Collins as your mistress even before our marriage."

"I see I must needs educate you in the way of the world, my dear." Oliver's voice took on a silky smoothness. "I have done no more than many another gentleman by keeping a woman in a private arrangement. Society accords us that privilege. But you, madam, you were a wife and mother, and as such you deliberately – wantonly – betrayed each and every value placed upon those roles."

"What hypocrisy!"

"It is the way things are, and you would have done better to recognise that fact before you chose to oppose me. I fear you were not well advised."

Kitty shook her head and looked away. "What's done is done," she answered quietly, "and I see no point in raking over it. We have said to each other all that there is to say on the matter."

"I think not. I want you to withdraw your petition to the courts."

"Oh – indeed? And if I did, then would you withdraw yours also?"

"That is what I have come here to discuss with you."

Suddenly the whole tone of this confrontation between them seemed to change. Oliver reached for a chair and sat down.

"Come, Catherine, let us behave like civilised people," he said, throwing his riding crop on to the table beside Mr

Jaggers's letter. "I will admit . . . yes, I will admit that I may have been at some fault in continuing my association with Sadie Collins."

Kitty watched his face. He appeared to be fighting some inward struggle with himself, and she could only guess what an effort it must have cost him to put that self-blame into words.

"The relationship is now at an end," he went on again after a moment. "I want you to know that. I have made – shall we say, other arrangements for Miss Collins and I shall not be seeing her again. There, I have made a clean breast of the situation so that you may judge for yourself whether or not you wish still to proceed against me."

Kitty digested this information in silence.

"Well – ?" he prompted with sudden impatience, vexed by the lack of response. "Have I not made myself sufficiently clear?"

"Yes, indeed."

"And – ?"

"And it would seem that we are both now in the same position as one another. My relationship with Jonathan Rivers is ended, and yours with Miss Collins. Yet adultery has been committed on both sides, and the guilt is equal – so why should it be I who must withdraw my petition, and not you?"

"I have told you! I cannot risk public notoriety and the damage it might do my reputation in the City. The name of van der Kleve Lindemanns is too well known for the press to ignore their chance to make a meal of a contested suit. And think of the loss of confidence it might inspire in our clients! *They* will hardly take well to the spectacle of one of their directors figuring in some acrimonious divorce case."

"Perhaps you should have considered all this," Kitty said calmly, "before you threw me out of your house."

Oliver stared at her. "What has happened to you, Catherine? You have changed."

"Because I choose to defend myself? I may still be your wife, but I owe you nothing now –" she marvelled at the levelness of her tone – "so if you have come to bargain with me, sir, then you do so at a waste of your own breath."

"My God, you *have* changed." There was something almost like admiration for her in the way he looked.

For a few moments neither spoke. The night wind had started to rise outside and its thin moan could be heard in the chimney, recalling to Kitty's fancy the plaintive sounds which had so frightened her earlier. Upstairs in the bedroom, the rattle of a loose casement added itself to the stillness.

She shivered a little.

"My dear —" Oliver leaned forward in his chair, resting his arms on the table. "I cannot forgive, nor forget, the way you chose to misconduct yourself. But in view of the circumstances, I am prepared to take you back again as my wife."

Now it was her turn to stare. "You mean . . . you mean, you would not proceed with your intention to divorce me?"

He seemed to hesitate, as though there were some final inner decision he must wrestle with.

Then he nodded. "I suppose that is what I came here to say tonight. No, let me continue —" as she made to interrupt — "I have been turning the whole matter over and over in my mind this last day or so, since receiving Humphrey Jaggers's letter. I am a proud man, Catherine. I make no bones about it. Your infidelity was an affront to all I hold myself to be, both publicly and in private. But by the same token I will admit that my own actions have not been entirely guiltless . . . and therefore . . . therefore perhaps we should each be acting in the best interests of the future if we allowed that guilt to cancel itself out."

He hesitated again; and then, awkwardly, reached his hand towards her across the table.

"What do you say? Will you come back to me? Shall we wipe the slate clean and begin afresh?"

Oliver's second thoughts about proceeding with his action for divorce had not been entirely prompted by considerations for his public reputation. True, the City tended not to like scandal, whether financial or domestic; but any slight tarnishing of the van der Kleve name resulting from a messy court case would have been forgotten within the year, and the Stock Market could easily absorb the slight ripples left in its wake.

The fact of the matter was that Kitty's absence from his life had made Oliver realise for the first time that he needed her. While she had been there at Sion Place he had grown accustomed to her presence, used to the sight of her face, the sound of her voice, that faint trace of her scent upon the air of their private rooms. And then, suddenly – nothing; his explosion of rage and jealousy had removed her as effectively as if she'd been dead, and this loss of everything that was familiar about his young wife affected Oliver in a way he had never thought possible.

He missed her. That was the truth of it.

His first reaction upon learning that she knew of Sadie Collins's existence had been one of extreme annoyance that this part of his personal life should have been exposed. But hard on the heels of annoyance had come a feeling of some shame, that had he not neglected his wife so often for his City affairs and his mistress, she might not have been tempted to stray into seduction by the likes of such a one as Jonathan Rivers.

A few nights ago he had dined at his club with Humphrey Jaggers – as well as his legal adviser, a friend of long standing – and candidly asked the other's opinion: should he proceed with this divorce, or should he not?

"In such a case, the argument falls either way," Mr Jaggers had replied. "The decision rests entirely on yourself. If you take Catherine back to live again as your wife, can you be sure she will not repeat her misconduct upon some future occasion. In other words, my dear Oliver, can you trust her? That is the crux of it. And to answer the question, you must first ask yourself another: how far was your own behaviour contributory to her adultery. *Facinus, quos inquinat aequat.* Which is to say, guilt places on a level those whom it contaminates."

Could he trust Kitty again? Oliver's first immediate response had been an emphatic no; but then, thinking about it later, he had found himself inclined to be just a fraction more lenient in his judgment. In all other things but this matter of unfaithfulness she had never shown herself to be other than a loyal, obedient and dutiful wife, and surely – he argued – having erred but this once she would hardly be likely to do so a second time, knowing the penalties there were to be incurred.

Supposing he *were* to take her back . . . what was wanted, perhaps, was another child to the marriage. No sickly daughter, but a healthy young son to keep her well occupied. Yes, that would supply the answer, no doubt of it; a fine lusty boy to keep her at home, keep her attention from idling into mischief; and this time without the interference of Beatrice, Oliver told himself. Beatrice was half to blame for what had happened before.

"Go and see Catherine," Humphrey Jaggers advised. "Talk to her. Judge how the land lies. Now that your anger has cooled to a rational level, you may view the situation in a somewhat better light."

He had. And setting his pride at nought, had asked her to return to him.

Sion Place,
May 31st 1867

Dearest Harriet,

Here I am once more, where least I expected ever again to be, and to judge by my reception, you would think that my absence had been occasioned by nothing of further weight than a sojourn in Town. Beatrice kills me with her looks, of course, and twitches her skirts aside at my approach as though I were Contagion, and squeezes out her words like so many drops of *lemon juice*; but I have drawn her sting, since she has been forced to surrender up her keys and I have charge of the Household in her place. I must admit, I had not expected that, but Oliver said that it must be done. His manner towards her has grown very *strained*, I cannot think why; – altho' no doubt my prodigal return has much to do with it, for she can hardly have received the news with any great expression of *delight*.

I am determined that things shall not be as they were before: I mean, I shall not meekly suffer myself to be 'first among my husband's servants', as once I heard a wife described. My meekness of spirit has in the past too often been taken for uncaring apathy, or else faint-heartedness, and therefore I shall throw aside that false delicacy too generally assumed by my sex and become a very Diana in my conduct and bearing.

As to my husband, I feel that we have reached a better understanding one towards the other, and therefore it is my intention henceforth so to discharge the duties with which he has invested me, as to promote his welfare, ensure my own, and preserve the affectionate respect of all the Household; (– saving, of course, my *sister-in-law*, whom I fear is beyond such sentiment!)

You know, more than anyone, my dear Harriet, how sensible I am of the faults and misdeeds into which a lack of proper judgment previously led me. Believe me when I say, that my conscience has caused me to suffer most grievously for the error of my ways, and I am now resolved to manage myself in such a fashion as to give Society no further cause for disapprobation.

Can this be the same Kitty, I hear you exclaim, who so short a time ago expressed herself heartily well rid of *husband* and *marriage* both? Ah, but do not allow your judgment to run on too hastily! Is not my position now a better one than heretofore? For instead of being cast in the role of despised creature, looking to a true and only friend for charitable succour, I am now Mistress of my house, and waited upon once more by respectable neighbours and gentry alike. Is that not more to be envied than a future barren of any expectation? These past months have taught me a lesson which was bitter in the learning, and I would be foolish indeed if I did not now turn it to my own advantage.

I will close my Epistle here, for I wish it to reach you by this afternoon's post, so that you will not think me negligent of giving you my news. Please convey my warm regards to Mr Dutton when next you are in Loxley Wood, and thank him on my behalf for all his kind attentions to my comfort. I will visit him in person when time and circumstance allow.

Your most affectionate friend – Kitty

Kitty *had* changed. A little steel had entered into her soul, forged there by the tragedy and sorrow which had followed so hard one upon the heels of the other; tragedy and sorrow which might easily have broken a spirit of less strength than hers. She was still only very young – a month away from her twenty-second birthday – yet already had experienced more than many women knew at twice or thrice that age. Who could say what latent traits of character might not have been inherited from her unknown parentage: not selfishness, certainly, but a sense of self-preservation, and the ability to take life's blows and learn from them without being crushed.

She did not love her husband; but she was starting to see

that love was not the be all and end all of a woman's existence. Love made one weak; made one vulnerable. It left one unprotected against so many, many little hurts. Far better that she and Oliver foster a mutual respect, if that were possible, and learn to tolerate that which they could not alter in each other.

Whatever his reasons – and they were complex – he had reinstated her as his wife, had given her back everything which she herself had thrown away on an empty dream. She had walked the road of unhappiness to its end, and she did not intend to walk that same road a second time.

26

Benedict Sidney Hendrik van der Kleve was born at Sion Place in April 1868, a lusty, strong-limbed boy whose delivery cost his mother no more than a morning's labour, the pain of which was swiftly forgotten in the joy of bearing such a healthy child. He was brought into the world by Dr George Manser, successor to the recently retired Dr Adeney; and given the forename Sidney in honour of his esteemed godfather, a member of the ancient and noble family of Sidney whose country seat was at Penshurst in the neighbourhood of Tunbridge Wells.

With this birth, Kitty's position as wife of Oliver van der Kleve and mistress of his house was established beyond any doubt or argument. The shadow cast by events of recent years appeared to fall but faintly now across her path as she went about her daily business as an accepted and well-liked member of local society; and if memory ever by accident intruded into her thoughts, it was instantly dismissed as foolishness and pushed back to where Kitty considered it belonged – in the past. Her new-found strength of mind and purpose was fed by a growing confidence which responsibility and the satisfaction of motherhood together gave her; and as her physical beauty matured, so too did the vibrancy of her character and that natural warmth of personality which had – all unconsciously – so endeared her to those who had known her in earlier days. Even Oliver was forced to admit to the fact that his wife was becoming quite extraordinarily lovely.

She had seen a great deal less of Harriet Seymour since the latter's marriage to Herr Doktor Hoffmann a few months before, at the start of the New Year. The couple's engagement had been unconventionally brief, and Harriet was now living with her new husband in Baden-Baden; but the friendship between the two young women continued as fondly as ever via the pages of a regular correspondence. Kitty's own circle of acquaintances had been considerably widened through membership of the local Ladies' Literary Society, and by her work with a church charity for the Relief of the Deserving Poor organised for the purpose of assisting those who, through no blame of their own, might otherwise find themselves thrown into the nearby workhouse at Pembury.

She had been invited to join in this philanthropic enterprise by the Reverend Mr Edward Terris, as a mark of his personal favour that she'd chosen to return to the fold of respectability with such little damage to the good name of St Bride's. It was regrettable, perhaps, that Mr Terris chose to express his approval in quite so significant a manner, for it contrasted sharply with his cold-water reception of Beatrice van der Kleve, who had volunteered her own services to the charity some time earlier and whose hard work and diligence had so far met with scant sign of the minister's appreciation. That her hated sister-in-law, who – if there were any justice in Heaven – ought by now to have been selling herself in the gutter where she belonged, should have wormed her way so neatly again into Mr Terris's good books, further ulcerated the sore of enmity and loathing in Beatrice's breast.

Her brother's action in abandoning divorce proceedings and taking his young wife back into his house, had served to snatch defeat from the jaws of her victory. At the very moment when her prayers were about to be answered, to Beatrice's fury he had robbed her of her triumph in seeing her rival cast off and publicly humiliated; and all for what? For the reputation of the family's title and standing in the City? Beatrice had rather doubted it. One need only to look at the way she had been made to surrender up the household keys at Catherine's return to see how shallow was that excuse of Oliver's. No, depend upon it, he'd been caught in the coils of his own sexual appetites, like a fly in a web, and the more he struggled, the tighter he managed to ensnare himself. Facts spoke for themselves, in Beatrice's opinion: he had begotten another child on that woman within a month or so of taking her again into his bed.

And another thing – Rose Maguire. Rose Maguire, whom Beatrice herself had dismissed from service three years earlier, was now re-employed in the house as lady's maid, the very position she'd set her sights on before her impudence caught her out. How galling it was, that Oliver should have given way on the matter and at his wife's behest allowed the girl to return – an action which could only cast doubt upon his sister's authority and judgment; and how it vexed Beatrice almost to the point of screaming, to have to see Rose Maguire's smiling, happy face about the place, and know that the happiness could not be struck off by a blow of the hand, as in the past.

Her only source of consolation was her own maid, Jane Perrins; and even Perrins was not to be trusted too much or too far in case familiarity bred a secret ridicule. The woman was of invaluable use, though, in that she kept an open ear and a closed mouth, and could be relied upon not to repeat the bitter words expressed to her in private; while at the same time she saw to it her mistress was fully informed of all the gossip of the area, especially any stray tittle-tattle concerning Mrs van der Kleve, knowing how much that was relished.

Beatrice's resentment bit deep, and like acid it had corroded her mind to such an extent that she viewed everything to do with her sister-in-law from a peculiarly distorted angle. The fact that her niece Angelina seemed of late to have forsaken her company in favour of Kitty's, for instance – to anyone of common sense, it would be the most natural thing in the world for a growing girl on the verge of womanhood to seek the guidance and friendship of an affectionate young stepmother; but Beatrice saw the desertion as nothing less than deliberate poaching and blamed Kitty for wheedling the girl away from her on purpose, to use as a pawn.

"It's becoming quite utterly intolerable," she said one day to Oliver, finding him alone in the morning room. "Why should I be treated so, as though I were a lodger beneath my own roof. It places me in a most embarrassing position."

Oliver glanced a little wearily from the paper he was looking through. The golden summer light from the garden windows fell across his features, lending the pale skin a flush of warmth.

"What is it now, Beatrice? As you see, I am occupied. Can it not wait?"

"So – even the newspapers must take precedence! What I have to say is of rather less importance, I suppose?"

"I did not mean to imply that. It is simply that I wish to finish reading something here before I go out."

"You are always going out just as I am coming in. And so is Angelina." Beatrice seated herself in the armchair opposite.

"I am beginning to think there is a conspiracy in this house to render me invisible."

"Is that your complaint?" Oliver shook his newspaper open again and spoke from behind it. "Yesterday, as I recall, it was one of the servants who vexed you. And the day before, you were dissatisfied with the seating arrangement at dinner."

His sister's strong, austerely handsome face tightened. "And am I not allowed to express an opinion of my own, without I must be always in the wrong? Rose Maguire was insolent, and as for the seating arrangement –"

Oliver turned over the page and made a sound that was somewhere between a sigh and a clearing of the throat.

"Indeed. You made your views perfectly plain. And what is it now that has happened to annoy you?"

"Angelina. She promised she would accompany me to Langton church hall to give a hand with preparing refreshments for our little fête this afternoon. She had only to slice and butter the bread – the Misses Daukins are overseeing the fancy cakes and pastries, and Edward Terris was most particular that I myself should have a care of the teas – but now the silly girl declares she does not wish to assist, and prefers instead to go with the baby into the park."

"And what harm is there in that, pray?" Oliver glanced round the side of his newspaper. "I find it most commendable that Angelina should choose to occupy herself in so fond a fashion. She is to be encouraged in it. Surely, if the problem is merely one of buttering some bread, there are others who might be called upon to assist?"

"But Angelina gave her word. Besides, the rest of the ladies already have tasks of their own to engage them. There is no one else to ask."

Beatrice stared resentfully at the front-page personal columns of *The Times* presented opposite, and after a moment went on again, "To be frank, I cannot understand your attitude, Oliver. There was a time when you would have chastised Angelina for such mannerless behaviour, but now she is permitted to do precisely as she pleases. The way she was dressed for church service on Sunday, for instance – that outfit she wore was *quite* unbecoming for a child of her age. Why you allowed her to appear in public so maturely attired, I cannot think. Mrs Brinsley-Jones for one was plainly astonished –"

"Mrs Brinsley-Jones makes a virtue of her own intolerance," Oliver interrupted. "And I am sorry that you must imitate her. Speaking for myself, I thought Angelina looked very presentable on Sunday. And if I may say, it is a pity that you must always criticise anything to do with Catherine –"

"I had not mentioned Catherine!"

"You had no need to mention her." He threw the paper aside and stood up. "It was she who chose Angelina's new dress, as well you were aware. Now if you will excuse me – ?"

"But I have not yet finished."

"Then please make haste and do so."

The coldness of her brother's tone stung Beatrice into an incautious excitability. She rose with him, hands clasped against the black bombasine swell of her bosom.

"Why am I not permitted to visit the nursery – answer me that!"

"I was not aware that such was the case."

"Indeed it is. I am not allowed to set so much as a foot within the door."

"At whose orders?"

"At the orders of your wife, of course."

"Then there must be good reason for her to issue such a restriction. Doubtless she has a care for the health and well-being of my son" – these last two words carried all the unconscious emphasis of a father's pride. "Perhaps she feels that the fewer visitors to his nursery, the less risk there is of infection being carried in from the street."

The logic of such reasoning failed to impress itself upon Beatrice. "If she fears that, why then is the boy put out into the garden each morning, where he may breathe in all the contagious air of the neighbourhood, and why is he exposed half-naked in his carriage in the park instead of being properly swaddled against the ill effects of sunlight? She is going the best way about killing the child –"

"Now that is enough." Oliver's face blackened with swift anger. In the act of crossing to the door, he swung about on his heel.

"I wish to hear no more of this! That you, Beatrice, of all people, should speak of such a thing in view of what happened to my daughter Henrietta – who, if I may remind you, was given into your sole charge. Whatever Catherine thinks is best for our son has my entire approval, and be sure of this – I will not tolerate anything further of your interference in the way my wife conducts herself. I trust that I make myself clear."

The German band was playing a selection of waltzes, and in the still, warm air of the summer's afternoon the music drifted beneath the trees of Mount Sion Grove to lend a haunting continental gaiety to the scene, reminding Kitty a little of Baden-Baden. Further off, beyond the edge of the park, the sounds of horse traffic carried from the high street, muted by alleys and high garden walls, and by the leafy spread of chestnut, beech and lime which formed an overhead canopy against the brassy glare of the sun.

This spacious area of grass and trees had been bequeathed to the townsfolk of Tunbridge Wells in 1707 by the Duke of Buckingham, as a 'pleasaunce' for their enjoyment. It was a peaceful place to walk, and Kitty came here often, almost every day, with her baby son to take the air and sit for an hour or so listening to the band.

He lay asleep now beside the bench, lulled into slumber by the gentle rhythmic rocking of his mother's hand upon the carriage. A handsome child just three months old, his fine dark hair was feathered in wispy curls on his forehead, and his small, strong fist lay folded against a rounded cheek. He seldom cried, and when he was awake would watch the world about him in contented wonder, amusing himself with little sounds of happiness. Everyone – or virtually everyone – adored him, none more so than his father, to whom this son was the fulfilment of so many harboured ambitions, so many hopes, so many dreams.

Surprisingly, in view of the resentment she'd borne towards poor little Henrietta a few years earlier, young Angelina had developed a marked fondness for her new half-brother. She had come out with Kitty on this afternoon's walk – something they'd done quite regularly together since Benedict's birth – and was seated humming a waltz tune along with the band while she idly twirled the silken fringe of her parasol back and forth above her head.

"Do you suppose –" she said suddenly, breaking off her humming – "do you suppose that Papa may be persuaded to change his mind? About sending me abroad?"

"To L'École Rambouillet?" Kitty glanced at her.

"Yes. Oh, I know it's where he sent *you* to be finished –" this was stated with a candour which held not the least trace of spite – "but truthfully, I've no wish to go. I don't want to leave Tunbridge Wells."

"Now that you're no longer attending Miss Meyrick's, I expect your Papa feels it would be benefiting your education to complete it in France."

"But I don't *want* to go," Angelina repeated, and a little of the old childish sullenness which she seemed to have outgrown showed itself for a moment in her expression.

Having reached the senior class of Miss Meyrick's Academy, she had left that establishment at the end of last term, and had hoped to be allowed to remain at home and be 'finished' by private tuition in dance, comportment and etiquette – the only social requirements likely to be needed by the daughter of a wealthy father. Oliver, however, had decided otherwise. For the next two years, until her nineteenth birthday, he intended that Angelina should be sent to L'École Rambouillet in Paris.

"I want to stay here at Sion Place with you and Baby." The sullen look disappeared, and in its place appeared one of yearning appeal. "Won't you speak to him *please* on my behalf? He'll listen to you."

"Do you think so?"

"Oh, yes!"

Kitty continued her rocking of the carriage. This past year or so, since their reconciliation, she and Oliver had lived on terms of tolerant respect for one another; some fondness, even, in view of the fact that they shared the same bed and engaged in regular marital intercourse. Since her husband never spoke of his feelings, however, she had no idea how he now regarded her; although since the birth of their son, she'd noticed a growing benevolence in his attitude which had been absent before. For her own part, she tended these days to accept Oliver simply as he was, and neither dislike him nor warm to him in any great degree.

It was an amicable arrangement.

"I'll speak to him if you wish, my dear. But I warn you, don't entertain false hopes that anything I say may induce a change of heart. He only wants what is best for you."

Angelina closed up her parasol and laid it aside on the bench. "The best for me is my happiness, surely? You've said so yourself – don't you remember? When we were talking one day about my misconduct? You said the reason I did silly, stupid things was because I was unhappy –"

"Yes, I remember. I also said that Papa truly loved you. And he does, you must believe that."

"Then why is he sending me away from him?"

"He is not sending you away in that sense." Kitty softened her answer with a smile. "He'll visit you often in Paris, and hopefully so shall I. I want him to be proud of you, my dear . . . and you should want that too."

There was a loud sigh. "It's not fair. I'll miss seeing Baby growing. He'll walk and talk, and I won't be there to teach him. And what about Arthur – ?"

"Arthur Russell?"

"Yes." Angelina turned her eyes upon her stepmother. During the months which had passed since her sixteenth birthday she had started maturing visibly from a plump, round-faced and rather plain child into a taller, slimmer, slightly more attractive young person. She would never be a beauty, but her features were regular and held a lively, intelligent expression; and Kitty saw to it that she was dressed in the colours and styles which most became her.

Lately the acquaintance between Angelina and Arthur Russell, whom the girl had met at their neighbours the Broadwoods a year last autumn, had ripened through frequent social contact into something closer approaching real friendship. Arthur was the first young man she had danced with, the first young man who'd singled her out in company to talk to, the first to make her aware of her fledgling womanhood.

"He'll forget all about me," she said bleakly.

"Of course he won't!" Kitty tried to sound reassuring. "He likes you far too well."

"Oh – does he?"

"I'm sure of it. I've seen the way he looks at you."

A tell-tale blush of confusion flooded the other's cheeks. It was true, though; Kitty had occasionally watched the pair of them together and noted Arthur's attentive expression, the eager awkwardness with which he moved to offer a seat for her stepdaughter at the Broadwoods' soirées, his too-ready laughter in conversation, his clumsy gallantries. Certainly, his presence in Angelina's life appeared to have wrought a beneficial change in her behaviour. Even Oliver had remarked as much. She'd grown quieter, more thoughtful; older.

The baby stirred in his carriage and Kitty leaned across to fold back his embroidered coverlet.

"May I suggest something, my dear?" she said over her shoulder. "Regarding Arthur?"

She sat back again.

"Consider what an opportunity this will give you for correspondence. You'll be able to write to him each week from Paris – interesting letters which will please him to read. There's such a lot can be said in a page – so many thoughts, so many little private confidences. He'll learn a great deal more about you that way. And when you return, why, just think how well you will have grown to know each other."

The prospect gave Angelina pause for thoughtful reflection.

The German band was reaching the end of its programme now, the final waltz being played before the toy-soldier bandsmen put away their instruments for another time and left the Grove to the peaceful hush of the summer's afternoon.

Kitty rose from the bench. Benedict was showing signs of waking, and would need feeding in a while.

"Would you make me a promise, Mama?" Angelina looked up at her. She had only recently started to use that title when addressing her stepmother, and it sounded a little awkward still on her lips. "If I *must* be sent abroad, would you do something for me – please?"

"But of course."

The girl took up her parasol once more and followed to her feet, brushing the creases from her skirts in a self-conscious manner.

"Would you – well, keep a watchful eye on Arthur for me, please? I mean, in case there's someone else he seems to admire? You'd write and tell me at once, wouldn't you?"

Kitty smiled. "At once – I promise. You've no need to worry, my dear, I'll make sure his affection doesn't stray."

It was so easily said; a reassurance so easily given. Neither knew it then as they began making their way from the park together, Angelina pushing the carriage, but those words would return to haunt them both in time to come.

27

"Ladies – gentlemen –"

The Reverend Mr Edward Terris waved his arms in a fussy manner to silence the rising swell of conversation in the church hall.

"– your attention a moment, if you please!"

Voices were hushed and heads turned expectantly in his direction; all except one, that of Mrs George Russell, who merely glanced round and then went on with what she was in the middle of saying to her neighbour Frances Broadwood.

"Ladies – *please* –" Mr Terris appealed again.

This evening's meeting of St Bride's committee for the Relief of the Deserving Poor had ended before the minister recalled to mind a final announcement he must make.

"– if I may be allowed –?"

Still talking, Mrs Russell looked over her shoulder towards the platform and was shushed by several others roundabout, fingers to their lips, a caution she acknowledged with a disarming smile and a little gesture of apology.

"Thank you." Having everyone's attention at last, Mr Terris held up a leaf of paper.

"Just before we all adjourn for refreshments, may I draw the committee's notice to a forthcoming event. A grand charity bazaar will be held in the grounds of Calverley House on Saturday, May the eighth. Now while this is not within our own parish, we have been most generously invited to participate if we so wish, to raise money for our own especial cause. I am sure you will all agree with me that this invitation should be accepted –"

Sounds of agreement rippled around the hall.

"– therefore it remains for us to decide what form our involvement might take. Perhaps you would care to – ah, set your minds to thinking upon the matter before the next meeting of the committee, so that we then will have some ideas for discussion."

Mr Terris made a courteous inclination signifying the end of his announcement, and turned to descend from the platform, his portly shadow thrown before him by the gasolier lighting overhead.

The swell of voices broke out afresh.

"Depend upon it, we'll have the usual crop of suggestions," Frances Broadwood commented laconically, glancing from Mrs Russell to Kitty van der Kleve, standing beside her. "The two Misses Daukins will want their cake stall, Colonel Legh will propose old books, and Mrs Stapley from the toy repository will put in a plea for Useful Goods and Fancy Articles."

Her gaze passed on to Arthur Russell, lounging against the back of a chair with his hands in his pockets.

"What we require is something completely different. Something new to attract the public's notice. Arthur – Arthur, dear, – have *you* anything to suggest, perhaps?"

Hearing his name, the young man glanced round quickly.

"Oh, don't ask Arthur!" his mother exclaimed with a laugh. "He'd have us all performing the most extraordinary antics. Ballooning, or worse."

Kitty clapped her hands. "Ballooning! But what a wonderful idea! I've always longed to ride in a balloon."

Everyone turned to look at her, not sure whether she was being quite serious.

"Think what an innovation it would be," she went on enthusiastically, "how much attraction we'd create for St Bride's by offering aerial flights across the Common."

Frances Broadwood smirked and leaned closer. "Can you imagine Mrs Brinsley-Jones in the basket of a hot-air balloon, my dears?"

With a gesture of the head she indicated a very plump, very dignified lady opposite whose features seemed set in a permanent sniff of disapproval.

"Or even – think of it – Mr Terris. *And* Beatrice. Together. Oh, what a glorious opportunity that would be . . . and who would cling tightest to whom, I wonder."

There was something slightly malicious in the way she laughed as she said that. Beatrice van der Kleve's fervid admiration of Edward Terris was no secret to the female members of the parish; just as Mr Terris's less than fervid response was the cause of much sly humour at Beatrice's expense.

Kitty shook her head with a dismissive smile. She was wearing a very becoming little hat which had attracted a good deal of envious attention this evening. "We should do *something* different, though. A bygones and curios stall, perhaps. Or – yes, or why not a fortune-telling booth?"

"Now there's an excellent suggestion." Mrs George Russell clapped her hands in turn. "A fortune teller! People adore that kind of thing. We could charge threepence a time –"

"And make a fortune, literally," her son observed drily, looking at Kitty. "Threepence sounds a bit exorbitant to me."

"Oh, but we'd get it, I'm sure."

"You'd need a gipsy, Mama. And a booth. And a crystal ball."

"Be quiet, Arthur," his mother told him, growing impatient. "I shall regret bringing you this evening if you can't say something useful."

"We could make a booth from one of the gardeners' huts," Frances Broadwood suggested. Having given Kitty's idea her consideration, and found it a good one, she was now prepared to make it her own. "And decorate the whole thing to look the part, with shawls and silver spangles and suchlike. And surely Mr Lawrence the photographer will have something among his studio equipment which we might use for a scrying ball."

"But where would you find an honest gipsy – and one with the gift of reading balls and crossing palms and all that?" young Arthur put in again. He had passed a rather dull evening kicking his heels about the church hall while his mother attended her committee meeting, but things were now beginning to look decidedly jollier. "I mean, you've got to make the performance convincing, or folk won't cough up their cash."

"Really, Arthur – I do wish you would refrain from using such common expressions. Papa would not have liked it."

It was on the tip of the young man's tongue to rejoin that Papa was no longer here to like it or not; but knowing such a remark would only hurt his widowed mother's feelings, he gave a little shrug of the shoulder and went back to lounging again against a chair.

"It's true though," Kitty came to the defence. "What would be the point of our advertising fortunes told if we had no one able to do the telling? Unless, of course –"

249

Just at that, whatever she was about to say was interrupted by the arrival of Mr Terris, cup and saucer in hand, come to remind them that refreshments were being served at the further side of the hall; and seizing the opportunity to steal more of Kitty's thunder for herself, Frances Broadwood said brightly, "Ah, Mr Terris – what do you think of this! Do let us have your opinion, pray. We have decided upon the very thing for the Calverley House bazaar. A fortune-teller's booth! So much more adventurous than cake stalls and what have you, wouldn't you agree?"

And before the other had time to gather his thoughts to respond, she gave him one of her winning little smiles and went on, "Our problem is, however, that we cannot think whom we might ask to do the scrying."

The minister cleared his throat. "The – er – *scrying*, Mrs Broadwood?"

"Yes. You know, the divinations. Reading the crystal ball."

"I see." Cup and saucer were laid aside. "I should perhaps remind you, ma'am, of the Church's teaching upon divination and all similar practices. St Paul himself had much to say against such things, describing their messages as being not from God but from Satan, Prince of Lies, and – no, Mrs Broadwood, permit me to finish, please –" as she made to interrupt – "in the book of Ecclesiastes it is written, 'divinations and soothsayings and dreams are vain. If they be not sent from the most High, set not thy heart upon them'."

Frances Broadwood rolled her eyes towards Kitty.

"Actually, the idea was Mrs van der Kleve's," she said sweetly.

"I see. Ah. Well, it is commendable in its way, I suppose, and – yes, we must thank Catherine for having the imagination to suggest something of such originality."

"I was about to wonder just now," Kitty came in, "whether perhaps one of us ladies might not play the part of fortune-teller. The thing doesn't have to be *serious*, after all. Whoever took the role, would need to do no more than invent one or two make-believe 'prophecies' to fit the face of each enquirer."

"But how would you propose doing that?" Arthur Russell wanted to know, intrigued enough to butt in again on the conversation.

Kitty made a hesitant gesture. "Well . . . if it were a young woman without a wedding ring, I'd say something about her meeting a handsome suitor. And to a married woman, that she must guard against gossip, perhaps, or against idle servants."

"And if it were a gentleman enquirer?" Even Mr Terris appeared interested now.

"Why, if it were a young gentleman, I'd tell him he was about to be lucky in love, and if an older one –" Kitty thought a moment – "that he must treat his wife civilly if he wished for peace in his house."

"Bravo!" Arthur applauded such inventiveness. "I believe you have found your gipsy, Mr Terris. Why seek elsewhere when you have such a ready talent here on your doorstep!"

"Arthur – remember to whom you are speaking," his mother admonished him sharply.

"But the boy has a point, ma'am," acknowledged the minister, himself now more than slightly taken by the idea. "Indeed, we should not be too hasty to dismiss Catherine's suggestion out of hand. I shall put it to the committee at our next meeting, and ask to have their reaction upon the matter."

He bestowed upon Kitty one of his avuncular smiles, and retrieving his cup and saucer, moved off in the direction of the Misses Daukins's fancy cakes, leaving Frances Broadwood to think of what cutting remark she could make on the subject of favouritism.

Arthur Russell had come into his majority in the spring of this year, 1869. Alas for his mother's expectations, he did not come into the large fortune anticipated from his father's estate. The reasons were several; namely that the late George Russell was not as wealthy a man as might on the surface appear; and the estate had been less than expected, leaving widow and only child while not exactly badly off, not exactly as well-heeled either as Mrs Russell wished her friends to believe.

Being a practical sort of woman, she sold the family house in Kensington – along with some of the more valuable of its contents – and in 1867 had purchased a more modest property at Mount Edgecumbe in Tunbridge Wells. To those who enquired her reasons for removing herself from the City, she answered merely that it was at the wish of her dear husband's cousin, Mr Henry Broadwood, in order that he might the better discharge those duties as kinsman which now fell to his responsibility.

The truth of the matter was, of course, that Mrs George Russell found it a good deal less expensive to live in the Wells than in Town; and the profit made from the sale of the house, sensibly invested, would do very nicely to keep her and young Arthur in the manner to which her friends were accustomed.

The mantle of the late Mr Russell's position as a mercantile investment consultant with the firm of Faber and Russell now fell upon the rather less sturdy shoulders of his son and heir. Arthur had joined the family firm at eighteen, and showing himself capable and competent, had advanced by degrees up the ladder of his career until he was now within sight at least of the boardroom door.

His next objective was to make a good marriage for himself; and to this end his mother had been most assiduous in her social spade-work to prepare the ground for a possible alliance with the van der Kleves. It helped, of course, that Arthur and Angelina van der Kleve liked one another. The girl was now seventeen, and attending a finishing school for young ladies in Paris. In another year she would be 'coming out' – making her début into Society – and Mrs Russell was determined to see that Arthur didn't drag his feet in proposing marriage, for fear some other candidate might appear on the scene to spoil his chances. One simply never knew with young women nowadays – they fell in love at the drop of a hat with the most unsuitable persons; and though her boy was conducting his courtship very properly by a regular exchange of letters, it did not mean an engagement to Angelina was a foregone conclusion.

In Mrs Russell's opinion, at least.

Seeing his mother move away with Frances Broadwood to the other side of the church hall, the young man deliberately held back as though wishing not to leave Kitty van der Kleve standing alone. She was preoccupied with writing something in her notebook, and it wasn't until she'd dropped book and pencil back inside her reticule that she realised he was there still.

"Aren't you having any tea, Arthur?" she wanted to know, glancing past in his mother's direction.

"No. I – er – don't much fancy the witch's brew that passes for refreshment here."

"Then you should complain to my sister-in-law. She's the one responsible for making it."

Embarrassment instantly coloured his face. "Oh, I didn't mean – I say, I'm most awfully sorry –"

"Don't be. I quite agree with you. I don't fancy it myself much, either."

Half-turning away to find a chair, Kitty went and seated herself, and with a gesture invited the young man to join her.

"Have you had any news from Angelina this week?" she enquired.

"Actually, ma'am, a letter came yesterday."

He sat down opposite, leaning back in a nonchalant manner and crossing one leg over the other. He wondered whether to ask Mrs van der Kleve if she would mind if he smoked a cheroot, then decided against it: a cheroot made him look a man of the world, but it also made him cough.

"We received one too, yesterday," Kitty said. "She must have posted them both together. Did she tell you about her visit to Versailles?"

"Yes. Yes, she did. Sounded very jolly. Especially the bit about giving old Mademoiselle Whats-it the slip in the Salle des Glaces."

There was a raised eyebrow. "Oh? Indeed? She neglected to mention that particular episode."

Arthur uncrossed his legs and folded his arms; and there was a moment's slight awkwardness before he asked suddenly, "Have *you* ever visited Versailles, Mrs van der Kleve?"

"Several times."

"And what was your impression?"

"That it's very beautiful." Then correcting herself – "No, perhaps beautiful is the wrong word. *Splendid* probably describes the place better. Splendid, and yet somehow rather dead."

"Like a mausoleum."

"Exactly. A mausoleum to a glittering world which no longer exists. Versailles was built to be a peacock's reflection in the mirror of its own vanity."

"I say, that's rather good!"

"Oh . . . someone else's quotation, not mine."

"The reference being to Louis the Fourteenth, of course." Arthur was pleased with himself for remembering his history. "Must have been a colourful show, don't you think – all those courtiers in brocades and satins clattering about the corridors on their scarlet heels. Can't you just imagine it?"

"Yes. Vividly."

Kitty looked away across the hall, her attention distracted for a second. "And what else did Angelina have to say for herself?" she went on. "Anything of interest?"

Sensing a hesitation in place of answer, she glanced back again. "No – don't tell me. It's private, I know. I shouldn't have asked. I'm sorry."

Again, there was a momentary awkwardness between them.

She gathered the ribbon-strings of her reticule and slipped them over her wrist, making as though to get up.

"Oh – don't go yet – please."

The words were blurted out before Arthur could stop them, and he instantly cursed himself for a fool as he caught her half-look of surprise, the slight widening of those lovely violet eyes turned upon him.

"I mean – well – Angelina said I ought to make myself better acquainted with you, Mrs van der Kleve. She wants us both to be friends. She's very fond of you, you know. In fact – in fact, she wrote to me saying I should be as attentive as possible whenever we happened to meet. So would you mind awfully –"

He came to an abrupt stop, his face colouring up again.

"Would I mind awfully what?" Kitty tried to keep the smile from her voice. It was transparently obvious that Angelina's little ploy was intended to prevent young Arthur's affections from straying during her absence by enrolling her stepmother as a focus for his interest. To provide a social distraction, in other words.

"Would you mind –" He collected himself, confidence returning. "Would you mind awfully if we stayed and talked a while longer? Mama's still occupied with Mrs Broadwood. And you don't have to leave immediately, do you?"

She gave this her consideration.

"No."

"Good."

"What would you care to talk about?" The smile revealed

itself in her expression as she looked at him; and emboldened further, he responded at once, "Why not about you, ma'am? I know so little – I mean, you never have much to say of yourself, do you?"

"Perhaps because there's not very much to know."

"Oh, I can't believe that!"

There was a pause while he hunted around for inspiration; and finding it, he went on again with renewed enthusiasm, "Angelina says that you yourself attended L'École Rambouillet."

"So I did."

"And also Miss Meyrick's Academy."

"And also Miss Meyrick's Academy." The smile was there still.

Arthur ran his fingers through his gingery-fair hair, leaving a small quiff standing up from his forehead. It had just this very moment occurred to him that there couldn't be more than a few years separating the two of them in age. How old was Mrs van der Kleve? Twenty-three? Twenty-four? It was a thought that hadn't struck him till now, and he found it oddly disconcerting.

"May I ask – were you born locally, ma'am?"

"Yes. At Tonbridge."

"Tonbridge? Ah. Is that where your people are living?"

Suddenly Kitty's smile became enigmatic. With a graceful fluidity of movement she rose to her feet. "I think that's enough of questions for one meeting."

"I say – you're not offended, are you?" Arthur followed at once, scraping his chair back noisily on the wood-block floor in his haste.

"Of course not." She glanced back at him. "But the evening's wearing on, and I have to think about going. Thank you for your company, Arthur."

She held out her hand. "Perhaps next time we might have a longer conversation? Would you like that?"

"Yes – rather!"

She inclined her head beneath its fashionable little hat and moved away across the church hall, leaving him with the thought that Angelina's stepmother wasn't half bad. No, not half bad at all.

28

Oliver had disposed of the opals which his wife so disliked
wearing, and in their place had bought her a set of sapphire
jewellery to mark the birth of their second son, Frederick Louis
Cornelius, in the summer of 1870.

Kitty intended showing off her sapphires this evening, at a
dinner party to celebrate the formal betrothal of Angelina van
der Kleve to Arthur Russell. It was a doubly felicitous occasion
for the family, for November the tenth also marked Angelina's
nineteenth birthday, and much forethought and organisation
had gone into the evening.

"Can I have your opinion, Rose?"

Fresh from the bathtub by the bedroom fire, and wearing
only corset and drawers beneath her wrapper, Kitty came into
the dressing room where the maid was folding away her
mistress's day clothes.

"Ought I to wear the cream satin tonight, do you think –
the one with the draped polonaise – or the pale pink silk with
the bustle?"

"Either of them suits you very well, ma'am."

"But which do you prefer?"

Rose Maguire straightened up and cast a look behind her
at the large mahogany wardrobe taking up a wall of the room.
Its double doors stood open to reveal a half dozen or more
draped muslin dust-protectors, each concealing a frothy con-
fection of pastel frills and flounces. Oliver liked to see his wife
expensively well-dressed; it reflected upon his own wealth and
standing that she should always appear so, for a gentleman's
social position was in part gauged by the jewels and finery of
the lady bearing his name.

"Well, ma'am, if you want the honest truth, the pink would
do you best. It's too cold a night for wearing cream."

Seating herself at the dressing-table, Kitty took up a hairbrush and gave her mirrored reflection a critical examination.

Her latest pregnancy had robbed her for ever of her willow-slim figure, but she was not displeased with the result, for that little extra roundness gave a softer, more feminine line to her face and shoulders.

"The pink it shall be, then," she said decisively, freeing her hair from its pins and shaking it loose. The lambent light of oil lamps in the room gleamed on its honey-gold smoothness as she started to brush.

"Bring the gown out, would you, Rose, and I'll try it on. You may need to re-sew a few hooks and eyes."

Oliver had had this particular evening gown ordered from a French dressmaker in London, made to the design of one of the very best *couturiers*. It had a low-cut neckline to be worn off the shoulders, and the delicate rose-pink silk was given a misty effect by the clever use of transparent gauze for the overskirts. At the back, a bustle softened by pleated frills created an undulating line from the high, round waist; and the short sleeves, neck and drapes were edged with velvet ribbon of a darker shade of rose.

The effect on any woman, however plain, would have lent enchantment; but on Kitty it was breathtakingly exquisite, and the moment she entered the Sion Place drawing room several hours later, every eye was turned towards her in total admiration.

Only Oliver seemed less than captivated by his young wife's appearance. Taking her aside for a moment as the champagne was carried round, he said, "I'm not sure the sapphires look well with pink, my dear. You would have done better to dress yourself in blue, perhaps. Or mauve. If I may say, the pink is a trifle sugary."

"The colour was ordered to your choice," Kitty reminded him lightly, inclining her head in greeting to a couple nearby.

"But not to wear with the sapphires."

"Then what a pity it is that I have no rubies to compliment such a very expensive gown."

She opened her fan with a deft little flick of the wrist, and giving her husband a cool look, left him to move over for a word with Dr Adeney and his wife who were just being announced into the drawing room by Nicholls. Since the elderly doctor's retirement from medical practice, she had not seen much of them socially, for the couple tended to spend several months at a time with a married daughter at Rye.

"And how is young Manser looking after you?" Dr Adeney wanted to know once greetings were out of the way. "He tells me your last confinement was the easiest one he'd attended."

"Well, he didn't have a great deal to do, that's true," laughed Kitty. "In fact, as I recall, he sat holding my hand and discussing whether or not the French would declare war against Prussia."

"I wonder you were sufficiently conscious to remember, my dear!" Mrs Adeney exclaimed, accepting a glass of champagne from one of the maids. "You must have been very brave."

"Not at all. I think Dr Manser's stratagem was to divert my attention from Freddie's imminent arrival. It certainly succeeded. The notion that England might be drawn into another war exercised my mind to such an extent that my son's birth was accomplished with hardly a moment's inconvenience. War is such a *dreadful* business –"

"I do agree!"

"And so many brave souls lost their lives in the Crimea conflict, it makes one fear to think how many more must die if we're drawn into another."

"I don't think that will happen," was Dr Adeney's opinion. "Britain has declared herself neutral, after all, in this affair between the French and Prussians. It will all be over within five minutes, you mark my words. Since Waterloo, France has lost the heart for a decent fight –"

He paused to take a sip of his own champagne; then, noticing someone over near the door – "Ah, here's young Manser now! I must go across and speak with him, if you ladies will excuse me – ?"

"And your two dear little boys, Catherine, are they both well?" Mrs Adeney enquired as her husband moved away.

"Oh, very well indeed. Benedict has learned to say so many words, you'd hardly believe it for a child who's not yet three. He chatters all day long and is such a darling. His father dotes upon him – and on Freddie, too. Though of course, being still in the care of a wet-nurse, the baby has yet to share equal honours in his father's affection."

The doctor's wife smiled at this eager demonstration of a mother's pride; then, leaning forward and lowering her voice so as not to be overheard by those around, she said confidingly,

"I'm so very pleased for you, my dear, that everything has turned out as it has, and that the good Lord has sent you happiness at last. If I may say, you are looking *radiant* this evening."

"Why – thank you, Mrs Adeney."

The other straightened. "And now I mustn't monopolise your company any longer. I shall go and sit down and enjoy this champagne."

Making sure that her guest was comfortably settled beside the fire, Kitty helped herself to another glass from one of the trays, and then went to join her stepdaughter Angelina, across the room by the windows. The heavy floor-length curtains had been drawn now, shutting out the chill November dusk, and the light of the gas-jets diffused by frosted globes shone warmly on the rich Venetian red of the velvet. Oliver had had the drawing room refurbished only this last year, and the result was one of graciously opulent taste.

"Oh, Mama – you'll never guess!" Angelina cried excitedly, linking her arm through Kitty's in an affectionate manner as she joined her. "Arthur has just told me. Mr Broadwood is to retire from the board of Faber and Russell, and guess who it is expected to take his place."

"But that's wonderful news! When did Arthur learn of it?"

"Earlier today. It seems that Mr Broadwood has been advised for the sake of his health that he should do less, and so he's decided to give up most of his board appointments in the City."

"I wonder what his wife thinks of that?"

Kitty turned to glance towards Frances Broadwood, seated side by side talking to Beatrice on the Chesterfield sofa. Henry Broadwood had suffered a mild heart attack earlier in the year and was warned that he ran the risk of another unless he altered some of his habits. Since those habits included a large consumption of brandy and a fondness for over-indulging himself at the dinner table, Mr Broadwood had not found the taking of such advice an easy matter, and his formal genial back-slapping bonhomie had begun souring to occasional bouts of testy short temper.

In the days when her husband had been a Member of Parliament and chairman of this-and-that, Frances Broadwood had held a high opinion of herself; and despite the fact that there was a difference of twenty-six years in their age, and Henry had something of a roving eye for a pretty ankle, her pride in her husband's position caused her to behave rather as does a doting mother towards a precocious child. Recently, however, as ill health took its toll of Mr Broadwood's capabilities and one by one his spheres of influence shrank, it was noticeable that his wife's easy-going if boastful manner was turning somewhat waspish.

When Kitty had first been married, Frances Broadwood had been one of her closest social acquaintances: not a friend, exactly, but someone she trusted sufficiently to confide in. During the past two years or so, she had sensed a coolness, a changing of attitude; and had put this down to Mrs Broadwood's having heard some whisper or other of her affair with Jonathan Rivers. Certainly, she had raised not a hand to help when Kitty had been forced to leave Sion Place in disgrace – indeed, she was probably one of the first to enjoy the scandal of the adultery. That business, and its consequences, had been kept a guarded secret, but servants talked, and who could blame Tunbridge Wells society for wishing to distance itself a little from the whiff of opprobrium. Had it not been for Oliver's tolerant demeanour and the fact that she'd borne him two sons, and was held in such obvious high favour by Mr Terris the parish minister, Kitty knew that she might well have found herself ostracised completely.

Not that she cared too much now. She had paid her debt, and locked the door on the past and all its memories.

Neither would she have been greatly concerned to discover that Frances Broadwood's growing detachment, her malicious remarks and little shafts of spite, were all rooted in a grudge against herself which had nothing to do with that past affair. The grudge had started long before, when Kitty's beauty had sufficiently infatuated Henry Broadwood for him to draw tactless comparisons with his own wife's form and features; and fed by jealousy, it had been exacerbated further as Henry's star waned while Oliver van der Kleve's glittered yet brighter in the City's heavens. Then Rose Maguire, whom Frances Broadwood had taken into service as a favour to Kitty, chose to give in her notice and return to Sion Place as lady's maid, leaving Mrs Broadwood the inconvenience of finding a trained replacement – which was no easy task when one was so *very* particular about cleanliness, honesty and nice manners.

These several different strands of discontent had together been woven into a single cord of ill feeling as a result of her growing friendship with Beatrice van der Kleve. The two women – one not yet out of her twenties and the mother of young children, and the other a spinster, middle-aged and now unmarriageable – had discovered a common bond between them both, rooted in enmity and rancour and directed against the same person – Kitty.

Catching her hostess's eye upon her now, Mrs Broadwood waved from the sofa and smiled before bending her head again to Beatrice's.

"I wonder what it is those two find to talk about all day," Angelina remarked innocently. "They've become very thick, haven't they, while I've been in Paris."

Kitty's response was a dismissive little shrug of the shoulder; then, looking round, she said, "I haven't seen Arthur for the last ten minutes or so. Is he with your Papa, do you think?"

"I don't know. I don't think so. He went off just now to fetch me something."

The young girl craned her neck to see across the room. Nearly all of the guests had arrived by this time, and were standing or sitting in threes and fours enjoying the preprandial conviviality of conversation and champagne until Nicholls was ready to announce that dinner was served.

"Oh – there he is now, look – over there with his mother and Mr Broadwood." She indicated the far side near the doorway, and as she raised her hand the gaslight caught the blaze of a solitaire diamond ring on her left finger.

Angelina had wanted this betrothal ring twelve months ago, when she'd completed her final year at L'École Rambouillet and returned home to Sion Place and to Arthur Russell's proposal of marriage. It was her father's decision, however, that she was too young at eighteen to know her own mind. Better to wait. If by her next birthday she and Arthur still wished to marry, then he would consider granting his consent and not before. One had to do these things properly, it was no good rushing into them: following the conventional betrothal period, the wedding could take place in 1872, when Angelina was twenty-one.

This past year had been one of marking time for both of

them – in different ways. Unbeknown to his intended bride, young Arthur had spent it sowing his wild oats around the London halls and learning how to gamble and drink like a gentleman. Marriage would alter his style of life considerably, and he wanted to cram as much hedonistic experience into these bachelor days as he could without quite ruining his health.

Angelina, on the other hand, had passed the twelve months quietly in her stepmother's company, enjoying the occasional day's outing to the coast or else to Town to shop in Knightsbridge. Paris had matured her; but it was love that made her blossom, gave the bloom to her cheeks and the sparkle to her eyes.

Tonight she looked at her best. She was nineteen, and promised in marriage to the one she adored. Noting the curve of her lips soften to a smile as Arthur Russell moved across to join them, Kitty prayed that life would treat her stepdaughter with kindness, spare her its knocks and blows, and keep her from anything that might change her present joy to future sorrow.

Arthur was enjoying himself immensely. He'd brought it off, by Gad – an alliance with the van der Kleves – a fingerhold on the first rung of that ladder to his dreams. Not long now and he'd be on the board of Faber and Russell; and in another – what, five, ten years? – they'd be offering him a banking directorship with van der Kleve Lindemanns.

Oh, life was good!

He leaned back in his chair at the dinner table and permitted himself a smile of self-congratulation. If he held on steadily to the same course he could be Lord Mayor of London by the end of the century – why not! Sir Arthur Russell. Yes, it had a good ring to it. Sir Arthur and Lady Russell.

Raising his wine glass to his lips, he glanced at the small white hand resting on the tablecloth beside him. It was waiting to be given another secret squeeze, and as he put down his glass again he dutifully obliged. It didn't take much to make Angelina happy – a wink, a nod, a whisper – yes, he'd made a good choice for himself, a damn' good choice.

He stifled a hiccup that tasted of roast beef and burgundy and smirked across at Frances Broadwood opposite. What a bitch *that* woman was; but what marvellously entertaining company – he did so enjoy hearing females tear one another's reputation to shreds while professing to be the best of bosom friends.

Frances and he had had a very interesting little conversation together earlier this evening at the Broadwoods' house. He'd stabled his carriage horse there after driving his mother from Mount Edgecumbe, and had been entertained by Frances while her husband doddered about doing something upstairs.

"So, my dear –" she'd said, "you've got what you want at last. My congratulations."

The cynical tone had made him a trifle cautious in his answer.

"I believe I am making Angelina very happy."

"But of course!"

"And I have her father's confidence."

"Indeed." Frances Broadwood had a way of narrowing her eyes like a cat when she smiled. "The father's confidence . . . and the stepmother's regard."

"Why, yes. That too. Mrs van der Kleve has shown herself – shall we say, interested in my courtship. In that respect she's been most encouraging."

"Is that so? From what I've seen of the way she behaves, I'd have thought the encouragement had a rather more personal motive."

"I'm sorry . . . I don't quite understand you."

"Really, Arthur! Don't you? And you such an *experienced* man of the world, too. You disappoint me."

Again, the cat's eyes smiled.

He'd felt the flush in his cheeks, concealed by the luxuriant growth of side-whiskers he now sported. "Are you by chance suggesting that Mrs van der Kleve has an interest in me other than that of future in-law?"

"By chance perhaps I am. She singles you out in company for private conversation, does she not? She pays you a great deal of notice –"

"Yes, but all of it on Angelina's behalf."

"Stuff! That's a ruse, a pretext. Her marriage hasn't been a happy one, you know. She enjoys amusing herself with young men closer to her own age."

"Is that so, ma'am. Then I must say that I've not

experienced such attentions myself." Arthur wondered where this bizarre conversation was leading. "Her behaviour towards me has always been very proper."

"Which is more than how one can describe her behaviour towards a certain other person. A drawing master, to be exact. Engaged to teach Angelina —"

Frances snatched her hand to her mouth in mock alarm. "Oh, dear — now I've really said too much. How naughty of me."

He'd been all agog for further detail. The idea that Mrs van der Kleve — the lovely, warm, feminine, untouchable Catherine — had been guilty of some sort of misconduct, suddenly opened new vistas of possibility to him.

The cat's eyes narrowed again into a sidelong look, and as casually as though she were discussing nothing more than the weather, Frances had continued airily, "I wonder you hadn't heard about it, my dear. *Quite* a little scandal at the time. She ran off with him, you know. Left poor Oliver in a most embarrassing position."

"But — but what happened? To end the affair, I mean?"

"Oh, well . . ." She examined her fingernails. "When the *grand amour* was uncovered, the lover simply abandoned the lady to her fate. Oliver had to take her back, of course. He had his reputation in the City to consider . . . at least, I believe that was the reason."

"Then he acted in the manner of a true gentleman," Arthur declared stoutly. Not for the world would he allow the malicious Mrs Broadwood to catch him out in an indiscretion. She'd soon see that it reached the ears of his prospective father-in-law, you could bet your life upon it.

"I think I shall forget this conversation," he added, just in time, as Henry Broadwood's mottled countenance showed itself at the door.

"La! But don't say I didn't warn you."

And she had moved past him, her smile now all for her husband.

Raising his glass to his lips again, Arthur eyed Catherine van der Kleve's reflection in the large wall mirror at one side of the dining room. Damned if she wasn't the most beautiful woman present tonight. The most beautiful woman in the

Wells, come to think of it. He'd always thought of her as being somewhere up on a pedestal, beyond the reach of that contamination of her sex which he'd witnessed and enjoyed so much of late; virtuous, a devoted mother and wife, and the epitome of domestic fidelity.

It just went to show how wrong, how very wrong a young fellow could be.

29

The carriage window blind had been drawn up, and the clear translucent light of the January day rimmed Kitty's profile with a sheen of pearl. As the train slowed on its approach into Chislehurst station, she leaned forward slightly to get a better view of the wooded slopes which rose away on the right, the winter-bare branches surmounted by the landmark of a shingled spire. Oliver had told her he'd heard some rumour that the defeated Emperor of France, Napoleon the Third, was proposing to spend his exile in residence here, at Camden Place.

But Chislehurst – why Chislehurst? – why not London or Windsor? Kitty sat back again. It seemed an odd sort of choice for such an exalted figure, to bury himself away here in the Kentish countryside.

Beside her on the padded leather seat, Angelina was reading, elbow cupped in one hand to steady her book against the jolting sway of the carriage. Opposite, stiffly upright, eyes closed, black kid-gloved hands folded in her lap, Beatrice van der Kleve sat in silent communion with her own thoughts. The three of them were travelling together into Town on a day's excursion to the shopping emporia; and Beatrice's presence – a last-moment arrangement – was owed to the fact that Perrins, her maid who would normally accompany her, was ill, and since Beatrice particularly wanted some lace for a new altar cloth for St Bride's, she was obliged on this one occasion to endure her sister-in-law's company.

It had been arranged that they would visit the drapery store of Marshall & Snelgrove, and the Pantheon Bazaar, both in Oxford Street, and Swan & Edgar's on the corner of Piccadilly Circus, before meeting Arthur Russell for luncheon; then afterwards, there was an abundance of shops by St Paul's Churchyard to call at, including George Hitchcock & Sons, whose plate-glass windows (the largest in London) were lit by gas chandeliers to show off their displays of silks, velvets, laces, ribbons, and Chinese shawls.

With another series of jolts, the train began picking up speed again as it drew out of Chislehurst and a cloud of sparks and sooty smoke swirled past the carriage window.

Beatrice opened her eyes.

"What book is that you are reading, Angelina dear?" she enquired after a few moments' scrutiny of her niece's bowed head.

Several further moments elapsed before Angelina looked up. "The book? Oh, it's Mrs Browning's poems."

She looked down again.

"I did not know that you enjoyed poetry," pursued her aunt.

"Oh . . . yes." This time the head remained bowed. "Very much."

"*Sonnets from the Portuguese*?" Kitty leaned to cast a glance over the pages opened beside her, and finding she'd guessed correctly, went on, "What pleasure I found in her verses too, at your age."

She paused, recalling; and then began to quote – "'If thou must love me, let it be for naught except for love's sake only.' How wonderfully Mrs Browning puts that!"

"Wonderfully indeed," Beatrice agreed acidly, looking away through the window.

Ignoring her aunt, Angelina took up the quotation. "'Do not say I love her for her smile – her look – her way of speaking gently – for a trick of thought that falls in well with mine –'"

"'And certes brought a sense of pleasant ease on such a day,'" Kitty completed the line. "Yes, I must admit, that was always my favourite. Although the third sonnet is almost as lovely."

"I hope that you are not about to give a rendition of that one also." Beatrice could not resist the opportunity for a little dig of spite. "It never ceases to astonish me that a thing learned parrot-fashion during infancy can be retained so long by the adult mind."

Kitty gave her a cool smile. "That surely depends upon the receptive qualities of the mind."

Then, to Angelina by way of a deliberate change of conversation – "Oh, I haven't told you, have I, that I received a

267

letter this morning from Harriet Hoffmann? You remember, she was Harriet Seymour before her marriage. Well, what do you think – she's had a baby. A little girl they're naming Edelgard – Ella, for short."

"Ella. That's pretty." Angelina placed an embroidered book-mark between the pages of Mrs Browning's sonnets, and closed them. "I suppose *I* shall be having to decide upon names in a few years more. I do so hope Arthur and I have a large family. Although –" she added hastily, a blush appearing suddenly in her cheeks – "we haven't yet discussed the matter of children."

"I should think not, indeed!" Beatrice appeared quite offended by the very idea of such indelicacy.

"When was Mrs Hoffmann's baby born?" Angelina wanted to know, pretending not to hear her aunt as their carriage rattled beneath a bridge.

"On New Year's Day," Kitty answered. "The perfect date for a new life, don't you think? Her husband, Doctor Peter Hoffmann, attended the delivery himself."

"Himself – ? Really?" This required a pause. "But didn't Mrs Hoffmann find that just a little . . . embarrassing?"

"Heavens above, no!" Kitty began laughing. "Why should she? Peter *is* her husband, after all, as well as being the child's father. What could be more natural than that he should be the one to bring his own daughter into the world?"

"I consider this an unsuitable conversation for Angelina," Beatrice interjected sharply, pinching in her lips and fixing her sister-in-law with a look of frigid disgust. "Confinements and the like is a subject fit only for discussion between those who are married, and most certainly not for the ears of young girls –"

"Or spinsters either, I suppose," Kitty couldn't help returning. Perhaps it was fortunate at that moment that the train reached a particularly noisy stretch of track where a number of suburban lines converged; and seeing it was useless to attempt further talk above the reverberating clatter of wheels, she picked up a copy of a magazine she'd brought with her, and started to read.

It wasn't much longer before the end of the journey; and descending from their carriage to join the mill of fellow-travellers streaming along the platform towards the station exit, the three women hastened to seek a hackney for hire at the cab stand outside.

The air here in the city was noticeably staler than the clear, cold winter freshness of the countryside. The daylight had a dingy yellowness about it, making everything appear slicked with a film of tarnish, and although it was still yet mid-morning, the first faint murkiness of a London fog was already starting to blur the distant perspective of buildings as their hackney cab travelled towards Piccadilly Circus. Once inside Swan & Edgar's, however, the bleak January weather was dispelled by the golden flare of gasoliers reflected in polished walnut surfaces, in bevelled plate-glass and lacquered veneers; while the malodorous stench of refuse and horse dung clinging to the streets was replaced by that rich, warm, interior smell of high-class emporia, a combination of perfume, beeswax, vanilla and hot-house flowers.

By midday, Angelina and Kitty had made most of their purchases and there only remained the altar cloth lace to buy from Hitchcock's after luncheon. Leaving the Oxford Street area, they took another hackney eastward along High Holborn and were set down in Ludgate Circus where it was planned they should meet Arthur Russell. It was just as well that Hitchcock's was close by, near St Paul's, for the fog was starting to thicken now, taking on that sulphurous opacity which had earned it the name of 'pea-souper'; and indeed, there was some discussion during luncheon whether or not it might be wiser to forget the lace for today and return to the rail terminus immediately they'd finished their meal.

Beatrice was alone in refusing to countenance this proposal. She had promised Mr Terris his new altar cloth for Sunday week; and if her sister-in-law and niece wished to journey back to Tunbridge Wells without her, why then they were perfectly at liberty to do so and she would follow by the next train. (This, of course, was out of the question, as she well knew: it was quite unthinkable that a woman of her class should travel unattended in a public conveyance. One read the most dreadful reports in the newspapers of ladies being molested, robbed and worse by ruffians taking advantage of the opportunity for crime which a closed carriage provided.)

So Hitchcock & Sons it was. Arthur Russell accompanied them, in case there might be some difficulty later in attracting a passing hackney cab to take them across the city. He'd be easier in his mind if he saw them safely himself as far as London Bridge, he said.

It was while the four of them were coming down Ludgate Hill away from Hitchcock's that an unsettling little incident took place. By this time the fog had grown quite dense in patches, like a dirty yellow veil of smoke filling up the streets from one side to the other, so that it was virtually impossible in places to see more than a few feet ahead. People loomed through the murk as nebulous outlines before being swallowed up again, and the noise of horse traffic was distorted and directionless so that one had to take care not to wander by mistake into the path of a carriage.

Kitty was walking just a couple of steps behind the others, keeping to the wall for safety's sake, when someone going past bumped into her and knocked the plaited-straw basket from her hand. Fortunately it held nothing breakable; but a few reels of silk thread just purchased and placed on top, escaped from their brown paper bag and rolled away across the pavement.

Calling to Angelina to wait, she bent to look for them.

"What's the matter?" Arthur asked, coming back to see. "What have you lost?"

He knelt beside her, and the fog seemed to embrace them both in its rolling dank cloud, shutting them off from the two women ahead. Kitty was just about to answer that she'd found what she'd dropped when Arthur said in a curious tone, "Aren't you a crafty one"; and as she rose to her feet, she felt his hand slip beneath her elbow to assist her.

It was what took place next that was so disturbing. Instead of releasing her as she thought, he put his arm around her and pulled her up against him in a hug, and before she could lean away he'd kissed her full upon the lips.

Almost at that same instant, just as his arm was falling from her waist, Beatrice van der Kleve appeared through the curtain of fog, peering forward in search of them.

"Aren't you a crafty one," Arthur repeated, grinning; and as he moved off, he gave a grotesquely exaggerated wink.

"It's starting to snow again," Oliver said, cupping a hand against the darkened window to look outside. "Just as well we

270

declined that invitation of the Broadwoods'. It's hardly a night for stirring abroad."

Seated in her wrapper by the bedroom fire, Kitty spared a glance from buffing her nails. Arthur Russell's mother had invited them to join the Broadwoods at her house on Mount Edgecumbe for dinner this evening, but pleading the discomfort of her monthly indisposition, Kitty had persuaded her husband that she'd prefer not to go.

"I'm sorry Angelina had to be disappointed," she said in answer. "You know, you could have taken her without me. I'm sure no one would have minded."

"*I* would have minded." Oliver let the curtain fall back across the window. "Henry Broadwood is a tedious old bore, and his wife – well, his wife would have taken advantage of the fact that I was there without you."

Kitty raised an eyebrow in amusement and paused to examine her nails before applying the ivory-backed buffer again. "You mean she would have flirted with you."

"She'd have done her best to embarrass me, that's what I mean. And I can hardly expect my own daughter to chaperone me."

He came over to the fire and sat down in the armchair opposite.

"Besides, it's my opinion that Angelina sees quite sufficient of young Arthur as it is. One evening spent apart from him won't harm her."

Something in the terseness of her husband's tone made Kitty cast another glance towards him. She hadn't mentioned that little incident in London last week, when Arthur Russell had kissed her in the fog. What would have been the point? To do so would only have stirred up trouble. And perhaps she had been mistaken; perhaps Arthur had been seized with a sudden spontaneous rush of affection for his future mother-in-law, and chose to demonstrate it in a somewhat clumsy fashion.

Somehow, though, Kitty doubted this. He'd obviously thought that she'd dropped the reels of thread on purpose, as an excuse to be alone with him for a moment; otherwise why should he have made that peculiar remark about her being – what was it – *crafty*? Had he mistaken her past kindness and attention for something altogether more personal?

She'd deliberately embroidered on her feeling of malaise this afternoon in order to avoid having to meet him this evening at Mount Edgecumbe. It was silly, of course. Arthur would not have dared do anything foolish in front of her husband and Angelina. But maybe if she were to keep her distance for a while, he might realise his error in supposing her interest to be motivated by anything other than her stepdaughter's own happiness.

Oliver leaned forward, elbows rested on his knees, looking into the fire. He had changed very little in feature since their marriage, and though the dark hair may have turned a shade greyer at the temples and side-whiskers which he wore just short of the jawline, the only concession to his forty-five years was the furrow of concentration between his brows and his occasional habit of forgetting where he'd put things.

For a while neither of them spoke. It was companionable to be here, husband and wife, alone at the end of the day, their two young sons soundly asleep in the nursery above; sharing together the peaceful stillness, the rustle of flames in the hearth, the soft whisper of snow at the window. It was simple little things like these which of late had seemed to bring them both just that bit closer to one another.

"Oliver –" Kitty said suddenly, breaking the lengthening silence. "Oliver, tell me truthfully – what's your opinion of Arthur Russell?"

"My opinion?" The question seemed to startle him by its unexpectedness. "Why – he's a pleasant enough young fellow. Sound head for business. Respectable background. What makes you ask?"

She gave a shrug. "I was thinking of Angelina. Whether it might not have been wiser if she'd had introductions to other young men first before accepting his proposal. Marriage is such a gamble, after all."

He responded with a searching look which seemed to say "who better than we should know that?"; and then, turning his gaze again to the fire, answered after a moment, "You think she should have been given the opportunity for choice?"

"I do. She's very young still."

"Well, she has another year or so in which to change her mind, that is why I insisted upon a long engagement."

There was a further silence. Oliver leaned back in his chair, crossing one leg over the other.

"Is there something about Arthur Russell which you dislike?" he asked.

Kitty avoided meeting his eye. "Not especially. As you say, he seems pleasant enough. My only concern is that he should make Angelina happy."

"And have you reason to suspect that he won't?"

The question was too near the truth for comfort. "Why, no . . . no, of course not. I'm sure they're both very suited to one another."

Another pause.

"Don't *you* think so?"

"Naturally I think so. I would never have consented to their betrothal otherwise. If you have your doubts about the young man, Catherine, then I hope you will have the sense sufficiently to confide them in me –"

"Oh, I have no doubts! None at all." She began to buff her nails again, little brisk movements which betrayed a certain amount of agitation. She wished now that she hadn't mentioned Arthur Russell.

"Did I tell you that Benedict learned a new word today?" she went on brightly, changing the subject.

"Yes, you informed me at tea." Oliver leaned forward once more. "What's the matter with you this evening, my dear? You appear very on edge. Is there anything wrong?"

"Wrong? Heavens, no. Why should there be? I'm feeling a little . . . out of sorts, that's all."

She made a delicate gesture indicating herself. Since the birth of their sons, she had actually suffered far less inconvenience at this time of the month; but feminine matters were one of the few remaining mysteries of marriage and a wife did not discuss such things with her husband as a rule.

His expression softened.

"Come here," he said, patting his knee. "Come and rest yourself against me and I'll soothe away some of the discomfort."

This was something he enjoyed doing when they were alone in the intimacy of the bedroom; enjoyed as much for the relaxation and pleasure it gave him as for his wife's own personal indulgence.

Kitty threw aside the nail buffer and moved across the hearth, curling herself on the rug between her husband's legs and resting her head against his knee. Gently he began to stroke her hair, his fingers moving over its softness in a slow, lingering caress, watching the way the firelight caught the honey-gold strands as the shadow of his hand lifted.

She stretched herself languorously, and sighed.

"Happy?" he murmured.

"Mm."

Yes . . . she supposed that she *was* happy. What more could a woman want of life than this – comfort, security, tenderness, warmth? Yet at the same time, she asked herself silently, what were all these without love – the one vital thing which held and bound together the wholeness and unity of marriage.

Love. Whatever else she might possess, that was what she did not have. Love . . . the imagination of the heart. And lacking it, she lacked all else beside; for the material comforts, the trappings of wealth, a husband's fond attention, were only an outward show worn for the eyes of the world, a veneer masking the emotional emptiness within.

30

My dearest Harriet,

What must you think of me, I wonder, for my neglect in not writing sooner in reply to your letter of last month! No doubt you have been wondering what could possibly be amiss to explain my long silence. To relieve your mind, let me say at once that it is not ill health nor ill fortune; – tho' I have been driven almost to both; – no, I have been sorely vexed by an *embarrassment* which is not of my own contriving, and it has so exercised my *wits* and my *patience* that, to speak the truth, I have been too distracted by its problems to apply myself to the writing of this letter until now.

At breakfast today I said to myself – "you will go directly to your room, madam, and provide yourself with pen, ink and paper; and you will remain there until you have remedied your omission of Affection to a faithful and best-loved friend" – Can you not hear Miss Meyrick's stern tones in that! – and so, dear Harriet, here I am fulfilling my self-command.

Firstly, let me reply to your News. What a pleasure it must have been, truly, that your brother William was able to make such a long visit with you in Baden. I believe the last time I saw him for myself was upon an afternoon at the Academy, when he came to fetch you home in his new carriage and pair, expressly that he might show off his *toy* to the world. How very handsome he looked, I do recall; and what a sad reflection upon the charms of womenfolk, that not one has yet succeeded in capturing his heart sufficiently for a lasting romance to blossom forth. Perhaps the

Fräuleins of Baden will prevail upon his affection where the *misses* of England and the Americas have so signally failed to leave their mark. I am sure that you will be more than happy to see him married, for as you say, William is heir to the family name and fortune, and at the grand old age of eight-and-twenty he has surely seen enough of the world to wish now to become more settled; and your dear husband is quite right to counsel him that "without roots there can be no sprigs". (I trust I have translated the German correctly?)

I can scarce credit that baby Ella is cutting her first teeth already! If she is fractious, I recommend rubbing her gums with honey, having found this a sovereign remedy; – but on no account allow her tender little mouth to be *lanced*, for I have witnessed the most fearful soreness resulting from this cruel practice, and it does not assist the teeth to erupt any the sooner.

Benedict is now growing to such a *big boy*! He is his father in colour and feature, but I am pleased to say that his nature is very loving and open, and he can no more do a wicked deed than could an Angel. His greatest joy is his rocking-horse, upon which he pretends that he is riding upon the pommel of Oliver's saddle (as he is allowed occasionally to do) and I believe it will not be long before his father permits him a pony of his own.

Little Freddie has found his feet now, and is into mischief everywhere one turns. The nursery-maid has been hard put to it to shorten all his skirts so that he does not stumble; – he tears the hems so *dreadfully* that I am in half a mind to put him into breeches before his birthday. It is a foolishness, do you not agree, my dear, that boys must be dressed as girls throughout their infancy? I cannot see the sense of it; tho' doubtless it has all to do with Convention and Custom, that pair of *antique bores*.

And now to the main burthen of my letter. I hardly know how I should describe the events of recent weeks, for so much of it may be mere suspicion only, or else the product of an over-fevered Imagination. You know how very *intimate* Beatrice has grown in her friendship with Frances Broadwood. They are as thick as two thieves bent upon the same crime, and not a day goes by but that one is not calling upon the other for the purpose of putting their tongues to some mischief. I am reliably informed by Rose Maguire that they spout all kind of calumnies against me in my absence; and yet when I am in company, they are both as *sweet as treacle* so that one would think I were the dearest friend of their bosom.

I hear you say – ignore them! And indeed, Harriet, I do, for their words are as worthless as their smiles; – and yet, as is the manner of all poison, the insidious effect upon my system is beginning to sicken me. What is it that they hope to achieve by linking my name so improperly with that of Arthur Russell? And what further must I do to show that my interest in that young man is quite impartial? I cannot *shun* him, for that would serve to wound Angelina; – and yet I dare not *smile* for fear he will but take it as further encouragement. I know not what I should do for the best, for whatever my action, it is apt to be misinterpreted by one party or the other.

On Sunday last, which was Easter Day, Arthur attended the service at St Bride's, and seated himself between Angelina and me. Imagine my discomfiture when I felt his knee pressed close against my own during the sermon – not once only, but *several times* – and in the most deliberate fashion. What was worse, I could not move away, for Oliver sat at my other side, and so I had to endure this intimacy without a sign of reproach to its perpetrator. But wait – read what was to follow! Upon leaving our pew at the conclusion of the service, I carelessly let drop my Prayer Book; and who else should it be but Arthur Russell who knelt to return it to me, at the same time *pressing my fingers* as tho' he would say – "what a sly one you are to make a purpose of what seems accident".

Indeed, upon reflection, there is so much which leaves my behaviour vulnerable to misconstruction. I must own to you, Harriet, that I fear nothing good can come of such a tangled web as Bea and her dear friend seek to spin for me; and upon this I must now close my letter, remaining ever your most affectionate –

Kitty.

No, I cannot do as you advise me, and unburden myself of
the situation to Oliver. Where is my proof? – What is
innuendo and suggestion when balanced against the risk to
my dear ones' happiness? I am determined instead to seek
a meeting with A. R., and in some private place where I
may speak my mind.

Yours in haste – K.

With the wisdom of hindsight, Kitty saw how all too easily
she had played into the hands of those who wished her ill. She
should have heeded Harriet's advice and gone to Oliver; it
might have spared her so much trouble. But at the time, the
simplest course had seemed to keep the matter entirely secret
from her husband, for the less he knew of it, the less unpleasantness there would be for everyone concerned, especially her
stepdaughter Angelina.

She would confront Arthur Russell directly with his misconduct, and by a little plain speaking leave him in no doubt of
his error, since the young man was obviously labouring under
some kind of false delusion about her feelings towards him.

How was their meeting to be arranged? Kitty pondered this
at some length. In the old days, during her affair with Jonathan
Rivers, it had been an easy matter to send her maid Dobby
with a note; but Dobby was gone, and she had no wish to
involve young Rose Maguire in anything similarly underhand.
A letter to Arthur Russell, addressed to him at his club in Old
Broad Street, would doubtless suffice for her purpose, and his
reply could be sent *poste restante* via the post office on the Parade
in Tunbridge Wells.

This was the stratagem accordingly followed, and if Arthur
felt any surprise, or indeed, curiosity, that his future mother-in-
law should write to him with such a proposition, his response
gave no hint of it but merely thanked her for her letter and
suggested that if it were convenient, they should meet at his
rooms in Hart Street, just a few minutes' walk from the Tower
of London. Kitty would have preferred a less intimately informal
venue, but since what she had to say was of such a very private
and personal nature, she agreed to accept this arrangement and

fixed the date for May the fifth – a Friday – when she knew Oliver would be away on business in Manchester.

It was a warm, rather stuffy afternoon and the smell of fish from the Billingsgate wharf hung unpleasantly between the grimy walls of tenements crowding the narrow, airless back-streets of the City. Kitty took a hackney cab across London Bridge as far as the junction of Eastcheap with Great Tower Street, and completed her journey the short way on foot into Hart Street, where she found Arthur Russell's rooms to be on the first floor of a large old building standing back within a cobbled yard.

"I would have come to meet you from the station," he said, ushering her into his sitting room from the corridor stairs and closing the door behind her, "had not your letter emphasised a need for discretion."

Kitty removed her hat and gloves and looked around. "It would have been imprudent for us to be seen together." The room smelled of dust and stale cigar smoke and macassar oil and there were signs that someone had given it a hurried tidying. "Thank you for respecting my wishes."

"I hope I shall always do that."

He took the hat and gloves from her and put them aside on a table; then, turning again – "May I offer you a glass of wine?"

She shook her head. "What I'm here to say won't take that long."

"Now you mustn't disappoint me, Catherine." The uninvited use of her forename jarred. It was a liberty he'd never taken before. "I insist you join me in a glass. I've some excellent champagne brought in especially."

"A kind thought, but I'm afraid I seldom drink, and certainly never before dinner."

"Ah well . . . as you wish." He gave her a strange look, half-humorous, half-appraising. "But you won't object if I have one? I must admit, now that we're together alone at last, I feel just a trifle overawed by the – shall we say *honour*, you've chosen to pay me."

"I would hardly call this visit an honour," Kitty said bluntly. "And neither will you once you've heard me out. I am not here to be entertained, Arthur –"

"No?" Again, he gave her that look, then smiled and went

across to the fireplace where the blackened ashes of burnt paper littered the hearth. Against the wall at one side stood a mahogany wine cooler, a handsome piece of furniture with fluted legs and lion-mask brass handles.

Lifting the lid, he withdrew a bottle of Bouchie Fils et Cie, and with his back still turned as he stripped the foil from the neck, he asked, "You're sure you won't change your mind and join me?"

She made no answer. Exasperation with this little performance of his was beginning to shorten her patience.

The champagne cork made a soft *pop* as it was eased from the bottle.

"I take it Mr van der Kleve isn't aware of this assignation of ours," he said over his shoulder.

"If you mean does he know of our meeting today – no, I preferred not to inform him, as I made perfectly clear in my letter."

"Just so. It would never do to tell one's husband everything."

He took up a wine glass and filled it as he moved away from the fireplace; then, standing with a bottle in one hand and glass in the other he raised a toast to Kitty.

"Here's to . . . expectations."

The chilly look in her eyes should have warned him that he was starting to presume a fraction too far upon the mannered control his guest had so far exhibited.

"I think," she said quietly, "that your expectations fly a great deal higher than the situation warrants. Unless, of course, you refer to your future with my stepdaughter."

He took a sip of champagne. "Let us be candid with one another –"

"Indeed!"

"– my darling fiancée has nothing to do with you and me being here together."

"On the contrary, she has *everything* to do with it. It's for her sake that I'm here at all, and I hope before we go any further with this conversation that you understand that quite clearly. I'm here on Angelina's behalf, and for no other purpose."

Arthur's expression narrowed as he raised the glass again to his lips.

"I wish I could get your measure," he said. "You certainly know how to play the game with a fellow. I'll tell you directly without mincing words – you've driven me almost to distraction with your behaviour and I think it's high time you dropped this pretence of being the virtuous wife and mother, because frankly, my dear, your cover is starting to wear a little thin."

Kitty's nostrils dilated at the gross impertinence of such a statement. "Do I take it you are implying that my conduct towards you was intended as an enticement?"

"What else am I to suppose? For the past two years you've done nothing but dance after me in public and generally make yourself as obliging as you decently could, not to mention all the little private signs of favour – no, wait a moment, let me finish! – all those smiles and intimate glances you've given me. After so much encouragement, why draw back now, Catherine? Why waste so much effort?"

"If you were not such an arrogant, self-conceited, shallow, ingratiating young puppy –" her voice shook slightly with the intensity of her anger – "you might perhaps have appreciated that my interest was solely for the benefit of Angelina's happiness. When she went away to Paris she asked me to ensure your affections wouldn't wander elsewhere. And I fulfilled that obligation. Do you imagine that I actually *enjoy* your company? Do you think I would jeopardise my family, my social position, in order to pursue some silly flirtation with a person I find not the least entertaining or attractive?"

Arthur Russell's face flushed dark red beneath the glossy auburn extravagance of his side-whiskers; and before she could go on, he'd flung back in a blustering, spiteful tone – "The truth of it is, I'm too good for you. If I'd been some hired drawing master employed by your husband, you'd doubtless have welcomed me into your bed with open legs."

There was a sudden stunned silence. Kitty felt the blood starting to hammer in her ears. To have that old affair dragged up so abruptly to be cast in her teeth – and in such an uncouth, unlooked-for manner –! The shock of it jolted her to the pit of her stomach.

Arthur refilled his champagne glass.

"Ha, that's taken some of the wind from you, hasn't it," he said with a smirk, seeing how hard his words had struck home. "You didn't think I'd heard about your little peccadillo, did you, Catherine dear. Doubtless you're wondering now who it was told me."

She did not look at him, but went to take up her hat and gloves from the table.

"Surely you're not going already?" Putting down the bottle, he moved to intercept her. "Why, the fun's not even started – you owe me a kiss, at least, for all the trouble you've put me to."

"Please allow me to pass," she answered tonelessly. "I have said all I came here to say and now I wish to leave."

She stepped to the left to avoid him, but he stepped with her; and when she attempted to move instead to the right, he followed again, blocking the way so that she had no choice but to stand where she was.

"Didn't you hear me, Catherine? You owe me a kiss."

He was close enough now for her to smell the wine on his breath.

"Touch me and I warn you – my husband shall hear of it."

Arthur laughed unpleasantly. "You'd never dare to tell him."

"Indeed I would. And I shall, if forced. Now let me pass."

"And what would you say? That you wrote to me at my club requesting a private meeting, and asking that my reply be sent discreetly? That you agreed to come to my rooms alone, and ensured no one would know of your purpose – pretending you were here in Town for some other reason? How would he respond to that, I wonder? D'you think he'll believe you if you say it was done for Angelina?"

"Why should he not believe me." But she knew the answer to that even before Arthur Russell said it.

"Because, my dear, you're an adulteress – and he'll simply conclude you're up to your old tricks again."

Kitty's hand came up in a stinging slap which caught him full across the cheek.

"You vixen –!" He grabbed at her arm as she went to strike him again.

"Let me go –"

"By God I won't. Not until I've made you pay for that."

Encumbered by the glass he was still holding, he tried to drag her against him, but she fought him off with a strength born of sudden fury, pummelling his chest with her fist so that he was pushed awkwardly off-balance. One of the pins holding her hair came out in the tussle, and several loosened strands fell forward across her forehead. In this dishevelled state, she snatched up hat and gloves and ran towards the door before Arthur could move to stop her again.

"You'll be sorry for this –" she threw back at him as she turned the knob. "I'll see you damned before you marry Angelina –"

She flung the door open and went out into the corridor, pushing the hair from her face, tears of anger and humiliation starting to well in her eyes.

A few yards away, just reaching the head of the stairs, were two women. And as she paused hurriedly to put on her hat, Kitty recognised them.

Arthur Russell's mother and Frances Broadwood.

31

"Mrs van der Kleve, miss?"

The nursery-maid shook her head.

"No, I haven't seen her at all. Leastways, she hasn't been up here this morning."

"You don't know where she is, I suppose," Angelina enquired.

"No, miss, I'm sorry, I don't. Perhaps Rose Maguire can tell you."

"It's Rose's day off."

"Oh – so it is. I'd forgotten."

The maid bent to pick up a scarlet and gold lead soldier from the nursery carpet, and turning to the small boy playing quietly on the window seat, chided him, "Now, Master Benedict, you'll have this trod on and broke if you leave it a-lying there."

Without a word the child slipped down from his seat to take his toy, then went and placed it back with its comrades in the wooden fort on the table against the wall.

"I'm sorry I can't help you, miss." The nursery-maid turned again to Angelina.

"It doesn't matter. I expect my stepmother's gone out somewhere."

"Aye, belikes that's the case. She'd be here normally, as a rule. Madam always makes a point o' coming up to play wi' the children while I go and prepare their midday meal."

Angelina looked across at her half-brother, and seeing his attention fixed upon her, gave him a smile in return as she said, "Well, now that I'm here, Emily, *I'll* stay for a while and amuse them if it would help."

"Oh, I'd be ever so grateful if you would, miss! Just to keep an eye on 'em both for me. I won't be gone above ten minutes – there's some soup from yesterday's dinner left over to warm, and I'll do 'em a bit o' beef toast each. They like that. Don't you, Master Benedict –" addressing the child – "you like a bit o' beef toast?"

Sucking in his mouth he answered her dutifully, "Yes, Em'ly."

"There's a good boy!" And turning to Angelina again – "Master Frederick's still asleep, miss, but seeing I were just about to rouse him, p'raps you'd do it for me, would you mind, please? He do get that contrary if he's woke straight to his food."

When the maid had departed about her errand, shutting the nursery door behind her, Angelina gave Benedict another smile and held out her hand.

"Shall we go and wake Freddie together?"

He gave this invitation solemn thought, then climbed down from the window seat a second time and came to put his own small hand into hers.

"Fweddie cwies," he informed her in his three-year-old's lisping speech as they crossed the sun-filled room. "Fweddie's naughty."

"Oh? Is he?"

A nod. "He cwies for Mama."

"And is that naughty?"

Another nod.

"Who says so?"

"Em'ly."

Not wishing to undermine the authority of the nursery-maid by commenting on this, Angelina said instead, "Do you suppose Freddie will cry when we waken him?"

This time the head beneath its mop of thick dark curls was given an exaggerated shake.

The van der Kleve children had separate sleeping places here in the nursery quarters at the top of the house. Benedict slept in his own little room along the passage; but Frederick, being hardly more than a baby still, had a cot in the maid's bedroom where she could attend to him if he were at all unsettled in the night. He lay there now, a large, pink, solid-looking infant with his thumb contentedly in his mouth, eyes shut fast against the lace-edged pillows propping him. Unlike his brother, he had his mother's fair colouring, but his nature was all his own, being bold and pugnacious and entirely fearless. Already his proud father was speaking of him as a future Army officer. (Benedict, of course, would follow the paternal footsteps into merchant banking.)

Angelina leaned over the cot rail and gently touched the back of her hand to the sleep-flushed cheek. There was a protesting little grunt and then a smacking noise as Frederick, eyes still closed, commenced to suck upon his thumb.

She stroked the duckling-yellow fluff of hair and said softly, "Freddie – ?"

This time the eyelids trembled.

"Fweddie!" Benedict echoed, standing on tiptoe to hold the top of the rail. "Wake up, Fweddie! Food!"

This had the instant desired effect. His brother's eyes opened into dawning attention; and after a moment's unfocused stare, they fixed themselves upon Angelina's face and a smile that would not have disgraced a cherub curved upon either side of the wet thumb.

"Hello, Freddie," she greeted him, turning back the coverlet and drawing the skirts of his day-gown over his sturdy, dimpled legs. "It's time to get you up."

Removing his thumb, the infant surveyed her a few seconds longer before responding in a curiously assertive tone for one so young – "Mamma!"

"No, Mama isn't here this morning." She leaned forward and lifted him to his feet, supporting herself against the cot-side.

"*Mamma!*"

"Mama will come in-a-minute, Fweddie." Benedict poked a hand through the rails and patted his brother in a reassuring manner, repeating, "in-a-minute"– a phrase he'd learned from Emily the maid and thought meant "soon, but not yet".

Seeing the baby chin begin to tighten ominously, Angelina swung Frederick up from his cot into her arms and carried him through to the next room. Here she went over to sit on the window seat, and settling him comfortably on her knee, proceeded to distract his attention from his absent mother by jigging him up and down and tickling him.

"Sing a song!" cried Benedict, following in a series of skips and hops across the square-patterned carpet. "Sing a song, 'Lina!"

"A song? Very well. Which song would you like?"

"Pat-a-cake!"

286

"Do you know the words?"

An emphatic nod.

Taking both little Frederick's hands in hers, she commenced to clap them together in time to the tune, singing softly and slowly, "Pat-a-cake, pat-a-cake, baker's man, bake me a cake as fast as you can –" while Benedict, clapping with them, joined in with a piping treble.

They were just beginning the nursery rhyme again when the outer door opened to admit Emily, carefully balancing a laden tray.

"Num-nums!" crowed Frederick, squirming round in Angelina's lap and wriggling to free himself. "Num-nums!"

"What an appetite that child has, to be sure," the maid exclaimed, setting the tray down on the table beside Benedict's wooden fort. "It's a wonder his little legs don't snap at the knees, the amount o' food he eats."

Then, coming across to take him from his stepsister, "I've asked Mr Nicholls if he knows where Madam is, miss. He says she went out early on, but she's expected in for dinner."

"Oh. I see. Thank you."

"And there's a message from Miss Beatrice. Will you go down to the morning room this instant, miss, she says."

"Oh? Did she mention why?"

There was a shake of the head beneath its white starched cap. The word 'trouble' formed itself in Emily's mind, but it wasn't for her to declare as much. It was something all to do with Mrs van der Kleve – she'd gathered that from the talk in the kitchen, where Jane Perrins was holding forth in her highty-toighty manner to Cook. Emily hadn't stayed to listen, priding herself on her loyalty to her mistress. Six years ago, when she'd been just a slip of a girl working as skivvy at the Young Ladies' Academy down the road, she'd attended on Madam the night before her marriage to the Master. And last summer, when she'd come here to Sion Place applying for the post of nursery-maid, Mrs van der Kleve had remembered her, and given her the position even though her qualifications weren't half as good as some of the others interviewed.

Let Jane Perrins rant and rail as she would: she was no more than Miss Beatrice's mouthpiece, and there wasn't one belowstairs but knew of the bitter ill-wishing *that* one harboured for the Mistress.

"Thank you ever so much for your help, Miss Angelina," the maid said as the other was going out at the nursery door. "I know Madam does appreciate it, the time you make to spend wi' these two little ones."

"You wished to speak to me, Aunt Beatrice?"

Angelina came into the morning room, wondering what was the reason for this peremptory summons from the nursery.

"I hope it's nothing too important – I'd planned to call at the lending library before they close for luncheon."

"That will have to wait, I'm afraid, my dear. Shut the door and come and sit here beside me on the sofa."

Beatrice van der Kleve's voice held a note that made her niece look at her twice. It sounded – sympathetic, almost. Quite unlike Aunt Bea's usual tone.

"Is there anything wrong?" she asked, deliberately going to seat herself in an armchair opposite.

The answer was made without preamble. "I'm sorry to say, there is. Frances Broadwood has been here just now to see me. What she had to tell me was –" a slight pause – "well, my dear, it was quite the most *dreadful* thing. Indeed, I hardly know how I should tell you of it myself."

"But what? What has happened?" A sudden thought occurred. "Is it – is it Arthur?"

"It concerns Arthur, yes."

Angelina's hand went to her throat. "There hasn't been an accident, has there? He's not hurt?"

"No, no, my dear, he's perfectly all right. But I fear his *reputation* may be in some danger because of what has come to light."

"What do you mean? I don't understand. What could possibly harm his reputation?"

Beatrice smoothed her hands slowly together, an odd gesture as though she were not so much wringing them as relishing what it was she was about to divulge.

"Yesterday afternoon, as I am informed, Mrs Broadwood and Mrs Russell were in Town to visit an acquaintance of the late Mr Russell. Finding they had time to spare before their journey home, they decided to call upon Arthur in Hart Street –"

"Hart Street? But surely he'd be at his office?"

288

"Ah, they had gone there first, to be told he had taken the afternoon off to deal with the matter of some important paperwork left at his rooms."

"I see."

Beatrice continued to smooth her hands.

"As the two ladies were approaching Arthur's door, they observed it open, and someone come out – a woman. Though in the half-light, Frances said, they did not immediately recognise her. It was only as they moved nearer, and noted her dishevelled appearance, that they realised with a thrill of shock who she was."

This time the pause was solely for dramatic effect.

"I am sorry that I must be the one to tell you this, my dear. But the person leaving your fiancé's rooms was Catherine . . . Catherine, your stepmother."

"Mama?" In her quick relief, Angelina uttered a laugh. "Is that all? Dear me, I was beginning to worry for a moment! Mama is free to visit Arthur if she chooses – it's hardly a crime. Heavens, Aunt Beatrice, I thought you were going to say something awful, that he'd had a woman of doubtful morals in his rooms!"

"And indeed, that is precisely the truth of it. You do not seem to appreciate, my dear, the implication of the circumstances."

Beatrice was somewhat resentful that her moment of high drama should have fallen so disappointingly flat.

"Arthur was not entertaining your stepmother. Quite the contrary. She had gone there yesterday to force herself upon him for a purpose which it does not behove me to describe."

The other stared at her for a second or two as the import of this sank in; then she threw back her head and laughed again, a little hysterically.

"What are you saying? That Mama intended to *seduce* my fiancé? Oh, but how droll! I know you and Mrs Broadwood hate her like poison, but really, Aunt Beatrice – coming even from you, such a suggestion is utterly ridiculous!"

"Arthur himself does not think so."

"No? Is that fact, or Frances Broadwood's opinion?"

Beatrice's hands ceased their smoothing and folded themselves together upon the lap of her steel-grey sateen morning gown.

Somewhat tightly she said, "I do not wonder you should

adopt such an awkward tone, my dear, and therefore I shall overlook your discourtesy in speaking of Mrs Broadwood so. She has your best interests at heart, believe me. We both of us do."

Angelina's voice took on an edge of mistrust. "Then why couldn't you have waited until Arthur had the opportunity to tell me about it himself? Why be in such an unseemly haste to cast mud at Mama?"

The aspersion was ignored. "I wished you to be aware of the situation –"

"It seems to me there is no 'situation'. Only gossip and hearsay."

"I see I must speak plainly." Vexation at this contrary attitude was tempered by the undertow of malicious pleasure running through Beatrice van der Kleve at the prospect of seeing her abominated sister-in-law finally brought to book. Frances's news, delivered not half an hour ago, had been like the kiss of life to her fading dreams of exacting revenge for the years of domestic snubs and slights.

A grimace that might almost have been a smile tugged thinly at the sides of her mouth.

"Mrs Russell was naturally anxious to know what had happened – your stepmother appeared so very distraught, and her greeting – well, Frances says it was quite as though she would have avoided speaking if she could, but since they must pass on the corridor, she had no choice but to acknowledge them."

"Yes, yes, but what did *Arthur* have to say?" Angelina came in again impatiently. "What was *his* explanation for Mama's state?"

"My dear, he made no attempt to disguise the unpalatable truth. Frances reported to me his very words – 'If Mrs van der Kleve is put out of temper, it is because I refused her what she wanted.' And when Mrs Russell asked what was meant by that, he told her your stepmother had been plaguing him with her attentions for some while, but he had not liked to say anything for fear of causing embarrassment to your father."

Angelina's round face began tightening into a little mask of hurt; hurt and something more – something not too far removed from the sullen, withdrawn peevishness she had turned upon the world as a child.

Seeing that look, Beatrice hurried on – "Oh, my poor, poor girl. If only you had heeded my words and not trusted your affections so openly to that woman! You see how she has served you? She is a canker in the bosom of this family, and she will not be satisfied until she has done all in her power to harm us. She caused your Papa untold anguish by her wretched affair with Mr Rivers – she has usurped my authority, turned even the servants against me – she has carried gossip of Mrs Broadwood around the town – and now she is determined to ruin the happiness of you and your fiancé by enticing Arthur into shameful misconduct. She is an evil, wicked, dangerous creature and the only consolation I can offer, my dear, is that this time she has over-reached herself. The minute your Papa returns from Manchester I shall see to it that he is fully informed of her disgusting behaviour."

"And *I* think you should mind your own business, Aunt Beatrice." The expression was still sullen, but now there were two red spots of temper in Angelina's cheeks, and any sudden suspicion of brightness in her eyes was due more to tears of anger than of misery. "It is not for you to meddle in what's none of your affair. You'll only paint things blacker than they seem. If there is any truth in this vile imputation, it should be Arthur who informs Papa, not you."

The heat of her words was matched by her aunt's reply. "Are you suggesting that what I have told you is a mere fabrication?"

"I should not be surprised to learn that it were. Ever since my father's marriage you have tried to manipulate events in order to cast the very worst light upon Mama –"

"Oh, do stop referring to her as your Mama! She is *not* your Mama – she is a stepmother."

"I shall refer to her as I wish!"

Aunt and niece glared at one another.

Then Angelina went on again, "For as long as she has lived in this house, you have tried to warp my mind against her – even to encouraging insolence and mischief. Have you forgotten how you praised me when I stole – yes, *stole* – things from her room? Have you forgotten –"

"Now that is enough!" Beatrice rose to her feet, her features working with outraged indignation. "I see how well that woman has played upon your innocence. And I pity you, my dear, because you are about to experience a most distressing awakening. I have a duty to this family, a duty to protect its members against those who seek to damage its stability, and I am sorry that the execution of that duty must cause you pain."

Angelina rose with her. "Until I hear from Arthur's own lips that Mama has behaved in any way improperly, I cannot believe that this – fantastic story is anything other than a spiteful exaggeration. Mama loves me! Why should she wish me harm?"

"Because you are your father's daughter. And old enough by now to realise that she has loathed your Papa since the day of their marriage. By hurting you she hits at him."

Lips pared to a bloodless line, Beatrice crossed over to the bell-pull by the fireplace.

Without looking at her niece, she said coldly, "I shall ask Nicholls to have a telegraphic message sent from the post office, requesting Arthur to come down at once. The sooner he is here with the proof of that woman's misdoing, the sooner perhaps you will come to your senses and realise how cruelly you have deceived yourself by trusting her."

32

The moment Kitty saw the surprise replaced by quick, sharp, spiteful curiosity in Frances Broadwood's eyes, she had known that a hornets' nest of trouble was about to be stirred up round her ears.

She had come home from London that afternoon only grateful that Oliver was still absent in Manchester, giving her time at least to consider how best to draw the sting of the situation, in the likely event that some garbled and highly coloured account of her visit to Hart Street would be relayed to her husband at the earliest opportunity.

She could go to him herself with the truth, of course; but it would be her word against that of Arthur Russell – the word of a wife who'd already proved unfaithful, against that of a young gentleman with both career and reputation to safeguard. On this alone, the balance of credibility would already seem to tilt in Arthur's favour, without the added weight of Beatrice and Mrs Broadwood behind him, ready to make as much capital of the affair as they could.

What she needed, Kitty decided after a sleepless night, was an ally; someone totally unbiased to support her; someone aware of her past, but equally also aware of her repentance; someone sufficiently on the side-lines to be impartial, yet at the same time well enough acquainted with matters to appreciate the dilemma in which she now found herself.

There was only one candidate suitably qualified for the role – Edward Terris; which was why Kitty had just risen to an early breakfast, dressed with more than usual care, and quitted the house before Fanny Broadwood, bursting at the seams with her news for Beatrice, should arrive for their daily morning ritual of tea and tattle.

Pompous he might be, but the Reverend Mr Edward Terris was unprejudiced; and the plum-voiced pulpit manner hid a mind which was altogether sharper and more perceptive than appearance might suggest. When first she had made his acquaintance, Kitty was inclined to dislike the minister, thinking him to be Oliver's pocket parson; but that was a misjudgment. He was no one's man but his own and God's, as she had come to appreciate during these past few years. The obsequious deference of his manner towards the more wealthy and influential of his parishioners was nothing more than a top-soil of social esteem to nurture their vanity and ensure the continuation of their guineas into his collecting plate – a necessary ploy, as he'd admitted in private to Kitty, for without their goodwill how could he feed the hungry mouths and clothe the ragged backs of those of his flock so very much less privileged?

Since becoming a member of various committees at St Bride's, Kitty had perforce been thrown much into Mr Terris's company, and had come to regard him with far greater respect than in the past. Thus it was that his should be the name which had suggested itself to her during last night's deliberations; and his was the judgement and advice for which she had now come to St Bride's vicarage to ask.

Requesting his housekeeper to bring them both a pot of tea, the clergyman showed Kitty inside to his study where last night's unfinished sermon notes lay scattered on the desk. If he were surprised to find her here so early in the morning, he gave no sign of it, limiting his curiosity to a mannerly enquiry after her health and that of her two small sons.

It was only when their tea had been served and the housekeeper retired again that Kitty put an end to the social chit-chat and as frankly and honestly as she could, outlined the reason for her call.

"So you see my situation, Mr Terris," she concluded, "and why I must appeal to you for counsel and guidance in the matter."

"Indeed!" Putting his cup aside, he leaned forward in his chair, elbows resting on arms, hands clasped before him. "Dear me, dear me, what a depressing picture is revealed of human nature, that envy and bitterness should breed such a lack of charity."

"Then you do believe me?"

"In all the years of our acquaintance, I do not think I have ever known you to give a deliberate lie. With you, my dear Catherine, it is either the truth, the half-truth, or silence.

Occasionally, I will admit, I have suspected an *embellishment* – but knowing your generosity of heart, this may be excused as a tactful avoidance of causing hurt to others. A little piece of flattery, nothing more. I practise it myself from time to time."

She managed him a small smile in response.

"Even so," Mr Terris went on, giving her a careful look over the top of his steel-rimmed pince-nez spectacles, "even so, I must ask you to search your conscience well before making me a categorical denial that you have ever misled Mr Russell into thinking your attentions were in any way equivocal. A glance, a touch of the hand, these things can be misinterpreted, you know."

"I have already searched my conscience – not once, but many times – and I can assure you, I have done nothing with which to reproach myself."

"*Nothing?* Can you swear to that?"

"I can. In fact, Mr Terris, I will do more –"

Rising to her feet, Kitty went to the minister's desk where a large leather-bound Bible lay open there for reference.

Placing her right hand upon the black-print page, she turned to face him again and said with some emphasis of tone, "I swear upon this holy book that at no time have I ever thought of Arthur Russell other than as the friend and future husband of my stepdaughter, and I further swear that I have never knowingly acted or spoken in a manner which might be construed as suggesting impropriety."

She removed her hand from the page, and the morning light reflected in at the vicarage window touched her features with an almost ethereal luminosity.

"There, Mr Terris. They may lay their tongues to what names they like, Beatrice and her friends, but surely even they would not stoop so low as to accuse me of perjury."

Her dramatic appeal found an answering chord. Taking off his pince nez to wipe them with a handkerchief from his pocket, and blinking rapidly as though to clear his sight, the clergyman responded with some emotion, "I did not doubt your innocence before, my dear. But now I know – yes, beyond all question and incertitude that you are quite, quite blameless of this repugnant allegation."

"As Heaven is my witness, I am!"

She sat herself down again, folding her hands upon her

reticule and presenting such a picture of loveliness and grace, Edward Terris thought as he replaced his spectacles, that only a mind blinded by the cataracts of malice could fail to see its purity of soul.

During these past few years, whenever he'd allowed himself to dwell upon Catherine van der Kleve, he tended always to imagine her as a latter-day Mary Magdalene – the fallen woman who 'because she loved much, therefore was much forgiven her' by reason of her true repentance. So it had been with Catherine. Like the lost sheep of the parable, this beautiful young creature had been brought back into the fold of the Church to become one of St Bride's chief adornments; and it vexed Mr Terris more than he could say that such as Frances Broadwood and Beatrice van der Kleve should attack her – they who called themselves Christian women because they attended Communion of a Sunday and thought that that exonerated them from the sins of their hypocrisy, their envy, their slander, and their lack of charity.

What was he to do with such lip-service sanctimoniousness!

"You say that your husband is as yet unaware of Mr Russell's – ah – regrettable leap to the wrong conclusion?"

Kitty nodded. "He returns from Manchester this very afternoon. By which time, of course, Beatrice will have been fully appraised of the details –"

"– of your visit to Mr Russell's rooms yesterday."

"Yes."

"Hmm. If I may say, my dear, you would have done better to seek my advice *before* you made that call upon the gentleman, rather than now when the milk has been, so to speak, spilt with quite such calamitous consequences."

"I appreciate that, Mr Terris. But I acted in what I believed to be the best interests of my family."

"'Best interests' are not always the most politic course to pursue. Tell me, Catherine –" he shifted in his chair, leaning sideways to rest his chin on his hand – "what is your opinion of Arthur Russell's character?"

She hesitated before answering.

"Why . . . he is agreeable, intelligent, ambitious – a trifle vain, perhaps –"

"Would you describe him as truthful? A person of high moral values? Faithful to Angelina?"

There was another, longer hesitation.

"I would hope, sir, that he is all of these things."

"Yet notwithstanding the social acquaintance there has existed between you for a number of years, you cannot say with any degree of confidence that Mr Russell manifests such qualities in his behaviour – qualities which are the virtues basic to a gentleman's morality."

"No. No, I cannot."

"You see, my dear, my point is this – there may well be something in his fibre of which we are unaware. A man does not suddenly accuse an innocent woman of attempted seduction without good cause – and if the cause does not lie with her, then it must, *ipso facto*, lie with himself! Do you take my meaning?"

And seeing the little frown upon her face, Mr Terris went on again, straightening himself up in his seat as he warmed to his theme – "I suspect that the clue to Arthur Russell's misconduct is to be discovered in the double life which he leads. Permit me to elaborate. When first his mother came to reside in Tunbridge Wells, Mr Russell shared the same house, and together they moved in the same local circles of society. Since he has taken these rooms in Hart Street, however, I have noticed a certain unfortunate coarsening of his manner. He is not seen here from one week's end to the next. What does he do with himself? Does he occupy each evening at his club? Does he belong to any particular clique or affiliation? Does he attend the theatre? Who are his friends? What manner of company does he keep while in London? No one knows! He arrives here of a Saturday evening, dines with Mrs Russell at Mount Edgecumbe, escorts her to church of a Sunday morning, takes luncheon with you and your family at Sion Place, spends his afternoon with Angelina – and departs again for Town by the seven o'clock train."

There was a pause; and then a gesture.

"So you see, my dear, it is quite within the realms of possibility that the Mr Russell *we* know is not the same young gentleman London society takes him for."

Kitty gave all this her careful consideration.

"You mean – you mean that he wears two faces, as it were – one for family and fiancée, and quite another for his City life?"

"Exactly so."

"Yes . . . yes, perhaps that would explain the offensiveness of his behaviour yesterday. And that other time, too, when we were caught in the fog –"

She gave a quick sketch of the incident, the day she and Beatrice and Angelina had gone up to Town to shop.

"I think, dearest lady, if I am to assist you," came the considered response once she'd finished, "I needs must make enquiry of my own – discreetly, of course – and see what's to do."

The minister made to get to his feet.

"Will you leave the matter with me?"

Kitty rose with him, smoothing out the mauve silk flounces of her skirts.

"Gladly, Mr Terris. But how would you advise that I act in the meanwhile? Once my husband returns, I cannot imagine Beatrice will remain long silent on the subject of yesterday's unpleasantness. She is bound to repeat Frances Broadwood's account of it word for word."

There was a sudden awkward little hesitation.

"Unless, that is –"

She looked across at him quickly, then away again.

"But no – no, I can't ask such a thing of you. It would be stretching charity too far."

He was all instant attention. "*What* can you not ask? What is it you have in mind – may I know?"

"I suspect you may guess."

"Ah." The minister's plump face assumed a most lugubrious expression. "That I visit dear Beatrice myself on your behalf, and request that she say nothing at all to her brother."

"She would listen to you! She admires you greatly."

"So I believe."

Kitty had to smile at the resignation in his tone.

"Oliver leaves again on Tuesday for a week's business in Amsterdam. If Beatrice could be persuaded to exercise discretion, at least until then, it would give me a little more time. Won't you ask her – *please*, Mr Terris? For my sake?"

She pressed her hands together on her breast in an unconscious gesture of appeal, and the look in those violet eyes would have melted a man far less captivated by her than Edward Terris.

298

He made a pretence of sighing and taking out his pocket watch to consult it for the time.

Then – "Oh, very well. I can spare a half-hour before luncheon. But I trust you appreciate, Catherine my dear, the peril you place me in by sending me upon so awkward an errand!"

Beatrice van der Kleve was in a thoroughly bleak humour. She had hoped to make her niece Angelina see the folly of continuing blindly to trust that corrupt and corrupting Serpent of Eden, Oliver's wife. But Angelina – always a difficult, headstrong child – had not wished to hear, quitting her presence in the rudest manner possible. The interview had brought on one of Beatrice's headaches. She would have to go to her room and lie down and request Perrins to make a cold compress for her brow.

Scarcely, however, had Nicholls the butler answered her bell in the morning room, than he was back again to say that Edward Terris had at this moment arrived to call upon her. Dear Edward – it was always a pleasure to receive him – but really, he could not have come at a worse time, just when she was upset, and extremely annoyed, and feeling quite, quite ill.

"Oh, very well, Nicholls. Show Mr Terris in."

She composed herself as well as she could. A glance in the wall mirror showed not a hair out of place, though vexation was written plain upon her features. She looked away from the unattractive image, the ache in her head growing worse.

"My dear Beatrice!" He came into the room with that little half-running step of his, and as always at sight of him her foolish heart instantly seemed to quicken. "And how do I find you this morning? Well, I trust?"

"I wish that I could say so, Edward." She indicated a chair for him. "But alas, I am feeling quite otherwise."

She seated herself, expecting some word of sympathy; but instead there came only a faint tut-tutting, as though the matter of her health was really of no great importance.

And then – why, she could scarce believe she was hearing aright! – he launched himself without further ado upon the account of a visit which he had but half an hour since received from 'dear Catherine' concerning that creature's 'misunderstanding' with Arthur Russell.

Misunderstanding, indeed!

Frances Broadwood had been scathingly specific. With her own eyes she had witnessed the woman leave Arthur's rooms – 'her features working with fury' she had said – and Arthur, poor, poor boy, hardly able to speak for the shock and the shame of what he had just been subjected to. That he should be propositioned in so outrageous a fashion – and by the wife of his future father-in-law! Frances had almost wept with indignation while telling of it.

And now here was Edward Terris, fresh from the hussy's seductive lies, her deceit, her cozening, defending her as though she were some very paragon of virtuous womanhood. Could he not see what a fool he was to himself to be so deluded?

"She swore her innocence upon the Holy Bible – most, *most* touching – I cannot tell you how it affected me, Beatrice – the vision of that dear lady calling upon the Lord as her witness. It will stay with me always."

What tosh. Catherine would not scruple to sell her own soul to the devil if she thought it suited her purpose.

"You are far too good-hearted, Edward. You see only the best, where others would recognise wickedness. I would suggest that you speak to Mrs Broadwood if you would learn the real truth."

Oh, but he did not think that was necessary. He had heard 'dear Catherine's' account and was perfectly satisfied with its veracity. There was no need to trouble Frances, or indeed, Mrs Russell. No need at all.

"And I trust, Beatrice, that you in your turn will not regard it as a matter of pressing duty to inform your brother of the – ah, incident – at least, that is, until it has been resolved to the satisfaction of those concerned."

Her poor head throbbed quite dreadfully.

"I am surprised that you should advocate such deception. Surely my brother is as much concerned as any?"

"But it would serve nothing by troubling him at this time with a hotch-potch report of the facts. Will you not wait a little until he has returned from his business abroad – delay the grievous hour –"

And forfeit her own pleasure in seeing Catherine served her just desserts? Never! Not even by so much as a day – an hour. Oliver should learn each and every detail of his wife's perfidious conduct the minute his foot was set across the threshold.

But what was this –? Edward had got up from his chair and was moving towards her. His hand was laid upon her arm. He was urging her to rise, to stand, to turn and face him. And of a sudden, her heart was fluttering like a captive bird within her breast.

"I cannot recall having ever before asked a personal favour of you, Beatrice . . . I am asking you now."

Ah, but this was the food of all her dreams, to have him hold her so, if only at arm's length, and gaze into her eyes with such beseeching candour.

"Give me your word that you will say nothing to Oliver – at least for the moment? I appeal to you, my dear. Believe me, I know the devotion you bear for your brother which prompts you to act in his best defence, and I admire you for such nobleness of spirit, more than I can say. Would that your admiration for me, your unworthy and undeserving friend, could but sway you half as much, and turn your mind to granting my request."

The very marrow of her bones seemed to melt at his touch. What transports of pleasure possessed her! Could he not feel her tremble? She had never swooned in her life before, but this . . . ah, this . . .

"Very well, Edward," she heard herself responding faintly, as though through a mist. "I cannot deny the appeal of one so dear to me. I will do as you ask."

33

James Randall was ambitious. He had to face the truth, though
– he'd never advance to being butler at Sion Place, not while
Mr Nicholls held the post; and it was plain as the nose on your
face the old fellow intended staying on until the Master either
pensioned him off, or he died.

Either way, Jem would have to wait a good long time if he
wanted promotion, in this household leastways.

He'd have given in his notice and gone somewhere else, so
he would, if it hadn't been for Rosie Maguire. He loved her,
and that was a fact; but it was also a fact that servants weren't
encouraged to marry – and if they did, they were out on their
ears pretty smartish, with no hope of re-employment except
maybe as handyman and cook to a family in Trade. And that
was coming down in the world, and no mistake.

Oh, he knew of fellows courting their girl for years on end,
and travelling half the country to see her every once in a while;
but he wasn't having any of that, not he. There was no one
else in the world like Rosie: if he went off and left her in
Tunbridge Wells, who was to say some clerk or shop assistant
wouldn't be sniffing around, stealing her heart away from him?

He was coming up for thirty now, and she was twenty-four.
Time was running on for them both.

A cousin of his had gone out to New Zealand back in '66.
He'd been a manservant too, like Jem, but had packed it in to
try his luck overseas, saving up the passage money out of his
wages; and now he was living the life of Riley (so he wrote)
managing his own hotel in a place called Otago where there
were gold-fields and good rich lands just waiting for a taker.

Why don't you come over and join me? he kept saying.
You're a mug to stay there, working your legs off for another
man when you could be your own master here.

Jem was sorely tempted, oh, he was! He could marry his
Rosie and take her off to a new life, give her everything she'd

never know in service, no, not in a hundred years. They could raise their kiddies in the fresh air of freedom, and under a roof of their own, where they wouldn't be beholden to Master and Mistress, wouldn't have to go cap in hand for permission for this and permission for that, wouldn't have to put up with the likes of Miss Beatrice treating poor Rosie like common dirt.

"The air's that thick upstairs you can cut it with a knife," he said that Tuesday afternoon, coming in at the kitchen door from the scullery stairs. Mr van der Kleve had left for Amsterdam yesterday morning early, and whatever it was had been festering between Miss Beatrice and the Mistress these past few days, it was bubbling up to a right old bickering match now the Master was out of the way.

He put down the silver-plate he'd fetched for cleaning, and reached over for the buff-coloured apron to protect his clothes, throwing a glance at Rose who was sitting near the window with some of Mrs van der Kleve's mending.

He'd spoken to her of his plans for them both to join Fred in Otago. She said she wanted to have a think about it. It was a fair old distance to travel away from her mam and family, after all.

"What's to do between the pair of 'em now, I wonder," he went on, addressing himself to the others in general. "There'll be ructions before the day's done, the way Miss Beatrice is letting her words fly about."

"It's some'at they've fell out over," opined little Susan Smith, scraping carrots at one end of the table. "Some'at about Miss Angelina's young gentleman."

"You get on wi' them vegetables –" As usual, Cook wasn't allowing any pertness from *that* quarter. "You'll last better if you says less and pays more heed to your work, my girl."

"But there *is* some'at going on wi' Mr Russell," put in Rose, not liking the way Mrs Reynolds was always slapping young Susan down. "You ask Mary Ellen. You ask her what she heard when she was serving at dinner last night. She'll tell you Miss Beatrice wasn't half laying the length of her tongue to the Mistress's character."

"She told *me* that, an' all," Susan ventured, hunching up her thin shoulders as though she expected Mrs R. to let fly at her with something.

"What did she say then, Rosie?" Jem went over to the range

grate and poured a kettle of hot water into a bowl to start washing the grease off the silver-plate. "What bee has the old biddy got in her bonnet this time?"

"You mind how you're a-talking, Jem Randall!" Mrs Reynolds exclaimed at him. "Old biddy, indeed! She'll old biddy you if she catches you calling her that."

"I'd call her a darn' sight worse to her face, given chance. Aye, and mebbe I will, too, before much longer."

He stopped himself there. No point in telling them all his business, not yet awhile. Leave it till he'd heard from cousin Fred in New Zealand.

"This house would be a cheerier place if she'd let the Mistress be, instead of rampaging on about her every time the Master's back's turned."

"She's saying now," said Rose, in answer to his earlier question, "that Mrs van der Kleve's been setting her cap at that young Mr Russell. I ask you! As if it's likely –" She caught herself up with a hasty glance at the staircase door. Jane Perrins had just that minute come through.

Then, in a know-what-I-mean voice she added, "There's some folk are never content wi'out they're stirring up trouble for others."

Perrins shot her a look that would curdle cream. She'd been standing out there with her ear to the door, no doubt.

"Talking about yourself again, Maguire?" she said snidely.

Rose returned her a smile – one of those face-pulling smiles, more of a grimace – and got on with her mending.

"I'll have to see about getting that keyhole raised for you." It was Jem who let Perrins have her answer. "Save you having to bend your back so far. There's a nasty draught whistles down those stairs."

Susan guffawed, hiding her mouth in her hand, earning herself the sharp end of Cook's elbow as the carrots were checked to see she'd scraped them clean enough.

"For your information," Perrins said, ignoring Jem's bit of sarcasm, "Mrs van der Kleve should count herself lucky Miss Beatrice has such a Christian nature as she has. If it was anyone else, she'd be finding herself put out on the street with no roof to her head. Again."

This last was added not so much as an afterthought, as a statement in itself.

"Go on – you don't say?" Jem had done washing the silver-plated ware and was drying the pieces. "What's Madam been playing at now, then?"

There was a sniff. "You might guess. The same as before."

"What, the very same? But I thought that drawing master – what was his name? Rivers? – I thought he'd gone and got himself married to somebody out in the shires. Didn't you tell me, Rosie? Didn't that friend of yours that works at Saltmarsh's mention something or other of Mr Rivers getting wed to a girl back home?"

All this was said in a deliberately obtuse, half-witted manner just to annoy.

Perrins rose to the bait. "Oh, it's not Mr Rivers this time. It's Miss Angelina's fiancé."

"Lord, you'll make me dizzy!" Jem clutched his brow in mock bewilderment. "I thought you were still harping on about that other old business. So it's Miss Angelina's fiancé now, is it? Well, I never! Who'd have guessed it. Mr Arthur Russell, of all folk."

The glint of anger appeared in Perrins's eyes. "I don't see it's any matter for levity. That engagement's well nigh ruined. Miss Angelina's ever so upset about it –"

"Poor young lady, so she would be, an' all," interjected Cook.

"She's got them at either ear, Madam and Mr Russell, each telling her a different tale. She doesn't know what to think."

"I know who I believe," said Rose, biting off a thread of cotton.

"*An'* me!" echoed young Susan, out of arm's reach at the scullery pump.

Jem dipped a piece of rag into the moistened plate powder and started rubbing at the sides of a teapot.

"The Master didn't strike *me* as being too bothered," he commented laconically. "In fact, he seemed in a rare good humour before he left yesterday. You'd think, wouldn't you, he'd have been more than a mite put out of countenance if his missus was playing beds and bolsters with his daughter's young man."

"That's because he hasn't yet been told," Jane Perrins answered, starting to set out a tray for her mistress's infusion of camomile. "Miss Beatrice thought it kindest to wait until he returns."

"Well there's a turn-up for the books!" Jem couldn't help but laugh at this. "Miss Beatrice, *waiting*? God help us, she's normally in such hurry to make trouble for Mrs van der Kleve, it's a marvel she hasn't broken her neck before now."

Perrins pressed her lips together primly. As always when she felt her nerves aggravated by the lack of respect and loyalty shown for her Miss Beatrice, the exaggerated refinement of her speech grew more pronounced.

"She's doing it at the request of Mr Terris the minister. He called upon her especially, to ask her out of the goodness of her heart to say nothing to the Master yet awhile."

"Oh, not yet awhile?" Rose mimicked her cruelly. "No wonder she's been like a scalded cat these past few days, if she's had to keep some'at like that under her bustle!"

"She fancies Mr Terris, does Miss Beatrice," said Susan, taking advantage of having the kitchen table between her and Mrs Reynolds. "I've seen that cushion she's making him, that 'un she's stuffing wi' her hair droppings."

"Have you been a-snooping about up them stairs again?" Mrs Reynolds made to thrust the sleeves up her plump red arms in a threatening fashion. "How many times have I told you! Upstairs is out o' bounds to you, my girl. Peoples as lives in this class of 'ouse has a standard to keep, and it's none o' your concern what Miss Beatrice does – nor whether she fancies the minister, neither."

"He doesn't fancy *her* much, though," said Jem, winking heavily at Susan.

He put the teapot aside for the paste to dry and took up a pair of decorated fish-servers; then added, "She could pray till her knees wore through to the bone, but it still wouldn't make a ha'pence worth o' difference. He's been too long a bachelor, has Mr Terris."

Just at that the stair door opened again, this time admitting the nurserymaid, Emily Duckett.

Throwing a hurried, flustered glance around the kitchen as she came in, and not waiting to shut the door, the girl blurted out – "Where's the clothes trunk, Jem? Mistress wants it taking to the nursery this instant. I've to pack the babies' things ready for 'em both to go away."

"Go away?" Instant curiosity. "Away where?"

"I dunno. Mrs van der Kleve didn't say. But I heard her telling Miss Beatrice not a minute since that she wasn't staying in the house a day longer and she's taking the little 'uns off somewhere – right away out o' the place."

It had been there all the time Oliver was at home, like an undertow trying to drag her out of her depth. She had felt it so strongly that it made her feel physically ill: Beatrice's malice weaving its spider's web around her, a watching, waiting hostility brooding on its revenge, longing for her destruction.

Mr Terris's intervention had gained her a week's respite at the most before her husband returned from Amsterdam. Kitty felt that she couldn't wait that long, not in an atmosphere as poisonous as this. No sooner had Oliver left than Beatrice turned on her, spewing out her hatred in words which had made Kitty run from the room in disgust.

Worst of all – and most unforgivable – Bea had forced Angelina to listen to Frances Broadwood, hear that woman's distortion of the truth; and not only Mrs Broadwood, but Mrs Russell, too, who could only parrot what her son Arthur had said to her. Lies, of course. Exaggerations. But even the smallest pebble will create a circle of ever-widening ripples, and the more the accusations were repeated, the larger they seemed to grow.

Little wonder Angelina avoided her now whenever she could. Poor girl, who was she to believe? The stepmother she'd only just grown to love – had for so long resented for taking her mother's place and her father's attention; or the fiancé with whom she'd planned to share the rest of her life in mutual trust and respect?

Kitty had no doubt at all that Arthur Russell must be regretting his own monumental folly in behaving as he had. She also suspected he found himself too far now up to his neck in the embroilment to extricate himself with any credit. At this late stage, who was going to believe him? It would sound unconvincingly all too like a gentleman's attempt to salvage her own good name from the mud.

Besides, there was the letter – the letter she'd sent requesting a private meeting, asking that his reply not be sent to the house but to Tunbridge Wells post office. In the light of present accusation, it looked a most suspicious piece of evidence.

This was beginning to be the Jonathan Rivers business all over again. Wounds might close with time and scars fade, but never quite completely. Like the memory of that past and finished love, they left behind some token of their pain, even though the hurt was now forgotten and the harm forgiven.

She had deliberately put away from her all thought of that dead affaire; had felt nothing even when she heard Jonathan had married his Susanna in Shropshire; but now it all seemed to be coming back to torment her again, the old blame, the old guilt. With one difference – she had learned to be a fighter; and for the sake of her sons she must get away from Sion Place for a while – find a haven for the three of them, at least until Oliver returned and this thing could be brought into the open and thrashed out once and for good.

But where should she go?

One place suggested itself. It was where she had gone before, and found there a friend in her need who had proved a friend indeed – Michael Dutton, the Seymour family agent at Loxley Green.

The Reverend Mr Edward Terris would never for the world have acknowledged the fact – not even to himself – but fact it was that he was just a little in love with Catherine van der Kleve. Had he not been, nothing would have induced him to act on her behalf as he had, swallowing his own fastidious pride to make a personal approach to her sister-in-law.

As he left Sion Place with the promise of Beatrice's silence, he had found the perspiration running from his brow at the thought of what encouragement he'd given her; and even at luncheon his hands still shook so that it was as much as he could do to deliver the food to his mouth.

He was well aware of the lady's regard for him – such foolish predilections were an occupational hazard for the Clergy – but dear Lord forbid that he'd overstepped the bounds of discretion and offered her cause for supposing he would marry her. Better a premature death than that.

Better anything!

So great had been his agitation that when next he met with Beatrice (she was arranging the lady chapel flowers, as it happened) his manner towards her was as cool as to be positively frosty. Not that it made the slightest scrap of difference: seeing him beating a hasty retreat down the aisle to the porch, she had followed at once, even forgetting herself so far as to clutch at the sleeve of his coat to detain him, and exhibiting a coyly flirtatious familiarity in her speech which astonished Mr Terris to hear, coming from such a respectable woman.

After Evensong that Sunday he had conveniently called to mind an invitation to spend a few days with a fellow cleric in Greenwich; and on the Monday had departed from the Wells, turning an unseeing eye to a note from Sion Place to take afternoon tea with 'ever your most affectionate Bea'.

Something in the minister's sudden reluctance to expand upon his avowal of undying regard, delivered in the morning room so short a time before, alerted Beatrice to the possibility that she might have misjudged his intention. And in the few days which followed, the more she brooded upon this, the more certain she grew that she had foolishly allowed her heart to rule her head. She had been used.

By the time her brother Oliver departed upon his week's business in Amsterdam – time during which she'd been forced to bite her lip to keep from crying out his wife's shame to his face – she felt as bitter as she could ever remember being. Not only had that creature Catherine cozened her husband, but she'd cozened Edward Terris too, making him a pliant accessory to the concealment of her own disgraceful conduct.

Beatrice had been glad to the point of jubilation, almost, when Kitty took the two little boys away from the house. With Mr Terris no longer in town to defend her, she was running from the scene of her guilt – yes, running to hide herself.

The fall of the dice of Fate must have been with Beatrice that week. Instead of returning to England upon the Saturday, as expected, Oliver van der Kleve cut short his business and was back again at Sion Place on Thursday – a full twenty-four hours before Kitty was planning to make her own return from Loxley Green.

His first enquiry on entering the house had been for his wife and sons.

And Beatrice's reply was calculated to cause all the trouble possible.

"I'm afraid Catherine is no longer here. She has taken the children and gone away with them. Packed every piece of their baggage and left."

34

"Left – *Left?* Left to go where?"

Oliver van der Kleve stared at his sister.

"What are you talking about, Beatrice? Explain yourself."

She met his look with one which barely disguised a smile of triumph behind the vindictiveness.

"Catherine has taken the children and gone away," she repeated. "She left on Tuesday. Randall drove the dogcart down to the station with all their luggage."

"But – I don't understand. Where have they gone? What did she tell you?"

"She told me nothing, Oliver, beyond the fact that she was leaving. However, I think that this may have a good deal to do with it –"

Like a stage conjuror producing a well-rehearsed trick from a hat, Beatrice dipped into the pocket of her skirts and withdrew an envelope which she held towards her brother.

"I think you should read this letter," she said, handing it over. "It will explain much."

Oliver glanced at the address. It was written in his wife's clear, generous hand and made out to Arthur Russell at his club, the City of London, in Old Broad Street, EC2. The top left corner bore the legend 'Private and personal' heavily underscored.

"Read it," Beatrice urged.

He glanced at her doubtfully, the crease of concentration between his straight, dark brows deepening into a frown.

"But this is addressed to Arthur –"

"Yes, yes. But *read* it!" She was almost beside herself, on a knife's edge of anticipation. "All of us – Arthur and his mother, too – feel most strongly that you do so."

The doubtful look became a searching one.

"Very well."

Drawing from the envelope a single page which was dated

almost a fortnight previously, he let his eyes scan rapidly over the lines; then went back to read more carefully.

My dear Arthur,
I wish to see you as soon as can be arranged, upon a personal matter which affects us both. Can you suggest somewhere discreetly private? Please do not reply to the house – let me have your note poste restante via the office on the Parade.
Yours – Catherine van der Kleve

Beatrice watched her brother's face, not missing a single flicker of expression as the page was replaced and he raised his head to look at her.

For a moment there was silence. Then he said, "What does this mean?"

It was all the cue she needed. In words which had been chosen and gone over until polished into sentences she knew by heart, she gave him the story – Arthur Russell's story – tricked out a treat with Frances Broadwood's trimmings and her own embellishments. The encounter in Hart Street added proof, if proof were required; but Beatrice kept the best, the most damning, till last, providing her own eye-witness description of an incident seen in the London fog, when Catherine deliberately lured young Arthur into her arms.

"She pretended to drop something – some reels of silk thread – and when he went to assist her, she caught at him in the most shameless fashion and kissed him full upon the mouth – I saw her! Doubtless she thought the fog was too thick, and would hide them from view. If I had not turned back –"

And so on, and so forth. Not a morsel of spurious detail was missed.

Throughout this recitation Oliver said nothing; but his features grew steadily more ashen, whether through shock or through anger was impossible to tell.

When she had finally ended, he turned away and for several long minutes stood gazing out through the window, as though there were something beyond in the evening-shadowed garden which required his total and utter concentration.

After a time Beatrice could bear it no longer.

"Well –?" she cried at the turned back. "What shall you do?"

His response, when it came, sounded curiously stifled.

"What shall I do? Uncover the truth, of course."

"But you have the truth."

"Your version of it, yes."

He looked round at her again, and she saw with a sudden catch of surprise that he was weeping. The sight of those tears unnerved her. She had expected rage – bitterness – indignation – the same response he'd shown when he'd learned of his wife's adultery with Jonathan Rivers. But not this naked suffering. There was something almost indecent about it.

To cover her own discomfort, she burst out loudly, "Don't, Oliver, don't – for pity's sake!"

And was answered at once – "It is for pity's sake that I am moved to weep. Could you not for once have left well alone? What is it about you, Beatrice, that makes you *hate* so much?"

Then, turning away to the window again, he went on more strongly, "Where is my daughter? Where is Angelina?"

"I – I believe she is out of the house at present. You were not expected –"

"In that case I shall go round to call upon Mrs Broadwood. If am required to judge my wife's conduct, I need some confirmation of events. Kindly ask Nicholls to delay the serving of dinner for an hour."

He left the room, moving with purpose now, and went upstairs to lave his face to remove the traces of emotion before going down again and out into Mount Sion, taking his hat from the table as he passed.

If the Broadwoods' maid, answering the door of Bowling Green House to his ringing, seemed bemused by the abruptness of his manner, it was nothing to Frances Broadwood's reaction when her caller was shown into the drawing room.

She guessed the reason at once; but what astonished her was the impression he gave of being not so much outraged by his wife's behaviour, as deeply annoyed that Beatrice should have brought it to his notice!

"I don't doubt what Arthur has been telling you," he said, seating himself with an ill grace at her invitation, "but how much of it may be verified as true must wait until tomorrow, when he comes down from London."

"My dear Oliver, surely the facts already speak for themselves." She seated herself in turn. "Once this whole sorry escapade was known, Catherine preferred to run away than remain here and face you."

"I can't believe that. My wife has never been afraid to admit responsibility for her actions. Had she been in the wrong, she would have stayed to make me a confession of it, and *then* gone away, perhaps. Not before."

Frances changed her approach and tried a different tack.

"It is hard to accept the worst of those we love – I know that from my own experiences with Henry. It hurts us to discover our trust has been abused. When I think of the many times in our marriage that he has gone astray, and repented, and sworn never again to wander – and then repeated his offence! I have needed to be a saint to swallow my pride and forgive him –" she smiled a little sadly – "and so I do sympathise with you, Oliver, indeed I do."

He did not want her sympathy. He had never cared overmuch for Frances Broadwood – even less once she became the intimate of his sister Beatrice. This whole story had the ring of concoction about it, as though the pair of them had put their heads together to make a mountain out of some minor molehill; yet for Arthur Russell to say it was true gave it foundation of a kind.

He could not bear to believe it . . . oh God, he could not . . .

Mistaking his silence, Frances went on, "My dear, I myself have seen Catherine flirting with Arthur – not once, but often – but said nothing, for fear I'd cause embarrassment. She is my friend, after all."

Had he not been in the grip of such bleak anger, he might have been tempted to laugh.

Instead, he asked tersely, "Give me an instance – one single instance of misconduct which you've witnessed."

"One? Good Lord, there've been so many." She did not need to search her mind. During this past week she and Beatrice had been raking over each and every nuance they could conjure.

"One will suffice."

"Very well." Again, the small sad smile. "At church on Easter Day, Catherine purposely dropped her prayerbook at Arthur's feet, and when he made to return it, I saw her cling

314

to his hand for quite some seconds, whispering to him before she moved away."

"How very observant of you."

"I was seated in the pew behind, as it happened. Indeed, I mentioned the incident to my husband, since it struck me as being so singular."

"And of course, you were at Hart Street with Mrs Russell, and being equally observant upon that occasion also, noted my wife's distress as she was leaving."

Something in Oliver's tone sounded a jarring note.

Frances shot him a quick, wary look from the corner of her eye. This wasn't at all how she and Bea imagined he'd respond.

"Tell me about it," he said. "Tell me precisely what you saw that afternoon."

"Why . . . your sister has already given you the account, surely."

"She only repeated a version of what you yourself described to her. I would prefer to hear the original – if you don't mind?"

Was he being sarcastic? She could not be sure. What a cold fish the man was; undeniably attractive – but so cold.

She gave a slight shrug of her elegant shoulders beneath the tussore silk. "Where shall I begin?"

"At the beginning might be as good a place as any."

"What, you wish to know the time of our train into London?"

"No, that is not what I mean." He said this with the kind of bored impatience one might use with a child. "You and Mrs Russell arrived at Hart Street. You entered the ground floor of the house. You mounted the stairs. And then –?"

"You wish to know *all* the details, Oliver?"

"So far as you can recall them."

"Oh, I can recall them!" Frances began to grow peevish. "Mrs Russell and I reached the top of the stairs at the very moment your wife was making her departure from Arthur's rooms. We both saw her quite clearly there along the corridor –"

"Was the corridor well lit?"

"Well lit? No, no, I don't think so."

"Nevertheless, you saw her quite clearly."

"We could not fail to recognise her! What astonished us was not so much the coincidence of finding her there, but that her appearance should be –" she hunted for the word – "so discomposed."

Some other description would have painted a more entertaining picture of the scene, but Oliver was hardly the audience for that.

"In what way discomposed?" He was watching her narrowly.

"She seemed angry –"

"Angry? Not – upset?"

"What's the difference? Yes, she looked upset. As though something had vexed her considerably."

"And when she saw you, what did she say?"

"Why, she scarcely said a thing! That's what struck Mrs Russell and me as so odd. Had she had some complaint or accusation to make, surely it would have made more sense to tell us both, than go rushing by as she did. Indeed, I would have followed her down the stairs if Arthur hadn't just then appeared at his door –"

"Yes – Arthur – how did *he* seem to you?"

"Oh, *shocked*! I have never seen such dismay upon a man's face. His mother immediately asked what was wrong, but he couldn't answer – obviously the matter was too indelicate – he wished to spare us both the embarrassment of learning what had passed between him and Catherine."

"But he did tell you shortly thereafter?"

"Once he'd finished the champagne."

This was a detail which she instantly regretted mentioning, for Oliver sat forward in his seat as though to pounce. "Ah, he was drinking champagne?"

"For his nerves. He was distraught. It's hardly a crime!"

"I grant you. But in the circumstances . . . However, we will let that pass. What was his confession?"

This should have been the high spot of her story, but by now Frances was starting to feel decidedly ill at ease under the cut and thrust of so many probing questions.

She examined her fingertips, head to one side, her sharp, slightly feline features showing resentment.

"Well –?" came the prompt.

"It isn't an easy thing to tell, especially to *you*!"

"I appreciate that, though may I point out that you've had the practice. According to Beatrice's account, the claim was made by Arthur that my wife had been making improper advances to him."

"Yes, that was what he intimated to his mother and me. He showed us Catherine's letter to prove it."

"I have seen the letter. It proves nothing."

"But she asked to meet with him alone – discreetly. What woman would do that unless she had something to hide?"

Oliver made no answer.

"He said –" Frances went on in a complaining tone – "he said that she'd gone to his rooms that afternoon to persuade him that they should . . . become lovers."

"Become *lovers*? Were those his exact words?"

"I don't recall."

"Please try. A great deal depends on it."

The coldness of the grey eyes fixed upon her was really quite frightening. She had half a mind to ring the bell and ask that her husband be called down; except that Henry had had another of his 'turns' and was presently asleep in bed, coddled with brandy and James's tonic powders.

She made an irritated little gesture. "I believe the expression Arthur used was – oh, something about becoming better intimately acquainted. Whatever the words, they amount to much the same thing."

"I disagree. However – the fact remains that he alleges Catherine made some sort of invitation, which he repulsed, whereupon she became abusive. Is that correct?"

"Yes. He was forced to restrain her, he said. Indeed, she struck him quite violently upon the cheek – I saw the mark of her fingers with my own eyes, and so did Mrs Russell."

A small muscle began to twitch at the corner of Oliver's mouth, the only sign of the terrible strain upon him to exercise self-control. He could not guess at Catherine's reason for wishing to see Arthur Russell, but he knew instinctively that this story needed standing on its head if he were ever to sort out the truth from the lies.

Abruptly he rose from his chair, noting the quick flicker of relief in Frances Broadwood's expression.

"Oh, you're leaving now?"

"Yes. Don't ring to have me shown out. There's no need."

He did not even have the courtesy to thank her for the

trouble she'd taken, she told herself, resentment starting to edge into spite as she acknowledged his brief goodbye.

Well, it was Arthur who'd set the cat amongst the pigeons. Let *him* take the blame. The whole thing was beginning to grow just a trifle boring, anyway.

Dinner was a silent affair at Sion Place that evening. Afterwards, Oliver took his daughter Angelina into the study. For the first time in his experience as father, he felt a need to share himself with this stranger-child whom he'd spent so many years holding away at arm's length, rejecting, ignoring; not even liking. Had it not been for Catherine's efforts to bring them together, he might never have grown to know her properly, might never have discovered that beneath the awkward ugly-duckling façade there was a pleasant and amiable young woman waiting to be noticed.

Instead of seating himself at his desk, as he always did, he went to stand at the study window; it was more informal, he thought, and was pleased when Angelina joined him there.

Yes, Arthur had told her what had happened, she said in answer to the question. To be honest, she didn't know what to believe, unless it was something which had started as a prank . . .

When she began crying, Oliver took her into his arms and held her head against his shoulder, glad that she could not see the tears in his own eyes. She was his flesh and blood, yet he had never held her before this moment; and it made him feel ashamed.

He talked to her quietly as she wept. She wasn't to worry – he'd get to the bottom of the business as soon as he'd interviewed Arthur tomorrow. No, he couldn't believe it, either. And no, he didn't know where it was her stepmother had gone, but he suspected he could guess. Rose Maguire would tell them. Rosie was bound to know.

In fact, in view of everything, it would be best if Catherine stayed where she was for the moment. He'd get a message sent first thing in the morning. There were going to be some unpleasant words – and worse – flying about during the next few days, and he'd rather she and the boys be kept out of it.

Whoever was responsible for trying to destroy his family's happiness, they'd be wishing they'd thought twice about it before he was finished. It was time for the airing of a few home truths. The situation here was going to change. He'd let things drift on long enough.

35

On either side of the narrow rutted lane, hawthorn hedges were hung with a shimmering mist of spiderwebs caught in the rays of early sunlight. There was a hint of warmth already in the air, promising a fine day to come: and as though rejoicing at this prospect, every bird for miles around seemed to be singing, every bough and bush and spray bursting with the sound of their sharp, sweet, liquid notes.

"It's like a morning in Eden," Angelina said, breaking her reverie.

Seated in front of her on the driver's bench, reins slack in his hands, Jem Randall nodded agreement.

"It is, indeed, miss!" Rose Maguire, sitting beside him, was more forthcoming. She turned to give their passenger a quick bright smile, then remembered herself and looked to the front again.

This was an odd excursion, to be sure. Rose had been sworn to secrecy not to tell a soul where her mistress had taken the little boys; but she could hardly refuse Mr van der Kleve when he'd asked her last night. The matter was very important, he said. She wasn't to think of it so much as betraying a confidence, as helping the family. Anyway, he'd seemed to guess for himself it was Loxley Green they'd gone, which made her feel easier.

"Hear that?" Jem cocked his head.

Far across the fields the call of a cuckoo came echoing through the birdsong on a two-note hiccup of sound.

"If you've got a penny in your pocket, Rosie, turn it."

"Why?"

"Don't you know? It's for luck. It'll bring you money in your purse."

He was in an excellent humour this morning. He'd had a letter from cousin Fred in New Zealand, with the firm offer of work and good prospects; and better yet, Rose had finally

320

made up her mind to go with him, to start a new life together.

What happier news could a fellow have than that? No wonder he felt like singing his head off with the birds!

He'd wanted her to give her month's notice straight away; but Rose had thought it best to wait until the mistress was home again and everything back to normal. That is, as back to normal as things were ever likely to be, the way they were going . . . No sooner had Mr van der Kleve told Jem to be up at first light today to take a message to Madam at Loxley Green, than he decided Rose must go too, to stay with her there till he should send for them; and then, to crown matters, Miss Angelina said she would come along as well, to see the children.

So here they were, the three of them, on as fine a May morning as the good Lord ever created, putting the miles between them and Tunbridge Wells at a steady trot in the dogcart and (speaking, at least, for himself and Rose) not a cloud to darken the future's horizon.

He tipped his girl a wink and started to whistle 'By the Green Grove'.

Angelina's thoughts were hardly as cheerful. She was glad to get away from Sion Place, from Aunt Beatrice, from the forbidding atmosphere which seemed to hang about the house like a shroud. She had no joy in anything of late; life had grown suddenly hateful and cruel, and from being entirely confident that Arthur Russell loved her, she now was beset by all manner of troubled doubts.

One of the legacies of her neglected childhood was a lack of self-regard which caused her to retreat into a shell when she felt herself being hurt – and the situation with Arthur was hurting her very much.

"Excuse me, Miss Angelina –" Jem Randall stopped his whistling to address her over his shoulder. "This looks like Loxley Green now – up ahead of us through the trees."

He indicated with his whip and, shielding her eyes against the sun, she leaned to look past him. The lane ran out from its leafy holloway towards a bank of cropped turf dotted about with daisies, and beyond that were the bleached thatch-roofs of a row of cottages.

Once their cart had breasted the rise, the view in front revealed a village green with pond and pump, edged round with a foot-track leading by more cottages to rejoin the lane further along where it dipped again into open country. Standing a short way off beneath a spread of beeches was a barn-like structure which looked like the smithy.

"Best we ask there for direction, miss," Jem said, using his whip again as a pointer. "I don't know whether the place we want is Seymours or Stillbornes. The Master wasn't sure."

Several women standing at the pump turned to examine them with tight-faced curiosity as they drove past, wheels scattering ducks aside in a flurry of white feathers. Rose waved a greeting; but only a child waved back, and was instantly called by its mother to 'come away'.

There was a young man with a dog outside the smithy, sitting on a log pile in the morning sunshine while his horse was being shod. As the cart drew up, he got to his feet in response to Jem's hail, and came across.

"Excuse me, sir. We're looking for a farm hereabouts. I'm not certain o' the name, but it's owned by a family from Frant called Seymour."

The young man treated the occupants of the cart to a cursory inspection, then removed his hat and inclined himself courteously towards the two women.

"It's the Stillborne place you want. Up along the lane a half-mile or so." He smiled at Angelina. "If you can wait another few minutes, I'll show you the way myself. I'm going in that direction."

Angelina returned his smile hesitantly. Though he was dressed like a countryman in jacket and moleskin breeches, his voice and his manner together spoke of breeding. Besides, she liked his looks: a square face full of humorous good nature, complemented by blue eyes and curling chestnut hair, all set above a compact frame of medium height and build.

"It's a fine day," he said conversationally, still watching her. "Have you travelled far?"

"From Tunbridge Wells."

"Ah."

He glanced back towards the smithy, checking on the progress of his horse.

"Forgive me if I seem presumptuous, ma'am, but may I ask who it is you're seeking at Stillbornes?" And noting her reluctance – "I only enquire because – well, it might spare you further journey."

Her cheeks were beginning to burn a little under his steady gaze. "That's kind of you. Thank you. But you're probably not acquainted with the person."

"Try me."

Jem Randall looked round from the driver's seat as much as if to say, d'you want me to deal with this? at the same time eyeing the stranger up and down to get the fellow's measure. Miss Angelina was his responsibility, after all.

She responded for herself. "It's a Mrs van der Kleve – though I'm sure that means nothing to you."

"Oh, but it does. Perhaps you're one of the family, are you, ma'am? If so, you'll have heard mention of a friend of Kitty's named Harriet Seymour." And with another smile and a theatrical bow – "Allow me to introduce myself. I'm Harriet's brother, William. And owner of Stillbornes, as it happens."

"Well, there's a coincidence if you like!" Jem said aloud, raising his eyebrows at Rose. Then, recalling his place, added – "sir."

"Is my stepmother still staying at the farm?" enquired Angelina.

"Oh, Mrs van der Kleve's your stepmother, is she?"

"Yes. Is she there still – with the little boys?"

"Indeed." William Seymour threw a glance at the dogcart. "Excuse me if I appear somewhat obtuse – I was under the impression they'd be returning home by rail this afternoon. I'd arranged to drive them myself to Crowborough Halt to take the two o'clock train."

"Everything's had to be changed, sir," Jem informed him. "Mr van der Kleve wants the Mistress to stay a while longer – if it's convenient. I've got his message here." He patted a pocket; and by way of further afterthought – "I'm manservant at Sion Place, sir. And this young person is Miss Maguire, Madam's maid."

The other acknowledged Rose with a nod before turning to take the reins of his horse from the blacksmith's lad, who had just led the animal out to him.

"Well, we'll soon have the matter sorted, I'm sure."

Counting some money from his breeches, he paid the boy

for the work, then, replacing his riding bowler, swung himself up into the saddle with an easy strength.

"If you'll follow me –?" he told Jem; and whistling his dog to heel, he drew his horse round and nudged the animal into a gentle trot away on to the lane.

Within less than ten minutes they had turned in through a pair of ornamental wrought-iron gates standing open between stone pillars, and were proceeding down an overgrown drive-way shadowed by woodland trees whose canopy shed patterns of dappled light along its length. Where the drive ran out from under the trees into sunshine at the further end, there stood a mellowed red-brick building of Elizabethan date.

"We don't use this way often," William apologised, helping Angelina down from the dogcart. "First impressions count, they say, but it's better than having you jolted in at the yard through a herd of cows."

He offered her his arm; and when she took it after some little hesitation, escorted her in a most civil fashion up the porch steps, leaving Jem Randall and Rose to follow them behind.

They discovered Kitty at the other end of the house, talking to Mrs Dutton, the farm agent's wife, in the kitchen. Her astonishment upon seeing her stepdaughter here at Stillbornes lasted only a moment before it was replaced by a fearful anxiety to know what on earth had brought her – and Rose Maguire, too.

"Papa arrived home yesterday –" began Angelina.

"And, ma'am, I had to tell the Master where you'd gone –" Rose continued.

"And he's sent you this –" concluded Jem, holding out an envelope.

She took it with some trepidation saying abstractedly, "the children . . . they're upstairs. They'll be so pleased to see you!"

The letter enclosed with it a Bank of England note. Hastily she began to read.

My dear Catherine,

My business abroad did not take as long as I had reckoned upon, and I arrived in Tunbridge Wells last evening. You will know what I discovered. I am determined to resolve the matter to my own satisfaction; and therefore I wish you to make arrangements to stay where you are for the present time, if that can be managed. With regard to your circumstances, and those of our sons, rest assured that I will do all in my power to bring you home again as soon as may be. In the meanwhile, Maguire will remain with you. I enclose herewith a bill of money, and should you require any further, let me know at once and I will send it.

I remain,
your sincerely affectionate husband,
Oliver van der Kleve

The tone of his letter, so considerate of her needs, so reassuring in its content, put a surge of new hope into her spirits. She had been dreading today's return to Sion Place, not knowing what she must face there, what further mischief might have been made of her absence. It was like some leaden weight being lifted to know that Oliver had learned of the situation, and far from judging her culpable, appeared to be taking prompt decisive action to defend her.

She felt a sudden unexpected rush of affection for him; and looking up from the letter, said almost on a laugh, "Well, William, I hope you are not wearied of our company. It seems I must presume upon your hospitality a few days more still."

"My dear Kitty – you are most welcome!" the other responded at once, and with pleasure.

He knew of the events in Tunbridge Wells. She had told him everything the first evening she was here, and being a warm-hearted young man, he had offered her the haven of Stillbornes for as long as she and her sons required it. It presented no problem that he was residing here himself at present, since the agent Michael Dutton and his wife shared a part of the house, and would provide the chaperonage demanded by social convention.

Having spent the last years abroad in the American States and in Europe, William had decided it was time to take up his inheritance at home, and become a gentleman farmer. He'd left Baden-Baden only a few weeks before, after an extended visit to his sister Harriet, so that it was an act of benevolent fate that he should be here at Stillbornes when Kitty arrived a few days ago seeking temporary refuge.

It was a mark of his character that his only annoyance

should have been that she'd hired a cart to bring them from Crowborough Halt and refused to allow him to pay the driver's charge.

"You may stay here for as long as you like," he now repeated himself, "– and Miss van der Kleve, too, if she wishes."

Angelina looked at her stepmother, and then at the floor.

"I can't, I'm afraid," she said with an abruptness which bordered on discourtesy.

"But why not? I've room and to spare –"

"No, I'm sorry. It's not possible."

William made a gesture of regret. "Then I'm sorry, too. If the invitation offended you, forgive me."

Immediately, colour flooded the young woman's face with embarrassment. "Oh, it wasn't that!"

She glanced at Kitty again.

"Arthur . . . my fiancé . . . he's down from London this evening."

"And you must return to see him. Of course." William quite understood the situation.

Making some light remark to put them at their ease again, he asked Mrs Dutton to prepare an extra-generous luncheon since there would be nine to feed, no less; then having directed Rose upstairs to unpack her box, he showed Jem outside to the yard to water the pony.

Left alone, Kitty found she had to be first to break the sudden silence between herself and her stepdaughter.

"Would you prefer that we talked together down here? Or shall we go up to Benedict and Freddie?"

"Whichever you wish."

"Then I'll fetch them both down, shall I, and we can go into the garden. It's too lovely a morning to waste indoors."

It was, indeed. It was also too lovely to waste on stilted words and awkwardness and hurt. As soon as they were seated in the arbour among Mr Dutton's roses, watching the two little boys playing on the grass, Angelina was first this time to speak.

"I don't believe Arthur has been telling me the truth," she said quietly. "I can't think why he should lie, why he should make up these stories, but I know it's all an invention."

"Have you told him so?"

"Yes."

"And what was the response?"

Her chin began to tremble. She concentrated upon the children, on Benedict romping in a make-believe game round and round the lawn.

"He said . . . that I could believe him or not as I wished . . . it made no difference."

Kitty reached over and pressed her hand tightly, understanding the misery she must be suffering. "You love Arthur a great deal still, don't you?"

There was a nod. "That's the worst of it. If I didn't I wouldn't mind so . . ."

"I'm afraid love's an emotion we can't control once we're seized in its grip. It's like a disease. The more we're infected, the more we become helpless to defend ourselves against the pain it causes. I hope you don't hate me too much, Angelina."

"*Hate* you – ?" The words came out as a little cry of protest. "But I don't hate you!"

"Resent me, then. Come, you must admit it. However unwitting the role I played in Arthur's lurid fairy-tale, you've surely wished at times that he'd never laid eyes on me."

There was a long hesitation before the answer came.

"Well . . . yes . . . I do admit that. When first he told me, I was . . . shocked – I suppose that's the word. I needed something – someone – to blame for ruining our happiness, and I turned on you, Mama, thinking that because you'd once had nothing, now you wanted it all for yourself. Everything. Even him. And I'm sorry   truly, I'm sorry for thinking that. It was childish and petty of me."

"But entirely understandable." Kitty gave the hand another squeeze before releasing it. "What was your father's reaction – I presume it was Beatrice who told him?"

"Naturally. I don't know what happened between them – I wasn't at home when he arrived – but he went round at once to Bowling Green House to see Mrs Broadwood."

Angelina would have added more, but just at that moment William Seymour came into the garden. Seeing the two women out there together, and tactfully wishing to avoid an interruption of their private conversation, he began instead to play with Freddie and Benedict, getting down on all fours to let the boys clamber on to his back and pretending to buck and rear about like a bronco.

"What a very amiable gentleman Mr Seymour is," Angelina observed inconsequentially as the squeals of delight grew louder.

And then, going on with what she'd been saying before, "Papa and I had a long discussion last evening. He holds you in no manner to blame. His only concern is to have you home once more. I don't believe you realise, Mama, how very much he cares for you."

She glanced down at her fingers, and Kitty noticed for the first time that her stepdaughter was not wearing any ring.

"As for Arthur . . . well, I have made my decision, and Papa agrees it is the right one. Though it grieves me to the heart to do so, I've decided . . . I've decided I should break off our engagement to be married."

She looked up again, towards William Seymour; and the knot of tears swelling in her throat seemed to ease a little.

36

Arthur was in it up to his neck; and he knew it. What had started as a misunderstanding – hardly more than a lark, really, a self-indulgent bit of fun – had got totally out of hand; and once Beatrice van der Kleve and Frances Broadwood began meddling in the affair, it virtually galloped away with them all towards disaster.

He'd been in half a mind not to come down from London this Friday evening – there was a girl at one of the variety halls in Vauxhall who'd been giving him the eye all week – but his mother was expecting him, and so was Angelina; and when duty called, pleasure must alas be waved adieu.

By Saturday morning, however, he was wishing he'd followed the siren lure of the Vauxhall beauty and stayed in Town. Oliver van der Kleve had called the previous evening just as his mother and he were finishing dinner at Mount Edgecumbe. Arthur had taken his cigar and glass of brandy on to the terrace, and was standing with an elbow on the rail, enjoying the balmy evening view across the Common, when the maid (they had no butler) showed the visitor out to him.

The next twenty minutes had proved extremely discomfiting for the young man. He put up a blustering defence of sorts, but everything he said was seized upon and questioned and cross-examined so exactly that he began tripping over himself, contradicting his facts and generally tying his own tale into tangled knots.

Angry at being made to sound callow and stupid as well as a liar, he tried to deflect all the blame on to Beatrice and her friend, protesting that the pair had got hold of entirely the wrong end of the story, and had dressed it up to such an extent that he'd been left with no choice but to play along with them.

"I mean, I could hardly accuse your sister of deliberately colouring the truth, could I, sir?"

"Any more than you could accuse my wife of behaving like a harlot?"

What could he do but retreat behind a smoke-screen of excuses, wishing the ground might open up and swallow him.

That wasn't the worst of it, though; not by a long shot. The Reverend Mr Terris had apparently been making it his business whilst in Town to initiate enquiries around the Hart Street area; and these ecclesiastic nosings had unearthed the fact that Arthur was known to entertain 'ladies' in his rooms.

Which just about put paid to further argument.

Bidding him a terse goodnight, Oliver van der Kleve had left the young gentleman to help himself a little shakily to another brandy and the task of explaining to his mother precisely why they would not be taking tea at Sion Place on Sunday.

Oliver was not by habit an immoderate drinker. At a time when the consumption of alcohol meant a man might have two or three bottles of wine to a meal and think nothing of it, he tended to be abstemious, preferring to keep his head clear for business and his wits unblunted.

This evening, however, he'd broken his own rule. Dining rather late with Mr Terris at the vicarage, he had made heavy inroads into the clergyman's cellar, and by ten o'clock was in that reflective state of inebriation when there steals into the mind a desire to unburden one's conscience in confession.

Throughout his life he had lived by the code of self-discipline: if a man could not control himself then he was not his own master, for if his head did not govern his more febrile inclinations, he lost purpose and perspective and thus became the slave of his emotions.

He had known Edward Terris for many years, both as priest and as friend, and could claim him amongst his closest acquaintances. Even so, being the type of man he was, Oliver had never chosen to discuss the deeper, more private aspects of his life, in particular his feelings towards Kitty – they touched too much upon a side of his nature which he would rather be held strictly in check, unexpressed and therefore the more easily contained.

Mr Terris was aware of the reasons for his friend contracting a second marriage in 1865, just as he was aware of the problems which had since beset that union – indeed, threatened some years ago to destroy it. Knowing both parties as he did, he could only hazard a guess at what darker undercurrents ran beneath the surface – the pride, the reserve, the disharmony of temperament; so that he was more than a little astonished to hear Oliver declaring suddenly this evening after dinner, as they sat together enjoying a final cognac –

"Something has happened to me, Edward. Something I can't account for. I have fallen in love with my wife . . . and I wish to God I knew how to deal with it."

The two of them were in the conservatory overlooking the vicarage garden, reclining among the cushions of their wicker chairs, glass in hand, reflections mirrored in the darkened panes in silhouette. Mr Terris grew his heliotrope and stephanotis here, and the air was heavy with a lush fragrance.

He did not respond to the other's statement immediately, letting its implications filter through his mind.

Then he said, carefully, "It is not an unnatural occurrence, for a man to feel some deepening of affection within marriage."

"I'm not speaking of affection, Edward. I'm speaking of being in love. There is a difference."

"Do you think?"

"My feelings at this present time assure me of the fact."

Oliver cupped the bowl of his brandy glass in his hands, rolling it slowly back and forth between his palms in studied concentration.

After a while he went on again – "I have never experienced an emotion such as this. It disturbs me more than I can say. I cannot even describe it, unless to liken it to some fever of the blood . . ."

He made to raise the glass to his lips; then lowered it untasted.

"I burn – yes, *burn*, with longing for Catherine. I lie with her, possess her, hold her in my arms – yet always she eludes me. There is some barrier between us which I cannot break through to reach her."

He seemed almost to be speaking to himself.

"And how long have you felt this?" Edward Terris asked quietly. "You have been married now – what – six years?"

There was a vague nod. "Six years last month. But this . . . oh, what can I best call it – this terrible helpless *need* of her

331

. . . it's come upon me only recently. I must be honest with myself, Edward. I've been aware for a good while that my affections towards Catherine were changing – since as long ago as the business with Jonathan Rivers. That opened my eyes, if you like. It was not until I thought I'd lost her that I realised how much she meant to me, even then . . . and realising that, I felt the pain of her betrayal twice as keenly. I don't mind telling you, the episode revealed to me more of my own nature than I ever knew existed."

He paused again, once more raising the glass and this time swallowing its contents at a gulp.

A large grey moth, attracted by the glow of the single oil lamp, battered itself against the conservatory windows in a futile endeavour to reach the flame.

Oliver watched it in silence for several moments.

Then he began to quote softly, almost sadly –

"Like moths which beat against a fastened pane,
Desiring most the thing that would destroy,
My thoughts are ever constant upon thee,
Shut out from that which is their greatest joy."

Mr Terris reached across to refill the emptied glass from the decanter on the table between them.

"Shelley?" he asked. "If so, the lines are unfamiliar."

There was the merest trace of a smile. "The lines are my own, as it happens. A poor effort which I wrote for Catherine whilst away in Amsterdam. Doubtless she would be amused to know it."

"I had no idea there was the poet in you, Oliver."

"Neither did I, my friend. You see to what a pitch I've been brought. Moths and I have much in common just now –" he raised his drink in salutation of the insect whose flutterings left a ghost-trail of dust across the panes. "We maim ourselves against some invisible hindrance which keeps us from obtaining what we desire – which if we but knew it, is no hindrance at all but rather a protection against something far more injurious to our being."

This was rather deep for Mr Terris, but he did his best.

"You fear that your – ah, love for your wife presents an obstacle to your happiness? But why?"

332

"Because the feelings are not returned. Nor will they ever be. Oh, she *likes* me well enough, I suppose . . . but when a man discovers himself for the first time in his life to be as much in love as I, then liking becomes mere toleration, and a torment."

"I don't . . . quite understand."

"Then let me explain." Oliver's eyes were still upon the moth. "Imagine you have gone without food. You are hungry. Someone offers you a crust of bread to eat, but far from being satisfied, your appetite is but made the more acute. Well, this is what Catherine offers me – crumbs of affection which leave me famished, as it were, for the feast for which I long."

Savouring a mouthful of finest French cognac, Edward Terris meditated in silence upon this analogy.

There had been a time in his youth, more years ago than he cared now to recall, when he himself had fallen headlong into love. The lady had been the sister of a fellow curate and he had worshipped at the shrine of her chaste beauty in mute and trembling adoration, fearing to declare his devotion in case such mortal longings might afright her. Alas, the Arcadian idyll of that Oxford summer had been rudely shattered by some low church cleric who boldly laid siege to his 'mystical rose of virtue' and swept her away; leaving the young Edward to sink into melancholic despair, roaming the scenes of his remembered joy to mourn its loss, and solacing his broken heart with the fruit of the vine and purple-passioned verse.

For a while he had toyed with thoughts of following in the steps of Newman and Keble and embracing Anglo-Catholicism, immolating himself upon the altar of perpetual celibacy so as to rise above the hurts of fleshly temptation; but the warm arms of a country alehouse wench soon cured him of that.

He never married. Whether it was because of his early disappointment, as he liked to pretend, or whether because he preferred the comforts of a bachelor's existence, who could say – perhaps the truth lay somewhere in between.

Clearing his throat with a dry little cough, Mr Terris said now, "May I offer a word of advice, Oliver?"

"I would be glad of it!"

"It is my experience of life that a man reaps what he has sown. 'Whatsoever ye do unto others, the same they will do unto you in like measure.' In the past, you have tended to hold Catherine at a distance – indeed, I would go so far as to say that your attitude has been one of cold reserve, therefore you cannot complain if she treats you in similar fashion. There can be no fire without some spark to light it. No, no, hear me out, I pray –" as Oliver made to interject something – "my point is this: if you would have your wife love you with the same real depth of feeling as you now love her, why then, you must show it – demonstrate your affection to her, treat her with tenderness and warmth – and given a little time and a little patience, you will see how she responds to you."

"But I am not a man easily moved to show sentiment –"

"Then you must practise it, my friend. A few fond words, a pretty compliment, a gesture – they never come amiss. And if I may say, Catherine is too sensitive and sweet a creature not to appreciate kindness when it is offered."

"I hope I have always been kind. It is consideration I've lacked. Let me confess something to you, Edward." The other shifted in his chair. "When first I set eyes upon Catherine, I did not see her as she was – some innocent, vulnerable child whose life till then had been spent with neither love nor any care beyond the charity of institutions – I saw a blank canvas in a beautiful frame on which I might create a picture – an ideal of the woman I desired for wife. I didn't enquire into her feelings. It pleased me better that she had none. It was not until after our marriage, after I'd had her educated and trained and conditioned – bred up, if you like – to conform to my own requirements, that I realised that under the china doll exterior there existed a young woman of whom I knew precisely nothing."

Oliver paused from his speech. The moth had wearied of its efforts to reach the lamplight and gone fluttering away into the darkness.

After a moment he went on again, bitterly, "Looking back upon my behaviour, I know now that I committed a terrible wrong against her."

"And you fear she may not forgive you?"

There was a helpless shrug.

Edward Terris removed his pince-nez spectacles and took out a handkerchief to wipe them. "Why not try?" he suggested. "Why not tell Catherine upon her return everything you have discussed with me this evening? There may never come a better time."

"A better time? In what way?"

"My dear fellow, have you not just demonstrated your faith and trust in her over this business with young Arthur Russell? That must surely dispose her favourably towards you." The spectacles were replaced. "Take my advice and grasp your chance – make a full admission of your conscience. It will act as proof of your sincerity."

"Is that what you would counsel?"

"It is."

Oliver leaned forward in his chair and setting his glass aside, clasped his hands between his knees in a gesture of frustration.

"If only I could find the words! If only I could say to her – Catherine, I love you – forgive me!"

"What words more do you need? You have said it all. Listen to me –" Mr Terris sat forward in turn, the better to make his point. "I would suggest that the greatest obstacle to finding happiness is your pride. You are frightened to expose your true self for fear that pride may be hurt by rejection. Am I not correct?"

For several long moments there was no response. Oliver's head was bowed, his features in shadow, expressionless. Some nerve of memory touched upon a scene from childhood, when a small boy had cried out to his mother for love, knowing himself unwanted . . . It was the chimera which had haunted him all these years.

He straightened abruptly.

"The child is father to the man, Edward. I carry a ghost upon my shoulder."

The words made little sense, except as an exorcism, perhaps.

Mr Terris waited for enlightenment. None appeared forthcoming. He decided to broach the conversation from a fresh direction.

With another of his throat-clearing coughs, he began, "There is one further matter which we have not so far touched upon this evening. I hope I may be forgiven for raising the subject, but it bears some relevance to the domestic situation at Sion Place."

There was a questioning look as Oliver reached to take up his cognac again.

"I speak of your sister Beatrice," said Mr Terris.

"Ah. Beatrice."

"What's to be done about her – have you thought?"

A humourless smile traced itself upon the other's lips. "You wouldn't care to marry her, I suppose, Edward."

"Alas, dear friend, I fear I must forgo that pleasure."

"A pity. It would have solved the problem perfectly. However –"

Oliver paused a moment from what he was going to say. Somewhere within the house the jangling peal of a bell began to die away.

"A little late for callers, surely?" he remarked; and then – "However, with regard to my sister, I agree that some action must be taken to remedy the position. Indeed, I've already considered a possible –"

He stopped again. The inner door of the conservatory had just been opened by Edward Terris's housekeeper.

"Excuse me, sir –" Her plain, homely features wore a look of concern. "I'm sorry to trouble you. It's a message from Bowling Green House. Mr Broadwood has taken one of his nasty turns, and would you go round there at once, sir. They don't expect him to live."

336

37

Kitty was in two minds whether to attend Henry Broadwood's funeral at St Bride's. She had never especially liked the man, and whatever friendship there'd been with his wife Frances – his widow now – had long since cooled.

It would be hypocritical to pretend she was saddened to learn of his death, and more hypocritical still to appear at the church as a mourner. Her only feelings were of sympathy for the two children, Alfred and Mary, who more often than not, poor things, had been left neglected in the care of the servants while their parents pursued an endless social programme of engagements.

Oliver had decided for her. Naturally they must go to the funeral – Henry Broadwood was a neighbour, after all, and it was only proper that they pay their last respects; but if Catherine wished, they would sit at the far side of the church away from the family party.

And Angelina – ? Ought she to accompany them, in view of the fact that her betrothal to Arthur Russell was now broken off? Her attendance might prove embarrassing, since the Russells would be there, of course, as cousins of the deceased.

In the event, Angelina made up her mind for herself and stayed away. And if Tunbridge Wells society wondered at her absence, it wondered even more that Beatrice van der Kleve should be seated amongst the mourners while her brother and his wife kept themselves pointedly at a distance.

That same society would have plenty more to exercise its tongue before the month was out.

Since Kitty's return from Loxley Green she'd observed a change in her husband. Whether it was the strain of recent upsets, or the pressures of the City, was hard to say: certainly, it could not help to have problems of a personal nature on his mind at a time when so much of moment was happening abroad, for the Netherlands had just ceded to Britain their territorial possessions in Guinea, and the business of van der Kleve Lindemanns, an Anglo-Dutch concern, was very much involved.

At night as the two of them lay together in bed, he seemed almost wary of enjoying the sexual intimacy of love-making, but preferred to hold Kitty in his arms, her head cradled against his shoulder, whilst he talked to her of political affairs in Europe. This was a thing he'd never done till now, and it puzzled her. Was a discussion of the Paris Communards and Stock Exchange reaction Oliver's way of saying he no longer found her desirable?

She decided she should humour him a little, and on the evening of Henry Broadwood's funeral as she was dressing for dinner she'd said casually – "I read in the day's paper that Ismalia has been annexed to Egypt –" and was quite taken aback when instead of some comment on adverse market prices, her husband burst into a sudden roar of laughter.

"I really could not for the life of me see what was so droll," she wrote afterwards to Harriet Hoffmann in Baden-Baden, "but Oliver said it was the sight of me standing there in my corsets (I should say rather, my *under-pinnings*) making the most profound and irrelevant observation upon the fate of some obscure little country. I have never known him to show so much amusement; – but oh, how *handsome* he is when he laughs!"

There were some things which one did not put into letters, even to a friend, some things too precious and private to share; and what she did not tell Harriet was that in the midst of his mirth Oliver had swept her up and carried her over to the bed, and there made love to her with more tenderness and desire than she'd ever known before.

Ismalia had broken the ice.

In the days following, Kitty noted how often his gaze seemed fixed upon her: whenever they were together, she would look up to find him watching her with a softness in his eyes which disturbed and yet thrilled her; and when she smiled back, his whole face seemed to light with some inner glow of pleasure.

He had always been generous, spending his money lavishly to buy her jewellery and clothes, but now there were smaller, more intimate gestures – a rose still moist with morning dew beside her pillow when she woke; a book she had admired, affectionately inscribed; and a linnet in a gilded cage to sing for her.

What could she give in return to show her gratitude? All she was, all she had, all she owned, had come from him, even her two little sons. She had nothing of herself; and her only real sorrow at this time, as the spring of 1871 crept into summer, was that she longed so much to show Oliver how truly she appreciated him as husband . . . yet she did not know how even to begin.

At the top end of Tunbridge Wells, beyond the Five Ways, the road to Southborough ran between tree-lined verges shading the gardens of neat suburban villas. This area was known as 'the Lew' and was considered an up-and-coming part of town to live, having the advantage of a fashionable new church, St John's, which was patronised by a number of the local gentry.

A few days after Kitty's twenty-sixth birthday, in the third week of June, Oliver van der Kleve astonished his sister Beatrice by suggesting that they take a carriage drive together the following afternoon. Relations had, not unnaturally, been very strained between the two since the Arthur Russell affair, and Beatrice had tended to avoid wherever possible mixing in family company, preferring to keep to her own rooms and make an appearance below only for dinner.

She was not a stupid woman by any means; far from it. She knew that the situation at Sion Place must be resolved one way or another, for it could not continue as it was, a household divided against itself into opposing camps whose hostilities were conducted in barbed silence.

This invitation of Oliver's was obviously rather more than a social courtesy between brother and sister: some design or other lay behind it, for he never did anything unless to suit his own purpose. She could have refused, of course; in fact, considered doing so. But there had been a note in his voice which said she'd be wiser to comply, if she knew what was best for her.

It was a bright day, warm but with breeze enough to keep it pleasant for their drive. Beatrice enquired where they were going.

"You'll know when we get there," Oliver answered briefly,

taking up the reins. He was using the gig, and the shared wicker bench-seat behind the pony made conversation easier, although hardly less constrained in present circumstances.

Touching the animal's flank lightly with his whip, he walked it out of the stable yard at the side of the house, and then with a "Gee-hup there!" urged it forward into a trot along Mount Sion, raising his hat in greeting to the Misses Daukins who were passing on the opposite pavement.

"If we are driving into the country," said Beatrice after a little while as her brother turned along by the boundary wall of Calverley Park, "I wish you had informed me. I would have worn a more suitable head covering."

Oliver glanced at the serrated straw bonnet edged with black lace frilling.

"What you are wearing will do well enough."

Another short silence; and then – "Perhaps after all we are *not* going into the country?"

"I'm afraid you must contain yourself in patience until we reach our destination."

Beatrice pulled at her net gloves in fretful irritation. "How very perversely you are behaving. I have a right to know where it is I'm being driven, surely?"

Her brother made no answer, merely giving the reins a slight pull to draw the pony over into the centre of the road to avoid a landau emerging from a gateway on the left.

After a minute or so, unable to hold herself, she burst out again, "And what *is* our destination, pray? I hope it is not far. I wish to be home in good time."

"Oh, you will be home, Beatrice. I promise you that, never fear."

They were now turning into Calverley Road, skirting the park on its northern edge and travelling in the direction of the Five Ways. Here the horse traffic was heavier, and as they approached the junction they were forced to wait while a large pantechnicon was backed across into the yard of Waymarks furniture repository.

"Had you taken the other way, we might have avoided this congestion –"

"I take the way I choose." Oliver silenced further complaint with a sharp chuck at the reins to get the pony moving again, and by dint of skilful driving succeeded in getting them through the press of vehicles and up the hill to bring them on to St John's Road.

Within another ten minutes he was drawing up outside a red-brick villa whose small front garden carried a wooden board announcing it 'For Sale'.

Applying the brake of the gig, he got down and helped his sister to the pavement.

"Well –" She looked about her. "Are we paying a call? If so, upon whom? For what reason?"

Instead of replying, he kept a firm hold of her elbow and reached inside the gate to open it; but as he made to conduct her along the path towards the front door, Beatrice reared away sharply.

"*Oliver* –" Her tone became more strident, and with a sudden edge of what sounded almost like fear. "I demand to be told what this nonsense is about!"

"All in good time."

He removed a key from his waistcoat fob pocket and stepping up to the door, inserted it in the lock. With his hand still tight upon her she had no choice but to let herself be ushered across the threshold into a long, dark, narrow hall that had the fusty smell of a place which had not been aired for some while.

There were no carpets on the boarded floor, and the noise of their footsteps echoed dully as they turned immediately off into the empty parlour.

Oliver looked around.

"Not a bad little room, this," he commented, releasing his sister's elbow from his grip at last. "Handsome plaster mouldings. All they need is a wash of distemper to bring them up. Gas jets already fitted, you'll notice. And that's Purbeck marble on the fire surround. Chimney probably needs a sweeping, though – I can see a patch of damp up there on the breast."

He gave his attention again to Beatrice. Her sallow, mannish face wore an expression that was part way between annoyance and a wary disbelief.

"Well, have you nothing to say, my dear? Nothing at all? I'd hoped you might like the place."

She appeared to deliberate with herself before answering. "But . . . what is the purpose of all this? Why should my opinion be required?"

"Because I should like to hear it, having gone to quite so much trouble on your behalf."

"I fail to understand."

"Ah. Then I see I must make myself clearer. To put it simply, dear Beatrice, I have bought this house for you to live in."

There was a frozen silence.

Casually, as though he were passing the time of day, Oliver went on again after a moment or two, "It's the perfect size for you and Perrins, wouldn't you agree? And convenient for St John's Church. I don't suppose you'll want to neglect your religious duties. Come —" he took her by the arm as before — "let me show you over the rest of the place to see how you like it."

"I will hear no more!" Clapping her hands to her ears, his sister pulled back as though stung. "I wish to go home, Oliver."

He regarded her steadily.

"My dear, this is your home. You have no other."

"I find your sense of humour in extreme bad taste. You have had your little jest. Now perhaps we may leave – ?"

"Presently."

He reached to take her hands, compelling her to go with him as he went again into the hall and along by the stairwell into the dining room at the rear.

Here, too, it was empty of furnishing and the single sash window looked out on to a small square of brick-laid yard with a wall beyond containing a door into the entry which ran at the back of the house.

"Kitchen and scullery are below," said Oliver, loosening her in order to indicate. "I won't take you down. There may be one or two dead rats – I've had to have some poison bait spread."

Beatrice shuddered visibly.

"Now, the place will be carpeted and curtained throughout," he continued in the same matter-of-fact tone. "I dare say there are several pieces of furniture at Sion Place which you'll want to bring with you. You may choose whatever you wish, within reason. As to your financial position, you have your own private income from Father's estate, and I propose to make you myself an annual personal allowance, together with the outright gift of this property, of course, and five hundred shares in the Suez Canal Company. I think you will agree that is generous."

Had there been a chair in the room, Beatrice would have collapsed on it with shock. It was quite obvious to her now that this was not some extended practical joke being played at her expense. Her brother was completely serious. He was removing her from the house where she had spent three-quarters of her life, the house where she'd reigned as Mistress until so recently, and was pensioning her off to this poky, common little villa as though she were some family dependent being retired from service.

The idea of it – preposterous!

"I suppose this is Catherine's doing," she said, trying to contain her rising anger. "I suppose it was *she* who has decided I should be evicted from beneath my own roof."

"Catherine knows nothing. I have not even discussed the matter with her. The decision is entirely my own."

"But doubtless she is the cause –"

"No, Beatrice. *You* are the cause. Had you not made yourself into my wife's most bitter enemy, you and I would not have reached this parting of the ways. Since the day of our wedding you have done your best to drive a wedge between Catherine and me. I gave you fair and clear warning some while ago – I was not prepared to tolerate your meddlesome interference any further. You ignored that warning at your peril, and now you're being called to pay the price."

"And I have only myself to blame, is that it?" Beatrice could afford the luxury of a little sarcasm: she recognised her own defeat in every word her brother had just spoken.

"Well let me tell you, Oliver – I have sacrificed my chances of marriage to give you the best years of my life as unpaid, unthanked, housekeeper – I reared your motherless child – promoted your interests – played hostess at your table –"

"And I trust I have shown my gratitude," he interjected, glancing at his pocket watch to consult it for the time.

"Oh, you have shown your gratitude well enough! I am to be tossed aside like some useless commodity – shovelled away out of sight and out of mind while you and Madam pursue a game of happy families –"

"Beatrice –" he interrupted her again, and there was no

mistaking the sudden hardening in his voice. "I have merely two words of advice to offer you. They are these. *Be content.* Because without contentment you condemn yourself to spend the remainder of your days an embittered and lonely woman – friendless, disliked and unwanted. The choice is yours."

He gave her a long look, then turned on his heel and went out; and in the empty echoing silence of the room Beatrice van der Kleve seemed to hear her own life sentence.

38

St Bride's annual church fête, one of the most important social events of the summer season, was being held this year in the grounds of Sion Place.

Everyone prayed for fine weather, none harder than the Reverend Mr Terris, for a cloudless day brought forth the multitude, and the remedy against the ravages of *xestobium rufovillosum* lay in their pockets. An examination of his chancel rafters had recently revealed that this destructive insect (more commonly called the death-watch beetle) was turning the timbers to powder, requiring immediate and costly work if the roof were not to descend upon his choristers' heads.

His prayers were answered. Saturday, the fifth of August 1871, dawned with the sunrise promise of a perfect day.

Among the various stalls and side-show booths which had been set up around the lawns stood a small striped canvas tent advertising *Madame Arcania – Fortune-teller* whose 'mysterious gipsy powers' might be released by the crossing of her palm with silver. Those curious to know their future destiny paid threepence for this privilege (a three-penny bit being silver, after all) and were greeted upon entrance by the sight of a shadowy figure in gauze veils and a turban sitting crouched above a crystal ball. To add to the mystic atmosphere, bowls of burning incense filled the tent with wreathing layers of hazy blue smoke.

By four o'clock, several dozen people had consulted Madame Arcania, and the lady was beginning to wish she could foretell when someone might think of fetching her a cup of tea.

"Here you are, Kitty –"

As though in answer, the tent flap opened and Harriet Hoffmann ducked inside carrying a tray in her hands.

"Heavens above –" she exclaimed at once – "what a fug! It smells like an opium den!" And setting the tray on the table beside the crystal ball – "I'll leave the flap tied back a way to let in some air."

"You'd better hang the 'engaged' sign out, as well," Kitty said indistinctly through her veils. "Otherwise we'll have some seeker after truth enquiring whether I read tea leaves."

She took off her turban and removed the mask of filmy gauze which hid the lower part of her face, fanning herself with it as she reached to pick up cup and saucer.

"Speaking of seekers," she went on when Harriet was seated, "Mr Terris, of all people, came in just now. And looking very furtive, too, as though he hoped no one would notice."

"You didn't read his palm for him – ?"

"I resisted the temptation. I told him instead that he was about to come into a great amount of money – which is true enough. The proceeds from the fête should show a very satisfactory profit."

She paused for a welcome sip of tea.

"I also told him that a certain dark lady had not long ago passed from his life. 'And thank the Lord for that', he said. Do you know, Harriet, I'm sure he took me quite seriously."

Her friend returned the look of amusement. Harriet had recently arrived from abroad to spend a month's holiday with her aged parents, and was staying at Sion Place as weekend guest of the van der Kleves. She'd been astonished to find Beatrice gone, and remarked as much again now; adding –

"I thought perhaps she might be here today, but I've seen no sight of her anywhere about."

"We weren't expecting her." Kitty finished her tea and replaced the cup. "And I can't say I'm sorry. Since she removed to St John's Road with Perrins, there's been no communication. She's flown into high dudgeon and refuses to have anything more to do with us."

"Well, that's her loss not yours," Harriet said with a sniff. "She'll come round in the end. I must say, my dear, the house feels *so* different now without her – as though it's been spring-cleaned of all its nasty cobwebs. And I'm pleased that Mrs Broadwood is going, too. She was another lurking spider."

No one had been particularly surprised by the news that Frances Broadwood intended to sell Bowling Green House. The place was much too large for a widow; and with the two children away at boarding school, there seemed little point in her remaining there alone. The only slight concern was some rumour that a local builder had been making enquiries about buying the property together with its neighbour Cumberland House, with the idea of demolishing them both to provide the site for a dozen or more terraced villas.

"I had someone else of interest come to consult me earlier." Kitty had to raise her voice a little as the sound of loud cheers from beyond the tent indicated a lucky shot on the coconut shy.

"It was Angelina – pretending she hadn't realised who Madame Arcania was. She had such trouble to keep a straight face that I could hardly speak for laughter."

"And what did the crystal ball reveal?" Harriet enquired, sitting forward eagerly.

"Oh – that she'd met a fine young gentleman whose initials were W. S., and that his friendship would bring her happiness of heart."

"Did she guess to whom that referred?"

"Of course! She knew it was your brother William, I could tell at a glance. She's contrived to see him on several occasions since they met at Loxley Green in May – he's probably told you?"

Harriet nodded. "And much taken with her he is. Oh, Kitty, wouldn't it be a wonderful thing if those two were to be married! I can think of nothing in the world I'd like better than for us to be united by a bond between our families."

She reached across impulsively and squeezed her friend's hand.

"Thank you, dear, for inviting William to your supper party this evening. He's delighted to accept."

"Well, I thought it high time he and Oliver should meet each other. Now –"

Kitty began masking herself in her veils again.

"There's still fortunes to be told and happy endings to predict before Madame Arcania folds away her tent."

She smiled; and from outside came the sound of further cheers as another well-aimed shot earned someone their prize.

The van der Kleves' supper party was an intimate, informal affair for a few close friends. When it was over and their guests had gone, Oliver and Kitty strolled around the garden while he smoked a last cigar, discussing this and that event of the day and the outstanding success of the fête – the best St Bride's had ever held, declared Mr Terris, delighted.

The night was clear and in the brilliant moonlight it was hard to believe that these deserted lawns had so few hours before been the scene of colourful, crowded activity. Now the trestles were stacked aside and the booths stood shrouded and empty, waiting to be dismantled for another time.

"Yes, it's been a good day," Oliver remarked quietly. "But this is the best part – sharing its end entirely alone here with you."

He tossed his cigar butt away, watching the dull red glow traced for a second against the darkened trees.

"May I ask you something, my darling? Perhaps it sounds foolish – but why does Harriet always speak of you as Kitty? Why does she never give you the name Catherine?"

"Oh . . . that's a long story."

"I should very much like to hear it."

His wife raised her face to look at him, and he saw the soft glitter of the moon reflected in her eyes.

"Kitty is what I have always called myself," she said simply.

He waited for her to go on; but she only turned her head away, as though there were nothing more to add.

"And is that all you wish to tell me of your . . . long story?" he prompted after a moment.

"It's a thing I've never spoken of to anyone."

He took the small hand resting on his elbow and raised it to his lips, conscious of feeling closer to her at this instant than he'd ever done before.

"Do you trust me . . . Kitty?"

The unexpected use of the name made her start a little, and she looked at him again, searchingly.

"But of course I do."

"Then may I not share your secret? There's so much about you that I still don't know . . . so much I dearly wish to learn. All these years I've been calling you Catherine, and not once have you told me of your preference for Kitty. Why not?"

She gave a little shivering sigh, as though something had been released within her suddenly, and pressed herself against him.

"I was a foundling . . ." she said, not answering directly.

348

"Foundlings are nameless . . . they have no identity . . . no family, no past . . . nothing."

Sensing her reluctance, Oliver drew her gently into his arms and held her there.

"The overseer at Tonbridge Orphanage kept a list of names," she went on in a low voice. "As each new child was registered, it was given whichever name was next on that list . . . I was Catherine."

"They had to call you something, my darling."

"Yes, I know. But it was the way it was done. Not a name, so much as a number. An institute label. I wanted to be different – I *hated* being Catherine – I wanted a choice of my own."

Again she paused. St Bride's Church clock down in the high street began striking eleven, its sonorous chimes carried on the still, warm air.

"I never seemed to fit amongst the others. I used to tell myself it was because I wasn't a foundling – my parents had mislaid me, that's all, or I'd been stolen from them – they were searching for me still, and soon they'd find me. It was a poor, useless, threadbare little dream, but all I had. A child needs hope, however slight . . ."

Oliver sensed the effort this was costing her, and he felt extraordinarily moved. He recalled his own experience, those long-dead days when hope was all he, too, had had to cling to: the hope that his mother would return again, the dream that she had never wanted to abandon him.

"I attempted to trace your background, you know," he said quietly, his cheek against Kitty's hair. "I thought I might be able to find some clue to your parents' identity."

"But there was nothing." She gave this as a statement, not a question.

"No. Nothing."

"It doesn't matter. I've found myself now. I know who I am at last."

She looked into his face again, and the sweetness of a smile curved her lips.

"I'm your wife, Oliver. The mother of your sons. And that's all I'll ever want to be."

He held her to him in silence, not knowing what to say, overwhelmed by the frightening intensity of his need for her.

349

The lush, heady fragrance of roses and night-scented stocks drifted from the shadows, mingling with the perfume of Kitty's skin.

"Let's go indoors," she said suddenly.

"Yes."

He took her by the hand, like any young lover, and together they walked slowly back across the lawns towards the house, their footprints traced behind them in the silvered dew.

An oil lamp had been left burning in the terrace room, and by its light they made their way through the darkened hall and up the double sweep of stairs. There was a tangible stillness everywhere, exaggerated by the steady, measured tick of the long-case clock below, and the faint echoing sounds of a horse and trap going down Mount Sion.

Oliver set down the lamp and closed their bedroom door behind him. The curtains had been drawn at the windows and the room, so familiar in its domestic comfort, seemed to wrap itself about them both in the intimate warmth of an embrace.

He felt himself starting to shake, whether with love or with longing he could not tell; and reaching out, he folded Kitty into his arms again and kissed her. To his astonishment, he tasted the saltness of tears.

"Dearest – what's this?" he asked at once, taking her face between his hands and searching it in concern. "Have I done something to make you unhappy?"

"No . . ."

"Then why are you weeping? Tell me –"

"Because . . . you're so good, so kind to me. Oh, Oliver, what have I done to deserve it?"

For answer he tenderly wiped the tears from her cheek; and then said very quietly, "I love you, Kitty. God knows, for years I have done you great wrong, pretending to myself that it wasn't love I felt but pride of ownership. I've wasted so much of our marriage, driving you away by my behaviour – ask me rather what you did to deserve *that*, my darling, not why I should show you a little kindness now."

He touched his lips again to her eyes, her brow, her mouth, murmuring between each kiss, "I need you for my own . . . I need you to be a part of me, and a half of me . . . can I hope you will forgive me for the way I've treated you?"

"What did you ever do that I should forgive? You are the

best and most considerate of men. Everything I have I owe to you."

"Perhaps."

"It's true."

She pulled away, placing her hands on his shoulders, looking at him almost as though she'd never seen him properly before this moment. The shadow of the lamplight brushed his features, softening the pain she seemed to read there; and something broke within her heart, some crystal of self-fear carried there since childhood, and she said on a little note of surprise, "Oliver . . . oh, Oliver, I love you. Is that enough to offer in return?"

Her words fell upon him like a blessing.

"I love you," she said again; and if there were fresh tears, now they were of happiness and joy as her husband caught her to him, crying out her name.

After a while she whispered against his mouth, "What a lot of time we have to make up for."

And he answered, "I adore you so much, darling Kitty, there will never be time enough."